an Trodai

by

John Breen Wren

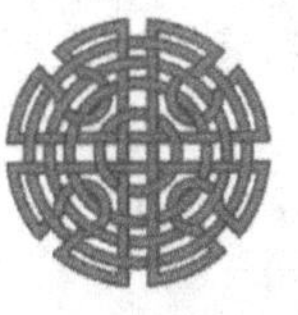

* * *

DEDICATION

To my father . . .

the quiet giant in my life who showed me how to stand tall, honor the past and feel pride in my heritage.

He will live in our hearts forever.

ACKNOWLEDGMENT

I acknowledge the counsel of editor and proofer; the patience of family, the access to friends; both new and old. I thank them for their help, their input, their CRITICISM, and their praise. Without them all, this book would not be.

A NOTE FROM THE AUTHOR

From a time before recorded history, Éirinn, Ireland was an island nation of many tribes, kingdoms and sub-kingdoms. Disputes between these groups pitted countrymen against countrymen in battle after battle and the alliances between tribes, clanns and kingdoms were forged and broken with regularity. Early settlements in Éirinn by people from the Iberian Peninsula, and later the Celts from central Europe, developed a race of people who quarreled and fought amongst themselves for centuries.

The invasions by raiders from northern countries dating from 795AD to the end of the first millennium aided in maintaining a near-constant state of warfare somewhere on the island. The battles fought, the men involved in those battles and their deeds are recorded in history and myth. Some of the characters cross the lines between the two, and today it is not entirely clear who and what is fact or myth.

My heritage on both sides goes back to Éirinn, sometime in the last 150 years. Members of my family have researched our ancestry and after a few generations, the lines often blur, and certain relationships are harder to define and confirm. The blood in my veins could be ancient Irish, Celtic, Viking, or a blend of all. There may also have been a traveler from some faraway exotic land who managed to leave his stamp on my family's history. One never knows.

The Irish are a proud people and the stories of ancient Éirinn have always intrigued me. Now that I have found time and incentive to write, I decided to take on this story about a family; a clann of warriors beginning near the turn of the first millennium. I begin the first part in the year 893AD, about a man with little definable heritage; a loner, nearly an outcast and build to a family united through several generations. A family, a clann that stands together through times both good and bad even in the face of extreme difficulty and warfare.

* * *

Part One

SCOLAI

1

893 AD Connaught, Ireland
Gudrik

A cold October wind carried a constant wash of wet, salty air over the sides of the longship as it made its way across the northern end of Connacht and south toward the inlet north of Munster. Olgar looked at the stars one final time as the sun began to hide them from view. "Gudrik, take the fore deck and keep an eye to the shore. A fire— movement of any kind, and we begin our day's work."

Gudrik moved to his post at the bow. He raised an arm high and pointed to the shore as he muttered, "I'll have a young one this day, and maybe more."

"Thorkel, turn to the shore," commanded Olgar as he looked to Gudrik for another signal. The helmsman complied and the longship slowly turned east, into the sun. "Lower the sail," commanded Olgar, "and man the oars."

The sail was secured, and each man took an oar, watching Olgar for his next order. In unison, the forty men responded to Olgar's raised arm and the oars dipped into the waves, moving the longship slowly and silently nearer the shore.

Gudrik signaled again from the bow and Olgar told Thorkel to ease the ship left and signaled the oarsmen to pull on their oars. They navigated into a small bay and the men on board peered over their shoulders at the shoreline, looking for signs of settlements close to the water's edge. As the sun finally broke full over the treetops, Gudrik signaled a sighting. The longship was steered slightly north of the settlement and moved steadily to the shore. Another hand signal from Gudrik told the helmsman which way to turn and then a signal indicated the water was getting shallow. Olgar commanded the oarsmen to slow their pull and allow the ship to glide into the shallows. As the hull gently touched the sandy bottom, Gudrik leapt overboard with sword and shield in hand. Twenty-nine other men followed and waded ashore in the early morning stillness. They were several hundred feet north of the settlement and as they assembled on dry land, each man checked his weapons, tightened his belt and prepared to begin their attack.

"I've a hunger for a young woman," Gudrik said quietly.

"We've come for gold and silver this time, fool. Not slaves," said Olgar.

"I don't want a slave, just a little time with a young woman," said Gudrik with a wicked laugh. "Just a little time."

"Gold and silver," returned Olgar, "and nothing else."

Gudrik was taller than any of his shipmates, his shoulders broad, his arms thick and powerful and he cared little for more than his immediate desires. He had joined this crew, three weeks earlier because he had exhausted his money and needed more. Having sailed with various Viking bands over the last several years, he was well known as a fierce pirate who helped himself to whatever he could carry and satisfied his lust with any female he could catch. Those few men who stood in his way paid the ultimate price.

Not accustomed to obeying orders, he muttered under his breath, "I'll take what I want and do as I please."

The raiders found the small settlement and prepared to surround the grouping of roundhouses. "They've no rath, no moat and I'll wager no men to defend this little village," said Olgar with a laugh. He addressed his men, "Stay quiet until we're close and don't burn anything until we've searched inside each of their houses."

They nodded in agreement and began to move quietly in groups of four or five around each side of the village. Olgar waited several minutes then whispered to his immediate comrades, "Now, we move in."

Each small group crept closer to the outer edges of the village until one was seen by an old man. The man stared at first, then shouted an alarm. The raiders sprang to their feet and charged. Looking initially for the men of the village, "Kill them first," Olgar had commanded, "and the rest will be easy."

There were few men in the village, only eight that presented any significant challenge. Olgar walked to an open area in the center of the village, looked down at three remaining village men and in his clumsy Irish he demanded, "Your men, where are they?"

The three remained silent and Olgar ordered them killed before again demanding of the assembled crowd, "Your men, where are they?"

Gudrik had a better grip of the Irish tongue and repeated Olgar's charge to a slight, young woman as he grabbed and twisted her arm.

"I'll tell you nothing," said Ceara with more grit in her voice than strength in her arms.

Gudrik pushed her to the ground and kicked her, "You'll tell me where your men are or I'll kill you."

"You'll kill me either way," snapped Ceara, glaring up at the hulking mass in front of her. She stared at Gudrik, expecting him to draw his sword and bring it down on her head. Trembling inside, she awaited the inevitable.

Gudrik, now angered by her defiance of his commands, grabbed her arm again, forced her to a stand and roared the same question in her face.

Ceara, repulsed by the stench of his breath, tried to pull away. Gudrik held fast, twisting Ceara's arm in his huge hand and hearing a bone crack, spat the question again.

Ceara felt the pain in her arm but remained defiant. She clenched her jaw and screamed through her teeth, "No!" as tears welled in her eyes.

Gudrik's free hand flew into her face, casting her to the ground, unconscious. He looked at her then turned to an older woman, "Where did they go?"

The older woman hesitated, looked at Ceara and turned toward Gudrik. She stared at him, not answering.

Gudrik grabbed Ceara's broken arm, drew his sword and poised as if to cut it off, "I asked you, where did they go?"

The older woman knew these men would kill everyone if they didn't get an answer, "Please don't hurt my daughter, she's very young."

Gudrik held his sword against Ceara's skin, grinned, and glared at the woman.

"They've gone with our chieftain, they battle the Dal gCais south of here," she said.

Gudrik grumbled, dropped Ceara's arm, turned and relayed the information to Olgar and scanned the crowd again.

Olgar, satisfied with the answer, turned to the crowd, "Bring me your gold and silver and I may spare your village. Deny my request and we will start killing you."

Gudrik, translated Olgar's words and continued to search the crowd.

The villagers understood the Viking's demands but were unsure if he would keep his word. They disappeared into their houses and brought out whatever they thought might satisfy the raiders. Olgar ordered a horse and cart to be brought to him and smiled as he saw the plunder build up in the cart. Very little gold or silver was found, mostly copper coins, weapons, tools and some leather belts.

The people had hoped that this Viking raider would not kill them, and they might see the sun rise again. The cart was loaded with all the raiders collected and Olgar assembled his men in the open yard. He counted faces, "Where is Gudrik?" he demanded.

"I don't know," returned Herlu, "last I saw, he hit the girl they called Ceara and knocked her to the ground."

Olgar looked to the place where Ceara had fallen. She wasn't there and Gudrik was nowhere to be seen. He looked angry, scanned the scene and said, "We leave, now. Gudrik may follow if he wishes, but we don't wait." He signaled the cart to leave, then turned to his men, "Kill everyone and burn the houses."

The villagers sensed the raider's intention and began to run toward the woods away from the beach. The Vikings hacked at the people as they ran, killing some and wounding more. Houses were set afire and as the loaded cart reached a turn in the path to the beach, the raiders stopped pursuing villagers and followed it to their longship.

As they ran through the wood to the beach, Olgar looked at Herlu, "Are they all dead?"

"I only know the ones I saw, I killed," returned Herlu.

"And Gudrik, is he with us?" demanded Olgar.

"I don't know, I haven't seen him," said Herlu and he continued to run toward the beach.

Olgar paused, turned and looked back toward the burning village once more. He drew a deep breath, smelling the burning thatch, he took in the aftermath one last time then hurried toward the beach and their longship. On the beach, he looked about, Gudrik was not among the band of pirates and when the boat was loaded, he ordered the men to push off to deeper water. The oars were manned but remained still as Olgar gave one last look to the shore, "Gudrik, I wish you luck," and he raised an arm, signaling the oarsmen.

The men pulled on the oars and as the longship eased out of the little bay, the sail was raised and secured, and a breath of sea wind pushed the longship gently north. Olgar sent Herlu to the fore station, "An eye to the shore and another settlement. The sun hasn't yet crossed half the sky and we've room for more plunder."

* * *

Gudrik spent an hour satisfying his hunger for a woman. Each time Ceara could, she resisted, scratching and clawing at his face and each time he laughed and backhanded her again. When he finished with Ceara, he threw her tiny, limp frame into a clump of bushes and picked up his scattered clothes.

Fully dressed and his sword in hand, Gudrik made his way back to the beach. He arrived well after the boat had set sail. "Damn," he growled. "I'm alone in this place." He knew the plan was to raid several settlements along the Connaught shore as they sailed north and homeward. He looked back toward the village and stared at the glow of fires still burning. He looked back at the shore, then up the coast, wondering how long it would take him to reach the next settlement. He sheathed his sword, slung his shield across his back and began to move north along the shore in hopes of catching up with his comrades.

Two hours of trudging over rocky shoreline and through heavy brush had Gudrik north several miles. He saw a large plume of smoke ahead, he paused and looked to the water, but didn't see the longship.

"They would've come ashore a little north of here, perhaps beyond those trees," he grumbled as he pushed aside more brush. He came to a clearing and slowly stepped out of the thick woods. The clearing stretched three hundred feet to a small roundhouse and a rath wall fifty feet farther. The house was burning, and several men carried buckets of water in attempting to douse the flames.

Gudrik stood still and watched from a distance. He didn't recognize any of the men and as he was about to melt back into the wood, one of the men throwing water on the fire saw him.

"Another," shouted the man. "I see another of them."

Several men dropped their buckets, lifted swords from the ground and ran in Gudrik's direction, yelling and screaming as they crossed the open area.

Gudrik turned into the wood and tried to run but was slowed by the heavy brush. He was tired, having spent the hour raping the girl and the next several hours plodding through woods to find his comrades. He was a large strong man and a great fighter, but the eight villagers who caught him had just repelled his fellow raiders and Gudrik was soon beaten to the ground and severely wounded.

"You should have run with the others," said one of the villagers.

"Now you'll die like your friends," said another.

Gudrik was dragged out of the bush, across the open field and stood at a tall thick oak tree. His back to the tree, his arms stretched behind him and tied, Gudrik was now able to see three other men tied to trees nearby. He strained his eyes and wasn't sure if he recognized the man tied to another tree only twenty feet away. It looked like Olgar, but beaten, bloodied, and probably dead.

As he looked about, trying to figure out how they might kill him, a boy approached with a length of rope in hand. He stared at Gudrik as he tied a knot in the rope, then he placed a loop around Gudrik's neck and walked slowly around the tree. The rope was again looped around Gudrik's neck, pulled snug and tied. The boy stood in front of him, with no expression.

An older man approached, "Do you understand our language?"

Gudrik knew enough of the Irish tongue to understand what was being said, but he didn't reply.

"Your people killed Lasair's father. Now it is his choice to kill you or let you rot standing at this tree," said the old man.

Gudrik looked at the boy and spit on the ground. Lasair walked behind the tree and tugged on the rope tied to Gudrik's neck. Gudrik gagged and coughed. Lasair pulled the rope away from the tree and put a stick between the tree and the rope, then walked around to look at Gudrik again.

The pair of nooses were pulled tighter around Gudrik's neck, and his breathing became more labored. Lasair looked at him for a moment, then spit on the ground in front of Gudrik and turned to walk away. The older man looked down at the boy, "Shall we kill him now?"

"No," said Lasair. "Tomorrow we will put another stick behind the rope and see if he chokes."

"This could take days," said the old man.

"Yes," said the boy, "it may."

Gudrik lived another two days with no food or water and finally the ever-tightening rope around his neck choked his last breath. The following day Lasair came to the open field with his bow and a handful of arrows. He stood thirty paces from Gudrik and loosed an arrow, striking Gudrik in his groin. The boy continued loosing arrows until they were all sunk deep into Gudrik's flesh.

2

894 AD Connaught, Ireland
Ceara

When Gudrik left the clearing where he had raped Ceara, she stirred, her body abused, a bone in her left arm broken and her eyes nearly swollen shut. She crawled out of the bush, saw some of her clothes and covered herself as best she could against the cold air. She stood in the shadows of the oak trees, feeling the pain of Gudrik's beating and abuse, gathering her thoughts and wondering if any others had survived. She staggered forward, holding onto branches with her right hand and allowing her left arm to hang at her side.

Slowly, she found her way back to her village. The fires had reduced most of the roundhouses to ash and there remained about twenty people tending to another twenty wounded and collecting what was not stolen or burned. A few carts were being dragged to the open yard for the bodies of the slain to be taken to a field where they would be buried.

The air was heavy with the smell of burnt thatch and death was everywhere. Ceara stumbled into the open yard and was seen by a friend. "Ceara, we thought you were dead," cried Soarla. She ran to her friend and helped her into one of the remaining houses.

"My mother," asked Ceara, "is she here?"

"No," replied Soarla, "she did not survive."

Ceara bowed her head, and more tears filled her eyes.

As Gudrik was being tied to the tree, Ceara was being helped by her friends. As a noose was placed about his neck, she was washed and bandaged. As the boy tightened the pair of nooses, her left arm was placed in a splint.

By the time Gudrik had been pierced with ten arrows, Ceara was rested, fed, and dressed, able to breathe easy and talk about her ordeal. "He was the large one who spoke our language," she told Soarla. "I was sure he would kill me, perhaps he thought he did," she speculated. "I wish I had a knife; I would have cut his eyes out and slit his throat," she said as she placed her right hand on the broken arm. She was still in pain, but she would heal.

Soarla's eyes went wide. She knew her friend was a fighter, but she was also small, and her attacker was huge. He might have been a warrior, but Ceara was the product of a long line of warriors and would have used any weapon she could lay her hands on in her defense.

As Ceara regained her strength she helped prepare the dead for burial. Her mother was one of the first to be buried and Ceara visited her grave every day. She cried at first, but the blood in her veins made her stand as tall as she could and consider her revenge, "I want to find that filthy bastard, cut off his head and kick it in the dirt."

As the days passed, she helped with the clean-up of the village in any way she could. Her arm was in a sling, and she spent most of her time probing the ashes of burned homes, looking for anything of value. Tools and weapons were most important. The raiders had taken most of the gold and silver, though some smaller pieces were missed, and her slow methodical search found a coin here and a bracelet there.

Searching the ashes of her own home, she found a dagger. It had been her father's. A warrior's dagger that had proven useful in close fighting situations. Ceara dwelled on the thought of this dagger in her hands. It was long and sharp. The handle charred and the leather wrapping nearly gone, but it was now hers. Her dagger, her weapon and thoughts of revenge welled up in her mind again. She thought about that brute as he abused her and could see his eyes, smell his sweat and filth and she saw herself pushing her new dagger into his throat. She slipped it into her crois beneath her deerskin vest. That evening Ceara cleaned the dagger, removed the remaining leather wrapping and found a scrap of cow hide to rewrap the grip. Finished and a new edge honed, she held it up in the light of the fire and breathed deep, "My dagger, may you find his blood and help it out of his eyes and his throat."

* * *

Six weeks passed and the new year began with the men of Ceara's village returning from their service to their chieftain. They had seen battle four times and lost two of their number. Their battles had met with success and now, they came home to a burned village and murdered families.

"We go to fight the Dal gCais to the south and we're attacked by foreigners from the north. Our village is destroyed, and there aren't enough of us to stand against another raid of this sort," said one of the men. "We should gather what we can and join our friends four miles north."

The dead had been buried, the wounded treated, and the remaining people herded their cattle in from the pasture, gathered their remaining belongings and trekked north to join another village. It was the same village where Gudrik and Olgar had met their ends. By the time Ceara and her friends arrived, fifteen weeks after their village had been raided, all that remained of Gudrik were bones— critters and crows had taken the rest. She listened to the stories of the raid and the pirates captured during and after the attack. She heard about the boy and the giant he killed with his nooses and arrows. She walked out to the tree where the last of the raiders had been tied and looked at the bits of clothing and bone on the ground.

Lasair, the boy who had tied the ropes around Gudrik's neck approached and said, "He was a big man, but not a giant. He died like any other man would." He looked at Ceara, "Did you know him?"

Ceara touched the dagger in her belt, "Not really, I think he's the one who broke my arm." She looked at the boy, "Did you see him tied to the tree?" she asked.

"Yes," returned the boy.

"Did he speak—, say anything at all?"

"No," said the boy. "He spit at my feet, and I tied the rope around his neck." He looked at Ceara with eyes that had looked into Gudrik's eyes, "I made the rope a little tighter each day until he couldn't breathe. Then I killed him again with my arrows."

She stepped closer to the boy and hugged him, "What is your name?"

"I am Lasair," he returned.

"That man beat me and left me for dead. I wanted to kill him myself if I ever saw him again. So, I thank you."

She put her hand on Lasair's shoulder, "Now he's dead, he won't hurt anyone else ever again." The two walked back to the rath together.

* * *

Ceara had recovered from the beating, but other problems were presenting. Her arm had mended but was still weak, her cuts and bruises all but gone save for a few small scars and her belly had begun to swell. The splint on her left arm had been removed and she should be ready to work in the fields in her new home when the planting began.

She was concerned that her child, fathered by one of the pirates, would not be accepted by the people of this new village or those from her old village and she wanted a better life for her baby. Her baby, this child would be her baby, not his and she knew that even though her friends were kind to her, her unborn child may not be so favored. She wrestled with her dilemma. Stay with her tribe and possibly suffer the child's hard life or leave, find a new village, a new tribe and begin anew. She decided to leave while she could still manage a trek south by herself.

"Soarla, have you traveled down to the river and the bigger town on the little island?" asked Ceara.

"Limerick, it's called Limerick. At least that's the closest town. There's another town if you go north on the river and that's called Ceann Coradh," said Soarla.

"I want to be where my baby might find a better life than I've had," said Ceara.

"You might find Ceann Coradh more friendly. It's the home of the king of the Dal gCais," Soarla advised her little friend.

"We had battle with them, I don't think they'd welcome a girl from Connaught," said Ceara.

"No more or less than a welcome in Limerick, and there are more Norse in Limerick."

"Ceann Coradh it is then, that's where I'll go and make a new, better life for me and my baby."

"You're a brave girl, how will you get there?" asked Soarla.

"I can walk, it should only take a few days, but I can walk," returned Ceara.

"Are you sure? Setting out on your own like this. Are you sure this is what you should do?" Soarla asked.

"I am," Ceara insisted, content with her decision.

"You've no need to feel shame," replied Soarla, "you are not to blame for what happened."

"I know, but my child will never be accepted here. Everybody will know the father was one of the raiders who murdered our people and burned our homes. If it is to be a girl, she will deserve a fair chance at life without the burden of that Viking father."

Soarla smiled and said, "And if it is to be a boy, what then?"

Ceara rolled her eyes, "If a boy, I pray he will not be like his father. But either way, this will be my child and I will raise him or her as free Irish with no mention of the father being a Northman who went Viking and took me as a prize."

Soarla hugged her good friend and said, "When you travel to Ceann Coradh, you shouldn't be alone, there are bandits, wild animals, and maybe even more pirates."

"There may be," said Ceara, "But I have nothing for them to steal and my belly says I've already been taken."

"Ceara, it's a long way, too long for you to be alone on the road."

"It should take no more than two days and I can't stay here any longer. People know whose baby grows in my belly."

That evening she made a small bundle of clothing wrapped around a loaf of bread, she had her dagger, a bow, and a handful of arrows and at first light, she quietly left the village, walking south toward the River Shannon. The road was longer than she imagined, and she paused often to rest. There was another settlement south of her old village; she had visited years earlier with her father. Perhaps no one would know her today, but she only intended to stay one night and be on her way south again. Her plan was working, and she found shelter in a stable, under a roof in the small village. Then again at the break of dawn, she continued on her way south. The road was quiet, she saw several other travelers, but managed to blend into the bushes and trees as they passed. She moved off the road four times the first day and several more the second, each time building more confidence in her decision to travel alone.

On the third day, as the sun reached high in the sky, the blisters on her feet began to break and bleed. Her swelling belly was more uncomfortable than she thought it would be and her newfound confidence began to fade. A small stream paralleling the road offered a cooling relief to her feet and as she pondered her situation, sitting at the water's edge with her feet gently splashing in the coolness, she muttered, "I'm alone, hungry, cold and very tired, I'd give everything I ever had if I could only make it to Ceann Coradh." She stumbled up the bank to a group of bushes and lay down out of sight of the road and the stream and quietly cried herself to sleep.

Sleep came easily in the shade of the trees, but her dreams were no comfort. She saw herself staggering toward Ceann Coradh in the dark of night, tired, hungry, and bleeding. She heard the sounds of wolves in the cover of the underbrush, stalking her. Suddenly a tall, slender woman in a dark cloak stood in her path, "Ceara, your child will be as his father," spoke the woman.

Ceara could see her eyes, bright as if on fire and the sword on her hip; brilliant steel, reflecting light that was not there, "Who are you?"

"He can be a great warrior, if I lead him through life. He will live long and be victorious in many battles, he will be a hero like few others."

Ceara saw herself fall to her knees and utter through her tears, "My son? A warrior?" She leaned forward and her head touched the ground, sobs racked her body.

The dark figure spoke again, "Give me your son and I will help you to Ceann Coradh."

"My baby," cried Ceara, "I want my baby to live and be free."

"Your son, Ceara, I will teach him," said the woman, "as only I can."

The pains in her back were overwhelming, her feet were cut, bruised, and bleeding. She was terrified as she defiantly addressed the woman, "My baby, I will die before I give him or her to you."

The woman seemed to float on a cloud of smoke as she approached Ceara without taking a step, her dark red hair streaming behind, "Give him freely or I will take him and leave you to die. I will have him and all his sons and theirs as well."

A noise on the road made the woman turn and look, the sound of a horse-drawn cart distracted her for only a moment, and she turned back toward Ceara, "When he is born, I will come back."

The sound broke the dream and Ceara strained to see what made the noise, who was on the road. She tried to stand and fell to the ground. She lay crying — then another noise.

She brought herself to her knees, fully awake now, the pains in her back gone, the cuts on her feet less painful than in her dream, and the tall dark woman had vanished. She heard another sound and crawled to the bushes, peering through the branches and leaves. A man was leading a horse to the water's edge and while the horse drank, Ceara watched, afraid to come out of hiding. She was awake, still afraid, remembering her dream of the woman in the dark cloak, "The devil," she thought aloud. "What did I promise?" She peered through the bushes at the intruder.

The man heard a muffled voice, then noticed movement in the bush and finally saw a young woman trying to hide. He turned his attention to his horse, away from the girl and faced the water. Then he said loud enough for her to hear, "You've no need to fear me, girl. I'm just watering my horse and I'll be on my way."

Ceara continued to look through the branches and leaves, trying to get a better look at the man. He slowly turned as his horse finished drinking and led him back toward the road.

"You can come out, girl, I'll be leaving now."

Ceara waited a moment, thinking about her dream, "Is that the devil, himself," she wondered. "Or could he be an angel sent to help me," she whispered. Then shyly, she stepped out from behind the bush and faced the man.

"My name is Bardan, and I'm traveling toward Limerick." He looked at Ceara, noticed her small frame and swollen belly and said, "Should you be out here alone, girl?" He paused; she was obviously not in any condition to walk. He held the reins and said, "My cart is empty, I've sold my vegetables and I'd be happy to take you toward Limerick or anywhere between here and there."

Ceara was tired, the trip thus far had been without incident until this morning, but she was still more than a day's walk from the river. "I'm on my way to the river and the town nearby. I think the name of it is Ceann Coradh."

"Well now, if you're referring to the River Shannon, then the town to the west is Limerick, where I'm going and the town to the east will be Ceann

Coradh. Now there's no sense in you walking that distance, so come with me, the horse won't mind an extra passenger or two."

His paternal manner brought her comfort and she agreed, "If it's no trouble, I'd thank you for the help."

Bardan helped her up onto the cart and noticed her feet. "Girl, how far have you traveled on those tiny feet?"

"I don't know, I've been walking for two days, but my baby makes me walk slowly and rest often."

"Well, now, you can rest as we ride and no more walking," said Bardan.

As they rode south, Bardan told Ceara about his farm and the kinds of vegetables he grew. They talked about trees and flowers and little animals. Then, when only a mile from the road between Limerick and Ceann Coradh, a wolf came out of the wood, stood on the road in front of them and bared its teeth. Bardan reined in his horse, reached for his bow and stood tall in the cart. The wolf stood less than fifty feet away and looked at them. Bardan notched an arrow and as he drew back, the wolf turned and disappeared into the brush.

"'Tis not a safe place to be for a young woman by herself," said Bardan. "without a weapon." He looked at Ceara, "We'll be moving on now, but be aware, where there is one wolf, there are usually more, and to them we are food."

As Bardan turned to put his bow down, Ceara said, "I'll hold the bow and have an arrow or two at the ready." She smiled, "My Da taught me to hunt and I've taken down a wolf before."

"Have you now," said Bardan, with a look of wonder.

Ceara sat up straight and continued, "Yes, I had just killed a deer and the wolf thought he might take it for himself. I didn't kill the deer for the wolf and another deer may not be easy to find that day, so I killed the wolf too, then pulled the deer onto my cart and brought it home."

Their conversation was lively, and the time passed quickly. As the air cooled and a hint of rain filled the sky, Bardan took an old cloak from the back of the cart and wrapped it about Ceara. Soon they neared the road that went to Limerick or Ceann Coradh, Bardan said, "Now where in Ceann Coradh would you like to go?"

"I don't know, I've not been there since I was a little girl, with my Da. He took me to buy things for the farm."

"Is he there in Ceann Coradh?"

"No, he died a few years ago, and my Mam just this last year."

"Why are you going there, then?" returned Bardan.

"It's the only place I could think of to go. After the raiders burned our village and our warriors came back from serving our chieftain, everybody moved to another village, and I didn't feel like I fit in."

"Your husband?" quizzed Bardan again noticing her obvious pregnancy, "What about him?"

Ceara thought for a moment, "I've no husband. The baby growing inside me is from one of the raiders. He was a large, brutal man. He hit me and I was unconscious. He dragged me into the wood, had his way with me, beat me and left me out there to die."

"So the baby is his?"

"No, no more. He went away, now the baby is mine alone and I'll see to him or her growing up right." She hung her head, "Not like the father."

"What is your tribe?" asked Bardan

"Aidhne," she replied.

"You know you are in the territory of the Dal gCais."

"I don't understand the difference, we're all Irish. What difference does the tribe we come from make?" Ceara asked.

"It depends on the year and who is making raids into whose territory."

"Well, then, I'm Ceara, just Ceara and I'm Irish."

"What about your baby? Won't he be a Northman?"

"No, Irish. He'll be as Irish as I and nobody need know the father was a brute gone Viking." She bowed her head and bit her lower lip, "I had a dream, back there where we met." She hesitated, "I hope it was just a dream."

Bardan saw she was uneasy with her dream, and he waited for her to continue. Several minutes passed and he said, "You're safe now, no need to worry about wolves or bandits."

"I don't know who she was, but she frightened me," said Ceara.

"Who frightened you?" asked Bardan.

Ceara sat up straight and blurted out, "She was tall and thin, wearing a dark cloak. She said my son would be a great warrior if she could lead him. He, his sons, and his grandsons would all be great warriors. Then you came and she disappeared."

"Had you ever seen this woman before?" asked Bardan.

"No, never. I thought she was a banshee, but she never wailed. She just spoke, then she was gone." Ceara hung her head, "Am I cursed?" A tear rolled down her cheek, "Is my baby cursed?"

Bardan thought for a minute, "You've heard the stories about people who live in the shadows?"

Ceara thought for a moment, "I have, but they're just stories. Aren't they?"

"They are, to be sure," said Bardan. "Just stories, but sometimes when we sleep and dream, they can seem very real." He noticed the wonder on Ceara's face and continued, "Scathach is a warrior woman from the Land of The Shadows. She is supposed to have taught the arts of war to great warriors, like Cu Chulainn."

"I've heard of him also, Bardan. Is he just a story?"

"Some of the stories we hear are just myths. Some others are all truth and then there are those that are a little of each. As stories go from one person to another, from year to year, a little embellishment by a teller now and again, can lead to a truth becoming a myth."

"So, how much truth is there in Scathach? asked Ceara.

"There may have been a woman warrior who could teach young warriors years ago, but did she make them invincible? Did she give them magical weapons?" He looked at Ceara, "I don't think so."

"But my dream? That woman who threatened to take my son, what of her?"

"You mean, was that Scathach?" He thought for a moment, then said, "If she ever was, it would have been 200 years ago or more. No, girl, anyone alive then would be long dead now."

"Even a god? If she was a god, she could still be here," said Ceara.

"If and if," laughed Bardan. "Are you a Christian?" he asked looking at her.

"I think so," she replied. "My mother was teaching me things she thought I should know, and she said I should be baptized soon so I could go to heaven." She bowed her head and thought, "I don't understand all the Christian things she talked about and when she took me to hear a priest talk a few times, I didn't understand most of what he said." She looked at Bardan, "Should I be a Christian, so I can go to heaven?"

"That's something you should decide for yourself, Ceara."

"Well, are you a Christian?" she queried.

"I was, when my mother was living, but now, I don't go to the churches much and I haven't been to a mass in a few years." He continued gently rolling the reins, steering the horse on the road and said, "Christians believe there is only one god, there is no room for Scathach as a god and if she ever was a real person, she wouldn't be one today."

Ceara sat quietly, thinking. "What about Cu Chulainn?"

"Again, if he ever was, I don't think he could have been as great as the stories tell," replied Bardan. "He could have killed a dog when he was known as Setanta, but there's no way he could have defeated an army by himself at any age."

"What else should I know about Cu Chulainn?"

"He was a great warrior, he had a harsh temper, he killed his own son not knowing it was his son and he died at an early age."

Ceara looked at Bardan. "He was trained by Scathach?" she said questioningly.

"That is what the legend tells us," he replied.

"She's a tall, beautiful woman with fiery eyes and wears a dark cloak?"

"Some have said she is."

"She wears a sword that shines even in the dark?"

"I've also heard about her sword."

Ceara stared ahead, thinking, "Scathach, it was her." She looked at Bardan, "She said she would take my son and leave me to die on the day he is born."

* * *

Bardan steered his cart toward Ceann Coradh and took Ceara to an inn. He led her inside and spoke to the owner, "Niall, I have a favor to ask of you, cousin." They sat and talked for an hour, Bardan telling Niall everything he had learned from Ceara. "She needs help, the kind of help you and Cairbre can give, and I cannot."

Niall looked across the room at Ceara talking with Cairbre. "Look at them," he said, "talking like two old friends who haven't seen each other in years."

Their conversation was animated, from very serious to laughter, often reaching across to touch the other's hands and Niall knew Cairbre would happily accept this young woman into their home. "There's your answer Bardan, I think it may already be decided."

Bardan fingered his small bag of coins and took out a few pieces of copper, "Take this, I wish I had more to give, but it will help". He stood and looked outside. The sun was setting and the clouds in the sky threatened rain. He looked at Niall, "Cousin, you have a guest for the night."

Cairbre led Ceara into the kitchen and said, "You help me with the dinner and let those two talk."

The morning came with sunshine and a warm breeze. "Tis time for me to leave," said Bardan. He looked at Ceara, "My cousin can help you and you can help him. I'll be back in the spring and see you then.

Ceara threw her arms around Bardan and with a tear in her eye, thanked him for all he had done for her. "Your cloak—don't forget your cloak," she said as he moved toward his cart.

"Keep it about you, girl," said Bardan. "Tis old and worn, but it'll keep you warm and the wind off your back." He motioned Niall to join him away from Ceara and Cairbre and told him of his meeting with this young girl and her frightening dream. "She's terrified of the Shadowy One and I tried to calm her by telling her that Scathach would have been dead long ago. She might never bring it up again, then again, she may tell everyone she meets." He went back to his cart and before he could climb up, Ceara came up from behind, wrapped her arms around him, squeezed hard, and said, "I thank you for all you've done for me, and I'll repay this debt someday."

Bardan smiled, "The smile on your face is more than payment. Tis not a debt, girl. It was a pleasure traveling with you." He climbed onto the cart and pointed his horse toward Limerick.

*　*　*

Niall, the innkeeper was a pleasant fellow who walked with a slight limp and often favored his left arm in lifting and carrying. Cairbre was a round woman with red cheeks and brilliant blue eyes. They welcomed Ceara into their inn, their home and took to her immediately. Cairbre suggested to her husband, "Ceara could help me in the kitchen, feeding our guests and when her baby arrives, it would be like our own grandchild."

Niall saw the hint of loss in his wife's eyes and remembered their son was near to taking a wife just two years previous, before he was killed in a battle, fighting against the Dubliners. "Yes," he replied, "She could be a great help."

Ceara was delighted with the opportunity to work and be useful. "I've never cooked for a large group of people before, but I've hunted game and brought home deer and rabbits."

"We can leave the hunting to our nephew, Brocc," said Niall. "You help in the kitchen and after the birth, perhaps you will go on the hunt with him."

Ceara worked every day, helping as she could and learning more about cooking and baking. She talked often about her wishes for her baby, "I want her to learn to read and write."

"Or him," reminded Cairbre.

Ceara would smile, "Yes, or him." She hoped for a daughter and feared a son may be like his father. "My baby's father was a very violent man, a great warrior, I suppose, but with a temper that would strike fear in the devil himself." She never told anyone other than Bardan she had been raped by a Viking raider. She allowed that her child's father was a warrior and nothing more.

The days passed and Ceara grew ever larger, until she had difficulty standing and walking. The pain of carrying a large baby in such a small body became overwhelming. The last few weeks of her pregnancy were very difficult and Ceara could not stand or walk about. Cairbre and Niall took care of her and when the baby was ready to be born, he was almost too big for a normal delivery. The damage to Ceara's body was more than she could tolerate, and she drew her last breath looking at her new son and holding him one time.

*   *   *

3

902 AD Ceann Coradh, Munster, Ireland
Scolai

Scolai ran ahead of Niall, his father, toward the open field where a crowd of about thirty boys had gathered. Most carried a stick of some kind, some with a flattened piece at the end. The discussion as Scolai arrived was about which stone was to be used in this day's game of hurling.

A tall young man held two stones, each painted white, and he finally said, "This one," as he held it above his head. "Now, let's set the goals." The boys followed him as he stabbed a pike in the ground and held another, ready to place several paces away.

"Spread out boys, we'll walk to the other end of the pitch and get all the other sticks and stones out of the way." He marked off six paces and stabbed the second pike into the ground. Then, he was handed two more pikes and with the boys stretched across the field, they walked toward the other end 100 paces away.

The goals set in place and the playing field marked, the boys began to migrate into two definite groups. Each group took an end of the field, and the tall young man tossed the white stone into the middle. They had only been playing for a few minutes before the first fight broke out. Two boys had collided, and tempers flared. As the tall young man tried to pull the two apart, another fight began and soon all thirty boys were wrestling, running or punching. Scolai was in heaven. He loved the fighting even more than the game, and Niall enjoyed watching his adopted son take on the biggest boys, sometimes even if they were on the same team. As he watched, a tall man stepped up beside him.

"That boy, there," said Lorcain, "He fights much better than he plays." He nudged Niall with his elbow and laughed, "That's my son he has wrestled to the ground."

Niall turned toward Lorcain, "I don't think I ever took you down when we wrestled, old friend, and I've worn many a bump and bruise thanks to you, so, yes, I enjoy my son being on top." Both men laughed as the brawl settled down and the game resumed.

Lorcain, a tall, hard-looking man with the scars of more than one battle looked at Niall and said in a serious tone, "I see you still have the crutch. Does your leg give you pain?"

"The pain is less than the day I was wounded, but the strength is not as it was and seems it never will be. Some days I need the crutch, some days I don't."

"I remember that battle well, we thought you were killed until you cursed and demanded your sword," said Lorcain.

"It was not my finest day." returned Niall.

"We won the day," said Lorcain "And you were still alive."

The two laughed at the memory and turned their attention to the game.

"You named him Scolai," said Lorcain. "In honor of your first son who died fighting against the foreigners?"

"Yes, in a way," said Niall. "His mother died before she could name him and Scolai came to our minds almost immediately."

"I heard you had a young girl living at the inn and she was with child about 8 or 9 years ago. Was that his mother?" asked Lorcain.

"Yes, her name was Ceara. She came here from Connaught to get away from the life she knew there."

"The boy, Scolai, he has the look of a Northman about himself. Do you think his father is Norse?" asked Lorcain.

"Ceara said it often, he's Irish, as Irish as she." Niall smiled, "She was a pretty little thing, as nice as a person could be. I never questioned her about his father, and she never offered, other than to say he was a warrior and was killed in battle."

"Well, good friend," said Lorcain, "this little Scolai looks to be quite a warrior himself." The two laughed again and continued to watch the match and the next round of fights. Minutes later, another warrior approached and pushed his way through the cluster of other hardened men surrounding Lorcain.

"Lorcain, the king, Finguine has died. We should be prepared to accept the next king of Munster," he paused, "it could be you."

Lorcain looked at Niall, "Enjoy the game, old friend. It seems my days of watching hurling matches may be gone. We will meet again soon." He turned and surrounded by nine Dal gCais warriors, headed for the palace.

* * *

The next game was played on the same field several weeks later. Once again, before the game was five minutes old, a fight broke out and a melee ensued.

Scolai was wrestling a larger boy to the ground when he noticed another boy watching him. He stood, releasing his opponent, and faced his observer. "You were here at the last game," said Scolai. "We wrestled then, did you come back for more?"

The boy watching grinned and said, "How did you knock me down last time? You did it three times and I want to know how it happened."

Scolai looked at him and said, "You play a better game of Hurling than I do, so, you show me how to play the game and I'll show you how to wrestle."

"What's your name, wrestler?"

"Scolai," he replied. "What's yours, Hurler?"

"Cennetig," replied the boy.

The two boys spent the rest of the day wrestling and moving the sliotar with their sticks. As Cennetig finally tossed Scolai to the ground, Scolai said, "Maybe I'll play better at the next game."

"Maybe I'll wrestle a little better at the next game," said Cennetig.

The two laughed and continued to push and prod each other as the day passed to night and they went their separate ways.

* * *

Scolai walked into the kitchen where his mother was preparing food for the guests at the inn and the family.

"Scolai, your eye is red, and your lip is bleeding. Have you been fighting again? That eye will be blue for a week," said Cairbre. "Clean yourself up, dinner is ready."

"He's got a lot of his father in him," said Niall. "He'll be a fine warrior, if he can control that temper of his."

"Let's not push him to learn the sword anytime soon," pleaded Cairbre. "He's such a nice boy. He loves to read, and I've heard him sing — perhaps he would enjoy the life of a monk, or a priest."

Niall smiled, "I watched him at the Hurling game a few weeks ago. He's a big, strong boy and loves to fight. I think the warrior blood runs strong in his veins. Someday soon he'll ask me how I came to be an inn keeper with scars on my leg and arm and he'll want to learn as the other boys here learn. He'll carve a wooden sword and make himself a shield." Niall smiled again, "There's Irish warrior blood in his veins, remember that."

They both knew the sandy-colored hair, the dark blue eyes and his greater sized strongly hinted of Norse ancestry, but Scolai was his mother's son, as Irish as she.

Another warm Sunday afternoon and another game outside the palace at Ceann Coradh was about to begin. Scolai arrived, anticipating a few hours of running around crashing into others. His excitement was even greater because of the things he had learned from Cennetig and he looked about for his friend, but didn't see him.

The game began, and the usual fights soon followed. Scolai was pushed into another boy and the two began to wrestle. His opponent was an older boy, bigger than Scolai and he seemed to enjoy the contest as much as Scolai. After several times being thrown to the ground, the two sat next to each other laughing. "My name is Scolai, what's yours?"

"Cassair," said the other boy, "Do you live here in Ceann Coradh?"

"Yes," said Scolai, "my father owns the inn. Where do you live?"

"Our home is across the river in Munster. We've come to visit my father's cousin, Lorcain, when Cormac comes."

"The King of Munster, why is he coming here?" asked Scolai.

"I don't know," answered Cassair. "I think he and Lorcain are friends. I come with my Da because of these hurling matches and all the friends I haven't seen in a while."

"Maybe we know some of the same people," suggested Scolai.

"Sure," Cassair said as he scanned the field. "I was hoping to see a few others that I don't see."

"Me, too. I know some of the others, but not all of their names," said Scolai. "Who are you looking for?"

Cassair punched Scolai in the arm and said, "No matter, let's get back in the game."

The day ended with Scolai returning home as the sun set with more bumps, bruises, cuts, and a huge smile. Cairbre shook her head and told him to clean up and come for dinner. Niall stood across the room, sharpening a knife and felt pride in his adopted son.

"Da, why does the King, Cormac come to Ceann Coradh?" asked Scolai.

Niall set his knife down and replied, "Lorcain leads our tribe, the Dal gCais and we have defended this land of ours and others south of here against incursions from the north, like the one led by Flann, the High King. He tried to invade our land here and would have continued south into Munster, but Lorcain defeated Flann's army here and Cormac didn't have to face them. Now Lorcain presses Flann by raiding up and down the river and gaining great plunder. Thus, Cormac favors Lorcain," said Niall.

"Someday, I'll be a warrior, and go with Lorcain up and down the river," said Scolai. "My friends talk about battles their fathers and brothers have been in and some of them have already begun training with the warriors from the palace."

Niall sensed the next question and he looked at Cairbre, "Scolai, we should talk about this training to become a warrior."

The three sat around a small table and Scolai began, "I know you were wounded in battle before I was born and that your first son was killed fighting near Dublin."

"My wounds were gained in a battle with the men of Connaught and Flann, a few years before you were born," said Niall. "They attacked us, and I stood with Lorcain and our warriors." He breathed deeply, "I was proud to be a warrior, to stand against the invaders with my friends and neighbors." He reached out with his good arm, touching Scolai's shoulder, "I fought, and I was wounded. I was lucky the man who cut my leg didn't finish his task. One of my fellows killed him before he could."

"Was Lorcain in the battle as well?" asked an excited Scolai.

"Yes, of course." replied Niall. "He may be a king someday, but he is still a warrior today and will be forever. He is still one of us and we all stood and fought as equals."

"Was anyone else wounded that day?" asked Scolai.

Niall sat up straight, "Battle is a dangerous business, Scolai. Men fight and kill for a number of reasons. I fought to defend our home and family and would again if I could. Some men fight for the plunder they may gain, some fight for the power of ruling others and some fight because they want to kill."

He paused and looked at Scolai, "Yes, many others were wounded that day, and many were killed." He hesitated again and continued, "I was lucky and I'm alive today. Three good friends were hacked to pieces that day and I can still see their faces and hear their screams."

He stood and slowly moved across the room toward the door, "If it is a warrior you wish to be, then you should begin to train now." He walked outside and stood in the open yard, looking at the stars as the night grew darker.

Cairbre looked at Scolai, "Have you thought of being a monk, or a priest?"

Scolai shook his head, "No, Mam, I've not."

"Then you will go with your father in the morning," Cairbre sighed, "and find a good piece of wood, to carve a sword."

*　*　*

4

905 AD Munster, Ireland
Wooden Swords

Three years passed as if in and instant and Scolai, now in his tenth year, had gone through a number of wooden swords. He had learned what Niall could teach him and as he played with friends, the cuts and bruises increased in severity, but lessened in frequency.

"He learns quickly," Niall said to his wife. "He and his friends play a game of hurling and save the fighting for a round of wooden sword play."

"He is big and strong for his age," replied Cairbre. "I don't suppose he has mentioned being a monk or a priest."

Niall smiled, "No, he hasn't, but he still reads every scrap of writing he can find. He's big and strong, but also intelligent and when he plays with other boys, he is usually the leader."

* * *

Another bright Sunday afternoon came and another Hurling match on the open field was scheduled. Scolai arrived with his hurley and his wooden sword. Cassair spotted him and seemed to have exciting news.

"My father began training me with the sword a few years ago," said Cassair, "but he now wants me to come here to Ceann Coradh and learn from Lorcain's warriors. He thinks I'm old enough and the training here is far better than running with a band of wild boys."

Scolai was excited for his friend but, questioned how this was possible, "I thought we had be in our thirteenth year to be trained by Lorcain's Dal gCais warriors."

"I don't know how they choose people to train, but my father is Lorcain's cousin, and he said that will allow me to be accepted for the warrior training."

Scolai thought for a moment, he reflected on what he had learned from his father, Niall. "My father was wounded in battle before I was born and can't teach me much more than he already has. He watches me practice with this wooden thing and allows me to use his short sword on a post. I would really like to join you and learn from them."

"We would normally have to wait a few more years before they would take us in training, but my father has opened that door for me," said Cassair. "Lorcain's son is our age, and he is already in training. That's why I don't see him at all the hurling matches.

Scolai only half heard Cassair's words, "How long may I have to wait," he asked.

"You're big for your age and that may allow you an earlier entry, but usually when we are in our fifteenth year, they think we could be ready," said Cassair. "You understand they take the sons of warriors and nobles first, then; they may accept others who look promising."

"I'd like to go now," said Scolai.

"You're strong and maybe even bigger than some of the warriors who would teach us," said Cassair. "Don't let that fool you, though. These men have all seen battle, and the training will be very hard, as real as battle, but without the sharp edge of a steel sword."

"Who could I ask, if I wanted to start now?" asked Scolai.

"Lorcain, if he thinks you're ready, he may allow it," said Cassair. "Your father, Niall. He was once a warrior. Maybe he could talk to Lorcain."

Scolai thought for a moment, "My mother has asked if I would like to be a priest. She may not like me beginning the training."

"The training is difficult," said Cassair. "And at the end there is a test to see if you are really ready to see battle. A very difficult test."

*　*　*

Scolai found his father cleaning a floor when he returned home. He sat on a bench and waited for Niall to notice him. "Da, can you teach me more of the sword?"

"My days of wielding a sword are long over, Scolai," said Niall. "I have shown what I can and perhaps I could watch you and tell you more, but if you wish to be a warrior, then we will have to find someone else to teach you. Perhaps some of my old comrades."

"I was talking to my friend, Cassair today and he told me that Lorcain selects a few men each year to be trained by his warriors. I would like to be chosen."

"Scolai, you are very young and have many years ahead of you," said Niall. "I will teach you all I can and try to have some of my friends teach you more. If you do well enough over this next year, I will speak to Lorcain."

Scolai accepted his father's words and set about carving another new wooden sword.

*   *   *

5

908 AD Munster, Ireland
Rioghan

Scolai was in his thirteenth year and had grown to a large, strong boy, appearing to be a few years older than he was. He still enjoyed the hurling matches and was getting better as time progressed, but not near as good as Cassair or Cennetig. His great strength on a team was his willingness to fight anyone and almost always with a smile and a slap on the back when the match was over.

His violent temper was held in check most of the time but fighting with him could be a very dangerous venture if one were to use a stone or a stick. Then he would not smile and several times, he had to be pulled away from his opponent. The summer was near over and a hurling match with a group of boys from another village had been arranged.

The game was played on the same patch of ground as in previous weeks. Each game was preceded with a scanning of the field and removal of sticks and stones as they were found. The ground was uneven, the grass in patches some long, some short made the game more challenging and constant cluster of players around the sliotar resulted in many players tripping, falling, and ending up in a fight.

When the game was over, three boys singled Scolai out and decided to settle a score with him, since he had wrestled two of them to the ground during the match. The contest began with one of the boys pushing him down from behind and kicking him in the ribs. Scolai's expression suddenly went from a smile to a blank stare and a narrowing of his eyes.

"Look, he's gonna cry," exclaimed the boy who kicked him.

Cassair was nearby and saw the initial push. He ran to help his friend, but Scolai was quicker. He was suddenly on his knees, then on his feet and immediately his fist struck the boy full force in his face. The boy went down, bleeding and his two friends charged Scolai.

Two more punches had the other two bleeding and Scolai delivered a second blow to the boy nearest him—the kicker.

Cassair reached the melee as the first boy received the second strike and he stood in front of his friend, "Scolai, are you hurt?"

Scolai's expression softened as he recognized Cassair, "Hurt, no. He kicked me, but I'm alright, I think I'll live." He paused, scanned the area and said, "Let's leave it be. He won't kick me anymore and I won't have to hurt him again."

"Crack his skull, Rioghan," prodded another boy from the other team as six of them arrived.

"Come back here and try your luck with me," said Rioghan.

"You and your friends?" asked Scolai as he turned to face Rioghan.

"No, just me," said Rioghan.

"I don't want to do this," said Scolai as he turned to walk away.

"You don't want to get hurt," laughed Rioghan.

"No," said Scolai. "I don't want to hurt you."

Rioghan stepped toward Scolai and tried to hit him. Scolai moved away from the punch and stepped in close with a strike to Rioghan's stomach. He slumped over and coughed. Scolai stepped away, hoping the contest was over.

Rioghan straightened himself, took a deep breath and attacked Scolai again. A flurry of closed blows delivered by both boys left Rioghan on the ground and Scolai kneeling over him. Both bled from their mouth or nose and Scolai paused with his fist ready to strike again, "Have you had enough?"

Two of Rioghan's friends tried to help as Scolai was grabbed and pulled away from Rioghan. They threw him to the ground. Then one of the boys kicked Scolai in his ribs. The small crowd that had gathered went silent as Scolai rolled off his back and regained his footing.

He didn't speak, he went directly at the boy who kicked him and punched him in his face. The boy went down and Rioghan grabbed Scolai from behind. Scolai moved quickly to his left and grabbed Rioghan's left leg near his ankle, lifting it up over his head and sending Rioghan to the ground. He immediately dropped his knee into Rioghan's chest and savagely punched him in his face. He turned, rose to his feet, and looked for the other boy who had kicked him. That boy was now over a hundred feet away and running. The other boys backed up, turned, and hurried away.

Several of Scolai's friends approached him cautiously, "Scolai, they're gone. All but that one, said one of his friends," pointing at the motionless Rioghan, "he won't bother you again."

* * *

Summer passed with no new incidents and as the air cooled and crops were harvested, Cormac issued a call to arms and assembled an army to march on Leinster. He was seeking payments of tribute due him as King which Leinster had refused. He led his army to Beallach Mugna to meet the forces of Leinster and force payments. Prior to the battle, Cormac sent for Lorcain and made it known that he favored Lorcain to be his successor as King of Munster upon his death.

"He thinks he may be killed in battle," Lorcain told his followers, "And he has stated his choice for me to follow him to the throne."

"A great honor, Da," said Cennetig. "What should we do now?"

"If Leinster continues to refuse payments and proper tribute, they will have battle. It would be better for all if they negotiated a settlement, and everybody went home."

"So, Cormac would remain king?" quizzed Cennetig.

"Yes, there's no rush to the throne, Cormac is a good king, and my time will come soon enough."

"I heard he has had a dream," said Fergal, "a dream which foretells of his death in battle—here."

"Dreams are just that, dreams," said Lorcain. "We will deal in what really happens. If the king dies, perhaps I will be next to occupy the throne. That will be decided by the leaders of several families." He paced the floor and finally turned and said, "We'll leave here in the morning. Cormac has a force large enough for his purposes and we leave the northern border exposed."

Lorcain found his son and Cassair practicing with their wooden swords, "Cennetig, come here," he commanded. "When we return to Ceann Coradh, I want you to see Tadgh. You will move to the next level of training. It is time you learned more of the other weapons we use."

Cennetig was excited, he smiled and said, "Does Cassair go with me?"

Lorcain thought for a moment, "Tadhg tells me he is more than ready, you both advance."

*   *   *

Cennetig and Cassair were walking to the hurling pitch on a Sunday afternoon. "This may be the last game for us," said Cennetig as he saw Tadhg approaching.

"Hurling today, boys?" asked Tadhg.

"We know this may be our last game for a while," said Cassair. "Are you coming to watch?"

"I always enjoyed playing the game, now I watch when time allows." As they walked to the game, Tadhg said, "I've already spoken to your fathers, boys, and all is ready for you both to begin this next phase of your training. We will begin tomorrow. Be ready."

"We will," said the boys in unison and they ran onto the open field where a hurling match was to begin. They found the sides already chosen and joined the team with obviously fewer players. The sliotar was dropped and the chaos began.

Play proceeded for a few minutes when Scolai arrived and Cassair called out to him, "Scolai, here, we could use you."

Scolai saw his friends and ran to join them. The game moved along for another few minutes when the inevitable fight broke out between two boys. Cennetig and Cassair were talking as Scolai approached, "I haven't seen you two for several days."

Cennetig was about to speak when four bigger boys approached, "You there," said one of the boys. "You hurt my brother a few weeks ago. I am here to teach you not to hurt my family or friends."

"Who's your brother?" asked Scolai.

"Rioghan," replied the big boy.

"I didn't want to hurt him," said Scolai, "but he kicked me, and I was not about to let him kick me again."

"Then you'll have to feel my foot cracking your ribs," said the big boy as he stepped toward Scolai, "I think I'll just kill you and not have to do this again."

As he moved quickly towards Scolai with his face turning red and fists clenched, it was obvious he intended to truly hurt Scolai, even if it resulted in killing him. The reaction on Scolai's part was without hesitation as he flipped his hurley in his hand, holding the thicker end and swung the stick hard at the big boy's shins. The stick connected and the big boy screamed out in pain. He stumbled to his knees and Scolai hit him again with the stick across his back.

With the big boy down, Scolai hoped the fight was over, but without pause the other three boys moved to attack Scolai. Each was as big as Scolai and each held a hurley. Scolai turned in time to see the three rush toward him and he quickly took the thin end of his hurley and met the three as he had met wooden swords in practice sessions. Cennetig and Cassair took up their hurleys and each intercepted one of the attackers. The battle was on and Cennetig bested his opponent quickly, Cassair also pushed his foe back and Scolai beat his opponent to the ground.

"Enough of this," said a booming voice. All six turned to see Lorcain looking very angry as he turned toward his son. "What's going on here, this is supposed to be a hurling match and you boys look to be killing each other."

Scolai immediately spoke up, "It is my fault, sir. I hurt this boy's brother a few weeks ago and they were simply trying to even the score."

Cennetig was about to speak when Lorcain raised his hand, "As I said, enough! Now hurling is in order, not killing each other. Go back to your game." He turned and walked away with several others.

The four boys who attacked them skulked back into the crowd and Scolai stood with his two friends, "Who was that?" he asked his friends.

Cassair smiled, looked at Cennetig, then turned toward Scolai, "You don't know him?"

Scolai shrugged his shoulders, "No, but he made them stop trying to kill me, so he's a good man."

Cennetig laughed, "Yes, a very good man. Now, as he said, hurling—that's why we're here." He held up his hurley and the three ran back to the game.

After the game as Scolai was walking home, two of the big boys stepped out of the shadows and one said, "You don't have him to save you now." They attacked and Scolai was alone against the two. The first slash with a hurley caught Scolai on his right shoulder. He stepped back away from his attackers and brought his hurley up to defend against another slash.

The boy to his right tried to strike Scolai near his hip, the other moved to deliver an overhead downward blow. Scolai stepped quickly into the first boys hurley with his own and continued the swing back against the second boys left arm. The cracking of bone and a scream of pain filled the air and the first boy tried again to slash at Scolai's mid-section. Scolai stepped into the swing and used his fist to strike the boy in his face. The two fell to the ground and Scolai struck him again in his face, forcing his head down hard against the ground. The boy fell motionless and Scolai knelt over him, poised with a closed fist ready to strike him again. He hesitated, he wanted to punch him again, but stopped and stood. One boy with a broken arm, the other unconscious. Scolai picked up his hurley and walked toward home.

*   *   *

Morning came with the news that a boy was killed after the hurling match and his companion had a broken arm. Scolai found his father and, making sure his mother couldn't hear, he told Niall what had happened. "I didn't know he was dead. They attacked me and I defended myself with this," he said holding up his hurley.

Niall looked at Scolai, "You know the road south along the river?"

Scolai nodded, "Yes, but I've only taken it a few miles south."

Niall continued, "There is a fork in the road several miles south. The north fork goes to Limerick and the south to Cashel. Take the south branch, about two miles on you'll find a farm and a man by the name of Bardan." Niall put his hand on Scolai's shoulder, "Tell him who you are, and your mother's name. He will know you and help you."

"Did I do wrong, Da?" asked Scolai.

"No, boy," said Niall. "You did as you should. What I fear is the dead boy's family will come looking for you and more blood will be shed. Wait here." He left the room and returned almost immediately with Cairbre. She was carrying a leather belt with a sword ring and Niall held his short sword.

Cairbre touched Scolai's cheek, "Now, there is no choice. You are a man, and you should be able to defend yourself." She handed him the belt.

Niall said, "This sword has served me well. I hope you don't have cause to use it, but if you do, remember the little I have taught you."

Cairbre busied herself preparing a bundle of food and Niall handed Scolai a knife and reached for a bow, "The road is well traveled between here and Bardan's farm, but you should remain out of sight as much as possible. If you see someone coming, turn into the wood, let them pass, and continue. It would only take one person saying they saw you and you could be in danger again."

Cairbre was holding a cloak and the small bundle of food, "Bardan put this cloak around your mother when they came to Ceann Coradh. Now it can keep you warm as you travel to him."

She put the cloak across Scolai's shoulders, "Please be very careful and don't draw attention to yourself." She put her arms around her son and said, "Go now, in time we will see you again."

Scolai left the inn and hurried to the road south. He pulled the cloak close about himself and didn't look at anyone on the road, appearing as any ordinary man going about his business.

* * *

6

910 AD Munster, Ireland
Mochta

Scolai crossed the River Shannon and wandered south, along the water's edge. The river turned east then south again, passing groves of young oak and ash trees and widened as it turned slightly westward. He continued to a narrowing of the river and saw the road to his left that would take him south to the low rolling hills of Tipperary. He walked several miles from the river and found a recently fallen tree with most of the branches cleared, he sat on the trunk, in the shade of another tree, opened his pack and began to eat the bread and apples Cairbre had packed for him. He scanned the open fields in front of him and saw a man herding a flock of sheep in the distance.

Biting through an apple, he relaxed, forgetting about the reason for his journey, and watched the sheep graze on the lush grass. The shepherd didn't seem to notice him, and he began to close his eyes. The sudden caw of a crow aroused him, and he looked at the bird, "No bird, I am very much alive, not a meal for you." He stood, shook off the haze in his eyes, and was about to resume his trek when he saw the shepherd coming his way.

He moved his hand to his sword, felt its weight and watched the man approach.

"A fine summer day it is," he said to the shepherd.

"That it is," responded the man. He was older than Scolai by several years; tall, broad-shouldered, and well-muscled. His skin was the color of tanned leather, his hair was black, short, and very curly. He smiled and his bright blue eyes sparkled in the sunlight. "Where are you heading on this fine day?" he asked. His voice was friendly, not threatening and he was unarmed save the large staff in his hand.

Scolai eased his grip on his sword, and it slid gently back into its ring, "I'm on my way to visit a friend of my family," Scolai replied. "I believe his farm is on this road a bit farther south."

"Who may that be," quizzed the shepherd.

"His name is Bardan," answered Scolai.

"Well then, that it is, about fifteen miles and on the far side of the road. I'll walk with you a while if you don't mind." He looked back at his sheep, "When we get to that stand of trees ahead, I'll leave you and tend to my flock." He smiled, "My name is Mochta."

"I'm Scolai, from Ceann Coradh."

"Ceann Coradh, is it now? I've been to Ceann Coradh, with your friend, Bardan," said Mochta. "We were both in Lorcain's army when we marched north to battle the foreigners in Connaught. That was the year Bardan lost his wife to illness, and his want to be a warrior. He's a good man and we remain friends."

"Do you still go to war with Lorcain and his warriors?" asked Scolai.

"I do," returned Mochta. "My family was from Connaught, my grandfather was a slave, freed because he was a better warrior than a farmer and my mother was a slave taken in a raid into Meath. The Dal gCais took the lot of us as hostages, along with others, about thirteen years ago and we the fit into the life at Ceann Coradh. My father joined a few raids into Connaught and when I was old enough, I went with them."

"Did you have the warrior training at Ceann Coradh?" asked Scolai.

"No, that was something to train the sons of the nobles and warriors. I built my skill in battle."

"A few of my friends are training with the warriors," said Scolai, "and I wish I was with them."

"I know many of the warriors there and your friends will learn well. Learn from them—learn from your friends," said Mochta.

"But they aren't teachers," said Scolai.

"It is not for them to teach, as much as it is for you to learn," returned Mochta. He stopped and held his staff in front of himself. "Look here," he said as he twirled the staff in front of himself, then around his waist, and stopped with the staff again in front of himself. "Now what did you see?"

Scolai shook his head, smiled, and answered, "I see you can do tricks with a shepherd's staff."

Mochta grinned, "No, my friend, you see a warrior spin his long-handled axe in an enemies face and ready to fight him."

"That's a shepherd's staff," said Scolai.

"Once again, no, my friend," returned Mochta. "Have you ever seen a shepherd's staff like this," with that he handed the staff to Scolai.

"It's heavy, very heavy. I thought staffs for herding sheep were much lighter."

"So they are, but this is a new shaft from my war axe. Before going back to Ceann Coradh and my next battle, I will trim its thickness, wrap leather around the place where I will have my hands, put the axe head on one end and remove the iron weights there now."

Scolai looked at the ends of the staff. Each end had several iron rings around it making the staff very difficult to carry and use as a shepherd's staff, "Why do you do this?" asked Scolai.

"I am home, not at war. I tend my sheep, not attack a shield wall. The things I do here at home, where it is quiet and peaceful, must not take away from my ability to kill my enemies when the time is right. I practice with this heavy staff, and when I go into battle, I will carry my axe as easily as I now carry this staff." He looked at Scolai, "I have not been taught, but I learn."

He smiled and continued, "When I saw you, I crossed a battlefield and attacked your shield wall, what you saw was a man calmly walking toward you and greeting you. I use everything about me to teach myself and now there is no better axe man in Lorcain's army than me."

Scolai puzzled a moment longer and tried to spin the staff. It fell to the ground and Mochta smiled. Scolai picked it up and handed it back to Mochta, "I should cut a piece of oak like yours and practice."

They reached the stand of trees where Mochta said he would return to his sheep and he stopped, "Perhaps we will meet again and talk more of your becoming a warrior."

Scolai looked out over the field and said, "Your sheep are scattering."

"No again my friend, my enemy is trying to escape, and I must capture them." He laughed as he bounded over the short stone wall and ran to herd his sheep. To capture his enemy.

7

910 AD Munster, Ireland
Bardan

Scolai continued 'til the sun began to sink behind the distant hills to the west. He found a sheltering stand of trees where he made a camp, built a fire, and finished eating the bread, apples, and cheese from his pack.

The night was kind, it wasn't too cold and the grass where he slept beneath the trees was still dry when he woke. He gathered himself and continued on his way. The air was unusually warm and dry, the breeze gentle on his face, as the sun rising in the east warmed his back. He passed groves of ash and oak, noting the occasional deer noticing him and not bolting, "A fine warrior I'll be," he laughed to himself, "I can't even startle a deer."

Sooner than he expected, he came to a farm where he saw an old man working in a field, harvesting vegetables. He approached and offered to help in return for enough to make a meal.

"I believe there is enough for a number of meals if you help me all day," said the old man as he noticed a stain and a tear on the young man's cloak.

Scolai smiled, rubbed his hands together and said, "All day? I'd be more than happy to help you all day."

The old man looked at Scolai knowingly and said, "You know who I am, Scolai? I haven't seen you in a few years, perhaps eight or nine, but I'd know you and that cloak anywhere." He rested his rake against an old cart, "What brings you this way?"

Scolai removed the cloak and handed it to Bardan, "I believe this is yours."

Bardan looked at it closely, held it for a moment then said, "I gave it to your mother. You keep it." He continued, "How is my cousin, Niall and Cairbre?"

"They're well, and said you may be able to help me," he told Bardan about his fight with the two boys and that one had died. "I didn't mean to kill him, only to make him stop threatening to kill me. Now Niall thinks his family will want revenge."

"Did anyone see you fight with these two boys?"

"No, the hour was late, and the sun was about to pass behind the western hills. By the time I was home, it was dark."

They talked for a while about the events leading up to the fight and Bardan said, "Niall was right to send you this way. Some people do not see the justice in this kind of thing. You were attacked and you defended yourself. I'm sure Lorcain would see it that way and rule accordingly."

Scolai forced a smile, "That's what Niall said."

"I see it still troubles you," said Bardan. "What could you have done differently?"

"I hit him when he was down, I could have let him get up and walk away, but I hit him and wanted to hit him again."

"You were not wrong in hitting him. Doing it a second time when it would not be necessary, that may have been wrong." Bardan thought for a second and continued, "What do you think you should do now?"

"I should stay away from Ceann Coradh for a while, until the family of that boy no longer seeks to do me harm."

"You're welcome to stay here with me, I could use some help with these crops and the animals."

Scolai told Bardan about meeting Mochta. "Yes," said Bardan, "a very interesting man and a good long-handled axe man. Watch him as he exercises."

They talked for a while longer and Bardan finally asked, "What do you intend to do with your life?"

"My friends and I talk about becoming warriors, we would fight for Lorcain—for the Dal gCais."

"A warrior must be able and willing to fight. He has to be ready to meet any challenge that comes along. But there are times when he must stand down, when the battle is over and there is no need to kill anymore." He looked closely at Scolai's face, "Why didn't you hit that boy a second time?"

"I didn't like it when I was kicked in the ribs, I was down and there was no need to kick me, other than to hurt me. It made me angry. It wouldn't be right to kick someone else when he is down." He looked at Bardan, "I know I have a temper and sometimes I get so angry, I forget what happens." He bowed his head, "Niall told me, my father was a warrior, and he also had a temper. But I try to be a better man, I try to control the anger that sometimes comes over me and I didn't hit him again."

Bardan stood, "The sun is about to disappear, help me put the rest of these vegetables in the cart and we can be in my house preparing dinner when the sun drops from the sky."

*   *   *

8

910 AD Munster, Ireland
Brighid

Scolai stayed with Bardan through the winter and into the next summer and the harvest. His urge to leave and go farther south was lost when he met Bardan's niece, Brighid. She was two years younger than him with dark brown hair, big brown eyes and a smile that made Scolai forget everything else about him. She lived only a mile away, on a farm that was named Cnoc Gorm, Blue Hill for the blue flowers that grew on the rise approaching the rath. The land overlooked a small river that flowed eventually to the ocean.

Brighid and Scolai often walked to a grove of oak trees at the top of a small hill that gradually fell away to the river where they would sit in the shade and talk. They were young, but they seemed destined to be together. They talked almost every day and looked forward to their next meeting.

Three weeks after meeting Brighid, a warm autumn day, as Scolai was working in the field with Bardan, a tall, angry-looking man approached. Scolai saw him coming and stood, looked for his sword and moved in its direction. The tall man was about fifty feet away when he spoke, "You there, is your name Scolai?"

Scolai stood as tall as he could, looked to Bardan, then turned toward the man and replied, "I am, and who may you be?" He looked back at Bardan and saw him smiling.

The man came closer and Scolai was still farther away from his sword than he liked. He spoke again, "I am Breasal, Brighid is my daughter." He was now only five feet from Scolai. The two were looking directly into each other's eyes, "My daughter has told me about you, and so has my brother." He stood looking at Scolai with no expression on his face, "You come from Ceann Coradh, who is your father?"

"My father is dead, and long before I was born," said Scolai. "I never knew him. He was killed in battle in Connaught. Niall mac Morann and his wife Cairbre raised me in their home after my mother died."

"What was your father's name?"

"I don't know, I don't think I ever knew. Niall has been my father—a good father to me."

Breasal thought for another moment and continued, "How old are you?"

"I'm in my fifteenth year."

Breasal stepped back, looking Scolai from head to foot, "You look older, you're big for such a young man. What will you do with your life?"

"I have always wanted to be a warrior. I plan to return to Ceann Coradh this year, or next, and join Lorcain's forces."

Breasal held back his amusement, "Lorcain, do you know him?"

"No, but I have met some of his warriors and in the hurling matches, many of their sons join in."

"Who have you met?"

"Two of my friends are Cassair and Cennetig."

Breasal raised an eyebrow, "Oh and do you know their fathers?"

"No, but I think one of their fathers was there the last time I was. He looked like a warrior, a big man. I saw him talking to my father earlier and at the last match he stopped a fight with a single word."

"Who was he?" quizzed Breasal.

"I'm not sure, but he stopped the fight and I appreciated that. There were four of them and they were a little bigger than us," said Scolai.

Breasal smiled, "Bigger than you?"

Scolai thought for a moment and said, "Maybe not, but definitely bigger than Cassair. Cennetig and I are about the same size and there were only three of us and four of them."

Breasal said, "So you don't know this warrior who stopped the fight?"

"No, but my friends did. When he walked away and I said he was a good man, both of my friends agreed. I guess it could have been Cassair's or Cennetig's father."

"Do you know their fathers' names?"

"No," confessed Scolai.

"When you return to Ceann Coradh, be sure to ask your friends who he is," Breasal advised.

Scolai looked at Breasal, "You say that as if you already know who it is."

"Perhaps," returned Breasal, "But I may be wrong."

"Who, then?" asked Scolai.

"When you return, ask."

* * *

The next year, when the harvest was complete, Bardan announced he intended to travel to Ceann Coradh to sell some of his vegetables and trade for some other goods. Scolai said he would like to go with him. "Enough time has passed," he said, "I should return and let Niall and Cairbre know I am well."

He found Brighid talking to her father and approached. "Well young Scolai has come to visit," said Breasal, "or has he come to help with our harvest?"

Brighid laughed and ran to meet Scolai, "You look as if you have something to say."

"I do," said Scolai. "The time has come for me to return to Ceann Coradh. Niall and I will leave in the morning."

Brighid bowed her head, "Will you be coming back here soon?" she asked.

"I don't know what will happen when I get there," Scolai answered. "Remember the reason I left, I killed someone and there will be questions and maybe someone will be seeking revenge."

"I worry about you," said Brighid. "Please be careful and come back soon." She hugged him and kissed him on his cheek, "I'll be here, waiting."

Breasal watched his daughter bid Scolai farewell and opened his arms to comfort her as he walked away, "He's a fine strong young man, daughter. I know he'll be back as soon as he can."

"I fear for him, Da, he goes to face whatever he must."

"Not to worry, girl, we have all spoken to Lorcain and the matter should be settled."

"Who spoke to Lorcain?" inquired Brighid.

"Your uncle and your cousin, Niall."

Brighid looked up at her father, "And you, Da?"

"Yes girl, I told Lorcain what I thought of the man, and he was pleased in what he heard from each of us."

*   *   *

Bardan and Scolai traveled to Ceann Coradh and a week later, Bardan returned. "Has he come with you, Uncle?" asked Brighid.

"No girl," replied Bardan. "But we hope he may someday."

"Can you tell me more about him, Uncle?"

Bardan sat down and scratched his beard, "Well now, Scolai is an interesting young man. I may know a little more about him than you have already learned."

"Tell me, Uncle, please tell me," begged Brighid.

They sat and talked for a while, Bardan relaying the story of his meeting a young girl on the road south to Limerick, "She was a lovely young girl and I saw some of my wife in her. I couldn't just leave her on the road to Ceann Coradh, so I took her to our cousin, Niall."

He told her of the wolf on the road and how she took the bow with confidence, ready to protect them both as they traveled. "She was a very brave young woman, younger than you are today." He allowed the words to hang in the air for a moment and continued, "Then there was her dream, a dream about the Shadowy One."

Brighid's eyes widened, "Scathach?"

"Yes girl, the teacher of great warriors," said Bardan.

*   *   *

9

910 AD Munster, Ireland
Returning Home

The trip to Ceann Coradh took two days and the conversation was more about Brighid than the trouble Scolai may face when they arrived. "Almost two years since I've seen Niall and Cairbre. It will be good to be home again, but I look forward to coming back here to see you and Brighid."

Bardan listened and smiled, the boy was becoming a man. The little that Bardan could add to teaching him more of the sword may not keep him up with his friends, but there had been definite improvement. The several visits from Mochta added to Scolai's abilities. He now carried a heavy staff, weighted at both ends, and learned to move the staff as if it were a long-handled axe.

"When we arrive, I have a few people to see and business to attend to," said Bardan. "You should visit with Niall and Cairbre, stay out of sight until we know if the air has cleared and if anyone seeks your head on a pike."

Scolai agreed, "I'm rather fond of my head and want to keep it a while longer, so I'll do as you suggest and not wander the town."

The hour was late as they arrived in Ceann Coradh and the darkening sky gave a little extra cover to Scolai's return, "Stay here with the cart while I see who may be in the inn," said Bardan. "Don't speak to anyone."

Scolai nodded and pulled the cloak over his bowed head. Bardan went into the inn and a few minutes later, returned with Niall. "Scolai," whispered Niall, "welcome home."

Scolai climbed down and Bardan said, "Remember, stay inside 'til I return." He climbed on the cart and urged the horse forward.

Cairbre was waiting anxiously as Scolai entered the inn. She threw her arms around him and squeezed as hard as she could, "I have prayed for your safe return from the minute you left us." She stood back, planted her hands on her hips, and looked Scolai up and down, "Well, the boy seems to have grown into quite a man," she said as a tear rolled down her cheek. "What is that tree trunk you carry," she asked.

Niall looked at Scolai and said to Cairbre, "He has met Mochta."

"Ah, the axe man," she smiled. "Well set it aside and come to the table, I've made a soup and there's warm bread."

Scolai sat and talked with his parents for an hour, talking about Bardan's farm, working with the vegetables, and his special friend, "A pretty little girl, Brighid."

The hour was late when Bardan returned, "Well now, we seem to have come at the right time," he said. "I've met with a few old friends, and it appears that the incident two years ago is all but forgotten."

Niall said, "Did you speak to himself?"

"I did," replied Bardan. "He has had several people talk to him, as well as us, about the incident and he knows Scolai only defended himself. It's over and done."

Scolai looked confused, "Who did you speak to?"

Bardan smiled, "The man who said 'enough', Lorcain."

*   *   *

Scolai went to the open field where the hurling matches were played on Sundays. He looked about, remembering what it had been like and wondering if the people he saw recognized him. He walked through the marketplace, where he saw an older man talking to several younger boys. They were talking about learning the sword and shield. He drew close and listened. The older man noticed him and said, "You there, are you interested in what we discuss?"

"I heard you talking about fighting with a sword. Are you one of Lorcain's warriors?" Scolai asked.

"I was, but I no longer fight, I teach others to fight. Do you wish to learn?" asked the older man.

"I'm able to stand and fight," Scolai told the old warrior.

"I'm looking for men with some experience," replied the old man. "These boys will someday be ready, you look old enough, you have the size, and you carry a weapon—that short sword. Have you ever seen battle?"

Scolai shook his head, "No, I've never been in battle, I've never had to, but now I'm grown, and I should be able to stand and fight with the warriors." He stepped closer, "If I had the proper training."

As they were talking, another young man approached. He looked at Scolai and said, "I know you; we've played at hurling several times when we were a little younger."

Scolai tilted his head, thought for a moment, and replied, "I remember you. We did more wrestling than hurling then."

The two laughed, "Yes we did," said the other young man, "it's been a long time, Scolai."

"So it has, Cennetig. It's good to see you again." He looked around and asked, "Is Cassair also?"

"He's still in today's training session, we may see him later," answered Cennetig.

Cennetig slapped his old friend on his shoulder, "Are you here to join us?"

"I was thinking about it. This fellow says he can teach me."

Cennetig smiled, "Tadhg, he recruits men to join the army we try to maintain, but you should join me in the warrior training."

"Is there a difference?"

"Yes, not everyone is put through the warrior training," said Cennetig. "The sons of nobles and warriors of rank are given priority. Cassair is almost finished. I think he will be tested in about a month. I've had too many breaks in training and will probably be closer to your completion date." He laughed, "Have you had any training? They will ask you to show them what you can do and decide where you will fit in the sessions."

"Some—from Niall and Bardan. I also met a man who taught me some of the axe."

"I haven't begun that phase yet, you may be ahead of me there. Let's go see Tadhg and his team, they'll evaluate you and decide where you fit."

"Cennetig, I'm not a noble, and my father died years ago in Connaught. I may not be allowed into this training."

"Scolai, you're my friend and I have some influence with the staff of warriors," said Cennetig. "Tadhg is gathering men who will be with the army. Most of them have some experience and do not get the same training as we do."

"Does Tadhg teach the warriors?" asked Scolai.

"Yes, he was a great warrior and has seen battle many times. Now he is old and the aches and pains, from his wounds of years past, visit him frequently, but he is a very good teacher." Cennetig looked at the old warrior, "Tadhg, is my teacher and he could be yours as well. So, would you like to join us?"

Scolai didn't hesitate, "Yes, what do I do?"

"Come with me," said Cennetig, "I'll see to getting you started."

Tadhg said, "You should ask your father, Cennetig, about a new fighter. We should also see how he handles that sword."

"Perhaps, old friend, but I remember this fellow, we played with wooden swords and hurling together. I know he will learn quickly and be better than most before the sun rises again."

As the two young men walked across an open field, Cennetig said, "You've grown since we last met. Your size and strength can be a great asset in battle," he laughed. "It can also draw more enemy to you, and you will have to fight harder than most. My father will be pleased to meet you and more pleased to have you join in our training."

Scolai looked at Cennetig, "Your father, is he also a warrior in this army?"

Cennetig smiled, "Yes, he leads this tribe."

Scolai stopped and looked at Cennetig, "Lorcain is your father?"

"Yes," said Cennetig, "he is. What of your family?"

Scolai lowered his head, smiled and said, "My Da, Niall was a warrior. He was cut deep in his leg, long before I was born and his arm also. He walks with a bit of a limp and sends me to lift and carry anything he can't with his one good arm."

"How was he wounded?" asked Cennetig.

"Some battle about twenty years ago, I don't know much about it. He says it was fighting the men of Connaught. They had to be pushed back north out of our territory. Now, he owns an inn."

The following day, Scolai returned to the marketplace and met Cennetig again. As they walked to the training center, Cennetig asked Scolai, "Your father, his name is Niall?"

"Yes," replied Scolai, "How did you know?"

"My father was leading an army against the King of Connaught, and he knows a warrior named Niall, a good friend who was wounded fighting at his side. The man now is an innkeeper, here in Ceann Coradh."

The two looked at each other, and Cennetig continued, "Our fathers were comrades in battle, now we will be comrades as well. You will come with me and learn the same things I learn." He paused, smiled, and said, "You taught me to be a better wrestler when we were younger, now I will help make you a warrior."

* * *

10

910 AD Munster, Ireland
Training

Lorcain was a tough taskmaster, Cennetig told Scolai, "My father has said, if you are to learn, then you should learn the right way. A warrior should learn to fight on his own, without help, but also learn to fight when a comrade is next to him." The two young men entered an open yard where a number of others were clashing with wooden weapons. "This is where we learn," said Cennetig.

The yard was as big as a hurling pitch with posts standing the height of a man scattered about, a pit with a sand bottom, a small hill with boulders on one side, and a shallow pond. The yard was enclosed with a picket wall over twelve feet high and a narrow walkway around the perimeter, over eight feet above the ground.

Scolai saw Cassair fending off two other young men with their wooden swords. "We will be with Cassair?" asked Scolai.

"No," returned Cennetig, "he's far ahead of us in the training. He may finish this year and we will be half done."

Scolai gave his friend a confused look.

Cennetig smiled, "I go with my father when he meets with other leaders and my training slows. I have to learn to talk as well as fight." He smiled and held his hands apart, then he nodded to a man across the yard, "You've met Tadhg, our teacher."

The old warrior approached the two, "Cennetig, your father told me you were bringing this young man to join us." He looked at Scolai, smiled, and said, "You have the size, now we will teach you the skill and see what kind of warrior you may become." He led the two to a table where there were a number of wooden weapons, "Choose one to use today," he told Scolai.

Cennetig selected a wooden sword and Scolai did likewise, "You'll use these weapons today and tomorrow—perhaps a different one," said Tadhg. "When you have finished here, you will be able to use a number of weapons.

Today we practice against other young men. At day's end, you will be battered and bruised, but better at the art of war than you are this morning."

"We practice every day," he said to Scolai. "We practice and learn. When we finally go into battle, we'll be better prepared than our opponents."

Scolai queried, "You practice with a wooden sword today, do you ever practice with one of steel?"

"Yes, we do," returned Cennetig, "but not when we fight our fellows. The steel is used at the practice post and will be used in battle, but here we use these wooden swords. They are heavy and clumsy so when we use our swords of steel, they seem light and cut easily through the air."

"When do we practice at the post?" asked Scolai.

"Time will determine when you're ready. Tomorrow I'll practice at the post, remembering the number of times they hit me with their wooden swords, and I'll kill the post. You'll see my friend."

Tadhg approached the two and put his hand on Scolai's shoulder, "It's your turn to be taught, boy. Come with me." He put his hand on Scolai's wooden sword and shook it loose from his grip. Scolai looked confused, Cennetig smiled, and Tadhg frowned, "That is your sword," he said pointing toward the ground, "it is of no use if not in your hand. Learn to never let it fall again."

Cennetig poked Scolai with his wooden sword and said, "It begins."

Scolai followed Tadhg to a circle of dirt, and they stopped, "You hold a sword in your hand, and I am your enemy. I intend to kill you, quickly. What should you do?"

Scolai looked at the sword and back at Tadhg, "I should kill you first."

"Yes, you should," said Tadhg as he raised his wooden sword and attacked Scolai. He hit Scolai's sword once then struck Scolai in the belly and again struck his sword, then hit him on his upper arm, then the sword again, and finally stopped with his wooden sword resting on Scolai's shoulder touching his neck.

"I have just opened your belly, cut into your sword arm, and taken your head. You are now dead." He looked at Scolai, smiled, and continued, "Now, before you kill me, learn how to stay alive."

Scolai looked at his friend, Cennetig who stood off to the side laughing, "Stay alive once and he may allow you to eat with us tonight."

Tadhg said, "Now, if someone is attacking you, look in his eyes, raise your sword in front of you, and hold it tight in your hand. Be ready to block a slash, a thrust, a lunge." He raised his sword again and slowly slashed at Scolai's waist. The slash was met with a casual blocking movement and the old man said, "Do not be gentle with me, hit my sword and knock it from my hand." He backed up and again made a slow slash toward Scolai's middle. Scolai swung his wooden sword hitting the Tadhg's sword and forcing it backward. "Better," he said. "Now again."

The session went on for over an hour and Scolai was tiring when the old man said, "A tired warrior will only fight one day. If you wish to be able to come back the second day, you must stay alive, so you will need to make yourself stronger and able to fight all day."

Scolai looked at Tadhg, "I'm tired. You've taken all of my strength."

"We'll do this again tomorrow in the morning until you're exhausted, then again in the afternoon until you're too tired to continue. We do this every day and soon you'll be able to fight all day as I do now. We'll make you into a strong warrior."

Scolai bent over with his hands on his knees, "Strong enough to fight with you all day?"

"Stronger," said Tadhg. "I'm old and can no longer do battle with a real warrior. You'll practice every day until I say you are ready for combat. Until then, I'll push you as hard as I can."

Two months passed and as the weather turned cold and the rains began, Scolai felt himself able to match Tadhg in combat with the wooden swords, "Am I ready now, old man?"

"You have taken great strides in your training, but you have a long way to go." He turned to greet a pair of younger men, each carrying a wooden sword, "These are two men who have seen battle and will help in preparing you for the same experience."

He led the three to the round sand pit where he trained Scolai, "In battle, you must be able to fight more than just one opponent. Sometimes there will be two or more attacking you. You'll use what I have taught you. We begin."

The two other young warriors moved apart and one approached Scolai with a slash at full speed. Scolai blocked that move and countered with a downward blow. The young warrior blocked Scolai's slash and backed away. He smiled and nodded at the other warrior, and as Scolai turned to see him the other warrior began an attack. The two alternated attacks for an hour and as Scolai's arms began to ache, the other two were still fresh and ready to attack again.

"Hold," said Tadhg in a commanding voice. The two warriors stopped attacking Scolai, "This afternoon we'll do this again." He looked at Scolai, "You'll be ready, eh boy?"

The days turned to weeks and the weeks led to the coldest time of the year. Biting winds, rain or sleet and an occasional snow marked the day and Scolai kept working at the training. As the spring approached, Scolai felt comfortable and at ease after two four-hour sessions with Cennetig at his side and the two facing four opponents, "These boys have learned what I can teach of the sword, they're good, very good," said Tadhg to Lorcain. "They're ready to move on to the axe and the spear. In time, perhaps years end, they will be ready for the test."

*　*　*

Tadhg's prediction was right, Cennetig's training was interrupted so many times, he needed two years to Cassair's one to complete. Scolai had learned enough of the sword from Niall, Bardan and Breasal that he passed over a number of sessions. The few times with Mochta gave him an advantage over all the other prospective warriors and even two of the warrior instructors. The year passed and the two young men were ready to be tested. Ready to become true warriors of the Dal gCais.

Lorcain walked into a practice session as the young men were finishing a series of arm tiring exercises with heavy steel swords. He smiled as his son and friend wiped the sweat from their brows and reached for water.

"You both appear ready for battle," he said, "ready but not yet tested against a live enemy."

He stepped closer to the two and continued, "Imagine facing a man in battle with the sun shining brightly, a cool breeze taking the sweat from your arms and back and your enemy falling politely at your feet. Glorious." The speech sounded familiar to Scolai, he could almost hear Niall and Bardan preaching the same advice.

"Now hear my words and keep your mind open. Battle is not polite. It is not glorious. It is, my young friends, hell, it is steel cutting through flesh, leaving men without arms, legs and heads. It is blood and bits of brain flying through the air with nearly every swing of another man's sword or axe. It is hearing the screams of men as they are hacked apart, smelling the blood, vomit, urine and feces soaking the ground at your feet and seeing your comrades split from crown to navel by an enemy's sword or axe. Battle, my friends is not beautiful, it is ugly and has turned very good men into babbling fools. You should know what you are about to see, about to face." He paused, looked at his son then at Scolai, "Now take up your swords and stand ready."

Lorcain nodded to Tadhg, "Test them."

* * *

11

912 AD Munster, Ireland
The Test

Tadhg signaled to another man, a tall gaunt looking man with no weapons, "Goban, these two are to be tested together against five."

"Yes, I have five that will do for this," he replied as he turned and walked away.

Lorcain looked at his son and friend, "You are both ready and this is your final hurdle. Do as Goban instructs and no less." He put his hand on Cennetig's shoulder, looked him in the eye, turned and walked away. Moments later Lorcain reappeared on the raised walkway around the yard. He was accompanied by Tadhg and his personal guard of ten battle tested warriors who had all helped teach both Cennetig and Scolai over the last months. The walkway then filled with men who all had the look of hardened warriors. Lorcain looked about the yard and nodded to Tadhg.

The two young warriors stood and waited, not knowing what was to come. Then five men came into the yard followed by Goban. He told them to stay where they were and crossed the open yard to Cennetig and Scolai, "These men are prisoners, taken in different battles with raiding Norse over the last few years. Each has been given a sword and a small shield. You will meet them in the middle of this yard, and you will kill them, all of them." He looked at the two young men, "Do you understand me? I said you will kill them. This is your test—there is no failure, there is only victory or death."

Cennetig and Scolai looked confused, then they both gripped their swords, looked across the open yard at the five prisoners and nervously said they were ready.

"Kill these men as quickly as you can, all of them," said Gabon. "When you have killed them all, take their heads and put them on the pikes there," he pointed at five pikes around the perimeter of the yard. "Then hack their bodies apart. This will be your first test as a warrior, kill and see the bodies torn apart, smell the blood and taste the air as it lifts their waste and vomit to your nostrils."

"Will they fight?" asked Scolai.

'Yes," replied Goban, "they have been told if they survive this test, they will be released, free to go as they wish." He looked back at the two, and said, "Lorcain is a man of his word, if they kill you, they will be free." He walked to the center of the yard.

Cennetig looked at Scolai, "I didn't expect this." His voice was dry and carried a quiver. "We can do this; I know we can pass this test."

Scolai nodded, "yes, we can do this," he repeated in the same dry, shaking, low voice. "I don't think Lorcain would put us in a position to be anything but successful."

The two young warriors knew the men they faced were weak, they had not seen battle in months and their chances of living through this test were very low. Cennetig and Scolai were well trained, well-armed and in prime condition.

Goban came close to the two warriors, "This is your first taste of real battle. Each of these men will try his best to kill you and they have all seen battle. Kill and be quick about it. Be quick and final. Do not waste time thinking or worrying. Kill one and move on."

He stepped away and signaled the five men to come closer. He looked at the five, "Kill these two, and you will be free." He backed away from the middle then said in a loud voice, "Begin."

The five men moved slowly, surrounding the two young warriors. Then before any of them could move to attack, Cennetig stepped into range of one and slashed wildly at his shield. The man stepped back; he was not prepared for as hard a strike as Cennetig delivered. Cennetig stepped again slashing hard and driving the man to the ground. All of a sudden two men moved toward Scolai and he reacted with his shield to his left and his sword defending his right.

Cennetig delivered another crashing blow to his opponent and without hesitation a slash across the man's head, opening his skull and spreading his brains across the dirt. Cennetig hesitated for a second, staring at the man's head, then suddenly, he turned facing the remaining two as they moved cautiously toward him.

Scolai had absorbed a blow on his shield and blocked a slash with his sword. He pushed as hard as he could on his shield, forcing that man back and suddenly changed direction to his right with a hard slash and a second downward slash, catching the man's left shoulder and opening a small wound.

Then another upward stroke, driving the man's shield out of his way and an immediate downward cut across the man's chest.

Goban watched intently as Scolai turned to his left and the other attacker. A hurried rush at the man had him backing away and Scolai delivered two strong blows to the man's small shield. Beaten to the ground, the man raised a hand in surrender and Scolai looked at Goban for direction. Goban stared at Scolai with no emotion. Scolai understood and with a great swing of his sword, he cut through the one hand raised in defense and opened the man's neck in a gush of blood. He quickly turned to see Cennetig thrust his sword through a man's throat. There was now one man left to oppose the two warriors. Cennetig and Scolai advanced on the man and in a flurry of slashes, removed an arm and split his skull. Scolai felt as if his heart would beat right out of his chest and spill onto the ground, joining the other blood and guts before him.

The two young warriors looked at Goban as he walked to one of the pikes in the yard. "One for each of them," he said, "and scatter the rest of them about the yard." He turned and walked away.

Cennetig looked at Scolai, "You already have one head to place on a pike and I will take this fool's broken skull for my first." He raised his sword and brought it down hard on the dead man's neck. A second hack completed the cut, and he picked up the bloody mess and placed it on a pike.

Scolai walked across the yard, picked up the severed head of his second victim and rammed it down on a pike. The other three heads were similarly placed on pikes and the two set about dismembering the headless bodies. An hour's work left arms, legs and torsos spread about the yard and the two warriors covered in spattered blood and brains.

"We are to leave them here like this and my father will see to it that we visit this yard every day for the next week," said Cennetig.

"Why should we do that?" asked Scolai.

"As the days pass, they will rot, and the smell will be near unbearable. We come each day to learn what a battlefield is like. We smell the stench of death and taste the air. It's not pleasant, but it's much better to see it here and not during our first real battle."

*　*　*

12

Practice sessions continued every day for a month and the daily visits to the yard where the five bodies lay scattered about became easier each time. The sights and smells were enough to turn most men away, but the young warriors needed to see, to smell and taste that air that would be at many a battleground. "Learn to know it and ignore it," preached Tadhg. "In battle there is no time for choking on your own vomit."

They were made to walk through the yard and practice at the posts surrounded by pikes with the heads of their victims staring at them. "The men you have killed are gone," continued Tadhg. "They no longer threaten you. It is the man who stands in front of you that should hold your attention. He has a sword or an axe and will surely put your head on a pike if you waver."

The sessions never eased, each time Tadhg pushed a little harder and then one day, the two warriors were told to help clean the yard. "Take the pieces of those you killed and fill that cart," commanded Tadhg, "the heads will stay on their pikes."

As they cleaned the yard other men came in and placed five new pikes in the ground, "More men for us to kill?" mused Scolai.

"No," returned Cennetig. "There will be other new warriors to teach this day. I think we are to watch—watch and learn more."

They continued their task of cleaning as Tadhg walked about the yard pointing at bits and pieces missed and to be cleared. "Cennetig, Scolai come with me," said Tadhg when he seemed satisfied with the cleaning of the yard. He led them to a water trough, "Wash the foul smell from your hands and go to the walkway. Wait for me there." He turned and walked away.

Standing on the walkway, the two were soon joined by Lorcain, his personal guard, and Tadhg first, then others. They waited and Goban appeared in the yard with three young men. They stood in the middle and Goban looked to Lorcain and Tadhg. Tadhg nodded and five men were led into the arena.

Each of the five held a sword and a shield, each had the look of the five Cennetig and Scolai had faced a month before.

"These men were all pirates, captured in various river raids over the last few years," Cennetig whispered to Scolai. "These are the kind of men we may face if we go on a raid."

The little battle began, and one of the three young warriors was suddenly down with a gaping wound across his belly. One of his comrades hesitated and began to move to help him. The mistake cost him as another of the five pirates found the young warrior's back with his sword. Two of the three were down and the third fought furiously, killing the man directly in front of him and turning to face another. All four remaining pirates turned their attention to the remaining threat.

"His name is Torna, a man with a very bad temper. He will not die easily," said Cennetig. "I have seen him practice with the wooden swords."

The battle was quickly over as two more of the pirates were felled and Goban raised his hand, "Stop!" he ordered. He moved to Torna and clapped his hand on his shoulder. Your day near done. Stay here." He went to the remaining two pirates, "You have earned your freedom. Drop your weapons and leave this place. If you are found in Ceann Coradh after this day is done, you will be put back in chains."

The crowd began to leave the walkway, as the duty of placing heads on pikes began. Scolai stood on the walkway looking at the open yard, remembering the day he and Cennetig were tested. As he looked at the heads on the pikes, one of the pirates stopped and stared at Scolai. "Move along," commanded Goban.

"That one," said the pirate. "He looks very familiar, like a man I knew years ago."

"What was his name?" asked Goban.

"He was Gudrik, a fierce warrior, and a pirate," said the man.

"His name is not Gudrik, and he is only in his eighteenth year," returned Goban, "What is your name, pirate."

"I am Herlu," said the pirate.

Goban pointed at the doorway leading out of the arena, "Go Herlu, go and don't look back." Goban returned to the task of supervising Torna. Two of the pikes were left empty and the bodies of the two fallen warrior trainees were carried out of the yard.

* * *

Two days later as Cennetig and Scolai were practicing at the posts, Torna was led into the yard. Tadhg approached the two and said, "You are now joined by Torna. He has earned a place in our army as have you two. Practice together, learn to fight together. Learn to trust one another."

Torna looked at Tadhg, "I lost two friends in this yard, one because he tried to help the other. What are we to do in battle?"

"There is a time to fight and a time to help. The two are not the same. As you saw, Osan did not deal with the immediate threat, he stopped to help Neasan, and they both died. A hard lesson, but one you should all learn. You cannot help your friends if you are killed trying. Stay alive, my young friends. Stay alive—then save your friend."

* * *

Late in the afternoon, Tadhg called Cennetig and Scolai to the waterfront, "We have a task for you two. You are to join a party going upriver in the morning to see what there is to see. A scouting party in advance of our next River Raid." He looked at the two young warriors, waiting for a reaction, "This is a scouting party, we want it to be secret, so no contact with the locals."

Cennetig looked disappointed, "When will we get to fight?"

Tadhg smiled, "Yes, battle. All young warriors want to see battle." He hesitated, looking at the two young men, "Battle will come soon enough. This mission is to be quiet; you will remain unseen."

"What are we to do?" asked Scolai.

"You will protect the men that go with you," said Tadhg. "They know what needs to be done and if they're discovered, then you'll protect them, get them back here so they can tell us what we need to know."

Scolai asked, "They are spies?"

"Yes, you could say that," responded Tadhg.

"So, we also are spies?" asked Cennetig.

"No, you are warriors," said Tadhg. "You are there to protect but do so very quietly."

"Like a spy," laughed Scolai.

Tadhg grinned and turned his hands up, "Yes, like a spy."

The two young warriors laughed and poked at each other, calling the other a spy.

The morning came with a misting rain and a cool wind blowing in off the Shannon. Lorcain was standing near a pier stretching out into the river. Tied up along the pier were eight sailing vessels of various size and shape, at the end of the pier was a larger ship, a ship captured from the Norse. It was wider than a longship and had three decks, a single mast and a large square sail.

"What is that?" asked Scolai as they neared the pier.

"I think that one is a Knarr, made for moving livestock and large things. If we take any cattle, we may put them on that ship. I think I heard my father say it can carry eight head and they have to be on the lowest deck. Then there is room for other things on the other decks and twelve men at the oars. That is the slowest boat in this fleet."

Lorcain was talking to several other men when he saw his son and Scolai approaching. He turned to them and said, "A fine day for a trek up the river to see what you can see."

"What should we look for along the river?" asked Scolai.

Lorcain smiled and looked at his son, "Cennetig, what do you think?"

"I think we will see things that mean nothing, and we will not see things that mean everything. So, we should remember as much as we can and when we come back, you'll ask many questions."

Lorcain smiled and looked at Scolai, "Everything—remember everything. That's why there will be three men with you. They will also look at everything and try to remember as much as they can. This is what they do. They look, they remember, and they tell us here what we want to know before we sail up the river."

The task was set, the three men joined the little group leading five horses. "Are we ready to go?" asked Cillian.

All five mounted their horses and Cillian led them out past the ringfort and turned north along the river. The group was quiet as they progressed.

"If we meet anyone, we are traveling to Lough Derg to visit friends. As we return, we will be on our way to Limerick to visit my Uncle Olaf."

"You have an uncle in Limerick?" quizzed Scolai.

"No," said Cillian as he smiled and nudged his horse to a quicker pace.

The trip upriver was uneventful. They passed one lone man on foot, walking toward Ceann Coradh. The group reached the lough, and the three men went ahead alone, leaving the two young warriors to stay quietly out of sight.

They moved the horses deeper into the woods, remained hidden and whispered until the three spies returned. The group then began their trek back to Ceann Coradh. The return was interrupted by a roaming band of four soldiers They stopped the travelers and began to question them, "Where do you go at this hour?" asked one of the soldiers, looking at Scolai.

"We go to visit my cousin's uncle in Limerick," he responded.

"Ah, where in Limerick?" asked the soldier.

Scolai smiled, "I don't know, this will be my first time in the town of Limerick."

"And where are you coming from?" asked the soldier.

"Meath," replied Scolai.

Another of the soldiers began to draw his sword, "I don't think you tell the truth."

"Think as you will," said Cillian, "we have a long journey ahead of us and the hour is late. We'd like to get at least near Ceann Coradh before we rest this night."

The soldier pulled his sword halfway out and Cennetig gripped his sword. Scolai looked at the first soldier and said, "I think we'd all like to go our own way and enjoy the night air. This horse is surely tired of carrying me and also needs a rest."

The soldiers now all started to pull their swords and Scolai reached for his, realizing a conflict could be more damaging to their mission than beneficial "There's no need for us to argue, we should be on our way." He pushed his sword back into its sheath and turned to move away.

The soldiers now all drew their swords and moved to face the travelers.

Cennetig drew his sword and Scolai dismounted, drew his sword and walked back to face the first soldier, "You wish a contest, as I have said. There is no need. We travel to visit our family and you block the road. I ask that you stand aside and allow us to move on."

The soldier scowled and raised his shield, "You will tell us who you are and where you are going." He looked at his comrades and all four moved to block the path.

Cennetig took his shield from his horse and moved to Scolai's right, "We wish to pass, not fight, but if you don't get out of the way, then it's a fight you'll have."

Scolai looked at Cillian and said, "You should go now, and give our greeting to Uncle Olaf in Limerick. Tell him we will be along shortly."

"You'll go nowhere," shouted the soldier and raised his sword stepping toward Scolai.

Scolai brought his shield up to block the soldier's slash and saw an opening to the soldier's midsection. He stepped toward the soldier, blocked his downward slash, and swung his sword at the man, opening his belly. The other soldiers started toward both Cennetig and Scolai and the two young warriors responded as they had been taught. Immediately Cennetig caught one soldier stumbling over his fellow's leg and crashed his sword on the man's head. The metal helmet offered little advantage and the man was down, his skull crushed and blood filling his eyes.

Scolai wasted no time on his first victim and charged another soldier. Cennetig did the same and both soldiers were cut down before Cillian and his fellow spies were out of sight.

"Scolai, drag them there into the bushes," said Cennetig as he took a soldier's feet and pulled, "we should leave no trace of our having been here."

The four dead soldiers were dragged off the road and deep enough into the bush that they wouldn't easily be seen from the road. The two warriors mounted their horses and hurried to join their companions.

The remainder of the trek home was uneventful and upon arriving at Ceann Coradh, Cennetig and Scolai were taken to meet with Tadhg.

"The hour is late," said Tadhg, "and I'm very tired. Let's make this quick." He sat across from the two young men and continued, "Tell me what you saw on your way to the Lough."

"There was little to see," replied Scolai.

"Ah, but your eyes were open, and you did see something; trees, the sun, birds—perhaps another traveler on the road."

Scolai thought for a moment, "Yes, a traveler coming this way, toward Ceann Coradh."

"A man alone? Or with another?" quizzed Tadhg.

"Alone," returned Scolai.

"A rich man or a poor man? An old man or a young man?" asked Tadhg.

"I don't know," said Scolai. "He was just a man—walking."

"So, he was not a rich man, a rich man would have been on horse." Tadhg watched Scolai consider this and continued, "What else about this man?"

"He was on foot, and we were on horse, but his height seemed to be near yours and less than mine. His shoulders showed strength, but I saw no sword, no shield. He wore a clean cloak, not covered in dirt, not torn and tattered. His beard was neatly trimmed, and his boots were well worn, but clean and in good repair," Scolai paused, looked at Tadhg, and continued, "he looked older than me and much younger than you. His hand, on his staff, was large and strong," Scolai paused again.

"So, you did see something," said Tadhg, "tell me more."

Scolai thought, "It was early in the day, and it had been raining through the night. His boots should have been covered in mud, but they were clean, and his cloak was wet," he paused again, "as if he had been on horse, but I saw no such animal."

"Could a horse have been concealed in the wood? A horse he would return to?"

Again, Scolai thought and replied, "The wood was thick at that point, there could have been ten men and as many horses in the wood, but I saw nothing."

Tadhg leaned toward Scolai, "You say he was coming this way. Are you sure?"

Scolai rubbed the top of his head, "No, I am not sure of anything now. When I first saw him, he was coming toward us—walking."

"Would you recognize this man if you saw him again?"

"Yes, I'm sure I would."

"Is there anything else I should know?" asked Tadhg.

"Yes," replied Scolai, "on our return, we met four soldiers."

"So, I have heard," said Tadhg.

* * *

The morning came again with a gentle breeze and a continuing mist. "Today, we sail upriver," said Cennetig. "There are cattle and horses to be had and who knows what other plunder we may find." He tugged at Scolai's shield, "The boats are ready we should find our place on one."

All eight vessels were being boarded and prepared to leave. Cennetig saw Tadhg near the end of the pier as he waved, signaling both Cennetig and Scolai to come to the Knarr. Tadgh greeted the two and said, "This is your vessel today. You will pull on the oars and when there are animals to gather on board, you will tend to them. Get them to the lowest deck and secured, then you will help load the plunder from the raid and stow it on the second deck."

Scolai looked disappointed, "Do we join in on the raid? Or just wait on the boat?"

"No," came an answer from another of the crew. "We bring this ship into a place where we can load the cattle, then we join in on the raid. When all is done, we get back to this boat first and get it loaded as quickly as possible, then we sail. The others will follow."

Scolai nodded and leaned back against the wooden planks. He let his mind drift to the months of training, the confrontation with the four soldiers and wondered what the fighting would be like this day. He sat up straight, leaned forward and asked Cennetig, "Why do we raid these people?"

"These Norse are invaders," replied his friend, "foreigners who have raided and plundered our country for many years. They have established settlements along the river and now we can raid and take back that which was ours. That and more."

Scolai began to lean back again when an old man ordered them to get their oars in the water. "Time to move this hulking mass out into the wind. Put your backs into it and we'll raise the sail."

"What about the others?" asked Scolai.

Several men nearby laughed as the old man said, "They will leave soon enough to pass us on the way. Don't worry about them, boy. Think about your oar and when I tell you, you'll ship the oar and help raise the sail."

The boat was pushed away from the pier and turned toward open water. The order was given to pull on the oars and as soon as the old man felt a breeze, he gave the order to raise the sail, and the breeze took over. The order was then given to the rest of the men to bring the oars in, and the crew turned their attention to light conversation and storytelling. The two young warriors were on their first river raid and questions filled their heads.

*　*　*

13

912 AD Meath. Ireland
The Raid

The first boat was much faster than the Knarr. It was small next to the bigger ship but filled with armed men and sped ahead of the Knarr. The sail raised and a fair wind allowed the Knarr to increase speed without the oars. Cennetig and Scolai watched as the other boats turned a bend in the river and disappeared. After three hours of gliding over a calm surface, the other boats were seen, anchored several hundred feet offshore with limited crews. The Knarr moved in close and lowered sail.

"There," shouted a man aboard one of the other boats, indicating the best location for the Knarr to anchor and await the return of the raiders. The oars provided all the power to maneuver the Knarr into position and the anchor was lowered. The water was shallow, and the remaining warriors aboard were anxious to get ashore. A small boat provided the final transport to shore and the group raced to join their comrades in the settlement.

The fighting was still in progress as the two young warriors raced up to join the battle. Cennetig and Scolai both eagerly challenged single settlers. The hacking and slashing by the settlers belied their lack of training and exhausted their strength, trying to overpower the raiders. Scolai accepted a series of four heavy blows to his shield and as the last of the four was delivered with less energy than the others, Scolai struck back with one heavy blow to the man's shield then a slash across his mid-section. The man was down and a final thrust through the man's neck left him the first of Scolai kills.

Cennetig had defeated his opponent and the two charged ahead again looking for their next victim. Scolai sighted a tall, slender man, walking casually toward him. "An easy target," he mumbled as he turned to face the tall man. He thought how easily he had defeated his first opponent and concluded this one would be the same.

"I am Karl, son of Halldor. You have come to kill us and take all we have, Irish," he said. "Not as long as I live." He shuffled his shield and brought his sword up, then moved in a slow circle to Scolai's right. He stopped, slightly lowered his shield, and stared at Scolai. "You're little more than a boy," he said.

"You should have stayed home, now you may never see home again." He stepped quickly toward Scolai and brought his shield up.

Scolai reacted with a wild swing at Karl's shield. Karl absorbed the blow and did not return the strike. Scolai was embarrassed. He had done what Tadhg had taught him not to do. *A wasted blow, did I leave myself open?* He stepped back, studied Karl and again posed for an attack.

Karl continued to circle him, now to Scolai's left, coming ever closer. He held his shield in his left hand and arm. The distance now only a few feet and he raised his sword.

Scolai responded, bringing up his shield, but Karl did not strike, instead, he took another step and raised his sword again, and again, Scolai brought up his shield. This time, Karl tapped the top of Scolai's shield with his sword and laughed, "You've a lot to learn, boy."

This angered Scolai and he reacted by lunging at Karl with his sword high.

Karl simply stepped aside and allowed Scolai to stumble forward. As he passed, Karl's sword caught Scolai's shoulder above his shield with a glancing blow. The wound was not deep nor disabling and as Karl stepped to finish the contest, a javelin was suddenly thrust into his back. Karl's eyes went wide and as he fell next to Scolai, Cennetig grabbed the javelin, put his foot on Karl's back and pulled the javelin free.

"We won't tell Tadhg about this, my friend. He would send you back to the first day of training." Cennetig turned and scanned the area, "Now, back on your feet, we still have work to do."

The two caught up to the rest of the raiding party as they finished their initial task. Tadhg saw them and ordered them to find a horse drawn cart and bring it to the center of the settlement. "Then you can look for cattle," he said, "Now go, we should work fast and be out of here as soon as possible."

The cart and horse were the easy part. Finding cattle proved more difficult. An hour's search profited the two warriors with six head of cattle. They herded them to the shore near the Knarr and waited for the rest of the raiding party to return.

The Knarr was moved close to the water's edge and a dozen wooden planks were stretched to the shore as a gangway. The cattle were loaded, and the other plunder secured on the middle deck, then the Knarr was rowed and pushed away from shore.

As the sail was raised and the Knarr moved out into the lough, Scolai and Cennetig sat on the edge of the upper deck, watching the cattle. "How do we divide the day's profits?" asked Scolai.

"We get to eat the cattle," laughed Cennetig. "Our part was to help on this boat, find the cart and the cattle and get everything loaded. This was our first adventure and some of the plunder will find its way down to us. We may be given a ring, or some gold chain, perhaps a few coins. This was our first raid and as we go on more of these, we will earn a place in the first group where we will be able to take what we wish." He smiled and added, "The cattle will go to my father's stock, and we really will be eating them soon."

* * *

14

The several river raids both Scolai and Cennetig joined that first year had them progressing and by years end, they were both on the lead ship. The raids were either north into Lough Derg and beyond into Meath or south toward Limerick and Connaught. Four raids total had brought thirty head of cattle and ten horses to Lorcain's livestock inventory. Gold, silver, precious stones, weapons and leather were also taken and as the two young warriors were now in the lead ship, their collection of wealth increased.

Over the next two years the fighting skills of both young warriors was honed and Scolai remembered the lesson of overreacting. His greatest problem was his temper. In practice, a mistake that cost him a bruise or a cut, didn't seem to bother him, "Every bump and scratch is a lesson. Better it happen here than in battle," he often said. But it was in battle that the little mistakes often threatened to become grand mistakes because of his temper.

The day he slipped on the slick rain and blood-soaked mud below his feet resulted in his temper exploding in a burst of slashes and crashing blows to four men and a woman defending their homes. Scolai fell in front of them as he approached their position. He screamed his anger in curses and regained his feet before the five in front of him could capitalize on his blunder. With two hands on his great sword, he charged and slashed at the terrified five, each of whom fell within a minute of his fall. The last to fall was the woman. She was backing away from Scolai as he advanced quicker, and his sword barely slowed as she tried to block a shoulder high slash. Her head rolled in the mud as he brought his sword down on her falling body, splitting open her chest. Anger overtook him as his breathing came in great gasps, Scolai turned to each of his victims and continued to mutilate the men already dead. Cennetig saw Scolai as he fell and by the time he neared his friend, Scolai had just decapitated the last of his fallen victims. He approached slowly, "Scolai, we should move on, there is more to be done."

Scolai turned to face his friend. The look on his face would have frightened anybody and Cennetig wasn't sure if Scolai was going to attack him. They stood for a moment staring at each other when Scolai shook his head and the tension eased, "Cennetig, I didn't see you . . ."

Cennetig maintained his distance and said, "We should move on," he pointed north, "there, with the others."

Scolai stepped slowly away from the butchered bodies and as his breathing eased, he said, "Yes, we should go."

Scolai had become a remarkable warrior, fearless, powerful and deadly with his sword. The others respected him and were always glad to see him join their raiding party, but none wanted to be near him in battle. It was feared that his violent temper would vent itself on both friend and foe, if his friends were not careful.

The day that Scolai had the opportunity to repay Cennetig for saving his life on their first raid came several years later when Cennetig was battling four men and they had cornered him between two large rocks.

Scolai saw his friend and raced to help him. The last several steps coming up behind the four men had Scolai roaring and drawing their attention away from their intended victim. The swing of his large sword was as if he intended to cut all four in half with one slash. The sharpened end of his sword connected with a man's upper arm and left him screaming in pain without his arm and a gaping wound in his chest. Scolai didn't slow, his sword was raised, and a second slash found flesh and bone on two more men. Cennetig now had only one man to defeat and as he plunged his sword into the man's belly, he saw Scolai finish with a thrust through one of the two he faced. Scolai turned to the last of the four. The man was in pain and could not continue to fight. Scolai looked at him curiously and slowly placed the point of his sword at the man's throat. The stared at each other and Scolai pushed his sword through the man's neck.

Cennetig stood and approached Scolai, cautiously. "Scolai."

He looked at Cennetig, "We should keep moving."

After the raid, as the two men rested on the boat as it sailed toward Ceann Coradh, Cennetig said, "Now we are settled. You saved me out there today."

Scolai grinned, "I will never cancel the debt I owe you. A friend today as we were two years ago and as we will be till we die."

Cennetig leaned toward his friend, "That temper of yours is a frightening thing to see, but when I was sure I was going to die, I was very happy to see it again."

* * *

15

916 AD Munster, Ireland
The Family Grows

The seasons passed with Lorcain ordering raids up and down the Shannon into Meath and Connaught. Every type of vessel that could transport warriors was used and the plunder was used in building Lorcain's forces. Cennetig, Cassair and Scolai were comrades, engaging in these skirmishes, primarily with the Norse, the foreigners who had invaded their country. Each year after a season of raids, Scolai would travel to Bardan's farm where he would spend a month helping Bardan with his harvest. Then he would visit Brighid and help her father with his harvest.

Breasal moved slower each time Scolai visited and finally, after they finished working a full day in the fields, the old warrior had a bowl of soup and laid down to sleep. His death was seen coming for some time and Brighid would often sit outside their roundhouse at night waiting for the wail of a banshee. The banshee didn't wail that night, but still, in the morning, her father didn't wake.

Brighid's mother was a small woman, not in good health and after Breasal was buried on a slope facing the river, she was uncertain of her future. "Can we handle this farm on our own, girl?" she asked her daughter.

Brighid didn't have an answer for her mother. The work on the farm was mainly done by Breasal and the two of them simply helped. He was the lifter of things heavy, and he knew what was needed and when. Brighid sat quietly thinking about her and her mother's future when Scolai came to help with the work that needed doing. He noticed Brighid didn't have her usual smile she normally had to greet him. Instead, her eyes were worried, and she had been crying.

"What is it that troubles you?" he asked.

Scolai went to the hillside where he and Brighid spent so much time looking out over the little river and the hill beyond. He dug a grave for Breasal and collected rocks to cover the burial, then went and sat with Brighid.

"My father managed this farm and neither my mother nor I can do as he did," said Brighid with concern. "We have to find a way to continue."

Scolai smiled, "I will help you. Whatever we don't know, we can go to Bardan and ask. He'll help us figure it out."

She looked at Scolai and said, "This farm is more than my mother and I can tend," she paused, then, "you could stay here, work the farm and we could raise a family."

Scolai stared at Brighid, "A family, children…" he looked at the little girl he had known for nearly seven years, the little girl was now a young woman in her twentieth year. The idea of spending the rest of his life with Brighid had occurred to him often, especially when he returned to Ceann Coradh each year. During the winter months, his mind often drifted to Cnoc Gorm, the blue flowers on the hill leading up to the rath and the pretty young girl who made him forget about battle and training with his friends. He took her hand and pulled her close to himself, put his arms around her and they stood quietly as the sun set.

* * *

Cassair returned to Ceann Coradh from a winter spent at his home near Cashel. He brought with him a beautiful young girl, Nuala, His bride of two months. Cennetig and Scolai teased Cassair mercilessly about being tied to only one woman when there were so many to be had. Then in June of that same year, Cennetig wed and when Scolai returned to help Bardan and Brighid with the harvest, he and Brighid wed.

Each of the three young men were blessed with children within the first year of their marriages. Orlaith, Cennetig's daughter was born first; Daigh, Scolai's son came next and Cairell, Cassair's son was last. The three men bragged about their offspring and each vowed to sire more than the others.

Brighid came to Ceann Coradh to be with Scolai. They lived at the inn and spent many hours with Niall and Cairbre. On a dark, rainy day when Scolai and his comrades were off on a raid, Cairbre took Brighid aside and they talked about the dream Ceara had years ago. "Do you think she was dreaming?" asked Brighid, "Or, could she have really seen Scathach on that dark road?"

"I don't know, girl," said Cairbre, "But, if it were a dream, look what has grown up in front of us. Scolai is a warrior, and his friends talk of his deeds when they come here and celebrate their victories."

"Do you think the curse of Scathach is real then?"

"I don't think so, I think Ceara was dreaming, but look at what has happened." Cairbre paused, looked around the room and continued in a low voice, "Ceara died less than a day after Scolai was born."

* * *

Daigh was an active, healthy boy, constantly moving. He loved to wrestle and as soon as he could handle a hurley, he was playing at hurling. Like his father, the game was more a reason to get together with a bunch of boys and crash into others, ending up in a fight. He came home with many a bloody nose and lip, but always with an accompanying smile.

In Daigh's seventh year his father was working in the fields with two other men when a roving band of about twenty men carrying ropes and grappling hooks started up the hill. Daigh was carrying a bucket of water to his father and three men working in the fields. Scolai saw the band of raiders and called to his three helpers. They all began to run toward Daigh and Scolai shouted at him to get inside the gate, "We're being attacked."

As Scolai crossed the bridge, behind Daigh and the last of his helpers, they pulled the door closed and set the oak plank in place against the door.

Scolai gave each of the men a sword and all of them strung a bow. They each grabbed a handful of arrows, hurried up the ladders to the walkway and spread out along the south side of the wall. Scolai counted the attackers, "Twenty-three," he said.

"I count the same," said one of his helpers.

Scolai was calm and looked at the three men and Daigh. "Notch an arrow and be ready, don't loose your arrow till the bastards are so close, you can't miss. Then carefully notch another and do the same again."

Scolai stood at the top of the wall, looking down at the men as they approached, "Go back where you came from," he shouted, but the bastards didn't seem to understand the Irish tongue. All five on the wall let their arrows fly and several of the raiders fell before they reached the moat.

Daigh was on the walkway and saw a grappling hook on a rope fly over the wall. Scolai was nearby and just looked at it, then drew his sword and stood ready for the raider to reach the top of his climb. As the man's head appeared between the pointed tops of the wall pickets, Scolai brought his sword down hard on the man's metal helmet. His sword glanced off the helmet and caught the man on his shoulder. He fell backward into the moat. It wasn't clear if it was the sword or the fall that killed him, but all of a sudden, between arrows and the one man in the moat, their number was cut in half.

Another grappling hook caught the top of the wall near Daigh and soon a hand and arm reached over the top. Daigh didn't want to wait and see the rest of the man, so he brought his sword down as hard as he could and caught the man near his elbow with the dull edge of the sword. The man screamed as he pulled his broken arm away from the wall, lost his balance and fell back into the moat. This time it was the fall that killed him. The brief battle ended with thirteen raiders dead and two more seriously wounded on the ground.

Brighid stood on the wall looking toward the running raiders as Scolai and his helpers walked across the bridge. One of the helpers tried to talk to the two wounded men, but they either didn't understand or were in too much pain to answer, so the helper killed them.

There were eleven raiders outside the moat who had been taken with arrows. Two more in the moat and the two survivors. Eight ran away and Scolai was unsettled for several days, wondering if the eight would return with a larger force. They didn't return.

* * *

Brighid watched as Scolai wrestled with their son. She sighed and muttered, "My two warriors," as they rolled on the ground, covered in dirt and laughing. The matches were a regular occurrence when Scolai was home and as the years lazed by, Daigh came ever nearer at besting his father. In the evening, after all chores were done, the family would sit around the fire and talk, Scolai expounding on the great battles of the past and the deeds of his recent comrades. Brighid would bring out the books she had and Daigh learned to read and write.

When Daigh reached the age of ten, Scolai presented him with a wooden sword. The practice sessions and play blended and Daigh showed great promise as a warrior. He carried his wooden sword everywhere, even to hurling matches on Sunday afternoons. As his father before him, he and his friends finished the hurling and began their swordplay. When he reached the age of fourteen, in 931, he was ready to begin the rigorous training to become a Dal gCais warrior just as his father had and he was taken to meet Tadhg.

Cennetig stood by the posts in the yard as Scolai and Daigh approached. He was watching his son, Latchtna, as he moved around a post and slashed at it, then moved again. Latchna paused as Scolai and Daigh neared, lowered his sword and raised a hand, "Daigh, are we to be together in warrior training?"

Daigh looked at his father, then turned to Latchna, "Yes, are there others?"

Cennetig walked over to Scolai, "Our sons, like our fathers, comrades."

Scolai slapped Cennetig on his shoulder, "Now, where is the task master, Tadhg?"

"Tadhg has had his day," said Cennetig. "He now spends his time in the garden, looking at the flowers and listening to the birds. He hardly knows us anymore."

"Who leads the teaching?" asked Scolai.

"An old friend, Cassair. He was sorely wounded three years ago and his arm can no longer hold a shield. His sword arm, however, is strong as ever, and he wants to lead this training."

As they were talking, Cassair entered the yard with six other young men in tow, "Scolai, I haven't seen you in years." He looked at the boy standing next to Scolai, "Daigh, you've grown." His eyes moved to Scolai, "Tall and strong, like your father." He smiled, "Now can he learn as well as his father? We will see if he can he fight as well."

* * *

The boys were led off to begin the two-year process of learning the weapons and actions of a warrior. There were several swords of varying length and weight, spears, pikes, axes, assorted clubs, daggers and slings. Anything that may be used as a weapon was taught and the young warriors learned.

Cennetig asked Scolai to accompany him through the afternoon and they could continue their conversation. "I have to remain relatively close to Lorcain. He's in his seventy-fifth year and I have to be ready to assume the role of leader of the Dal gCais at any moment."

"Is he ill?" asked Scolai.

"No," said Cennetig. "He is stronger than most of our warriors, but he insists that I stay close." Cennetig laughed, "He's wise and I would do whatever he asks, so I stay close, I see, hear and learn."

"Seventy-five," said Scolai. "A good age, longer than most men live, I hope we are as lucky."

Cennetig laughed, "We're warriors, we'll be lucky to be alive tomorrow." He looked at Scolai, "I've heard a story, about your mother. Did she really meet the Scathach?"

Scolai looked agitated, "I don't know, I may have been there, still in her belly, but I think it was all a dream in her head."

Cennetig looked at his friend, "Well you're as good as if the Shadowy One actually had trained you."

They laughed at the idea and then talked about their sons.

"Daigh is a fine-looking boy," said Cennetig. "He's big and strong, are there more little ones coming any time soon?" asked Cennetig.

Scolai smiled, "I think not. Brighid has lost two in birth and no more have come our way in the last five years. What about you?"

"My daughter, Orlaith and five more brothers thus far. The youngest, Mathgamain is not yet at his first year. So, who knows? There may be even more to come."

The training went as it had for Cennetig, Cassair and Scolai. In the end, their sons were ready to join the warriors and Cennetig had entered three more of his sons into the realm of a Dal gCais warrior.

* * *

16

934 AD Munster, Ireland
A New Warrior Generation

Daigh mac Scolai finished his warrior training along with his friend, Latchna and four other young men. They took their places in the river raids and other skirmishes of the Dal gCais against invaders. On a number of occasions, Daigh stood between a comrade and certain defeat. His sword was well known and the rumors about the Shadowy One having a place in his training proliferated.

At the end of the summer raiding into Meath, Daigh was prepared to return to Cnoc Gorm when Morann caught up with him. "Daigh, are you leaving already?"

"That I am, Morann. This year's harvest won't wait and we've two farms to clear."

Morann said, "My father can no longer stand in battle and so he has retired to our cousin's farm near Cashel. I'll be traveling there in a month. Maybe I'll stop and see this Cnoc Gorm you favor over a celebration with friends."

"In a month, I'll be looking for an excuse to sit down and talk. I'd welcome the visit," said Daigh.

Morann grinned, "I'll probably not be traveling alone, there may be two of us."

Daigh assumed Morann meant he would have a woman with him, "A friend of yours is as welcome as you." The two talked for a minute or two and Daigh set off on his journey home.

The harvest of both Cnoc Gorm and Bardan's fields went well. The weather was warm and dry and the three men, Bardan, Scolai and Daigh had gathered vegetables in the barn, ready to be cleaned and sorted and were concentrating on hay for the animals.

Scolai and Daigh had cut a new picket for the rath wall from the nearby wood. As they were cleaning off branches and bark outside the rath wall, two people on horse came up the rise from the main road. Daigh paused, set his axe down and shaded his eyes.

Scolai looked at the two on horse, "A man and a woman. He has the look of a warrior, she carries a small package."

Daigh recognized the man, "Morann and his friend. We have visitors from Ceann Coradh, Da." He wiped the sweat off his brow and arms, picked up a shirt and walked toward the approaching couple.

Brighid came across the bridge over the moat and greeted the woman as Morann continued toward Daigh.

"Morann, tis good to see you," said Daigh as he looked past Morann at the young woman. "You're a very lucky man. She's beautiful."

Morann laughed as Saraid joined them, "I won't argue that, my friend." He put his hand on Saraid's shoulder, "Daigh mac Scolai I'd like you to meet Saraid, my sister."

Saraid smiled, "My brother has spoken of you often. Are you as great a warrior as he claims?"

Daigh was taken aback, "I can't say I'm a great warrior because we've fought no great wars." He nodded toward Saraid, "I've not heard of you before now, has Morann kept you hidden from our lot because he knows I am attracted to beautiful women with bright red hair and blue eyes?"

Saraid hesitated, took a shallow breath and returned, "You saved my brother's life in battle. I'll call that a great deed even if in a small war."

"An act any of us would have done for him as he would for any of us," said Daigh.

Morann looked at Daigh, "I've never properly thanked you for that."

Daigh looked at Saraid, "Smile, young lady and I'm repaid."

Saraid blushed, smiled and turned toward Brighid, "I've brought you a little gift from Cairbre."

The two of them walked across the bridge and Brighid turned toward Daigh, "Bring the lady's horse when you come in."

Scolai slapped Daigh on his back, "Wash the dirt and sweat off yourself, then come in. I'll take care of the horse."

Daigh looked at Morann, "Your sister?" He took a deep breath, "She's very nice."

Morann laughed, "Yes, and there are a number of men looking at her with thoughts of talking to our father. She doesn't impress easily and wanted to get away from Ceann Coradh for a few weeks. So, we travel to visit our family near Cashel."

Daigh looked at his friend, "You could stay here for a while. I could use help cutting another picket." He walked down the hill away from the road toward the river, waded into water up to his waist then dove under and swam for a minute and emerged, bathed.

"How long does it take to cut a new picket?" asked Morann.

"As long as it takes—an hour or two, or more if there are other things to do," replied Daigh.

Morann smiled, "So, a day or two, depending on how much time you spend with my sister."

Daigh shrugged, "Or, that."

That evening Daigh walked out across the bridge and looked across the open fields to the south.

"A beautiful sight," came a young woman's voice.

Daigh turned to see Saraid standing only a few feet from him. "I come out here each night and think about what I have…a family, a home and view of the distant hills," he held out his arm and brought Saraid closer, "and now a new friend."

She stepped closer to him as he pointed west, "The sun will soon leave the sky there and give us a beautiful view. His eyes went from the western sky to her eyes, and he gently pulled her closer.

Three days and two sunsets later, Morann and Saraid continued on their journey. "We'll be back in a month," said Morann as they mounted their horses and rode away. Another two pickets cut and cleaned and Daigh wondered what he could put in front of Morann to keep them there longer on their return.

* * *

17

936 AD Munster, Ireland
Saraid

The raids on the River Shannon continued and Cennetig became less and less available to his friends. Lorcain shifted greater responsibility on Cennetig's shoulders and kept him busy with leading raids or sitting in council with the warrior leaders. The day-to-day business of being the king or chieftain of the Dal gCais took more time and left little time to visit with friends.

The summer of 936 showed little promise of new raids and Daigh decided to remain at Cnoc Gorm to help his father replace several pickets in the rath wall.

Morann came to visit Daigh and stayed for several days, helping with the pickets. "How do you find these logs?" he asked Scolai.

"As big around as a young boy and as tall as four men. Straight and with as few branches as we can find. We cut one or two each year and keep them in reserve till they're needed. Then we cover the part that goes in the ground with pitch and sharpen the top to a nice point."

"Have you ever had to defend this rath?" asked Morann.

"A few times," replied Scolai. "The last time was ten or eleven years ago. It was this wall that kept us safe and allowed us to defeat that band of men."

Daigh said, "I remember it well. It was my first real encounter with an enemy, and we all had to help defend the rath."

The conversation drifted on into the night and Morann finally asked Daigh what he thought of his sister, Saraid.

"She will be a real prize for the man who can win her favor," he answered.

"I have to tell you, Daigh," said Morann, "she has asked about you more than once or twice and she told our father about you. Now he asks me about you."

Daigh was surprised at the attention he had gained with Saraid. "She could do much better than me," said Daigh. "I'm not a rich man and probably never will be. I fight for Lorcain and Cennetig, for the Dal gCais and my future is very uncertain."

"Saraid is not interested in being rich, she's tired of these men, these boys who think more of their possessions than of their family," said Morann. "You hold a higher place in her mind than any of the others."

Daigh didn't know what to say, or what to do. He looked at Scolai and his father said, "This is your life, boy. You make choices and live with them." He looked at Brighid, "Some of us are very fortunate in finding someone with whom they may share their life."

Brighid smiled and added, "You could travel to Cashel, talk to Saraid and meet her father." She stood, walked toward Scolai, touched his shoulder, and said, "I married a warrior, he had nothing but a strong arm and good heart when we met. Now look at us, we have you."

The following morning, Morann and Daigh left Cnoc Gorm and traveled to the home of Morann's cousin. As they approached the little village, Daigh could see a young woman with red hair, standing in front of a roundhouse. "She's here," he said.

"Yes," said Morann, "and so is our father."

Their father was a formidable man, battle tested and wounded as both Bardan and Niall had been. His lot in life was now the farm that had been in his family for several generations, his farm and his daughter.

Their wedding was a simple affair, both families were there, as were several of Daigh and Morann's comrades. Daigh brought her back to Cnoc Gorm and they built another round house within the rath wall.

In the second year of their marriage, Saraid bore a son, Garbhan, and two years later a second son, Laoghaire. The year after Laoghaire was born, Daigh was at Ceann Coradh when Cennetig joined his warriors to celebrate the birth of his newest son, Brian.

Saraid and Daigh's third son, Tanai was born another year later, but there were no celebrations in Ceann Coradh, Lorcain was killed in a battle with the foreigners. Both Scolai and Daigh had answered the few calls to arms in those few years, but practice with the sword was always an important activity. "The day will come when we'll be thankful for these sessions, Daigh," said Scolai. The day did come.

Cennetig was now the King of Tuadmumuh and with the change in leadership came new challenges.

* * *

18

944 AD Munster, Ireland
Gort Rotachain

Cennetig crossed the open yard where the warriors trained and found Scolai talking to Cassair. He was unsettled and called his two friends to a quiet corner, "I have concerns about parts of our territory south of here and Cellachain's interest in the same. He moves to seize it and push us out." He paced back and forth, ignoring the rain on his bare head, "I'm calling a council this afternoon with several of our warrior leaders, and I want both of you there." He didn't wait for an answer but turned and walked away.

Scolai looked at Cassair, "He is angry with Cellachain. First the man's mother pleads with Cennetig to allow the man to take the throne of Munster without challenge, now Cellachain wants to take our lands."

Cassair shook his head, "I've known Cennetig all my life and he has always treated people fairly. Now, the man who is King of Munster because Cennetig allowed it, is invading our territory." He thought for a moment, "This territory includes my family's land." His right hand began to massage his left arm where he had been wounded.

"This will mean a call to arms, we will probably march south as soon as our troops are assembled," said Scolai. "I know you would stand and fight even with only one arm, but let's wait to see what Cennetig has in mind. It may be our presence in the disputed land will be enough."

The two men continued to talk quietly as they made their way to the meeting. They arrived and found twenty other warrior leaders assembled and muttering as Cennetig made his way to the middle.

"Friends, men of Thomond, we are threatened with an invasion of our southern territory. I have briefly spoken to all of you, and I now call our warriors to arms. This intrusion will not be tolerated. Prepare yourselves, assemble your units and be ready to march in two days." He pushed his way through the crowd and left the room.

Cassair saw four of Cennetig's sons in the room and went to them. "Your father is very angry, we should stay close to him, help him, be sure all is properly prepared for this march and the battle that may follow."

Finn reached out and touched Cassair's shoulder, "Will you march with us?"

Cassair didn't hesitate, "Yes, I will do all I can to support this venture."

Scolai stood next to Cassair and said, "Your sword has no shield to help it in battle, but your words to these young warriors and your advice to our friend, Cennetig will be even more powerful."

The room heard Scolai's words and swords were raised in a supporting shout. Then the room emptied, and the men went to prepare for the march.

* * *

The Dal gCais had marched south through the day into the disputed land and arrived near an open field. The scouts reported a force from Cashel was about a mile away, making camp for the night. Cennetig gathered several leaders and began to plan the attack.

"We could strike now, but the sun is about to disappear till morn, there are clouds in the sky, and we can't depend on the moon for light. I think we should wait, sleep now, rise well before the sun and be ready to strike before they can wipe the sleep from their eyes."

There were no fires, the men quietly rested, took food, and slept. As the sun was about to crack the darkness, a sentry went to wake Cennetig and found him standing, tightening his belt and ready to begin this day.

The leaders gathered outside Cennetig's tent, "The scouts—have they anything to report?' asked Cassair.

"The morning mist is heavy, and visibility is reduced to only a few feet," said the first scout.

"All was quiet from the other camp," said the second scout, "they still sleep."

Cennetig stood next to Cassair and nodded, Cassair told the scouts, "Go back and watch, at the first sign of stirring in their camp, one of you bring word. If they begin to move before we are in position to attack, the other is to come back."

The scouts hurried out of the camp area and Cassair looked to Cennetig, "I have my sword, and I will strap a shield on my other arm. You will not fight this battle alone."

Cennetig smiled, "I need someone I trust to stay back and collect reports from all sides. Someone who can move our forces around as the battle progresses." He paused, "and if the battle goes poorly, we must be ready to retreat."

Cassair nodded in agreement, "I'll stay out of the way and do as you ask."

The several units were aligned and the Dal gCais began to move through the fog into a thicker wood. Before long, the first scout appeared out of the mist. "They stir, less than a half mile that way," he said pointing through the fog.

Cennetig cautioned the troops, "Quiet, be careful where you step."

The Dal gCais moved slowly through misty wood and soon the second scout stood in front of Cennetig, "They move, but not toward us, they move in that direction," he said pointing off to Cennetig's left.

Cassair stepped closer, "How many? And how far?"

"A quarter mile away, about eight-hundred men." He paused and looked at Cennetig, "The mist, it makes a count very difficult, at least eight hundred, but there may be more."

Cassair looked at Cennetig, "We should turn our line and advance, allowing our right flank to engage first."

"Agreed," said Cennetig. "Dub, Finn, Scolai, you hear the plan? We turn and Scolai, your group will see first blood. Hurry, they're close."

The two armed forces crept through the mist and woods, coming closer and closer. Moving slowly, deliberately—both armies were trying to be quiet, thinking the other had not spotted them.

Discussions were at a whisper and every cough, cracking branch or tripping warrior, startled everyone, on both sides. Scolai had a band of twenty men including Daigh. To his left was Dub mac Cennetig with another forty

Dal gCais warriors. The center was led by Cennetig with near one-hundred warriors and Finn was to Cennetig's left with more than thirty men.

"Where are we?" whispered one of Scolai's men.

"I don't know," came a low reply.

Scolai turned and gruffly whispered, "Quiet!"

The men kept moving forward knowing the other army was somewhere in this mist, also inching forward. They would come face to face at any time and as Cennetig stepped over a fallen log, he saw a flash of light, a reflection off a sword or shield, there was movement ahead. Then the sounds of men burdened with heavy mail and metal helmets, carrying shields, and drawn swords, clanking through the fog, gave away Cellachain's location. They were seen and the Dal gCais prepared to attack.

A brief hesitation, a series of hand signals and the Dal gCais force was ready to strike. They began to move slowly, deliberately, carefully and the inevitable cracking of a branch or bump of two shields alerted the foe to their presence. An alarm was shouted and the Dal gCais had their signal, they charged through the brush—the few remaining yards to the other line. There was no shield wall in this tangle of trees, bushes and fallen logs. Each man met one or two from the enemy and the battle raged.

The ground was wet and uneven, scattered with rocks and fallen branches. Before the Munster forces could fully react, Scolai's group had attacked and threw the men of Munster into confusion. Six of the Munster force were killed before any of the Dal gCais. Scolai charged ahead with vicious slashes of his sword, taking the arm of one man and cutting deep into another's neck. He forced his way ahead, killing two more men and drawing the attention of several others. Two of the Munster men charged Scolai and a third hefted his javelin, then waited for an opening. Another Munster warrior moved to Scolai's left side and made annoying strikes to his shield. These were not intended to hurt Scolai, but rather to open his sword side to greater advantage of his attackers. Scolai reacted by stepping backward, drawing the annoying man with him, then suddenly charging in his direction. The man fell backward and as Scolai was about to send him to the other world when a javelin found purchase in Scolai's back.

Cassair received a report that Scolai's group was facing more resistance and the entire center of the Munster line had turned into that flank. The Dal gCais was not able to reposition their left flank in time and they were left standing with no one to face. He sent the messengers back telling them to move to support Cennetig in the center. The time needed to reposition troops proved disastrous. The Munster men were pressing Cennetig, forcing him backward and the reinforcement from the left flank had to negotiate brush and trees to come close to positions of advantage.

The contest between Scolai and the four Munster men changed when the javelin struck Scolai in his back. The big man went down and as he raised his shield to block the thrust from a sword, another spear was driven into his chest. His last sight was that of a Munster man with an axe, about to take his head.

Daigh broke free of his match with a blow to his opponent's ribs and he rushed to Scolai's side. It was too late to save his father, and the man about to decapitate Scolai was himself a victim of another's axe. He fell on top of Scolai and as Daigh tried to move him, he was slashed across his shoulder and again above his knee. He fell to the ground and was struck on his head by a club, rendering him unconscious.

Father and son had marched under the banner of Cennetig mac Lorcain against Cellachain Caisil and the men of Munster in this battle over lands claimed by both the Dal gCais and the king of Munster. The Dal gCais forces were facing defeat with heavy causalities, bringing the brutality and cost of battle home to Daigh and Scolai. Both had seen battle many times over the years, experiencing victory more often than defeat. The scars that marked their bodies were mementos of the wounds they had suffered, but until Gort Rotachain, none serious, none fatal. The bruises and scars, the aches and pains after each battle, had given them bragging rights amongst their comrades. These two warriors had seen death up close many times and managed to keep him at bay. Both had earned the praise of their fellows; both had carried the day in more than one skirmish. Both were honored for their heroic deeds and now Scolai had paid the ultimate price of a hero.

Cennetig had pushed his unit ahead and as he engaged the center of the Munster force, their right flank turned to the center and Cennetig and his men were pushed backward.

As the battle continued, the fog began to fade, and the carnage could be seen more fully. The Dal gCais had an advantage early on but that was slipping away. Scolai was dead, Daigh was struck on his left with wounds to both arm and leg and the remainder of their force was trying to retreat to better ground.

Cennetig and his force were pushed back through the brush, tripping and falling over logs and branches they'd carefully traversed earlier. The battle was all but lost. Cennetig saw his son, Finn, as he made a charge through several ranks of the Munster force, and he too was cut down.

Cennetig's line was holding at the top of a small rise and soon both sides pulled back. The battle was over. Cassair and Cennetig surveyed the battlefield. They found Cennetig's sons, Finn, and Dub, and carried their bodies to the rear. Daigh was found, near death and Scolai already dead. Nearly three hundred of the Dal gCais were killed. The wounded were collected, those able to walk did and those not able were loaded onto carts for the trek home. Some of the dead were gathered as there was room on the carts to carry them.

* * *

Cennetig led the remnants of his force into the town of Ceann Coradh. "We were hard defeated," he told his wife. "Dubb and Finn are killed, my old friend Scolai—dead. More than three hundred of our warriors—slaughtered, and hundreds more wounded. This battle was a complete disaster.

Be Binn and her husband struggled with the loss of their sons, and it wasn't until the next day that Cennetig gathered his warrior chiefs to plan the re-build of their force.

"I've lost two sons in this last battle. I want our force better prepared to meet these bastards on the battlefield." He considered the rest of his family. His eldest son, Marcan was in the monastery, Latchna and Mathgamain had already been battle tested and Brian was still too young for the warrior training.

Viking raids on their home had resulted in numerous losses within the tribe and his family. He decided Brian was to be sent to the monastery of Clonmacnoise for his own safety. "I want to send him to the monastery, to learn Latin and Greek, to keep him out of harm's way as we regain our strength."

The remainder of his army was sent home to bury their dead, heal their wounds and allow more men to be recruited. He sent for Lachtna, "Stay close to me, son. I hope for good days to come, but we should be ready for any turn of fortune. The burden of leadership may fall to you long before we wish, and you must be ready."

* * *

Morann, with the help of two other warriors, placed Scolai's body on the horse-drawn cart that would carry him home. Daigh sat up on the seat next to Morann and remained quiet as the little procession slowly moved along the road to Cnoc Gorm. At a halfway point, one of the warriors was sent ahead to let family and friend know of their imminent arrival.

* * *

Somewhere in the lush green hills of Tuadmumuh that roll across the western side of Éirinn and south of the River Shannon, between Limerick and Ceann Coradh, Cnoc Gorm lies on a gentle rise covered in blue wildflowers. To the east of the rath is the road to Corcaigh, to the north, planted fields, pastures and a stream beyond, flowing to the Shannon.

In late afternoon, the small procession finally turned and plodded slowly up the path with blue flowers on both sides, the last rise to the rath, to Cnoc Gorm. Daigh mac Scolai, wounded and forever crippled in the Battle of Gort Rotachain, and his father, Scolai, killed that same day had been taken home, Daigh to heal and Scolai to be buried.

Word of their return had reached Bardan. He came to Cnoc Gorm at once, arriving as the small procession approached the gate and as the sun was about to set. The warriors and the cart stopped outside the rath. Brighid was standing on the bridge, her head held high, her face into the wind and the tears blown back to her flowing hair. She waited for the cart to stop next to her. She stepped close and lifted the bear skin that covered Scolai's face. His eyes were closed, and no sign of pain showed. He looked as if asleep and Brighid touched his cold cheek. "Welcome home, husband," she said quietly. She looked at Daigh, "Your wounds, Daigh, are they beginning to heal?"

"They will, mam. They will," he replied. "Tis father we must attend to now and we'll talk of my wounds later."

Bardan ordered the men to carry Scolai into the roundhouse where he would be prepared for burial. He helped Daigh down from the cart and gave him a shoulder to lean on as they went into the roundhouse.

The next morning Morann led three of his comrades out to the hillside where Breasal had been buried. They dug another grave and collected a number of large stones to cover the mound of earth.

Two days passed and a gathering of friends and family stood on the slope to witness Scolai's burial. Daigh was able to stand with a crutch and a helping hand from Morann and his oldest son, Garbhan. Saraid was next to Garbhan holding on to Laoghaire and Tanai.

*　　*　　*

Part Two

DAIGH

19

945 AD Munster, Éirinn
Cnoc Gorm … Blue Hill

Daigh's days as a warrior had ended at Gort Rotachain and the family's lives were changed forever. Daigh, no longer able to be the warrior he was, now would be a farmer with the help of Saraid, Brighid and his three sons.

On the day after the burial, Daigh stood in silence between the oak trees and Scolai's grave, thinking about his life, the sudden changes and how he would continue. Saraid came over the rise and down between the oaks, she stood next to Daigh, looking out beyond the stream, then turned toward her husband, and said, "I see why your family called this place Cnoc Gorm. The wildflowers are beautiful."

Daigh remained silent, and Saraid continued, "Tis a fine house, a lovely hill and a sturdy wall that we have, Daigh." As she spoke, their three sons came through the oak grove and stood next to Scolai's grave. She walked over to the grave, joined her sons, and said, "We'll say a little prayer for Senathair each day and he'll hear us in heaven." She touched Tanai's shoulder, "Your voices will give him comfort."

They lowered their heads and Saraid led them through a short simple prayer. One they could remember and say themselves. She walked back to Daigh as the boys ran back through the oaks. "Daigh, we've three young sons, your mam, this beautiful farm and your wounds will get better by the day. Our life is good, and our sons have a good life ahead of them."

"A fine thought, girl. To many others, a dream that would be," replied Daigh with a look of near defeat, "I heard the stories when I was a little boy about my grandmother meeting Scathach, and I dreamt of Scolai or I being another Cu Chulainn. Now just look at us, himself in the ground and me, a fine warrior I turned out to be, too late to help m'father and now, too crippled to hold a sword and shield, let alone walk without a crutch."

"Daigh mac Scolai," said Saraid, "I've known you twelve years and never a word of complaint before. You're very much alive, not dead. Yes, you've been sore wounded, but you'll be better each day and someday soon you may manage without that crutch. We should thank God for what we have and not cry over what we don't."

She stood tall with her fists planted on her hips, her hair, red as fire, pulled back, tied behind her and falling to her waist, and her dark blue eyes sparkling in the sunlight. "Now, this is our home, there's work to be done, and no time for complaining, so stand straight on that one good leg and do something of use." She turned and strode briskly back through the oaks.

Daigh took a final long look at Scolai's grave, turned and limped back to the rath. The boys were playing in the dry moat, chasing a rabbit when Daigh reached the bridge. He looked at his sons and gruffly said, "Buachailli, there's chores to be done. Now let's get at them." He looked at his oldest son, "Garbhan, see to the firewood." He turned to his second son, "Laoghaire, 'tis time for the cattle to be in their pens." Finally, he looked at his youngest son, "Tanai," their eyes met and Daigh paused, "go help your mam."

*　*　*

20

945 AD Munster, Éirinn
Teaghlaigh … The Family

The world of tenth-century Ireland demanded that young men learn to defend their families and stand in battle with their clan, their tribe. As the three brothers grew, Daigh began to teach them everything he could about the farm and the sword.

In his teaching, Daigh tried to downplay the glory of battle and stress the dangers in close combat. Scolai was a great warrior but when surrounded by four men, a javelin thrown into his back and a spear thrust into his chest, he fell.

"Battle is a brutal business," Daigh often said, "and the men who fight in these contests are as violent and barbaric as they need to be to remain alive."

* * *

In 950 AD Munster was invaded by Congalach Cnogba in the eighth year of his reign as high king. The Dal gCais fought in the battle to repel the invasion. Two sons of Cennetig mac Lorcain, Donncuan and Echthighern, were killed. The following year, 951 AD, Cennetig was killed in a battle with the Norse foreigners and his son, Latchna mac Cennetig succeeded him as tribal chieftain.

Brian, now near his tenth year, was brought home from the monastery of Clonmacnoise where he began to learn more of the warrior life. Two years later, Lachtna was killed in battle and the leadership fell to Mathgamain mac Cennetig.

* * *

The years drifted by and Daigh's injuries improved little. He managed short walks without his crutch but had no real strength in his wounded leg or arm. He tried to teach his sons all he could of the sword, but his damaged limbs limited what he could demonstrate and the vigor he felt in years gone by was no longer there. The boys found their lessons with the sword more play than hard training and it affected each differently.

Garbhan the oldest, now in his twelfth year, saw himself as the realization of his grandmother's dream. He believed he was destined to be a great warrior and thought he had learned all his father could teach. He'd learn whatever else he needed with Scathach's help and he wouldn't have to overly exert himself. He was a tall, strong boy, bigger than many men, but as time passed, he proved to be overconfidently lazy.

Laoghaire was different, he doubted the existence of a mythical figure who would give him anything he hadn't earned on his own. He constantly tried to improve in his weapons training, always doing more than he was asked to do. Always pushing himself to be better and he enjoyed the fact that the harder he worked, the stronger and better he was for it. Initially he laughed at his older brother's relaxed approach to training. Later he watched Garbhan closely and saw where he could defeat him.

Tanai was again different. He enjoyed the daily chores about the farm and tending to the animals. He practiced with his weapons as he was told, but not with the same enthusiasm as Laoghaire nor the arrogance of Garbhan. He watched his older brothers closely, knowing he would never be as good a warrior as Laoghaire, nor as much a braggart as Garbhan. Tanai saw himself as a better farmer than his brothers. He enjoyed working with his hands and often took on Laoghaire's chores about the farm, allowing his brother to practice more with his weapons.

As the summer months turned to autumn and the light of day became shorter, the family spent more time around the fire pit inside the roundhouse, talking, cleaning tools and weapons or just relaxing. Laoghaire and Tanai often played a board game or shared a book, or scroll, reading in the light of the fire.

Garbhan wanted to hear more of *The Shadowy One* and the boy, Setanta who became Cu Chulainn. He envisioned himself in a chariot, with a magical spear and boasted to his mother and grandmother, he would fight in many battles, kill hundreds of men and be a great hero.

On this night, Garbhan sat calmly pulling splinters from his wooden sword and smoothing the edges with a stone. He asked his father if he thought it was time for him to join a group of other young men, learning the ways of a warrior.

"No!" exclaimed Daigh. "You're too young, you need four or five more years before you see battle. No."

Saraid touched her husband's arm, looked at Garbhan and said, "There will be plenty of time for battles when you're full grown, boy. Don't be in such a hurry to die."

Daigh added, "Or come home wounded and useless like me."

Saraid frowned and squeezed Daigh's arm, "Not useless, not able to fight, but there are other things in life."

Brighid, Daigh's mother, turned away from the discussion and bowed her head. Saraid moved closer to her and whispered, "Does something trouble you, mam?"

Brighid answered quietly, "Five years, or is it six now since Scolai has rested on the hill above the stream." She looked at Saraid, then glanced at the others, turned back to Saraid and whispered, "The story we have all heard about Scathach and Scolai's mother, Ceara. It comes back into my mind, into my dreams and I used to ask Scolai about her, The Shadowy One. He would laugh and say it was just a dream. Then when Daigh was learning from the warriors at Ceann Coradh, they would say he was going to be great, Scathach would make it so, and I wondered again and worried." She paused, looked at Saraid and continued, "Then came Gort Rotachain …Now, I wonder about your sons." She nodded toward Garbhan, "He's so young," she looked at the other two boys, "They're all so young. I fear she will come and take them away."

"Brighid, Scolai was right, it was a dream and no more than that," returned Saraid. She moved closer to Brighid, "She was so young, alone, pregnant and had no idea where she was going or how she would manage by herself with a new baby."

"A dream, yes, but look what has happened. Ceara died, Scolai became a warrior in Lorcain's army as did Daigh. Now, I look at those three boys and wonder, I worry about them." She looked up at the roof and continued, "I wish there were no more battles, I wish we could live in peace." She looked to see the boys were not listening and continued, "She said they could become great warriors, but they would die young, in battle. Scolai always laughed at it, but he was trained in Ceann Coradh for two years and he became a Dal gCais warrior, maybe even a great warrior."

Saraid took Brighid's hand, "He was a great warrior, the men who marched with both Scolai and Daigh have said as much. I am very proud of Daigh and what he has done just as you should be proud of Scolai and his deeds."

Brighid looked at Saraid, "Scolai taught Daigh all he could and Daigh went to the same place in Ceann Coradh to learn from the best we have, and he too became a Dal gCais warrior. His friends celebrated his victories. He was a favorite among his comrades. They told stories about Daigh saving their lives, more than one of them. He may have been one of their best. Then there was Gort Rotachain." Again, Brighid hung her head, "They tell me Scolai fought well, very well. He died a hero, after saving two other men from certain death. Now he's dead and we have the memory of him."

Saraid put her arms around Brighid, hugged her and let her drift into a dream.

Brighid then lifted her head, sat up straight, sighed and said, "I see him in my dreams, standing very tall next to his friends in battle, then I see him here at Cnoc Gorm, playing with his son when Daigh was a little boy. I see him with me as we walked through the fields of wildflowers when we were young." She turned and looked at Saraid again, "And I see him as he was when we prepared him for burial." She turned away and her head lowered as she quietly remembered Scolai, and tears filled her eyes.

Saraid went to Daigh and sat close to him, "Your mother feels the loss of Scolai and fears the loss of her grandsons. She speaks of Scolai briefly and she cries."

"Time has eased the pangs of sorrow, but they still remain, less and less each passing day. He was a good man, good to his wife and good to me. I miss him as well, but I also see him as a great warrior who died doing what he was born to do."

Saraid sat quietly for a moment, then, "Your friends still tell stories of you in battle. They're all proud to call you friend as I am proud to call you husband." She touched Daigh's sword hanging on the wall behind them and said, "The time is coming when our sons will want to join the warriors at

Ceann Coradh. Both Brighid and I fear for their lives." She looked at her sons and continued, "Daigh, will they be ready?"

"I've shown them what I can of battle," returned Daigh. "Garbhan is in his twelfth year and thinks he is ready now, but he's not. Another two years and he may be ready to go to Ceann Coradh to learn from the warriors there."

"What of Laoghaire and Tanai?" asked Saraid. "I know the day will come, but I wish for it to be far in the future."

Daigh paused then said, "Laoghaire will follow the sword. He's big and strong and practices with his wooden weapons with skill and hard work." He paused again and continued, "Tanai is different. I think he enjoys the farm and would prefer to stay here and work with the animals and grow vegetables."

Saraid touched Daigh's shoulder, "Garbhan, I worry about him."

"He doesn't listen as the others do," said Daigh. "He sees himself as that hero in Seanmháthair's dream."

Saraid puzzled for a moment, "Do you believe that it was Scathach?"

"It was a dream," said Daigh. "She probably heard stories of *The Shadowy One* when she was little, and the dream came at a time when she was very weak."

"But she died as the dream said she would," said Saraid.

"I don't pretend to understand why she died," said Daigh. "It happens to far too many young women as they give life to a child, and she was just one more."

They sat in silence for a moment and Daigh picked up his short sword, looked at it and said, "I'll ask my old friends if they can help me teach the boys more than I have already." He put his arm around Saraid, "Mochta lives nearby, he has a son near Garbhan's age, perhaps I will speak to him. The two boys could learn together and maybe Laoghaire could join them, he's growing fast and learns quickly." He paused, held Saraid close and continued, "We will give them all we can and hope when they are ready, they can go to Ceann Coradh to learn from Cennetig's warriors."

*　*　*

21

951 AD Munster, Eitinn
Garbhan

Another year passed and little had changed. Garbhan was in his thirteenth year, Laoghaire in his eleventh and Tanai his ninth. Each passing day had the boys doing their chores about the farm and practicing with their wooden weapons. The farm required constant attention in more than the vegetables and livestock. The roofs needed periodic thatching repairs, the walls of the roundhouses where daub had fallen away from the wattle were patched and as the rath wall pickets succumbed to the elements, they needed to be replaced. Some years the pickets all passed muster, some years one or two would not and the chore of removing the old picket and wrestling a new one into place demanded attention.

A practice initiated by Breasal, years before was to have two or three pickets cut, cleaned, stored inside the rath and ready as needed when one in the wall could no longer stand.

Daigh and Saraid walked about the dry moat outside the rath, talking about their three head of cattle and if one would be better used as food than a source of milk. As they walked, Daigh was looking at the pickets and tapped those looking weak with his crutch. The sound on one indicated a weak spot in the wall and Daigh looked at Saraid, "A fine day to walk the woods and cut down an oak for our wall," he said.

"A fine day, indeed," returned Saraid, "but a man with one bad leg and one good arm might do well to seek out a smaller picket, perhaps one for the walkway support, rather than a thicker one for the outside wall."

"A wise choice," said Daigh, "or perhaps I could search for a branch to carve a new wooden sword for Garbhan."

Saraid smiled and as they continued their walk around the rath, she began to count the pickets. Daigh paused, tapped another suspect log, turned to Saraid as she halted her tabulation, and said "I've walked the middle of the moat several times and think it's fair to say it's about 250 paces around for a man with no crutch."

She folded her arms, looked at the picket wall, thought for a moment and said, "About 600 pickets then, husband."

"A fair estimate and perhaps a few more," returned Daigh, thoughtfully.

"I know what you're thinking, Daigh," she said. "You've found two that should come down and we have just that many in the rack. Tis time to cut one or two more."

"Garbhan can bring down a tree with his axe," said Daigh, "and the horse can drag it to the rack. Laoghaire can dig out the old, rotted log and perhaps a friend may be able to help us set the new one in place."

Saraid nodded in approval, "Mochta is a good man, he's helped us before and if I can bring down a deer, a hearty meal of venison, new bread with milk and honey, he just might help replace the entire wall."

Daigh laughed, "Today, a walkway support or a sword for Garbhan, then I'll take a little trip down the road to visit Mochta. Perhaps we do the large picket in a week or two."

The morning sun had dried most of the dew off the open fields, but the woods were still damp and cool. Daigh and Garbhan walked through the wood in search of a suitable oak tree.

"There," said Daigh as he pointed toward straight branch near the base of an oak tree. "We'll take that branch. Cut it off, Garbhan and we'll have a good piece of oak that we'll carve into your sword."

Garbhan cut the branch as his father instructed, then trimmed it where Daigh pointed. He immediately held the piece of oak like a sword and complained, "It's too heavy, Da. It has to be lighter."

"So it will be, Garbhan," said Daigh. "We have to carve away the parts we don't want and find the sword hidden inside."

Garbhan was confused, but he grinned and said, "Will you help me carve away those parts?"

"That I will, boy," answered Daigh. "When we get back to the fire pit we will cut away the extra wood, feed the fire with the bad pieces and find your sword." He took the piece of oak, holding it in his one good hand and waved it about as if he were being attacked.

Garbhan laughed as Daigh stumbled along, fighting imaginary foes with Garbhan's new sword. "Let me take the sword, Da. I'll protect your back and kill a hundred invaders." He held the oak limb with two hands and swung it about, pretending to kill enemy soldiers as the two made their way back to the rath and the large fire pit.

The carving was a chore for Daigh with only one usable hand and Garbhan's help holding the piece of oak steady. He cut away pieces and slivers of wood, eventually revealing the crude shape of a cloidem, a short sword. Daigh tried to smooth the surfaces as best he could by scraping the handle and the blade with a knifes edge, then he rubbed the surfaces with a stone and finally he took an old cloth, dipped it in water and sand, then rubbed the handle, smoothing the wood surface a little more. Finally, he handed it to Garbhan.

Garbhan took the sword and began to move it about, "Look at me Mam, I'm a warrior and I'm going to kill hundreds of invaders." He charged out of the roundhouse threatening Laoghaire and Tanai as if they were his enemy, then over to the practice posts in the yard and he slashed and lunged at the posts as his brothers watched.

"Soon it will be Laoghaire's turn to have a sword," Daigh said to his wife. "They grow up too fast and will soon be joining the other young men in Ceann Coradh and fighting in real battles.

Saraid squeezed her husband's arm, "Do you think Scathach will take all three boys from us?"

Daigh smiled, "I think Scathach is an old story, and our sons will choose their own path in this real world." He looked at Garbhan killing imaginary warriors, "If he is to learn the sword well, I must have others teach him all they can and then hope he is good enough to go to Ceann Coradh for the final training." They continued to watch Garbhan with the two younger boys, Laoghaire, smiling, watching intently and Tanai often with his head bowed as if in prayer.

* * *

Time passed and Garbhan reached his thirteenth year. Daigh, with Mochta's help, and a few of his friends had taught the boys, Garbhan and Mochta's son, Ronan, everything they could of the sword. He could stand in mock battle with his father and his father's friends and the time for him to advance was fast approaching, but Daigh was not ready to let him go to Ceann Coradh. "Another year, maybe two, and you'll be ready. Not today."

Garbhan was never happy to hear this news, he saw himself as a great warrior, invincible and ready for full on battle. Daigh decided to allow Garbhan to use a bronze sword he had found on a battlefield after an engagement. "I took this after a battle, years ago. It was left on the field, and I assume the man who wielded it is no longer alive."

Garbhan reacted as he had with his first wooden sword, threatening his younger brothers, only this time Laoghaire did not smile and marvel at his older brother. Instead, he stood tall, not flinching as Garbhan threatened him and Tanai with his new sword. Laoghaire watched every step, every move by his brother, seeing where he was strong and where he was weak. Tanai kept his head down, sometimes standing behind Laoghaire and folded his hands in prayer.

"I'll become a great warrior," boasted Garbhan. "*The Shadowy One* will watch every step I take, and I'll kill hundreds of men in battle."

Daigh cautioned his son, "Training is one thing, battle is another. Your grandfather was a great warrior, and he was killed at Gort Rotachain. I was considered as better than most, but still these wounds that I suffered are real and I'll never be able to stand in battle again. The training I give you will only take you so far, you'll need the hand of active warriors to teach you and test you."

Garbhan became less and less energetic in both his chores about the farm and his practice with the sword, stating often that Scathach would teach him all he needed to know. "When I go into battle, other men will turn and run. I will strike fear into the foreigners, and I will kill any who do not run." As he boasted, he struck the practice post a glancing blow then announced to his younger brothers, "There, I've killed another enemy. Are there no more men to stand against me?"

Laoghaire grinned and Tanai laughed at their brother's boasting, but Daigh knew this to be no laughing matter. "You hardly struck the post, boy. That blow may do no more than scratch an itch on a man's back. You must strike hard, hard enough that a second strike may not be necessary."

Garbhan winced at the criticism, but dutifully bowed his head and said, "Yes Da, I know…always strike hard enough to kill." He listened to Daigh, but less each time. He saw himself as the next Cu Chulainn, the mythical hero even as his father cautioned him, "Remember who you are, always, boys. We are men, not gods. Our training comes from other men, not some woman from the *Land of the Shadows*. There is no magic that will help you, it must be your hard work, your strength and your will to win that will carry you through battle."

The summer promised to be long and painful for Garbhan, he was big, strong and had the ability to be a good swordsman. He was young, but others his age had gone into battle. He was inexperienced, but so to were others before their first battle. He wanted to go to Ceann Coradh, he wanted to be a hero.

* * *

A warm day in mid-July seemed just right to Daigh. "I've spoken to Mochta, and he can come help us with the new picket a week from now," Daigh told Saraid. "I'll take the boys out today and cut another new one."

Saraid smiled and wondered if Daigh was taking on more than his lame leg and arm would allow. "Why not wait till Mochta comes, then go cut the picket?"

Daigh stood, took his crutch and put his good hand on Saraid's shoulder, "You've said it yourself, girl. I'm wounded, not dead. Now, there's a tree in the woods, waiting for me and I won't disappoint it."

He pulled his wife in close and held her with his good arm, then hobbled out the door.

He called his sons to the yard and handed Garbhan an axe. He told Tanai to bring the horse and Laoghaire to get the large, long rope out of the barn. "We're going for a walk into the woods, boys and find a new picket or two for the rath."

"Why that Da, the wall looks fine to me." said Garbhan.

"This farm and all that's in it are very defensible behind that wall," Daigh said to his sons. "But even sturdy pickets like these on our wall don't last forever so, we find a few new ones each year, cut them to size, drag them home and store them inside the rath till they're needed."

"Do we need one now, Da?" asked the youngest of the three.

"Yes, and you never know when another one will rot out and fall over, boy," said Daigh. "We should always be able to replace a picket when needed."

Won't there be plenty of time when we see one weakening, to cut a new one?" asked Garbhan.

Daigh stopped and looked at his three sons. "A strong wall is what we need, boys." They had never seen an attack on their home. He sat on a log and motioned for his sons to sit on the ground. He cleared his throat and began, "When I was a very young boy, this place was raided by a band of Norse. I don't remember it, nor the next time before I reached my fifth year. The one I do remember happened when I was about Garbhan's age." He paused and saw the three boys were listening closely. "I was carrying water to my father and three men working in the fields when a band of about twenty men carrying ropes and grappling hooks started up the hill."

All three boys turned quickly toward the path through the blue flowers leading to the gate in the rath. Daigh continued, "Seanathair, grandfather Scolai and his three helpers began to run toward me and he shouted at me to get inside the gate, we were being attacked." The boys turned again to look at the gate.

"As Scolai crossed the bridge, we pulled the door closed and set the oak plank in place against the door." Daigh paused again and the boys looked at him for more, "He gave each of the men a sword and all of us strung a bow. We each grabbed a handful of arrows, hurried up the ladders to the walkway and spread out along the east wall there," he said as he pointed at the wall. "Seanathair counted twenty-three men coming across the field of flowers." He paused again, "This was the first time I saw battle and knew what was happening. Your grandfather taught me to use a sword as soon as I could hold one and the bow as well."

"What happened then, Da?" asked Garbhan.

"Your Grandfather told us all to take careful aim, wait till the bastards were close enough to be sure of a hit. They were close enough, soon enough and we all let our arrows fly and notched another then another and again."

Laoghaire leaned in closer, and his eyes widened.

"He shouted at them," said Daigh, "Told them to go back where they came from, but the bastards didn't understand the Irish tongue." Daigh paused again and all three boys fidgeted and leaned in closer again. "I was on the walkway and saw a grappling hook on a rope fly over the wall. Seanathair was nearby and just looked at it, then drew his sword and stood ready for the poor bastard to reach the top of his climb. As the man's head appeared between the pointed tops of the wall pickets, He brought his sword down hard on the man's metal helmet. His sword glanced off the helmet and caught the man on his shoulder. He fell backward into the moat. I don't know if it was the sword or the fall that killed him, but all of a sudden, between the arrows and that strike of Scolai's sword, their number was cut in half."

"Did you use your sword, Da?" asked Laoghaire.

"Yes, I did, boy. Another grappling hook caught the top of the wall near me and soon a hand and arm reached over the top. Now, I didn't want to wait and see the rest of the man, so I brought the sword down as hard as I could and caught the man near his elbow with the dull edge of my sword. He screamed as he pulled his broken arm away from the wall, lost his balance and fell back into the moat, landed on his head. The brief battle ended with thirteen raiders dead and two more seriously wounded on the ground. One of Seanathair's helpers tried to talk to them, but they either didn't understand the Irish tongue or were in too much pain to answer, so the helper killed them."

"What about the others, Da? Were there still eight of them?" asked Garbhan.

"They ran to the bottom of the hill, out of range of our arrows and I never saw them again.," said Daigh.

"You killed one with your sword, but what about the arrows? How many did you kill with your bow?" asked Tanai.

"After they left, we counted eleven of them outside the moat with arrows in 'em. I don't know if I even hit anybody with my arrows. I used all of them as quickly as I could and grabbed my sword," he replied. Daigh stood, stretched and said, "Time to move on boys. There's a tree waiting for us out there and we have to find him."

The boys stood and the four continued to the woods, Daigh on his crutch, Garbhan with axe in hand, Laoghaire with the rope draped over his shoulder and Tanai, leading the horse and mumbling a prayer.

"Here Garbhan. This is a perfect tree," said Daigh. "Tall and straight. As big as a boy is around and as tall as four men. Cut it down."

When the tree fell, Garbhan handed the axe to Laoghaire. "There, brother, I've done the hard part, now you can clear the branches."

Laoghaire took the axe, slowly approached the fallen tree and cleared branch after branch, often with a single swing of the axe. "Done," exclaimed Daigh when the tree was cut to its proper length, "Now to drag it home, Tanai, bring the horse."

As the horse dragged the new picket homeward, Garbhan paced his father and said, "Da, I think I'm ready to join Cennetig and I'd like to go to Ceann Coradh."

Daigh was an old warrior and hearing his eldest son say he wanted to follow in his footsteps made him feel pride in his son, but the boy was not ready. "Not this year, Garbhan. You've still much to learn and you should allow yourself time to grow bigger and stronger."

"But Da," protested Garbhan, "I can best you with my wooden sword, and you were a great warrior."

Daigh knew he was no longer the warrior he once was and had seen other young men, not much more than boys, walk into battle full of thoughts of glory, only to be cut down by a tried and tested warrior. "No boy, another year maybe two," roared Daigh. "You're not ready."

The picket was across the bridge and full in the open yard as Daigh positioned the horse to drag it onto the rack along the walkway. Garbhan, angry or frustrated or both, kicked at the dirt in front of him and turned to walk away. As he crossed the open yard, he picked up the axe he had used to cut down the tree and proceeded to casually hack at the training post in the yard. Then suddenly, as if he envisioned an enemy attacking him, he charged at the post with three vicious swings of his axe. The top of the post fell to the ground and Garbhan buried the axe blade in the top of the remaining post and stormed away. Daigh sighed and continued to guide the horse, pulling the picket onto the rack.

*　*　*

Garbhan was unusually silent for the rest of the year. He did not heed his father's words and in the spring of the next year, as Cennetig was gathering troops to defend against an invasion by the high King, Congalach Cnoba, Garbhan secreted himself away from Cnoc Gorm, ran off to Ceann Coradh and joined their tribal chieftain.

Cennetig and Garbhan were both killed in that conflict along with many others and when Daigh was told of his son's fate, he was furious. "He didn't listen. He wasn't ready and now he's dead." Daigh bowed his head. "He was good, but not good enough," Daigh bellowed as he limped around their roundhouse on his crutch.

Garbhan's body was recovered from the battlefield and sent home to Cnoc Gorm. As his mother and father were preparing his body for burial, Daigh noticed the wounds in Garbhan's back. He had not faced his killer but appears to have been running away when slashed and stabbed. Daigh turned away from his son's body, threw his crutch against a wall, cursed and stumbled across the floor, falling into a large chair. Saraid walked over to her husband, sat next to him, and leaned into his chest. Daigh put his arm around his wife and the two sat in silence.

*　*　*

22

952 AD Munster, Éirinn
Roghanna …Choices

Garbhan was buried on the hillside with his grandparents, Scolai and Brighid and the days following the funeral were some of the hardest for Daigh. He knew full well his second son, Laoghaire would work hard and learn everything he could teach him, but Daigh wanted more. He wanted Laoghaire to be the best he could possibly be, to be a great warrior, a true warrior who would stand in battle and not run away. He also wanted Laoghaire to grow old and raise a family.

"I'm broken, not dead," Daigh told his two younger sons, "Now we practice with the sword every day and you should learn the axe and the spear as well. If you want to stay alive, you should learn every weapon you may be able to use and every weapon you may have to defend against. You learn and practice, and you may end up better than me."

When either of his sons slowed in their training, Daigh reminded them, "You need to work even harder. A battle is never done until the last of them is down. Remember, as long as a true warrior can breathe, he will fight. Stay alert and you may stay alive, always look where you cannot see, face your enemy and never show him your back." He didn't use Garbhan's name, but Laoghaire and Tanai both knew their father did not want to lose another son for lack of training, He pushed them both as much as he could.

"They learn," said Daigh to his wife, "but I'm not going to send either of them off to Connaught to prove himself." He stomped about, then paused, "Now Laoghaire, he is still young, but could probably come back from Connaught with his sword bloodied." He paused, turned to his wife and said, "You were right, Tanai is different, he's more a farmer than a warrior and that's good to know before I send him off to do battle."

"Perhaps he sees the church as a vocation," hinted Saraid, wondering if that may be an option.

"A priest, a monk," scowled Daigh, "No, I've said it before, not one of my sons. We're warriors and farmers, not priests."

"So you will allow the boys to decide what they want in life, Daigh," returned Saraid. "You've said it yourself, Tanai's a good boy and not gifted as Laoghaire with size and strength, but he knows the farm and enjoys working it."

Daigh knew Saraid was right. Tanai was not destined to be a great warrior. More than likely, if he would go into battle, he'd become one of the first casualties. Daigh hobbled out through the gate in the rath wall and made his way to the top of the rise then down between the oaks and stood looking at the graves.

Saraid came over the rise and stood next to her battered warrior. "There's no shame in being something other than a warrior," she said. "Tanai would stand and defend this home to the best of his ability, but not as Laoghaire could or would. He's good with the animals, good with the crops we grow and that's important as well."

Daigh stood silent for a moment, then, "A farmer? Better than being a monk."

* * *

The boys grew older and each showed improvement in their weapons, but Tanai spent more time working the farm and less at his sword. Daigh finally took him aside and said, "Tanai, you should choose what you want to be. If that is a farmer, then you will be the best farmer I can teach you to be. If a warrior, I will teach you all I can about weapons and battle."

Tanai smiled, picked up his sword, "Yes Da, I do wish to be a farmer, not a warrior, but I've also got to be able to defend this house and all the people in it."

Daigh was at peace with that and turned to Laoghaire, "Now you, what do you want to be?"

Laoghaire let his arm fall to his side, still holding the short sword and an axe, "I know I should learn about the farm, Da, but tis these weapons that draw me in and it's battle I want to see."

Daigh looked at both of his sons as he felt great pride swell in his chest, "I've raised two fine boys," he said to himself, "Two fine men," he said aloud.

* * *

Part Three

LAOGHAIRE

23

955 AD Munster, Éirinn
Mochta

Daigh, limited with his wounds, had taught Laoghaire all he could of the sword and axe and there was still much more for him to learn. He stood, watching as his son practiced on a post in the open yard, crossed the open space and called to Laoghaire, "you're built for battle, tall, strong and you handle these weapons as if they were part of you." He took the axe from Laoghaire's hand and continued, "The axe, it suits you, but perhaps a longer one may be better in your hand." He was thinking again of his old friend, Mochta and continued, "When I was young, I learned from one of the best, our friend Mochta. He handed the axe back to Laoghaire, "Perhaps he can teach you more of this weapon than I ever could."

In the morning, Daigh took the horse and cart down the road to visit his friend and two days later, Mochta appeared at the gate in his cart with a boy near the same age as Laoghaire. Saraid saw them as she came up the hill from the planted fields, carrying a basket of turnips. "Mochta, welcome," she said as Mochta and his companion stepped down from his cart. "Daigh and the boys are in the field gathering more vegetables," she said looking at the boy, "and who may this be?"

Mochta unhitched his horse and let him run in the pasture. "You know my son, Ronan."

Saraid's eyes widened as she looked at Ronan, "You've grown, boy. The last I saw you; you were half this size." She stepped closer to Ronan and put her hand on his arm, squeezed gently and continued, "And a fine, strong man you've become."

Ronan smiled and looked toward the field as Daigh and Laoghaire approached. He walked toward Laoghaire, "I haven't seen you in a while, my Da says you've been training with the sword and we're here to get you started on the axe."

"Are we going to work together?" asked Laoghaire.

Mochta grinned, "Ronan has been working with the axe for a few years now. As soon as he could hold a small one, I began to teach him, now he will help me teach you."

Daigh, walking with his crutch, finally reached the gathering and greeted Mochta, "Ronan, thank you for bringing your father to visit."

"Today, I've come to see if this boy of yours can handle an axe," said Mochta, as he took his long-handled weapon from the cart. "Daigh thinks he's ready to learn, and I'm ready to teach."

Ronan went to the cart, pulled a long piece of oak from the cart and a bag of iron rings. "We've brought you a gift," he said to Laoghaire as he handed him the oak staff and gave the bag of rings to Mochta.

"We'll cut it to size and add the rings when I see how tall you are, and how strong your arms are," said Mochta.

Laoghaire looked at the staff and said, "I remember the story of the heavy shepherd's staff."

Ronan pulled another staff from the cart. This one was shorter than Laoghaire's and had iron rings at both ends. He twirled it around, moving it from one hand to the other with ease.

They went through the gate to the large fire pit and Mochta placed the bag in the hot coals. It immediately burst into flames, and he nodded to Ronan, "Another log or two, boy, to heat these rings."

Ronan added two logs and took the staff back from Laoghaire, "first we see how tall you are and how long this staff should be."

Mochta smiled as his son measured Laoghaire and marked the staff about a half foot shorter than Laoghaire. "Too long and you won't be able to move it around easily," He poked the fire and saw the rings were heating nicely. "When these rings are hot enough, we'll put some on your staff to give it some weight. The number of rings depends on the strength in your arms."

Laoghaire was already over six feet in height and well-muscled. He held the trimmed staff next to himself and Mochta nodded, "This one will do for now, but as you continue to grow, we will cut you a longer staff." He poked iron rings again, "Soon."

Daigh and Mochta sat near the fire as the rings gained heat and size. Ronan showed Laoghaire some of the basic movements with the staff, all designed to give him strength and flexibility when he held a war axe.

"I miss the men and the marches to meet the foreigners," said Daigh. "Here I have raised my sons, trying to teach them all I can about battle." He bowed his head, "I failed with my oldest son, Garbhan. He wasn't ready when he joined Cennetig, and I'll not allow my other two boys to see battle until I've taught them everything I can." He took a deep breath, "Laoghaire is the one you can teach, Tanai is more the farmer and that's what he'll be. Laoghaire is the warrior, you'll see."

"Well then," said Mochta, "the sooner we begin, the better." He poked at the iron rings in the fire and said, "Almost ready?" He looked at the two boys and called them over to the fire. "Ronan, get the tongs, the larger ring and the hammer."

Ronan returned with the tools and poked in the fire, drawing out one of the rings. He placed it over the end of Laoghaire's staff and tapped it with the hammer, then he placed the larger ring against the hot one and drove the heated ring farther onto the staff with his hammer. He looked at Mochta, "He's strong and should have at least three rings at each end."

Mochta nodded and Ronan repeated the process until there were six rings on the staff, three at each end. Ronan then dipped the ends of the staff in water and carefully touched the metal rings. It was heavy, bulky and not easily moved about. "Perfect," said Mochta as he placed a small metal wedge at the end of the staff and drove it in with the hammer, then did the same at the other end. "Now, Ronan, show Laoghaire the practice moves we do with this staff."

Ronan went through a series of spins, stretches, reaches, slashes and thrusts with his staff and Laoghaire tried to duplicate the same movements. After several drops and stumbles, Laoghaire was finally getting the rhythm of the movements and could feel the weight of the staff, straining at his arms. The exercise went on for an hour and both boys were breathing heavily and sweating.

"Enough for now," shouted Mochta, "rest for a few minutes and we'll do it again." He looked at Daigh, "We'll need a taller practice post. As tall as Laoghaire or maybe a little taller."

"For the axe?" quizzed Daigh.

"No, not yet," replied Mochta. First, we learn the movement of the axe using the weighted staffs. Soon enough they'll be using the real thing, but not yet."

* * *

Ronan and Laoghaire's intensive training began immediately. Tanai would practice with his sword for an hour each day and take over most of Laoghaire's farm duties to allow he and Ronan the full day to practice. He was happy to do so. All three boys were doing what they wanted to do.

Mochta handed Laoghaire a sack and said, "You will put a few handfuls of little stones in the sack, then carry it over your shoulder as you run around the moat five times." He handed Ronan another sack and smiled. Ronan knew what that meant, and he immediately put several handfuls of stones in the bag, then took off running after Laoghaire in the dry moat.

Mochta looked at Daigh, "More stones than I intended. They'll get very heavy, very soon."

Daigh smiled, "Yes, they would for most men."

The two boys finished the five turns around the moat and returned to the open yard, still carrying their sacks and both breathing easily. Mochta looked at Laoghaire, then at Daigh, "For most men, eh." He turned again to Laoghaire, 'Here, boy take your sword and show me what you'd do to this post if it were your enemy."

Laoghaire did as his father had taught him, attack and look around, then attack again. Mochta watched closely and after three solid attacks on the post, he tossed Laoghaire a wooden sword, "Now, boy attack me."

The two dueled for several minutes and Mochta backed away. "Daigh, you've taught him well," he said as he held up a hand in surrender. "This boy is better than most men."

Daigh grinned and turned toward his son, "Are you getting tired, Laoghaire?"

Laoghaire looked at his father with sweat flowing from his forehead, wiped his eyes, smiled, and replied, "No, Da, tis too much fun to be tiring."

Ronan laughed and said, "We should try the staffs."

Mochta said in return, "Well I need a rest, so you two go ahead and we'll stop you when we have something else for you to do."

Ronan showed Laoghaire where to put his hands and how to move them as he changed positions when making different strikes. "Begin with your right hand higher on the shaft and your left hand in the middle of the grip."

Laoghaire did as he was told and grinned like a child with a new toy. He looked at the placement of his hands and asked, "Can I change my hands, with my left hand higher?"

"Try it both ways," replied Ronan, "hold it as I showed you and approach the practice post with a slash. Then try it the other way, and see which way feels better for you."

Laoghaire did as he was told, striking the post from both sides, then looked back at Mochta, "I don't know which is better."

"All the better, boy. You'll learn both ways," returned Mochta as he leaned back again. He turned and looked at Daigh, "This is a good thing, he'll be able to use the axe from both sides. A very good thing." He looked back toward Ronan, "Now, boy, do battle with the post from both sides. Two or three swings from the right, then two or three from the left."

Ronan demonstrated then stood back as Laoghaire did both sides, smiled and looked at Ronan. Before he could say anything, Mochta bellowed at him, "Another three from each side again, then spin around and do it again, then spin around to face Ronan and be ready to defend yourself."

Laoghaire did as he was told and Mochta prodded the two to change places and repeat the same process over and over. Finally, Mochta shouted, "Enough, boys. The post is dead."

Both boys stopped, dripping sweat, and breathing heavily, they looked at Mochta and Laoghaire asked, "Now what do we do?"

Mochta put up his hand toward Laoghaire, looked at Daigh and said, "I like this boy, he will do well, very well." He looked at Laoghaire, "enough for today, boys."

Laoghaire led Ronan down the hill to the stream, waded out till he was waist deep and fell over backwards. Ronan dove in and the two splashed for a few minutes, washing away the dirt and sweat of the day.

The two men sat back and watched as the boys came back from the stream, dripping wet, talking and laughing. "They work well together," said Daigh.

"That they do," agreed Mochta. "Now we should develop a full day's work for them and start in the morning."

"They can run the moat first," said Daigh.

"Yes, then the staffs and follow that with some basic sword work," said Mochta. "The axe I use in battle is long and has a wide curving blade. Ronan has learned some of its use and is ready to move on. His sword is not as strong as Laoghaire's, so as I teach Laoghaire the axe, you can teach Ronan the sword."

The boys returned to the fire pit, clean, dried, dressed and very tired. Mochta looked at Ronan. He was holding his staff and he looked at Laoghaire, "Your staff, where is it?" asked Mochta.

Laoghaire leapt to his feet, hurried across the yard to the practice posts, picked up his staff and came back to the fire pit.

Mochta looked at Laoghaire, "I want you to carry this staff with you wherever you go. Use it in everything you do, it is now a part of you, get used to its weight, its size. Move it from hand to hand, spin it around and toss it in the air. Catch it with one hand and keep it moving. Remember this isn't a staff, it's an axe. As you get used to this big, heavy staff, the axe will become more and more comfortable in your hands."

The practice sessions went on for several days, each day beginning with Laoghaire and Ronan running the moat with the sack of stones and each day the sacks were made a little heavier. Even as Mochta added another lap or two around the moat, both boys seemed to enjoy the exercise all the more.

The practice sessions grew to both Laoghaire and Ronan facing Mochta with wooden swords, then their heavy staffs as if they were axes.

Tanai joined in the contests, making both boys face one, two or three opponents. Both boys acquitted themselves very well. Both were developing into expert axe men.

As Daigh and Tanai were watching the early morning ritual of running the moat, Tanai said to Daigh, "Da, the practice post needs replacing. Maybe we could use one of the pickets cut in half." He thought for a second, then, "Or we could put both halves in the ground and have two that we could attack."

"Or leave the one there already and add the other two. Two new, big, strong warriors and one little beaten poor soul."

The two laughed and Daigh said, "Three posts, spread apart and all three of you could practice at the same time."

"Then it's done," said Tanai. "I'll drag one of the posts off the rack and cut it in half now." He looked at his father, "Of course a little help would be appreciated."

"Three posts," exclaimed Mochta. "A very good idea. We should arrange them in a triangle and the boys could move from post to post or one could stand in the middle and turn in any direction."

Ronan, Laoghaire and Tanai began to locate the post locations and dig the holes. Mochta and Daigh watched. "Are you too old or too tired to help?" laughed Daigh looking at Mochta.

"Both," returned Mochta, "and getting older every day."

In the following days, all three boys ran the moat and attacked the posts. They each took a post and when Mochta shouted a direction, they moved to the post to their right or left.

The sessions grew in intensity and finally, Tanai sat down next to Daigh and said, "Da, I don't know how they do it, but I can't keep up with them any longer."

"I know your calling is to the farm, Tanai," returned Daigh. "You practice as much as you can and tend to the farm as it is needed. Your brother and Ronan will continue at the posts and weapons."

*   *   *

A few weeks into the training process, Mochta expressed a concern to Daigh, "Laoghaire, is very good, young, very strong and has the size of a big man, but does he have patience? Will he stay the course and learn everything we can teach, or will he see he is better than most and want to join in battle before we have finished?""

"My oldest, Garbhan," said Daigh, "he didn't have patience, now he's dead." Daigh paced a little and continued, "Laoghaire is different. He's a thinker. He knows his limits and strives to stretch them. Every day he grows, every day he is better than before. He will learn what we teach, and he will stay here until we send him to Ceann Coradh." Daigh smiled, "He will be a great warrior."

"I know about Garbhan. I know he thought more of himself than he was. I know he wasn't ready; he did not have patience. He has learned much thus far," said Mochta, "and there's much more we can teach him, but if he is as his brother was, then we'd be wasting our time and his."

"He'll stay on course," said Daigh. "He'll keep training and practicing until we tell him the time is right for him to move on."

After several more weeks of intensive training and sparring with Mochta, Daigh and Tanai, Laoghaire and Ronan would often best the three of them. It appeared they had learned everything the two old warriors could teach and now they hungered for more.

"Your son, he's all you said he'd be," said Mochta. "That and more. Now I think it time to call in a few of our old friends to give both of these boys a real challenge." He looked at Daigh and scratched his chin, he knew several men who were still alive because of Daigh's actions in old battles, "There are others, you know," said Mochta, "Others who would come help train these two." He put his hand on Daigh's shoulder, "I know a few men who feel indebted to us both and who would be here now, if asked."

Daigh looked at Ronan and Laoghaire, then back at Mochta, "Then ask, old friend and I will be very grateful."

* * *

Mochta left for Ceann Coradh in the morning and returned to Cnoc Gorm a week later with three other men.

"Daigh, old friend, it's been too many years since we marched together," said Cassan. "I hear there are two boys who need to learn to fight like warriors, so, we've come to help you two old men."

Daigh leaned on his crutch, "Cassan, you were wounded and being dragged from the field when I last saw you. It seems all your wounds have healed."

"Most have," said Labhras, "But not the one to his head," he laughed.

Mochta looked at Daigh, "You remember Ross. Tis your sword that kept him alive a few years ago and his that has saved me more than once since."

The five men gathered about the fire pit, sat on logs, and reminisced about battles fought, the men no longer with them and life at Ceann Coradh. The conversation finally got around to training the two boys.

"How old are these boys?" asked Cassan.

"Laoghaire is in his fifteenth year," replied Daigh.

"As is Ronan," added Mochta.

"Fifteen," said Labhras, "Old enough to join us today, if they can hold a sword." He looked at Daigh, "Does your boy have your size?"

"Is he any good with the sword?" asked Ross.

Mochta held up his hands, Laoghaire is a big strong boy, still growing. He is taller than Ronan by an inch or two and Ronan is bigger than each of you. They both handle the sword better than most men I know; Ronan may be better than me with an axe and Laoghaire, he is new to the axe, but he fast approaches Ronan's ability."

Daigh looked around the open yard, "Where are they?" he wondered aloud.

Saraid was standing behind her husband and said, "The boys have gone to the village, they'll be back soon." She patted her husband's shoulder, "Would you men like something to eat. I've made a soup and there's new bread still warm from the baking."

As they ate and the sun dropped from the sky, the conversation wound back to old battles and old friends. The hour grew late, and the three men fell asleep with full bellies and thirst quenched.

Morning came and the three men woke to the shouts of both Mochta and Daigh prodding Laoghaire as he ran the moat. They walked out into the yard to see a tall, powerfully built young man take a final swing at a practice post and stand next to Mochta. He dipped a cup into a bucket of water and drank, then splashed the remainder across his face.

"Friends," said Daigh, "this is Ronan.

The three men stood in awe of this tall young man, "I see why you wanted help," said Ross.

As they were looking at Ronan an even taller, broader man with a sack across his shoulders came across the bridge, tossed the sack to the ground, grabbed a long-handled axe and attacked the three posts.

Mochta turned to the three men with his hand extended toward the three posts and said, "Laoghaire."

They watched, quietly as Laoghaire finished his morning routine. Cassan leaned down and tried to lift the sack of rocks with one hand, and let it drop to the ground, surprised at the weight. Labhras stood next to the practice posts, looking at the strike marks. The three men came together, and Ross said, "This is interesting, Mochta, very interesting." He waved the group of five men together, "They're big, strong, and very good with each of their weapons. These two are each a better warrior than most I know. I don't know what we are here to teach them."

Mochta spread his hands, "Friends, neither of these boys have yet been tested in battle. They appear to be ready, but only true combat will define them. What we are here to do is simple, make them the best warriors we possibly can."

Daigh leaned on his crutch and added, "My oldest son, Laoghaire's brother, was not ready and lasted less than a day in battle. Laoghaire and Ronan have worked long and hard to develop their fighting skills, now we will test them with wooden swords, try to find weaknesses and make adjustments. They will be better than any one of us and maybe better than all of us together."

Laoghaire and Ronan were put through hell, learning how to stay alive in a battle. "The man who fights the hardest, does not relent, pushes his opponent into the ground and kills in as few strokes as possible will last the longest," preached the old warriors. They pushed them in several directions at once, often surrounding one of them with two, three or all four seasoned warriors and teaching them how to stay alive.

"When you are faced with three or four, take the weakest of their number, and kill as quickly as possible," the boys were told. "That will give them pause, a very brief pause." The mock combat continued, "Then take the best of the rest and attack — hard. Push him to the ground and give him no mercy. Kill and be quick about it as the others will not wait, they will attack. Turn and meet them before they can strike."

Mochta circled about as the boys trained, "Be alert," his voice gruff. "Know your battleground, know where your enemy stands, and where he can fall. Know where others can attack you, look where you do not see," his voice getting louder and rougher as he continued. "Take the fight to your enemy and do not hesitate."

The four warriors left and returned several times, each time to realize Laoghaire had gone beyond Ronan. He had grown bigger, stronger, and smarter. The beatings he inflicted on his teachers were finally more than they could tolerate, and they proclaimed both as ready as any warrior could be. "We've done all we can do," said Ross. "Send these two to Ceann Coradh and let Mathgamain see what you have created."

Two weeks later Mochta and Ronan arrived at Cnoc Gorm with a gift for Laoghaire. Mochta handed him a long-handled axe. It was as tall as Laoghaire with a large, curved axe blade, offset with a hammer and a pike rising between the two a full foot above the tip of the axe. The handle was a long oak shaft with three small iron bands spaced evenly and a leather wrapping between the rings. The base of the shaft ended with an iron plug that gave balance to the staff.

Ronan pulled another, identical axe from their cart and stood next to Laoghaire. "I think we are ready for the final phase of our training. We're ready to go to Ceann Coradh and stand with the warriors." Laoghaire looked at Daigh, "Da, have we learned enough?"

Daigh stood without his crutch and took the axe from Laoghaire, "You'll never stop learning, but you have learned all we can teach the both of you here. Now, Mochta will finish what we have started when you go to Ceann Coradh." He felt the heft of the weapon and looked at his son, handed the axe back to him, "A fine weapon, use it well."

"It is that," replied Laoghaire as he took the axe and twirled it as he had the weighted staff. "I like the feel of it and I can reach out a fair distance, farther than with my old axe, tis much better."

Mochta said, "I will go to Ceann Coradh in one week's time, both you and Ronan are ready to go and join the others I teach. In this last week, both of you exercise with your axes as you have practiced with the staffs."

Laoghaire was now nearly six and a half feet tall and Daigh told his wife, "He is no longer a boy, Saraid. He's in his eighteenth year and has learned everything we are able to teach him here. He wants to join the men at Ceann Coradh and stand ready for battle."

Saraid knew her son would leave some day but had hoped it would wait a few more years. "We've lost one son, Daigh. Are you sure this one is ready?"

"That he is, girl. That he is." Daigh stood, leaned on his crutch and continued, "Garbhan was not nearly as prepared as Laoghaire. He didn't ask, he thought he was ready and probably knew I'd say no if he did." Daigh hung his head, "I've no want to lose another son, but this one is better than I ever was and the men I've brought to help train him can no longer suffer the wrath of his strength." He raised his head, "Yes, Saraid, our son is ready."

"And he wants to go, husband?" quizzed Saraid.

"He's not said as much, but I know he does," replied Daigh. "It's what he is, what I was years ago and what I wish I still was today. Saraid stood next to her husband, touched his hand on his crutch and said, "And a fine warrior he will be."

* * *

24

The training regimen at Ceann Coradh was hard, but both Laoghaire and Ronan had a solid foundation in training. They were ready, they both passed the challenges and tests that were put in front of them and in the late summer of 958, they were both called Dal gCais warriors.

Laoghaire left Ceann Coradh and went home for the winter at Cnoc Gorm. He was now a full-grown man, as large as he would ever be, well trained and well-armed. His mother and father were very proud of their son, possibly the warrior that Garbhan had wanted to be, possibly the warrior that Ceara's dream had predicted.

He stayed through the winter and in the spring, Laoghaire traveled back to Ceann Coradh. He arrived as a group of ships was being loaded with supplies and found Mochta near one of the captured longships directing a group of laborers. "Mochta, where are you going?"

"Laoghaire, welcome back," smiled Mochta. "You're just in time to join our expedition."

"Expedition? Just where are you going?"

"We'll be going upriver today, my young friend," he replied. "To visit a site or two on the shore of Lough Derg. Would you like to join us?"

"Visit?" questioned Laoghaire.

"We'll try to chase the foreigners out of there. Push them farther north. They're constantly trying to move closer and closer. Eventually they'll be all over this island and we'll be outnumbered."

"Push?" asked Laoghaire.

"Yes, we attack them, force them to move back. After enough of these raids, maybe they'll just go home and forget about living here,"

"They've been here more than 100 years," said Laoghaire.

"True enough," admitted Mochta, "And about time for them to go home." He turned toward a row of buildings and directed Laoghaire to a door into an Inn. "Come in and meet some of the others who will be going today."

They entered a small room, overcrowded with some twenty men. Cassan, seated near the center of the room, stood and said aloud, "Friends, you have all heard me talk of this young man," he gestured toward the open door, "Laoghaire mac Daigh."

The men in this crowded room turned and quieted as Laoghaire and Mochta entered. Then a low murmur and one man stood, "Does the son of Daigh mac Scolai come to join us? We've heard stories about you."

Another man stood and said, "Yes, we hear you can best four of us with your axe."

Mochta speaks highly of your ability in battle," said another, "But you've never seen real battle."

As another man was about to speak, a door on the opposite side of the room, opened and a tall young man entered. "Who has never seen battle?" asked the tall man with a commanding voice.

Mochta was about to speak when Laoghaire stepped forward and answered the question, "My name is Laoghaire mac Daigh, and I am here to be one of you." He stepped to the middle of the room and met the tall man. "You know my name, now what is yours?"

The young man stepped closer to Laoghaire, extended his hand, smiled and said, "Brian, and I welcome you."

* * *

Mochta introduced Laoghaire to a number of other warriors, and they found a place in the crowded room to sit and continue talking. "Brian is Mathgamain's younger brother," he told Laoghaire.

"Brian mac Cennetig?" asked Laoghaire.

"Yes," returned Mochta, "The youngest son of Cennetig, the king killed on the same day as your brother, Garbhan." He looked around and quietly said, "Brian and his brother don't agree on everything. They often argue about the Norse of Limerick, about using horses in battle and ships. Brian likes to use the ships we have to move troops about." He looked around the room again and quietly continued, "Brian is a good man, a great warrior and a better leader. These men in this room would follow him if he wanted to attack Cashel, Limerick, Dub Linn or hell itself."

"So, who do we follow, Mathgamain or Brian?" asked Laoghaire.

"Tis all the same," smiled Mochta. "They may argue behind closed doors, and we all know they do, but in front of us, they're united."

"So then, these river raids are by Mathgamain's orders?" Quizzed Laoghaire.

"I'm sure these are more Brian's ideas than the king's, but once again, those two are one voice," replied Mochta. He scanned the room again, "Well now, will you be joining us on this little raid this morning?"

"I came here to be part of Mathgamain's force, and the sooner I join in, the better," said Laoghaire.

"Good," said Mochta, "I'll tell Brian we'll have another axe on this little trip and I expect Ronan will be here too."

*   *   *

Brian was a tall, powerful looking man, a few years older than Laoghaire. His long red hair and dark blue eyes reminded Laoghaire of his mother's family and that was somehow comforting. Brian approached Laoghaire and said, "Mochta tells me you wish to join our ship on this expedition."

"I do," responded Laoghaire. "I came here to be a part of Mathgamain's army, not watch you and these others sail up and down the river. So, the sooner I get involved, the better."

Brian smiled, "Then, once again, welcome," and he was off pointing and directing men boarding the several longships.

*   *   *

Mochta slapped Laoghaire on his shoulder, gestured toward one of the two longships in the harbor and said, "Let's go aboard and see where you fit, we all pull an oar till the sail is set and God's breeze pushes us along."

They walked across the plank, boarded the ship and Laoghaire heard a familiar voice, "It's about time you got here," said Ronan.

The two men found oars across from each other and talked as the rest of the crew boarded. Laoghaire puzzled over the oar and Ronan said, "I'll help you get started, it's simple enough, you use your back, not your brain and once we're out in the wind, we relax."

As the longships began to move away from the shore, the motion of the waves was a new sensation for Laoghaire. The others laughed as he seemed to change colors and leaned over the side. One of the other warriors slapped him on his back and said, "You've still some things to learn, boy."

Laoghaire spit out the last of his discomfort, stood tall in front of the warrior, "Then teach me, old man."

The entire crew laughed, and they set about pulling on their oars. The longship moved out into the river and the wind finally filled the sail. The ship turned north and sailed into the widening waters of Lough Derg.

"We're heading for a settlement along the west side of the Lough," said Ronan. "It's one we haven't attacked before, and our purpose is to rid our country of these foreigners."

The raid was simple. The longship moved close enough to the shore for the warriors to quickly wade ashore in very shallow water, and race to the settlement. The conflict was brief, a number of people were killed, and their homes burned. Laoghaire was not willing to kill old men, women or children and he settled for chasing a woman carrying a child into a nearby wooded area where he slowed allowing her to run farther away. He returned to the settlement where the bodies of those caught were strewn about the burning buildings.

The raid bore minor looting and the men were returning to the longships. Laoghaire walked through the little village and caught up to the other raiders as they boarded their ships. He casually walked up to Ronan, "This is not what I imagined a warrior would do. These were defenseless people, and we were no more than those miserable raiders I have heard about."

Ronan came close to Laoghaire and quietly said, "This is all part of what we do. The Norse have invaded our country and we are trying to rid the island of their kind. There will be battles where you will face true soldiers, warriors and your skills will be fully used. We will come back here in a week or two and be sure this settlement is gone forever. We may be able to capture a few head of cattle or horses. We shall see."

The next week a raid was conducted south on the river, away from the Lough about halfway to Limerick. There they met opposition from a band of Norse soldiers and engaged in three skirmishes. Laoghaire met his first true match as three men approached him in an open field. They approached with less caution than they should have, believing the three of them could easily defeat this single warrior. Laoghaire readied himself as Mochta had taught him and as the three neared he noticed a slight hesitation on the part of one. He moved quickly slashing both left and right making those two back up a step or two and he charged the man in the middle. He moved quicker than the middleman could retreat, and his axe found the man's shield only offered casual resistance. The second blow cut through the man's shoulder at his neck and Laoghaire spun quickly to meet the other two already recovering from the initial charge. Laoghaire feinted toward his right and quickly turned with full force to his left, meeting the man only an axe length away. Again, his axe found flesh and he again turned to face the third man. Three steps had Laoghaire smashing the man's shield and a second slash finished the contest. He turned to see Ronan and Brian coming his way and his second victim trying to reach for his sword. He had been cut through his midsection and death was only moments away.

Ronan stood over the man as he put his hand on his sword and brought his axe down on the man's neck. He turned and nodded toward Brian.

Brian walked up to Laoghaire, "The stories about you are true. You bested three men here, three experienced Norse warriors."

Laoghaire said, "I also saw you do as much with your sword. Are all raids as easy as these two have been?"

Brian smiled, "No, my large friend, not all river raids are as successful and the losses to the Dal gCais have been significant. We raid to rid this land of invaders," he bowed his head and continued, "The losses we have suffered have taught us more about our enemy and how to fight him. In that sense, even our battles lost are victories."

He nodded to Ronan, "Your father and Daigh have trained him well, my friend. Perhaps we should try training more young men like him." He nodded to Laoghaire and hurried back to the others near the river.

The battles along the River Shannon lessened and over the next few years and a peace treaty was negotiated by Mathgamain with Ivar, the king of Limerick in 963. Brian, however, was not pleased with this arrangement and the arguments with his brother increased. "They're not our friends," argued Brian. "They are our enemy, trying to take this entire island from us. They treat us as dogs, and you are bowing to them."

"The deed is done, brother," said Mathgamain, "Ivar and I have an agreement and the raids into our lands will cease as ours into their lands will cease."

Brian was furious, he stormed about the palace grounds, thinking and cursing. Laoghaire and Ronan were relaxing under a tree when Brian approached. "Brian, what troubles you?" asked Laoghaire.

"We have given up too many lives and property to the Norse, and I will not be treated as a whipped dog." He stopped and stared at the clouds for a moment, then sat with his friends. "I'll not be a part of this farce, sleeping and eating with our enemy." He looked at his friends, I'll find as many men as I can of a like mind and we'll challenge the Norse of Limerick.

Laoghaire looked at his friend, "Brian, I have no desire to be a part of this truce. We have spent years fighting these bastards and I'll not break bread with them now. I'm with you."

"First, we have to gather as many men as we can, leave Cashel and Ceann Coradh, go to the hills of Tipperary. There we can conduct a war on the Norse of Limerick. We may be no more than a thorn in Ivar's side, initially, but if we begin to have an effect on the Norse, others will join us."

"How many do you think we may have?" asked Ronan.

Brian thought, "I'd guess more than 100 and less than 300, at first."

"When do we go?" asked Laoghaire.

"In the spring," said Brian. "We'll use the time between now and then to gather men and supplies. I think we should keep this quiet until we're ready to join in battle. Talk only to people you trust, and even then, do so very quietly."

*　*　*

25

We may not be enough to defeat him initially, but if we attack and run, then attack again, always when he least expects it or when we find a smaller force outside of Limerick, little by little we can lessen his numbers and perhaps increase our own till the day when we can challenge him with equal numbers." He looked at his two friends, "Are you with me?"

Neither hesitated, "I am," they said in unison.

Brian smiled, "We're only a few now, but I expect we'll be more before we leave."

"There are others," said Ronan, "this peace with Ivar does not set well with everybody."

"We have to keep this quiet, talk only to men you trust. There are those who may run to Ivar or my brother and tell them of this plan."

Laoghaire sat quietly for a moment, then "Brian, you should leave soon, take all you can with you and find a place where we can meet. Ronan and I will stay here another day or two, then join you with as many as we can muster."

"I'll finish this day here and leave," said Brian. "When I find a place, I'll send someone back to tell you where we can meet."

Ronan looked at Laoghaire, "And you thought we were going to have a quiet summer." He leapt to his feet, picked up his staff and twirled it around, "I'm off to find a friend or two who may want to join us. Laoghaire, I'll be back here tomorrow about this time, and we can plan our next steps."

Laoghaire stood, looked at Ronan, "Tomorrow, this same place, I'll be here." He looked at Brian, "Tis a dangerous course you have set, Brian." He put his hand on Brian's shoulder, "I came to Ceann Coradh to be a part of Mathgamain's army, to fight against the Norse and now, I choose to follow you and continue that fight."

Brian looked at his friends, "They come here for Ireland, we'll give them a piece of hell."

The next day Ronan and Laoghaire returned to the same place, each with a following of several men. "I could stay another day," said Ronan, "and perhaps gather more men."

As they were speaking, a small, older man approached, looked at both and said to Ronan, "I knew your father, long ago. We gave battle to the foreigners in Connaught and up into Meath." He looked at Laoghaire, "and Scolai, your seanathair, I was with him at Gort Rotachain. He was a good man, a great warrior." He sat down and continued, "Brian asked me to lead you to him. This is all I can do now, deliver messages and the like." He looked around, "We should leave here in smaller groups, as not to attract attention. When we're away from curious eyes, we can travel together."

Laoghaire and Ronan arrived with twelve men, bringing their total to 187 men including Brian. "Tis a small army, sure enough," said Brian, "More would be wonderful, but with this gathering of warriors, we'll be able to attack smaller groups of Norse and slowly carve away at the force in Limerick."

"When do we begin?" asked one of the old warriors. "The day is still young and I'm eager to spill a little Viking blood."

The men nearby raised an approving rumble and Brian replied, "Tomorrow will set out and look for their early patrol to the south of the city. If we match up with them, we attack."

The morning came with warriors anxious to find and meet a Norse patrol. Brian sent four scouts to the city gates. "We need to know their number and their direction," he told the scouts.

One of the scouts returned with word that the morning patrol was coming out and heading east along the river. "I counted 82 men in mail with shield and sword, afoot, save the leader, mounted."

"We go now," said Brian. The entire force assembled and began to move through the hillside, north to meet the Norse. An hour into their trek a second scout found them and reported to Brian.

"Only minutes away, more east than here. They stopped to harass a farmer and two of their number are taking him back to Limerick for God knows what."

Brian looked about and called one of his men, "Take five good men, catch the bastards and free the prisoner."

"The soldiers?" quizzed the old warrior.

"They are the enemy," replied Brian.

The old warrior understood, waved at five men and they hurried off in the direction of Limerick.

Brian checked with the scout, then drew his sword and pointed in the direction of the patrol. The rush to meet their enemy was chaotic at best and when they burst from the cover of woods and brush, the Norse had precious little time to form a defensive posture. They tried to form a shield wall, but the undisciplined Irish were on them before shields could link or even swords drawn. Armed only with swords and no spears or pikes, the Norse defense was splintered, and it was more a slaughter than a battle.

Laoghaire charged a shield striking with his long-handled axe. The Northman behind the shield was driven to the ground and Laoghaire drove the pike end of his axe into the man's chest. He turned to see another opportunity and swung his axe into another shield. This time the shield shattered, and the Northman was left with a battered arm and his sword. Laoghaire didn't hesitate, bringing his heavy axe down on the man's head, driving the edges of his mail into his head.

It was over almost immediately; several Norse were on their knees pleading and Brian signaled his warriors to kill them. He turned to several men with brief conversations and then faced the larger part of his army.

"We've lost six of our number and three more hard wounded, but we've killed 80 of them and gained a number of long swords and," he smiled, "a horse."

The bodies of the Norse were stripped of anything of value and the 80 were left to rot in the sun.

* * *

26

The celebration after this initial victory was loud and drunken. The dead were honored, and the wounded sent home to heal, then the drinking and bragging began. It seemed as if each man claimed at least two kills, which would have put the enemy force at over 300.

Laoghaire was quietly cleaning his axe when Ronan raised his arm, "friends, we should honor the true heroes of today's battle. I salute Laoghaire, I saw him destroy two men in an instant and would not doubt he killed ten more."

Another man stood and said, "I saw Laoghaire split a man's shield."

Another again said, "He drove another man to ground with a single blow."

Another stood, "Laoghaire mac Daigh, I know his father and Scolai, he comes from a line of great warriors."

Then another stood, "The stories about Scathach, are they true?"

Laoghaire raised his hand, "Friends, I'm no different than any of you, I met two men in battle today, no more and Scathach was a dream of my grandmother's. I learned to fight from my father, Mochta and the warriors of the Dal gCais."

Brian raised his arm, "Laoghaire has been with me for six years and I have seen him in battle a number of times. He is indeed a great warrior. There are few who could challenge him and less could defeat him." He lowered his arm and drifted into thought, then turned and walked away.

The men gathered saluted Laoghaire and again mentioned others who had fought well that day. Laoghaire watched Brian leave the gathering and decided to follow. He saw Brian walk aimlessly and watched him from a distance. Finally, after an hour, Brian returned and saw Laoghaire watching him. "Laoghaire, I have a plan, come, join me. I have to select a few good men to lead smaller groups. You are one of my choices."

The two men went back to the celebration and Brian spoke in a clear voice, "I need you and you," he said, pointing at two older warriors. Then he selected another sixteen men similar to the first two. "Come with me, I have a plan and you are an important part of it." They left the gathering and reassembled out of the way of other men wandering about.

"Each of you will pick nine men," said Brian. "Men who will follow you into battle. Men you know and trust." He allowed that to sink in and continued, "We're going to fight a different type of war. We're going to use the trees, the bushes, tall grass and uneven ground as our allies." He studied the group of warriors, "We will attack in smaller groups of nine or ten men when the enemy is not prepared to fight. We will fight when we are ready. We will attack and retreat quickly, don't give them a chance to lock shields and form a wall." He again watched the eyes of the gathered men.

Laoghaire listened and thought, then, "Brian, will each smaller group act independently, or will we receive instruction from you?"

"We will have an overall plan, a strategy. Then as the engagement develops, I will talk to you men, individually and you will lead your groups accordingly."

Brian's small army conducted raids as he planned, small groups of men attacking from cover, striking when least expected. Victories were few, but each skirmish taught the group more about fighting the larger and usually better armed force of the Limerick Norse.

"We fight till we win or see that victory will not be ours," said Brian, "then we run and live to see another day."

Each man proved his worth in these small battles, but their losses mounted, and new recruits lessened. Some fought better than others and Brian was among the best. He led his men in front, often being the first to strike and his example kept the group together.

Laoghaire followed the example set by Brian, fighting like a wild-eyed beast, lashing out at the enemy with a ferocity that terrified not only the enemy but his comrades as well.

Following an engagement with a group of the Limerick Danes, Brian noticed Laoghaire standing over a vanquished opponent, frozen, looking down at his last kill. Brian approached him cautiously, "Laoghaire, are you wounded?"

He turned toward Brian and realizing the battle was over, he relaxed, heaved a sigh and replied, "No Brian, this day is ours again. Have we lost anyone?"

Brian stood next to Laoghaire, put his hand on the tall man's shoulder, "Two, Torna and Morann. They were good men and will be missed." Each battle had been costly, and their numbers fell as men were killed, severely wounded or lost interest in continuing.

The two were approached by a young warrior, "Brian, more Danes are comin' this way," said Brogan.

"Their number, Brogan?" asked Brian, "Do we know how many?"

"I stopped counting at twenty, but more were behind," he managed as he caught his breath.

Brian looked at Laoghaire, "We should leave now."

Laoghaire tossed his axe to Brogan, "Carry this for me boy, I'll take Torna across my back."

Brian placed his sword in a belt ring, handed his shield to Brogan and said, "And I'll carry Morann."

*   *   *

The group had now dwindled to less than twenty men and the two men killed that day would be sorely missed. They moved through the woods and over the nearest hill heading south to their camp.

The rest of the men left in different directions to mislead anyone attempting to follow in their tracks. Two hours later they had regrouped in a well-hidden cave. As the men gathered around a small fire, Brian stood, "Winter is near, the rains and snow will soon make our work more difficult. Perhaps we should retreat farther south and try to increase our numbers for the spring," he said.

As he spoke, Brogan came into the cave. He walked over to Laoghaire. "I've news from home, Laoghaire. Your father has been taken ill and may not live to see the sun rise again."

Laoghaire looked at Brian, "I'll leave now and see you in the spring at Killaloe."

Brian thought he may have seen his good friend for the last time, placed his hand on the tall man's shoulder and said, "You have served us well good friend. Before you return, be sure your family is cared for." Brian remembered the battles of the last years and wondered if he could ever replace the big man's axe.

The others gathered their belongings and all dispersed, each leaving in a different direction for their homes. When Laoghaire arrived home, his father was in the final throes of a sickness that finally stole his breath and stopped his heart. The funeral was simple, Daigh was buried on the slope north of the rath next to the graves of his mother and father. Laoghaire stood with Saraid and Tanai as Saraid quietly said a prayer for Daigh.

Daigh was gone and Laoghaire was prepared to remain home to help his mother and younger brother with the farm. Ready, but not wanting to leave his comrades in their war against the foreigners.

Saraid knew her son Laoghaire was a warrior, dedicated to the cause for which he had fought over the last several years. She knew he would stay at Cnoc Gorm even though he wanted to be back in the hills of Tipperary.

"Laoghaire, I am happy that you are home and safe," said Saraid, "but I also know you want to be with Brian fighting the foreigners from Limerick." She stood in front of her son as she had on many occasions with her fists planted on her hips, and her back straight, "You're a warrior, a very good warrior and your place is with your comrades, doing what you have trained all your life to be." She paused, put her hand on his arm and said, "I want you here, home and safe, but that's not where you belong, go back to Tipperary, be with your comrades and fight the good fight."

"The winter is near, I'll stay till the spring, then decide what I'll do, where I'll go."

Saraid sat with her sons that evening, enjoying a meal and said to Laoghaire, "You're a warrior, I cannot hold you here. Stay long enough to put some fat on your belly and let me remember your face."

Tanai looked at his older brother, "I've never been as good as you with a sword, but I am good at working the farm. As long as we have this place, you have a home to come back to."

Saraid looked at Laoghaire, "Tomorrow I'll be takin' the cart into the village to trade for a few things. You should come with me; I could use a strong back to lift and carry."

*   *   *

27

964 AD Ceann Coradh, Ireland
Deirdre

The village square was a busy place when Saraid and Laoghaire arrived in the morning. The chill in the air was just warming to the cloudless sky and the dew had already misted away. Saraid had several places to visit and knew her son would be bored with her banter with old friends and her bargaining with vendors.

"Go, walk about the market, find something to purchase or an old friend to talk to, enjoy the sunshine and the fine cool air. I'll be here before the sun is high and we can stay longer if you'd like or be on our way."

Laoghaire smiled, "I'll be here." He strolled down the open area between the vendors and craftsmen, looking at everything and everyone.

She was a tall dark-haired beauty, arguing with a vendor. Laoghaire paused, looked, and smiled. The vendor noticed the tall warrior and said to the young woman, "Is this giant going to make me give you the cauldron?"

She turned and looked at Laoghaire, "No," she replied turning back to the vendor. "We agreed on a price last week and now you want more. I've no need of help from the likes of him or anyone else. Now are we going to argue, or will you honor your word from last week?"

The vendor looked at Laoghaire and was about to speak when Laoghaire held his hands apart and said in a low voice, "I don't know the young lady, and I don't think she needs any help from me."

She turned, looked at Laoghaire for a second longer and turned toward the vendor again, "Well old man, what'll it be?"

The vendor looked at the woman, then at Laoghaire, then back to the woman, "Deirdre, take the cauldron for the price we set last week."

She handed him a few copper coins and reached down for the large iron pot. It was heavier than she remembered, and she stood with hands on her hips, drew a deep breath, and reached for the pot again. Laoghaire had stepped closer, leaned over, and lifted the cauldron with one hand before she could move it, "I'd be more than happy to help you move it."

Their eyes met and they both froze for a moment, "Where would you like me to put it?" asked Laoghaire.

"The cart, there," she replied pointing to a small horse-drawn cart, "and I'll thank you for that."

Laoghaire placed the cauldron in the back of her cart and moved to help her climb on. She was quicker than he thought, and she turned toward him and said, "Thank you again, tall man," as she nudged the horse forward.

Laoghaire stood tall and watched as the horse pulled the cart away. He smiled, turned, and wandered back to find Saraid putting things in their cart.

"There you are," said Saraid, "I've gotten all I came for and we can look about more if you'd like or be on our way home."

Laoghaire loaded the last few items and helped his mother climb onto the cart. As he joined her, he said, "I met someone today." He told his mother about the vendor and the woman named Deidre.

"Deirdre, I know her. She lives east of here with her father, Fearghal on their farm. Oh, she's a lively one. Not one to cross, a quick wit, an intelligent tongue, and a strong hand." She looked at her son and smiled, he seemed to be dreaming.

Deirdre arrived home with the cauldron and her father walked to the back of the cart. He hefted the cauldron to the ground, stood straight, took a deep breath, and lifted it again to carry it into their roundhouse. "Did that old man help you lift this thing," he grunted as he set it down.

Deidre stopped, thought for a second as her father exhaled and looked at her. "No da, a tall man helped me."

She smiled and Fearghal noticed, "A tall man, eh daughter. What was his name, girl?"

Deirdre stopped and her smile faded, "I don't know," she hesitated, "I didn't ask."

"Well, what did he look like, girl?" said Fearghal as he hefted the cauldron.

"A warrior, a very tall very strong warrior," she replied.

"A warrior, eh. Are you sure?" he asked as he took another rest.

"Well now Da, I've not seen him about before. At first, he looked a little like Tanai mac Daigh, but this one is bigger and wears the scars of more than one battle."

Fearghal stopped, his face drained as he looked at his daughter and stepped toward her, "Laoghaire, I'll wager it was Laoghaire mac Daigh."

"I've heard the name, da, but wasn't he killed years ago?"

"No, girl. That'd be his older brother Garbhan." He sat next to his daughter and said, "I marched with his father at Gort Rotachain. He was a boy then and his father was sore wounded that day. He never went to battle again." He looked at his daughter, "This Laoghaire, he fights with Brian against the *foreigners* of Limerick. I've heard stories about him. A beast in battle. A very dangerous man."

Over the winter, Laoghaire met Deidre several times. He seemed lost in her bright blue eyes and engaged her in conversation as often as he could. Within a month, he had met Fearghal and stated his intentions. "Your daughter, sir, is a bright light on the dark road I travel. I'm a warrior before a farmer and have joined Brian mac Cennetig's marches over the last few years. I have property nearby, a house and animals, fields used for grazing and my mother and brother tend the lot as I go to war. I look at Deirdre and think now about being a farmer more than a warrior."

Fearghal approved of Brian's exploits and admired Laoghaire for marching with him. "You have my attention, young man. My daughter seems equally taken with you and I respect your service to Brian, to Éirinn. I will speak to my daughter and hear what she has to say."

"Thank you, sir, I'll be leaving to join Brian again in three months," said Laoghaire, "I'll see you again before then."

Fearghal took his daughter aside and began the conversation, "Daughter, this man, Laoghaire."

She interrupted him, "Yes father, Laoghaire. I wish to wed. As soon as possible."

152

Fearghal's eyes widened, "Deirdre, you've only met the man, a month or two ago, do you know him well enough?"

"Father, I know you," she replied. "I know my three brothers and I know a number of other men, from the village, friends of yours, friends of my brothers. This man is the one I wish to call husband. I know my mind and now you've heard it."

"Has he asked you to be his wife?" asked Fearghal.

Deirdre smiled and said in a singing voice, "No, not yet. But he will, soon."

* * *

They were wed in the spring of 967 and Laoghaire was drawn closer to the life of a farmer. He was a warrior, battle-tested and well-proven and he believed in Brian's cause. The desire to remain at Cnoc Gorm with his family as opposed to going off to battle the Norse kept him awake on many a night.

One moonlit night, as he was pacing about the practice posts, Deirdre saw him and approached, "What troubles you, Laoghaire?"

He turned to her with one hand on a practice post, "I have slain these posts many times and now they give me peace. I can think as I walk about them and I wonder about our lives, what we have here and what I have done for years as a warrior." He turned to Deirdre, put his arms around her, held her close and said, "I want to be here with you, I want to see battle again, and I can only follow one path."

Deirdre stayed close and said, "I don't wish to see you go back to the hills of Tipperary, but neither do I want to hold you here. You're a warrior, not a farmer. I married a man who goes off to battle every year and I know someday you may not return, but that is all part of why I love you." She pulled herself in closer to him and continued, "You will go again, and when you return, I will be here, I'll always be here."

* * *

28

967 AD Munster, Ireland
teacht le chéile … Reunion

Laoghaire once again went to the hills of Tipperary to meet with Brian and what was left of their band of warriors. He had joined the small band each year as they waged their raiding war on the *Dark Foreigners* of Limerick. Each year was a lesson in guerilla war and each year they paid dearly for those lessons. When Laoghaire met with Brian that year, their number was less than 20 men. Brian was determined to continue his war, but their numbers might not withstand another full season and he decided to try once again to convince Mathgamain to join in this war on the 'foreigners'.

Brian, Laoghaire and the rest of their band made their way back to Cashel where Brian sought out a number of Dal gCais tribal leaders. The conversations with a few chieftains were brief. Some of the results, disappointing, but other conversations were positive. Brian turned to Laoghaire as they left one meeting, "We may have an ally here, good friend. He sees the *foreigners* as we do and if nothing else, he may join our campaign with forty warriors this new spring."

The two men laughed as they approached another chieftain. "We know the peace with Ivar cannot last," said Brian, "And we will soon be facing their swords in the field."

Laoghaire added, "We have faced their forces many times and with the proper numbers, we know they can be defeated."

The two warriors visited another four chieftains and delivered the same arguments. Leaving one of the sessions, Laoghaire said, "I think if Mathgamain is ready to listen, even more will join our cause."

Brian smiled, "Well then good friend, is it time to approach my brother?"

Laoghaire laughed, "No need to ask me, Brian. I'm ready to talk to the Ard Ri himself, if I thought it would do us some good."

Brian turned to his friend, "This is one I must do myself, Laoghaire."

"I know, Brian. And I'll wait outside till you've had your say. No matter what happens, I'm ready to go back to the hills and continue our battle, our war."

*   *   *

When he approached Mathgamain, Brian had already found substantial support among a number of the tribal chieftains. He presented his arguments with confidence and well-planned force. Mathgamain initially was resistant but soon saw the advantages pointed out by his younger brother. "Brian, you have swayed my thoughts. I hear your arguments and will talk with the tribal leaders. The *foreigners* of Limerick have never truly respected our people, our property or our rights. As you have stated, they tolerate us. We will talk again after I have met with the other chieftains, and they all have had their say."

Brian smiled, "I could ask for nothing more, Mathgamain. I'm confident they will see the Limerick Norse for what they really are."

Brian left his brother to consult with his closest advisors and met Laoghaire outside near a tree. Sitting in the shade, resting, Laoghaire saw Brian coming toward him with a confident look and stride, he stood, and they both smiled, "You've done it," said Laoghaire.

Brian was animated as he answered, "I think I have. Mathgamain was more receptive than he has been in the past and he is now talking to the other tribal leaders."

"We know their minds, Brian," said Laoghaire. "And we may soon have more than a few new allies." Laoghaire breathed deeply and put his hand on Brian's shoulder, "Now we can plan a real campaign against the *foreigners*."

Brian thought for a moment and said, "We should continue our talks with the other chieftains. Tis not the time to rest just yet old friend, tis time to add wood to the fire we've started."

*   *   *

Faced with solid arguments from Brian, and enthusiastic responses from a number of other tribal leaders, Mathgamain was finally convinced of the value of his brother's war. He sent for Brian who was still talking to other leaders, and he called a meeting of all the chieftains. As the gathering grew, the chieftains realized the purpose of the meeting. Most had been in conversation with Mathgamain, Brian or Laoghaire and the rumblings began before Mathgamain spoke.

Mathgamain joined the assembly and found the common theme of conversation was "The time has come to stand against the Norse." He moved to the center of the gathering and quieted the crowd. "I have had conversation with my brother as many of you have and I see the value in his words. The time has come to break from the Norse and not live under their foot any longer."

The initial response was not unanimous, but as Mathgamain continued to talk, more tribal leaders raised their arms in approval and the entire assembly was soon together.

Brian met with Mathgamain at length that night talking about his war with the Norse and his vision for the future. His vision included using the ships already in their control, cavalry in combat and the guerilla techniques he had developed over the last several years.

Laoghaire wandered about for a short while, thinking about the new configuration of their force. As a rain began and a storm was visible on the horizon, he found shelter in an inn where he found several of his old comrades. He wanted to tell them about the reunion of Brian and Mathgamain as they shared food and he said, "Soon we will be a much larger force and the *foreigners* of Limerick will run from us," proclaimed Laoghaire.

Brogan, one of the younger warriors, said quietly to Laoghaire, "We should be careful of what we say, even here. These walls, these roofs have eyes and ears. Much of what is said may reach the ears of Ivar. Be careful of what you say, Laoghaire."

"Young, but wise," returned Laoghaire. "We should keep quiet and let our actions make the noise when the time is right."

*　*　*

Mathgamain called his brother to a war council and Brian brought Laoghaire and Brogan with him. The three battle tested warriors stood and listened as Mathgamain talked about the current state of affairs with the Norse of Limerick. He noted the numerous incursions into the land and property of the Dal gCais by the Norse and Brian's guerilla war with Ivar, king of Limerick. "My brother comes to us today to speak of his war, which he says is our war with the Norse. I ask that you all listen to him, hear what he has to say and we will discuss his ideas."

Then Brian stood, walked to the center of the room and spoke, "Brother, chieftains, friends, I've been at war with these Norse for four years. They are not my friends, and I don't think they are your friends. They treat us as lower cast people and take from us at will. They have plundered some of your villages, killed our people," he paused, looked about the room. "They have killed people close to me, and I cannot accept them as friends or as rulers." He paced the middle of the room, "This is our island, our Éirinn and they are the invaders; the *foreigners*." He paused as his words sunk in and he again paced the floor, then continued, "We should unite our warriors, take up our arms and drive these Norse out from our home, from our Éirinn."

The muttering and grumbling began and rose as Brian again paused. "I have spoken to a number of you over the last few days and I know there is much agreement with my words, you are not so many sheep to be herded and sent to slaughter. We are better than that and it is time we stood together and let the invaders know who we really are. We are Dal gCais. We are no longer going to live under their boots."

The assembly was still divided, but more on the side of Brian and fewer on the side of maintaining the peace with Ivar. Mathgamain sat and listened, noticed the reaction of the chieftains, saw his younger brother stand in front of this collection of men and sway their thinking. He motioned to Brian, "Please continue, little brother, your words are very interesting, and these men need to hear more."

Brian looked at his brother then to his two friends and he continued, "I know where the Norse are weak." He looked at Laoghaire, "We've met them in battle in open ground, and been defeated. We've met them in the woods and defeated them, they prefer to fight in a formation with their shields together forming a wall. In open ground, that is very effective. In the woods, they can't easily stand together, trees and bushes are our allies and they're weaker." He paused, allowed this to sink in and paced the room. Then he said, "We attack them from cover when they don't expect us," again he paused. "We make them pursue us over uneven ground and through heavy brush. We carry only what we must, they are burdened with iron mail, large shields and long swords," he paused, paced and continued, "We attack, strike and fade back into the forest." He looked at Laoghaire and continued, "We have taken their weapons and used them against them, Laoghaire fights with an axe, Brogan with spear and darts, I fight with one or two short swords and sometimes a small shield." He scanned the room, the others listened to this experienced warrior, "We are not big enough to defeat their army, but we continue to cut it down, two, three, five at a time. A few here and a few there. We strike and fade back into the woods. It has been a long and difficult war, but now with greater numbers, numbers that rival theirs we can strike harder and be more effective."

One of the chieftains looked at Laoghaire, "You, tall man, how do you see these Norse? Are they fierce warriors to be feared?"

Laoghaire stood slowly and walked to the center of the room, thinking as he walked. "I have been with Brian in this war for four years. We have met many smaller groups of Norse and engaged them in battle. These men are not to be taken lightly, nor are they to be feared. We fight them and we have lost many good men in this fight, but we will never stop until they are defeated."

The chieftain stood and raised his voice, "But do you fear them?"

Brian was about to speak when Laoghaire turned toward the chieftain and moved in his direction, "I fear no man. Not any of them nor any here in this room. It is not fear or the lack of it that visits me in battle, it's respect. If you would raise your sword against me, I would not fear you, but I would respect the fact that you are a warrior, one who has seen battle and still stands. You are to be respected and fought as if we are equals."

The crowd rumbled in approval and Brian stepped next to his friend. "This man has never shown fear in battle, but as he said, he meets each challenge with the same caution and ferocity. Laoghaire is a great axe man, one who strikes fear into those who oppose him, and justly so." Brian paced the room as Laoghaire returned to his place next to Brogan. "Brogan is another of our number who has been with me for three years. Ask him if he fears the Norse, if you like," said Brian.

Mathgamain stood, "We have heard my brother speak, now it is time we discussed his thoughts."

The room quieted down. Brian spoke, "I'll review the possible configurations of our united force and have a plan to present to you tomorrow when I return."

The three men left the assembly and walked across the open yard. "How many men do you estimate we may have now?" posed Brogan.

"More than yesterday and hopefully less than tomorrow. We'll make a plan that includes only those we are confident will join us," returned Brian.

Laoghaire cleared his throat, looked back at the gathering of chieftains and said, "I roughly count as many as a thousand in our force." He lifted his eyes and looked at Brian, "But if we are, as I suspect, we may be closer to seven hundred."

Brogan thought for a moment, then smiled and said, "When last in Limerick, I estimated their total force at about one thousand men."

"That sounds right, so that's the number we will use in our planning tonight," said Brian. "We'll not be attacking the walls of Limerick and if we were to meet them on a battlefield, their number of a thousand would be more than I would like to face with only seven hundred." He paused, looked about the grounds and continued, "But when we meet them in the woods, on uneven ground and can move about better than they, we are much more effective. We have to draw them out of their walled city, away from wide open fields and into the woods." He hesitated again, "Perhaps we could find a way to draw them out of the city. Think hard my friends, we have this night to plan and tomorrow we will present our thoughts to Mathgamain."

Laoghaire said, "If we divide their force, we will eventually have to deal with the remainder of their troops." He looked at Brian, "I'd rather have their entire force in the woods at once."

Brian thought again and responded, "Agreed, the more we draw away from the city, the fewer we will have to contend with later."

The three men walked out of the fortress and stood on the top of a rise overlooking rolling hills an open plain and a forest. Brian scanned the horizon and said to Laoghaire, "You know the hill called Sulcoit?"

"I do," replied Laoghaire.

"Not far from here," said Brogan.

"Yes," said Brian. "And the at the base of the hill is a small clearing, then thick woods and uneven ground," he looked at his companions. "Our kind of battlefield."

"But how do we get them to meet us there?" asked Brogan.

"We invite them," smiled Brian, "We invite them."

The three men looked at each other and Brian continued, "If they saw a small band of our men lurking near Limerick, they would pursue us with a force larger than ours to be assured of defeating us."

Brogan smiled, "So we let them see enough of us to draw out a large force to chase us?"

"Yes," said Brian. "And we lead them to a place like Sulcoit Hill where we have the larger part of or force lie in wait."

"A trap," said Laoghaire, "With some of us as bait."

"Yes," repeated Brian. "Now we have to figure out how many men would be enough to tempt their entire force out of Limerick."

"We have fared well against them in the woods, Brian," said Laoghaire. "So, if they saw a force of twenty, they may send fifty to destroy us."

"And if they saw a force of one hundred, they may send five times that number to chase us," added Brogan.

"Yes, but I want all one thousand to come after us, so we must look more like two hundred or more when they see us," said Brian.

Brogan put his hand on Brian's shoulder, "Brian, if we were to set up a camp near Limerick with two hundred men and make enough noise or set too large a fire, we would undoubtedly be seen by one of their scouting parties."

160

"Well said, Brogan," said Brian. "We could set up a few scouts of our own, be ready to move on a moment's notice and when Ivar sends his troops after us, we move out to Sulcoit as we talked about, where the other five hundred of our men would lie in wait."

Brian turned toward his two friends, "We're seven hundred and they're one thousand, but if we can manage to get them to Sulcoit, we would have the advantage."

Brogan grinned, "Yes, and they will pursue us through some very uneven, rough country. We will travel light, be able to move over the ground between Limerick and Sulcoit quickly, easily. They will be in mail and bulky armor, carrying heavy weapons. We can leave most of our things at Sulcoit with our friends. When we get there, they will be tired, we will pick up our weapons and with our well-rested friends, in our woods, we will have an advantage."

"We'll have a victory," said Brian. He looked at Brogan, "I like the way you think."

*   *   *

29

967 AD Munster, Ireland
Sulcoit

The morning brought a cool rain and a gentle breeze across the open yard at Cashel. Brian and his friends entered the meeting area with a well thought out plan and the confidence of battle tested warriors. They were greeted with a rousing chorus of grunts and battle cries. "We are together, Brian," said Mathgamain, "and ready to hear your plan to meet Ivar's troops.

The plan was laid out for Mathgamain and the tribal chieftains and met with approval. The initial task was to select a group of two hundred men who could move quickly through the countryside from Limerick to Sulcoit staying ahead of the pursuing Norse, but never losing them.

"Are we a foot or on horse?" asked one of the men.

"Initially, on horse," replied Brian. "But as we approach the hill, the horses may be more trouble than advantage. We'll have to see when we get there."

Brian noticed smiles on the faces of half of his men. "We'll be the bait in this trap, we'll travel light, move fast and let these invaders see us and pursue us. When we get to the hill, we'll turn and fight with the rest of our numbers."

The warriors all agreed, this is a good plan. Each man among them had fought the foreigners and knew friends who had died in this cause. Each man wanted to be part of the deception.

"Not to worry, old friend, I know I am running to a fight, not away from one," said Laoghaire with a laugh. "And we've selected only the fastest of us, we'll be at Sulcoit as soon as the 'foreigners' can gather their armor and heavy shields and plod along after us." The two men laughed as they went in different directions, Brian to Sulcoit and Laoghaire to Limerick.

The bait team drifted close to the river and the city walls. They set up a camp and prepared fires that would be visible from the city walls at night. As the sun set and darkness covered the countryside, the fires were set and as planned, were seen by sentries walking a post in Limerick. Word filtered back through the troops in the city and finally reached the king, Ivar. He was told a scouting party investigated and saw a band of Dal gCais warriors who were probably going to attack the surrounding countryside. Ivar assembled his troops and in the morning, they set out to surround and destroy the Dal gCais.

The Norse left the city and moved toward the Dal gCais. As they neared, Laoghaire pulled his force back away from Limerick, moving southeast and the Norse followed. "I've seen more than one hundred men," said one of the Norse scouts to his leader. "But they move back into the wood, so I am not sure how many more."

"They may be two or three hundred," returned the leader. "Send word to Ivar that they may be a much larger force than we have met in the past."

Ivar received the message. He responded, "We still outnumber them, even if they are three hundred."

"They run toward Cashel, to his brother," said one of the Norse leaders. "We must move faster, catch them before they reach The Rock."

The full force of near one thousand men under Ivar moved closer to the retreating Dal gCais and finally the distance was down to a few hundred feet. "We have them," said one of the Norse leaders to Ivar. "They're slowing; we should begin an all-out assault immediately."

Ivar raised his arm and indicated a charge toward the Irish, then he moved to the rear of his troops, to watch from safety. He leaned toward one of his guards, "Send word, take no prisoners, kill them all." At that moment, he saw an opportunity to eliminate a constant thorn in his side.

Laoghaire carefully led his men through the wood, slowing at the meadow before the hill to allow the Norse to begin a charge. Brogan was at their rear, watching the actions of the Norse and when he saw them begin to assemble for a charge, he quickly moved closer to Laoghaire and signaled him. Laoghaire immediately stepped up the pace of their movement through the woods and the Norse hurried their charge. As the Irish moved up the base of the hill, Laoghaire looked about for signs of their larger force when a familiar voice said, "We saw you coming about an hour ago."

Laoghaire looked to his left and saw Mathgamain leaning against a tree. "You've done well," continued Mathgamain. "I see you've brought their entire army with you."

Laoghaire walked over to Mathgamain, "Where are the rest of our people?"

A quiet laugh caused Laoghaire to turn to his right, "Brian, are we ready?"

"We are good friend, now you and your men move to the rear, rest a few moments and be ready, it will begin soon."

The bait team all passed by the hidden Dal gCais troops and collapsed on the ground, laughing, "We've done it. Now for the finish."

The Norse moved slowly through the heavy brush and trees, trying to stay together as much as possible. Ivar was seen at the rear on his horse and as soon as the last of the Norse was seen entering a small clearing at the base of the hill, Brian signaled his troops to move both flanks, surrounding the Norse on three sides. The movement of men higher up the hill was seen by Ivar's troops and an alarm was sounded.

"No more hiding in wait," said Brian as he stood and hurled a spear at the approaching Norse. The barrage of spears, darts and stones flying down the slope into the confused mass of Norse began.

Brogan lifted a stone and laughed as he tossed it as high as he could. He looked at Laoghaire, "We've the advantage of height and even I can now hurl a stone or two."

Laoghaire laughed as he picked up a large stone and launched it into the air. The two men watched it as it came down on the shoulder of an advancing Northman. The man fell to the ground and was obviously in great pain. Brogan handed Laoghaire another stone, he sent it into the air as he did the last and the two men watched as this stone found the metal of a foreigner's helmet. The helmet did little to protect the man as the stone bent the metal helmet, driving part of it into the man's skull.

"That's two," said Brogan as he hefted a smaller but still heavy stone to his shoulder. He hurled as high and far as he could and saw it come down on another advancing Norse.

The two found three more stones worth throwing, hurled them skyward and watched them hit two more attackers. Brogan looked about for another but only found one the size of his fist. "Last one, then we have to use our swords," he said looking at Laoghaire. He threw the stone striking another attacker. This one however seemed to bounce off the man's shoulder and he looked up with a savage, angry look. "That one's all yours," laughed Brogan as he picked up his spear and shield.

The advance up the rise was short lived as the Irish came down the hill and attacked from three sides. Brogan drove his spear into a man's belly and couldn't retrieve it. He drew his short sword and hacked at another Northman. As the Northman raised his hand in defense, Brogan slashed as hard as he could, striking the man's hand with the end of his sword. The man screamed as four of his fingers tumbled to the ground and blood gushed from the stumps left on his hand. Brogan took one more slash at the man's throat and left him dead with his fingerless hand raised over his body.

Laoghaire passed between a pair of trees and brought his axe down on the outstretched arm of a man. The axe struck just below the shoulder and pushed the man's coat of mail deep into an almost dismembered arm. He wasted no time on mutilating the man, a simple thrust with the sharpened end of his long axe handle through the man's exposed throat. No time to waste as three others approached Laoghaire. He feinted toward one on his right and with his axe extended, he began a swing of his axe to his left with all the strength he could bring to bear. The axe struck the second of the men at his knees and he lost a leg in the blink of an eye. The third man came at Laoghaire with his sword raised over his head and Laoghaire rolled to his left, lifting his axe and regaining his feet. The third man stepped toward Laoghaire, and he took a half step backward. The man sensed fear and withdrawal. He took a long stride toward Laoghaire and that was his last step. Laoghaire stepped twice into the man's path, swung his axe and found the man's neck.

The advantages of thick trees and bush favored the Irish style of combat. The initial height over the pursuing Norse allowed the Irish to inflict more injury than usual with stones, darts, and spears. The Norse never assembled an effective shield wall, and the battle was in the favor of the Irish from the beginning. The battle lasted only a few hours and the remnants of the Norse running to the rear, trying to find their way back to Limerick bought them no mercy. They were pursued and when caught, killed. Few if any made it far from the battlefield.

Mathgamain approached a group of warriors around Brian, dismounted and approached Brian, "Ivar, has anyone reported on Ivar."

"I saw him early in the day," returned Brian, "But not since."

"Perhaps he has run away," said one of Mathgamain's guard. "This day was ours from the beginning." There was a roar of approval from warriors nearby as one of them yelled, "Ivar probably saw his troops losing the battle ran home to his walled city."

Mathgamain and Brian consulted for a moment and looked at Brogan, "You've been in the city recently, Brogan?"

"Yes Brian, I have," he answered.

"Their troops, did they leave any in the city," asked Mathgamain.

Brogan pondered the question, looked at the battlefield and with a smile replied, "No sir, I think they took nearly everybody to chase us down here," he looked back at the battlefield. "There they are, Brian, nearly every one of them."

Brian and Mathgamain looked at each other, and in unison the said, "The city is undefended."

The march to Limerick took several hours and the Dal gCais found the gates open and the walls undefended in the morning. The town was entered and plundered. The pillaging and killing went on for most of the day. The city was then burned, and the Irish left it in ruins.

Laoghaire walked through the streets of Limerick as fires were being set. Several men approached him with looted valuables in hand, one with a scroll and two books. Laoghaire stopped him and asked what he was going to do with the books and scroll. "I'll trade them to a priest at the first monastery we pass, or I'll burn them if I feel cold."

Laoghaire had a hand-full of copper coins, he held them out and said, "If it's trade you seek, look no further."

Brian saw Laoghaire trade for the books and scrolls, "You are now a scholar and an axe man, eh, Laoghaire.'

"My wife reads everything she can lay her hands on and these will increase her collection."

"And you, old friend, do you read them as well?" asked Brian.

"I read the Irish writings but struggle with the Latin and Greek. Deirdre reads them all then talks about what she has learned."

Brian smiled, "If I could, I would put all the books and scrolls back in the monasteries from which they have been stolen over the last hundred years and more. I think we should all learn to read, perhaps I have a book, or two Deirdre would like."

* * *

30

969 AD Munster, Ireland
Muirin

Laoghaire returned home to Cnoc Gorm to find his wife near birthing their first child. Saraid was with Deirdre as her labor began and stayed by her side until the baby was feeding comfortably. She walked out of the round house to find her son pacing about the yard tapping the practice posts with his axe.

"Laoghaire, your wife is feeding your daughter," announced Saraid. "You should be with her, not out here with your practice posts."

"A daughter, I have a daughter?" quizzed Laoghaire.

"Yes, you've made me a grandmother of a beautiful, healthy girl," said Saraid. "Now go to your wife and give the baby a name."

Laoghaire stepped clumsily, handed his axe to his mother, and said, "A daughter, her name . . ." he plunged into the roundhouse to find Deirdre laying on a pile of furs, nursing a small baby. "Deirdre, I don't know what to do. What do you need, or want?" He reached into a pouch draped over his shoulder and produced two books and a scroll. "I brought you these," he stammered as he stretched out his arm.

Deirdre saw the gifts he had brought, smiled, and replied, "They are very nice, but this little bundle is more important right now." She held the baby up toward Laoghaire, "Here, take your daughter."

He stared, then reached for the baby, "Are you sure I should hold her, she's so small, and I don't want to hurt her." He held the little bundle away from his body and Deirdre told him to rest her on his chest and shoulder.

He did and the baby fell asleep. He looked about with a look of uncertainty, not quite panic but the fear of dropping or squeezing the baby too tightly. He stood motionless for a few moments as Deirdre adjusted her clothing, smiled, and stood.

"Relax, husband, the little one is asleep. She must feel warm and safe on your shoulder."

Laoghaire smiled and said, "We have to give her a name, Deirdre. What name do you like?"

"When you came home from your battles a year ago, you talked of sailing on the River Shannon and someday sailing out onto the great ocean. Then, when you were away again, I thought about the sea and how calm the sound of the waves were when I last saw the coastline. As our daughter grew in my belly, I often thought about the sea. It gave me comfort on many lonely nights."

Laoghaire put his free arm around Deidre's shoulder and pulled her in close. Then Deirdre spoke again, "The name Muirin, it means from the sea, and I like the sound of it. What do you think of it?"

Laoghaire held the little bundle and repeated the name several times, "Yes, a beautiful name and Muirin it'll be."

*   *   *

Laoghaire was home with his family. He set aside his axe and took up the tools of a farmer. There was no call to arms in the spring and Laoghaire remained at Cnoc Gorm through the summer. Life was peaceful and easy. He hunted for deer, helped in the fields and made repairs to the roundhouses. Toward the end of summer, as Tanai and Laoghaire were replacing a picket in the rath wall, Tanai told his older brother he had met a woman he felt good about.

"She's a good woman and makes me feel a better man," said Tanai. "I've seen you and Deirdre together and I think I can have the same happiness you two enjoy."

"Brother, that's more than most men can claim," said Laoghaire. "Do I know this woman?"

"I think you know her father, he was with our father at Gort Rotachain, his name is Aonghus."

"Yes," said Laoghaire, "He spoke of her often, her name's Eadan."

"Yes," returned Tanai, "I'd like to bring her here to meet you and Deirdre."

"Then make it happen, brother." Laoghaire leaned against the picket as it settled in its new home, "I suppose her father will come as well."

"It's only proper, brother," said Tanai.

"It is that," said Laoghaire, "Tell Deirdre and we'll make ready for their visit."

"I've already told her," said Tanai.

Laoghaire laughed, "Once again, I'm the last to know." He slapped his brother on the back and hugged him. "I wish you the best, brother, the very best."

* * *

As the days passed, Laoghaire began to practice with his axe and sword on the old posts in the yard. There was no call to arms, but he was determined to be prepared when it did come.

Saraid spent much of her time with Muirin. She fell ill just after Muirin was born and recovered before the new year only to be afflicted again in late spring. The summer months were warm, and she seemed to be improving, but with the winter came a recurrence of her illness. Spring again brought hope that Saraid's health would improve, but just as Muirin was beginning to talk, Saraid slipped into a deep sleep and after two days, passed away.

She was buried on the hill overlooking the stream flowing to the Shannon, next to Daigh.

* * *

"Peace comes in little pieces and never lasts long enough," said Deirdre, quietly to herself. She was looking out through the gate in the rath wall and watched a rider approach. She turned and walked back to the animal pen where Laoghaire and Tanai were repairing a support. "You have a visitor," she said to Laoghaire. "Mochta approaches."

Laoghaire looked at Tanai and Tanai nodded. Laoghaire walked over to his wife and together they went to the gate. Mochta was dismounting as they crossed the little bridge.

"Mochta, have you come to visit or to drag me away to Ceann Coradh?" asked Laoghaire.

Mochta looked at Laoghaire, tilted his head, raised an eyebrow and turned to Deirdre, "You're looking wonderful."

Deirdre shook her head, "So are you, you old crow. You've come to take him away again, haven't you?"

"We shall see. First, we have to talk, then perhaps we can decide if you will journey back to Ceann Coradh."

They walked over to the fire pit and Deirdre sat with them. Mochta began, "Mathgamain has claimed the throne of Munster and he is considering a march into Connaught."

"Why does he raid Connaught?" asked Laoghaire. "They're not a threat to us and I don't see the advantage." He paused, looked at Mochta, "Is this a call to arms?"

"No," returned Mochta. "I came to tell you that I will not be making this march. I'll remain here and return to Ceann Coradh later in the summer. We have new men to train, and I would like you to help me, after all, I'm getting old and slowing down."

"If it's not a call to arms, I think I'll stay here and finish this wall with Tanai. Spring will come soon enough, and I'll return to Ceann Coradh then."

* * *

Laoghaire returned to Ceann Coradh in the spring of 971 to help in the training of new warriors. His daughter, Muirin had just begun her third year and he wanted to be home more than he wanted to be in battle with the foreigners. Deirdre knew what he was, a warrior and she would not stand in his way when there was a call to arms. Each time he left their home, she stood tall in the doorway and smiled as he rode away. Each time he rode away, she worried for his return.

This time, he returned to help train new warriors. He understood the need to be prepared when going into battle. His younger years were all in preparation for war and now, after nearly ten years of engaging the Limerick Norse, his reputation had spread throughout the Dal gCais Community and the rest of Munster. He was respected, looked up to by the new recruits, making teaching easier.

The years passed with little to do but teach. Then came the year of the heavy rains and Laoghaire like many others remained home to care for his family, his home and their crops. Some poor souls lost nearly everything in floods. Many crops saw too much water and were lost. Laoghaire and his family were fortunate. Cnoc Gorm was almost entirely on higher ground and the rains flowed across the planted fields and into the little river that flowed to the Shannon.

They had food, the rains didn't destroy as many plantings on the higher ground that sloped gently toward the river. As the ground became saturated, the lower elevations where land was flat, water pooled and destroyed many plants. The rain forced deer and other game to higher ground, often farther away from people and harder to hunt.

Fewer crops and scarcity of game made life for many much more difficult. Laoghaire was accustomed to living off the land, hunting or fishing as needed. His skill with the bow was not as good as the archers in Brian's army, nor Deirdre's. She could easily bring down a deer, but it was Laoghaire who would carry it home.

A rainless day drew Laoghaire's attention to his bow, "A good time to find a deer, I think I'll take a walk about the farm and see if I can find a fat one."

Deirdre laughed, "Best if I came with you, your axe may be a great weapon against men, but a deer wouldn't let you within throwing distance and your skill with a bow leaves much to be desired."

Laoghaire laughed and said, "It's meat we're after and I won't argue about who may be better with the bow." They took a few pieces of bread and some dried meat, "No telling how long we may be out there."

Three hours of walking through the damp brush and sidestepping bogs found the pair several miles from their home and the rains began again, this time with a stiff wind and shelter was in order. They found a recess in a hillside with an overhang raised high enough for Laoghaire to stand up, away from the wind and rain. The recess was dry, and several small branches lay strewn about. They were both soaked through and feeling the cold.

Laoghaire looked around, noticed the dry sticks, and said, "If you start a fire, I'll gather a few more sticks to keep it going." He stepped out into the rain and disappeared into the brush and mist. A few minutes later, he reappeared with an armful of larger sticks and dumped them on the ground. "We'll need more than these few sticks to dry off," he said. He looked around their shelter and continued, "The rainwater is running away from this cover to a little stream about twenty feet away," he told Deirdre. "You stay here and I'll be right back," he paused, then "You're cold, girl." He took off his shirt and handed it to her, "I've spent many a night in this kind of weather. Wrap this shirt about yourself and I'll gather a few more pieces for the fire." He touched her cheek as he handed her the shirt and turned out into the rain again.

A few minutes later he returned with enough firewood to burn through the night. Deirdre stood with his shirt wrapped about her and the rest of her clothes spread out over a rock to dry, deeper in the recess. Laoghaire fed the fire, stood, and pulled her close to him. The fire burned warm through the night and in the morning, Laoghaire woke looking out through a dissolving mist and watched as Deirdre finished splashing water over her body in the little stream. As she walked back toward him, he thought he'd like to stay another night even though the rain had stopped, and the sun was breaking through the scattering clouds.

* * *

The rain had stopped, their clothes nearly dry and they stepped out into the morning sun. Laoghaire went back to be sure the fire was out, and Deirdre gathered her bow and the handful of arrows she had brought with her. She casually scanned the surrounding area and froze. Slowly she raised her bow and notched an arrow.

Laoghaire stepped out of the recess as her arrow found its target, "A young male," she said quietly. "There's enough meat on him to last a while." She notched another arrow and began slowly moving in the deer's direction and Laoghaire drew his knife from its sheath, ready to finish the kill if needed.

Laoghaire gathered the young buck around his shoulders and the two turned toward home. He looked toward the western sky, "perhaps it will rain again before we get home."

"Another fire tonight, tall man," she said, "whether it rains or not."

* * *

31

The following year, Laoghaire and Deirdre were blessed with a second child, a son. A very loud and healthy boy, he was given the name Earnan, iron. Laoghaire was thrilled, he had a son. On the next trip he made a trip to Ceann Coradh to help in training new warriors, he bragged about his new son.

"Have you carved him a baby axe?" asked Ronan with a laugh and a slap on Laoghaire's shoulder.

"Does he run about his home with a sack of pebbles?" asked another fellow warrior.

"When will we see him here?" asked Deaglan, a young trainee in his fourteenth year, still a year or more before he should see battle.

The teasing pleased Laoghaire, his friends made him laugh while he really wanted to be home with his family. He took every opportunity to travel home and by summers end, he went home for the winter.

Earnan was a healthy and happy little boy. Very curious and very quick. He could find an opening in the rath wall as soon as it appeared and loved to run in the pasture, chasing the horse and the goats.

Muirin was in her eighth year and Earnan in his third when Ronan came to visit. This was not a friendly visit; the news was bad. "Mathgamain was invited to a feast at the home of his rival Donnabhan mac Cathail," said Ronan. "The promise of safety, guaranteed by a churchman, was broken, Mathgamain has been betrayed, taken prisoner and, we believe, delivered to Máel Muad mac Brain."

"Is there ransom?" asked Laoghaire.

Ronan hesitated, "No, no ransom. We have spies who report that he has been killed."

"Did he travel with his guard?" asked Laoghaire.

"It was a banquet, there was supposed to be a discussion with Donnabhan about their differences. We thought he was under the protection of a bishop. There was no need for guards, and his confidence in Donnabhan was betrayed," replied Ronan. He paused, looked at Laoghaire and continued, "Máel Muad has now reclaimed the throne of Munster."

Laoghaire paced the floor for a moment, then, "Brian, what has he said of this?"

"Brian is angry. His brother murdered; his brother's throne claimed by his murderer. Yes, Brian is very angry, and he calls us to Ceann Coradh."

"Is this a call to arms?"

"No, my friend," returned Ronan, "this is a call to council. We will talk first, plan and then act."

* * *

32

977 AD Munster, Ireland
Cathair Cuan

Every battle brought new faces to the fore and saw other faces vanish. As when Laoghaire was younger and his father saw greatness in his son, he advanced it by training him, so too did Laoghaire see potential for improvement and perhaps even greatness in a number of young warriors over the years. Now that he had a son, one who may want to follow his father into the life of a warrior, he became more aware of the young men about him.

Ronan was watching a small group of aspiring warriors practice with wooden swords when Laoghaire approached, "What have we here?" he asked.

Ronan turned to see Laoghaire standing behind him, watching. "I'm remembering the days of being yelled at by old nasty battle tested men as we learned the weapons and ways of a warrior," said Laoghaire. "Now, I see these boys in need of the same harassment."

Ronan turned back toward the young men for a moment, then looked at Laoghaire with a pained expression and said as he looked again at the practice session, "Stop what you're doing, come here …listen and learn." He motioned to Laoghaire to join him, "Laoghaire and I have watched you beat each other with your wooden swords. Now it is time to learn how to use those swords properly. You will work hard in these coming training sessions, you will listen, you will learn, and you may live long enough to become Dal gCais warriors."

All three boys looked at the two men with a degree of awe. "I've heard of both of you," said a tall, young man, looking at Ronan. "I hope someday to be as skilled as you two are with the axe."

"If that is what you want," said Ronan, "Then you should train like we have, and practice as we do every day." He looked at Laoghaire, "As we were taught, now he and I will teach you. Are you ready?"

"Yes," replied a tall young man, without hesitation.

Laoghaire sensed something in this young candidate, "What's your name, buachaill?"

The young man smiled at the insult, 'boy'. He stood as tall as he could, "Deaglan mac Aod."

The other young men followed Deaglan's lead and gave their names.

Ronan looked about the training yard and decided they would first replace the practice posts and mark off a running course. He disappeared and returned moments later with several empty sacks.

Posts were cut, holes dug, and several additional wooden swords were carved along with a few blunt spears and axes.

"We will begin with the sack of stones," announced Ronan, looking at the three young men. "You will each carry a sack of small stones as you run this course five times at the beginning of every day, then we will introduce you to the sword and other new weapons as you progress through this training process."

The training was intense and soon Cassan, Ross and Labhras joined in to help. As more young men joined the group of aspiring warriors, additional practice posts were installed. Soon there were twenty-three young men running with sacks of pebbles, attacking the practice posts and learning how to thrust, slash and defend against both with wooden weapons. The days were full of small victories and equally small defeats.

The mood was infectious, soon, even the older warriors were spending time in the training yard, practicing their skills.

"We do these exercises every day to keep our bodies strong and our movements quick," Ronan told an assembled group of young candidates "When battle comes, we will be prepared to fight longer and better than anyone we face." He put his hand on Laoghaire's shoulder, "We begin to win each battle here, in this yard and finish on the battlefield."

* * *

Brian had spent several days, thinking, developing a plan. He finally called his warrior leaders together to discuss this plan for an attack into Munster, an attack on Donnuban mac Cathail.

"I plan to lead a Dal gCais force in pursuit of the remnants of the army of Limerick Norse following Donnuban mac Cathail," said Brian. "I plan to find them and destroy them and their leader, Donnuban."

"He has the support of Aralt mac Imair," said Ronan, adding to Brian's statement. "We're not sure of their numbers, but we have a larger force than them and the advantage."

Brian spoke again, "They aren't as organized as they were before Sulcoit, and we have been getting stronger by the day."

"Where do we meet them?" asked a tribal leader.

"We don't have an exact location, but we know they're south of here, so we'll march toward Corcaigh," returned Brian. "We've already sent scouts out ahead of this force, we'll find them."

The discussion continued for another hour and Brian ended with, "The bastard betrayed my brother, delivered him to a murderer and claimed his throne. This will not be allowed to stand."

Men left the meeting grumbling about Donnuban and cursing him. Laoghaire and Ronan made their way back to the training yard and Laoghaire asked, "Do you plan to join in the battle, Ronan?"

Ronan smiled, "Thank you for thinking I might, but no. Brian has asked me to remain behind in any skirmish and help coordinate the overall effort."

Laoghaire stopped, "And Brian—will he stay in the rear?"

Ronan shook his head, "I don't think anyone could take the sword out of his hand. No, my friend, Brian will not allow you to do all the fighting."

"He's a great warrior, but now he's also our leader, our king. We should protect him," said Laoghaire.

"You can try to tell him that if you want, but understand, he is very angry, and will want to be in the center of the battle, right up front," said Ronan. "He's angry enough to take on their whole army by himself and he'll want to take Donnuban's head himself."

The following morning found the Dal gCais force moving quickly south toward Corcaigh. Brian sent out additional scouting parties to locate the Limerick army as he formulated the final pieces of his plan.

Mid-morning found the force taking a break along the banks of a small river and Laoghaire was told Brian wanted to talk to him. He found Brian pacing angrily in a clearing away from the rest of the force.

"Brian, you look troubled, what is it?" asked Laoghaire.

Brian looked past his friend as if expecting others, then stepped closer to Laoghaire and said, "Death comes to us all. We die in many ways and if Donnuban had met Mathgamain in battle and killed him, then I could accept it and move on." He continued to pace, holding a sword and slashing at trees as the young warriors did in practice. He stopped and turned toward Laoghaire, "But to offer him the protection of a bishop and then betray that trust." He slashed at another tree, turned again toward Laoghaire, "and hand him over to be murdered, that I do not accept and for that both Donnuban and Máel Muad will answer to me."

Laoghaire faced Brian and said, "I will stand next to you in this, I agree this was cowardice and cannot be ignored, but be sure you keep a calm approach, or this battle could well be disastrous." Laoghaire put his hand on Brian's shoulder, "Keep the anger, but leave the temper behind. You're a great warrior, don't let a fit of temper defeat you."

Brian looked sternly at Laoghaire, "You talk to me as if I were one of your trainees."

"Yes, Brian. A trainee, my friend, my king."

They stood in silence for a moment, then Brian smiled and said, "I've called a council meeting to put the last pieces of my plan in front of all the commanders. They should be here now."

As he spoke, several of his commanders arrived and soon after, the rest. Laoghaire listened to the battle plan, thinking about protecting Brian and when positions on the front line were discussed, he put himself and his unit to Brain's immediate left. Brian looked at Laoghaire, smiled and said, "Yes old friend, having you and that axe on my left will give me comfort."

The several other commanders were assigned locations along the front, such as it was. The terrain would not allow a smooth battle line for either side and as the Dal gCais force approached the Norse army through the trees and brush, their line would be anything but even.

"It is our fight, and we will do it our way," said Brian. "We'll attack them immediately, before they can fully prepare for battle. They'll expect us to watch them as they form and think we'll be attacking their flanks first," he paused, "We'll not disappoint them." He looked at two of his commanders, "Gilleagan, take three units to our right flank, make noise but maintain a distance." He looked at another of his commanders, "Curnan, take the left flank and do the same." He looked at both commanders, "It is important that you appear to be more than you are, many more. We will have our main group directed at their center, but they won't see us, they'll see the formations on the flanks and think we are attacking from two sides. Meanwhile, we'll move our main force as close as possible in the center, approach slowly and quietly, then as we attack their middle, their flanks will have to turn toward the center and that's when you'll attack." He looked at Laoghaire, "When it is our time to attack, we must do so causing as much confusion in their ranks as possible. Our center will quietly approach as close as possible before we attack, then when we hit the middle of their line, our flanks will close in. It'll be the opposite of what they expect." Does anyone have any comments, suggestions?"

The gathering was quiet, everyone knew Brian had thought this out and the enemy this time was responsible for killing Mathgamain. This was Brian's battle, and no one wanted to challenge him. He looked at Laoghaire, "You've said little this time Laoghaire."

"I see the plan working well as you've laid it out, there's little to be said." He stood, put his hand on Brian's shoulder, "Mathgamain was a good man, a bit stubborn at times, almost as stubborn as you and we will defeat Donnuban. Now I'll find my unit and meet you back here."

Laoghaire gathered his unit and sat them down for a quick pre-battle talk. They were told enough, but not everything. Both Brian and he agreed that information was easily transmitted to an enemy, sometimes intentionally, sometimes not. Thus, the less the individual soldiers knew, the less the enemy could learn. They gathered their weapons and assembled at the center of the battle line.

The march south into Munster of over one thousand men would not be secret for long and Donnuban was made aware of their arrival in an area known as Cathair Cuan. The initial meeting was between two scouting parties, each more concerned with reporting the sighting to their leaders than engaging the enemy. Several spears were thrown, and nobody was hurt. The scouts returned to Brian and reported their findings.

"How far ahead is the bulk of their force," asked Brian.

"Less than a mile," reported the scout.

"The ground, trees, brush, open…?" asked one of the older warriors.

The scout smiled, "Uneven ground, and a bog to their right. Small trees, some brush and a small stream behind them."

Brian looked at his commanders, "We move ahead, leave everything we don't need here, and we follow the plan as discussed. The center will attack as soon as we can. They know we're here, so let's not keep them waiting."

The afternoon sun was high in the sky as the center of the Dal gCais line advanced toward the Norse. Laoghaire and his unit were on Brian's left as planned and hurrying through the countryside to meet the Norse army.

Suddenly the Norse were seen, they had not yet formed up in a defensive position and Brian order all to stay low, out of sight. He called a scout to his side and ordered him to tell Curnan and Gilleagan to move their units as planned. "We wait, give them time to get into position and make some noise."

A scout returned from Curnan's units, "Almost there," he reported. "Only minutes and they will begin."

Brian, breathing heavily, looked at Laoghaire, "I've never been this nervous before a battle."

Laoghaire said, "Tell the men to rest now for a few minutes, and that we'll be moving very soon."

Brian half smiled, slapped Laoghaire on his arm and turned toward another of the commanders, "Pass the word, rest now we move in a few minutes." He looked back at Laoghaire, more relaxed, "Thank you, old friend."

Within five minutes, another scout returned, "They are in position."

Brian looked at the assembled Norse from their position of cover. They were moving about, unaware of the larger force watching them. They suddenly began preparing to answer a threat from two opposite sides and started to move elements to form a shield wall to face each threat.

"Now," said Brian, "Stay low and quiet as long as possible."

The main Irish force moved forward quickly and quietly through the trees and brush. The two Irish flanking forces made more noise and started banging their shields as they stood and started to walk slowly toward the Norse. As the main force neared the area between the two shield walls, they were seen. An alarm was sounded, and the Norse became aware of their exposed backs.

Then, as soon as Brian realized they had been seen, he jumped to his feet and led a running assault into the confused and disarrayed Norse lines. There was only about 100 feet between them when the Norse spotted the Irish and they couldn't respond quick enough to fully reform a shield wall to face Brian and his charging troops. Brian was one of the first to strike the inadequate shield wall and Laoghaire was less than a second behind. Laoghaire's axe opened a hole in the wall, and he charged through, swinging his axe and killing two men before they could respond. Brian was through another opening and battling two Norse when a spear from one of his men took out one of Brian's opponents. As the center was collapsing and the men who had turned their attention to the flanks, tried to regroup and return to the center, the Irish on both flanks pressed inward. The Norse were in complete disarray, bumping into each other and stumbling backwards as the Irish pushed through the wall in several more weakened points.

The battle was beyond question and Brian looked fiercely around the field, "Donnuban, has anyone seen Donnuban?" he shouted.

Laoghaire heard the shout and sent two of his men to look for Donnuban. He approached Brian, "I've sent men to search the field for him."

Brian calmed and looked at Laoghaire, "I want that bastard's head on a pike," he said in a low voice.

"If he's here, we'll find him," returned Laoghaire.

As they were talking one of the men Laoghaire sent in search of Donnuban approached, "Laoghaire, I heard Donnuban left the field when the fighting began. He saw his line collapse and ran for his horse."

Brian heard the report, "Damn," he paused, "send riders after him. Find him and bring him to me if you can."

As the battle settled down to a slaughter of the cornered Norse, Laoghaire sent more men to scour the battlefield and gain all the information he could about Donnuban.

"He ran at the first clash of swords," said one of the Dal gCais warriors.

"I saw him at the beginning, on his horse, at the rear of his troops. Then he was gone," said another.

The consensus was, "He ran as soon as he could."

"Brian, we've searched the battlefield and talked to a number of the men," said Laoghaire, "he's either dead on the field and cut to pieces or he ran. I think he ran and is probably halfway to Dubh Linn by now."

"I want him, Laoghaire," said Brian with anger in his eyes. "I want to kill him myself."

* * *

33

978 AD Munster, Ireland
bhaile arís … Home Again

The battle was over, the Dal gCais had a victory over the remnants of the Limerick Norse. Now it was time to resume the training of new warriors, time to allow the wounded to heal and the dead to be buried. Time to visit families and to prepare for the next confrontation.

Laoghaire returned to Cnoc Gorm for a few weeks, then came again to Ceann Coradh. He reviewed the improvement of those young warrior candidates and noticed Deaglan took the training very seriously, more so than most of his companions. He often continued working at the practice posts well after others had stopped. Each morning he put more stones in his sack than others and each day ran a longer distance.

As days passed into weeks the training began to show results in the abilities of both the new crop of warriors and the older veterans who helped in the training or allowed that they too had things to learn. Brian frequently came to watch the sessions, he was impressed and encouraged everybody to join in the training regimen.

The value of the training became obvious as the warriors in general seemed to walk taller, talk bolder and were able to remain at the practice posts longer swinging their swords with greater vigor and destroying the posts quicker.

*   *   *

The Battle of Sulcoit, the sack of Limerick and the Battle of Cathair Cuan were now history and Laoghaire was frequently praised for his feats in the field. He remained with Brian and his team of warriors for several weeks as Donnuban was hunted throughout the territory of the Dal gCais and the nearby regions. No success in that endeavor was discouraging but understood. Soon life at Ceann Coradh returned to normal with the exception of the increased training and practice sessions by warriors new and old.

Laoghaire found Brian talking to his wife and holding a small child. "You're a fortunate man, Brian," he said. "I've a daughter and a son I've not seen in a long while and I'll be going home for the rest of this year." He patted the small boy on his head, "Spring will come soon enough, and I'll return."

Brian could not criticize this man who had stood next to him for so many years. They fought the guerilla war against the Norse of Limerick and was at his side in every major engagement since then. He wondered if Laoghaire would come back again when he planned to challenge Máel Muad. "You've earned a long and happy rest, old friend. You've trained enough young warriors to fill the gap you'll leave when gone." Brian embraced his good and loyal friend and thought this was their final farewell. "Go, enjoy your family."

Laoghaire left Ceann Coradh, riding south along the Shannon and south to Cnoc Gorm. His service to Brian became less and less important in his life as his daughter grew to seven years old and Earnan neared his third year.

* * *

34

978 AD Munster, Ireland
Bealach Leachta

There were many unfamiliar responsibilities for Brian as the new king of Munster and his closest advisors and leaders were called into service. Laoghaire returned to Ceann Coradh in the spring and sat in on counsels for Brian. A campaign against Máel Muad was being planned and Laoghaire debated about his continued service. He was in his 37th year and the wounds from past battles had slowed him down. He was not the same man he was years ago and he wanted to see his son and daughter grow up. He determined this call to counsel and to arms was going to be his last and planned on telling Deirdre on his return home. After a day-long meeting with the other chieftains, Laoghaire found Brian sitting alone in a garden. "You look deep in thought, Brian."

"Laoghaire, please come and sit with me," he replied as he gestured toward another bench. "We've come a long way in these last few years. We've had many battles and lost too many good friends." He paused, "I look forward to the day when we have driven the foreigners out of Éirinn and we can be at peace with our neighbors." He looked at Laoghaire, smiled and continued, "Do you think either of us will live to see that day?"

"I have every intention of seeing my son and daughter grow old and give me grandchildren. If we can achieve peace on this island, that dream might become a reality, it is why we have fought and why we continue to fight."

"Ah, yes, but we are growing older," said Brian. "How much longer can we stand in battle and continue this fight?"

"I've still got life in these arms," replied Laoghaire, "and this campaign against Máel Muad is yet to be completed." He paused, thought for a moment and continued, "I'll see this one through, then we can talk about our next step and perhaps I may take some time with my family."

* * *

Brian led an army south toward Corcaigh to confront Máel Muad mac Brain and the Norse that had joined him. Camped north of a river near Bealach Leachta the night before the armies met, Brian called his leaders to discuss the plans for battle. Laoghaire was one of twenty-five leaders invited to the counsel. Plans were made and the group finished the evening with food, drink and talk of their homes and families.

Morning came with a cool breeze and a cloudy sky. The chance of rain and thus a muddy field concerned some of the warriors. They were more comfortable on firm ground where the footing allowed their charge into a shield wall more effective. The sun shone a dull grey light on the field at first as the two armies moved closer to each other. A challenge was issued from the Norse ranks and two men broke ranks to step into the opening between the walls of shields. The contest was over quickly as the Viking's sword found the flesh above his opponent's knee, sending the man to the ground. The Viking finished the contest with a series of hard blows to the fallen man's head and shoulders, almost severing his head. The Viking then raised his sword and shield above his head to the shouts of his comrades.

Laoghaire saw one of his warriors begin to move forward. He put his hand on Deaglan's shoulder and said, "The man begs for another challenge. Don't allow him to draw you out to the middle." He turned to his group of warriors, "Today is not a day for challenges. We have worked hard preparing for this day and we should not waste our training on these little contests. We need all of you together when we break their wall." The young warrior was disappointed and relieved at the same time as he stepped back and nodded at Laoghaire. His companion leaned into his shoulder, "Don't worry Deaglan, we'll be in it soon enough."

Brian's army was made up of men of all ages from those past their sixtieth year to those only sixteen and a few even younger. Deaglan looked older than his seventeen years and this was to be his first real battle. He was anxious to show what he could do and carried a sword and shield like most of his fellows. Some used two swords, some wielded an axe, some carried spears and still others used slings, pikes, and hammers.

The two armies slowly approached and when in range, the kerns began to throw javelins and darts from the rear of both sides. The first casualties on both sides inspired a quicker pace and the shields soon clashed. The battle began in earnest as the sun moved higher in the sky and the clouds parted. The fighting lasted most of the day with high casualties for the southern Munster forces and their Norse allies. Máel Muad and many of his followers were killed. The battle had serious casualties on both sides.

Laoghaire was near the center of the battle line and crashed through the wall of shields. The opening in the wall allowed the Dal gCais to pour through and begin to inflict damage to the ranks of the enemy. Deaglan moved close to Laoghaire as he fought. His sword found flesh several times and he contributed four men to the list of causalities. Laoghaire faced five men at once and Deaglan was blocked from helping him by another three. Laoghaire's axe separated a man's leg at the knee, and he turned his attention to the other four. The man downed still held his sword and managed a slash at Laoghaire's leg, cutting deep into his calf. He stumbled and with two men attacking him from the front, he could not back up. Another violent swing of his axe caught one of the men to his right at the neck and nearly removed his head. Laoghaire was not able to move, and his leg was bleeding severely. The last three men attaching him took advantage of his wound and surrounded him. He couldn't turn and was slashed across his back, and another was able to lunge at Laoghaire and plunge his sword deep into Laoghaire's left side. He stumbled and as he began to fall, Deaglan and another young warrior both freed themselves from their contests with killing blows and moved to help Laoghaire. Deaglan prevented the third man from delivering a final blow to Laoghaire by throwing his sword at him. The other young warrior delivered the killing stroke to the third man's neck as the fighting seemed to be moving away from their position. Deaglan rushed to Laoghaire in the lull and saw he was seriously wounded. His comrade yelled, "Deaglan, they come again."

Deaglan looked for his sword and Laoghaire pushed his axe to him, "Take it, and fight as I have taught you. Go and don't look back, I will be alright here if you fight and win."

Deaglan was on his feet and hefted the long axe, looked at Laoghaire one final time and turned to continue the battle. Laoghaire was more seriously wounded than he realized and had lost a great deal of blood. Another passing enemy slashed at his neck missing but striking Laoghaire's chest as he ran farther away. Laoghaire felt a chill, his breathing shallowed as he tried to breath deep. He lay on the field, blood flowing from each wound and the sky seemed to darken. Sleep, he wanted to sleep and the world around him quieted, grew darker and soon sleep came.

The battle was over, the Dal gCais had won and the remaining enemy were slaughtered where they stood. Physicians and the younger warriors were scouring the field for wounded friends and Laoghaire was found, staring at the sky and not breathing. Still, he was taken to a physician's tent to be treated as if he were only wounded. "This is Laoghaire," said one of the young warriors. "He must be healed, do your magic, physician and give him back his life."

* * *

The defeat and death of Máel Muad allowed Brian to claim the throne of Munster. This was cause for a celebration and during the feasting and drinking, the deeds of a number of warriors were shouted out to their fellows. In that context, a man stood and held his hands high. "I hear the praise of men who fought well this day," the crowd cheered. "Someone even mentioned my name," another loud cheer. "But I have yet to hear of Laoghaire." The gathering of warriors rose to their feet and roared in approval. "Laoghaire fought today as he has in every battle," another cheer. "He stood like a stone wall and slew more of them than any of us," another cheer.

Brian raised his hand, "Where is my old friend?"

The crowd stilled. They looked about and didn't see him. Then Brian spoke again, "We win these battles because of men like Laoghaire. We should honor him, find him, and bring him here," demanded Brian.

Deaglan stood and said, "He was wounded when I last saw him, unable to stand. We were moving away from him, pushing the fight back down the hill."

Another man said, "I was behind Deaglan by some distance and thought I saw him carried to a physician's tent."

Ronan left the celebration and went to the several tents set up around the battlefield to treat wounded men. He found Laoghaire being attended to by a frightened physician with a young warrior holding a short sword behind him.

190

Ronan approached the pallet where he lay and spoke, "Brian wishes you to come to his tent and be honored, Laoghaire."

Laoghaire didn't hear the words and couldn't reply. The physician stepped closer to him and looked at the guard, "I can't bring him back." He looked at Ronan, "Tell Brian he has lost his old friend, I couldn't heal his wounds this time. The great axe man is dead."

When Ronan returned and told Brian, this great warrior had died from his wounds, the room fell silent. Then Brian spoke, "I remember Laoghaire's words of advice before this battle and his talk of family and farm. He was going to go home and live the rest of his life with his family." Brian fell silent for a moment, then he spoke again. "This man was my kin, my friend and a great warrior. He gave us great service," he said, and he ordered two warriors from their tribe to place him on a cart and escort him home. He called for a poet to compose a poem about Laoghaire and his great deeds in the battle. "Announce this to all who will listen, Laoghaire was a great warrior."

Laoghaire was cleaned, his clothes washed, and he was placed in a horse drawn cart for the trek home. As the cart was about to leave, several warriors stated they wished to accompany this hero home.

"Tis only fitting he be so honored," said Brian. Two with the cart and four to follow. Ronan, you were his good friend. Lead this group and see to all the proper preparations at his home.

After the small procession left, Brian told his son, Murchad to fill a purse with silver and copper coins, "It is to be given to Laoghaire's widow after all have left her. He served me well and now I serve him. He has left a wife and two children on a farm; this will sustain them until his son grows to a man."

* * *

35

978 AD Munster, Ireland
clann Laoghaire

Ronan rode ahead of the cart carrying Laoghaire's body. He stopped outside the rath at Cnoc Gorm, dismounted and walked across the bridge where Deirdre met him in the yard.

"Ronan, you come alone?" puzzled Deirdre.

"No, the others follow," he replied in a quiet voice. He was not smiling, not his usual self.

Deirdre immediately knew Ronan came with bad news. She stood straight, her face lit by the sun and her eyes sparkling as bright blue as ever, "Laoghaire, is being brought home?" she said with a strong voice.

"Yes," replied Ronan. "He was a great warrior, true to the stories of his father and grandfather," he continued. "None could stand against him in battle alone."

"And now?" wondered Deirdre aloud.

"Now," said Ronan, "he will be remembered and honored."

Deirdre felt the strength in her legs falter. She reached to her right and touched a walkway support, drew a deep breath, and said, "My children, please call my children." She touched her slightly swollen belly and sighed, "Our children."

Ronan turned toward the roundhouse and saw Muirin and Earnan carrying small sticks for kindling to the roundhouse. He called to them.

Muirin set her armful of kindling down near the door and walked over to Ronan and Earnan followed his sister. Muirin smiled and asked Ronan, "Have you returned with my father?"

Ronan looked at Muirin and replied, "Come with me, girl. Stand with your mother while your Da is brought home."

Muirin had seen other men brought home, often severely wounded and more often dead. She lost her smile and ran to Deirdre, "Mam, is Da coming home?"

"Come here to me, girl," she said to Muirin, "and Earnan. Where is Earnan?"

"Here, Mam," came a small voice behind his sister. "Is Da comin' home?"

Deirdre steadied herself, placed a hand on each of her children and stepped across the bridge toward the approaching cart. She didn't need to be told any more. She knew her husband was dead and that was all that mattered.

Two familiar warriors escorted the horse drawn cart up the winding path to the gate and stopped. They dismounted and stood on either side of the cart in silence.

Deirdre straightened her back, drew a deep breath and walked to the cart by herself. He had been escorted home and she knew he had died well, in battle. "Children, your father has fought his last battle and now he comes home to rest," she said, holding her head high.

Muirin had seen other men, killed in battle brought home on carts. She stepped close to Deirdre and hugged her, then reached her hand to Earnan.

The little boy stood looking confused. He was in his fourth year and didn't understand what was before him. He didn't understand his father would no longer lift him over his head, carry him across the open yard wrestle with him and make him laugh. He didn't understand his father would soon be so much dust and bone, no longer a tall strong man. No longer a giant in his life.

*   *   *

Ronan broke the silence, "Deirdre, I'll help prepare him for his final rest. The others should be here any time now."

At that moment Muirin said, "Mam, more men are coming."

Deirdre looked to the road and saw four fully armed warriors approaching on horse. They rode to the top of the hill, dismounted and surrounded the cart.

She stepped closer to the cart and Ronan nodded to the six warriors, "Give her time with him," he said.

They stepped away, "All the time the lady wants," said one.

Muirin came closer, "Can I see him?" she asked Ronan.

Deirdre lifted her head, "Come here daughter."

Laoghaire was lying in the bed of the cart with his arms across his chest. The blood had been washed away from his wounds and the wounds covered, but not bandaged. His body looked clean, his clothes washed, and his hair combed. His axe lay to his right and a sword to his left.

Deirdre reached for his hand, touched the cool skin that had last been warm and comforting. Her hand moved to his face and tears came to her eyes. She put her head on his chest, held his hand and closed her eyes.

Muirin stood quietly next to her mother and reached up to her hand. Deirdre turned to her daughter and brought her closer to the cart to see her father. Muirin looked at him and said, "He looks like he is sleeping." She touched his arm and saw the end of a large wound on his chest. She lifted the cover and saw the wound that had spilled his life on the battlefield, "Oh Mam, he was hurt, is this the wound that killed him?"

Deirdre didn't know what to say and looked at Ronan. He shook his head and said, "If that were the only wound, we could say it was, but there are more." He put the cover back over the wound and looked at Muirin, "You don't need to see them all, girl. Know that he was a great warrior, and it was five men who killed him, not just one." He turned and saw Earnan, lifted him to his shoulder and let him see his father. "He was a great man, Earnan. Never forget him."

* * *

The six warriors lifted Laoghaire's body and carried him into the roundhouse and placed him on a large table. They stood silently for a moment as if in prayer, then walked outside.

Ronan asked one of them to ride south several miles, find Tanai at his farm and bring him back to Cnoc Gorm. Then, he asked two others to dig a grave on the hill below the arc of oak trees.

Laoghaire was prepared for burial, his sword heated in the fire and bent, then cleaned and placed in his hand. His great axe was polished to a brilliant shine and hung on the wall of the roundhouse. All was ready when Tanai arrived with Eadan and a priest.

The next day Laoghaire was carried to the hillside and laid in the grave. As the priest was saying a prayer, another rider arrived. This was a young man, tall with red hair and broad shoulders. Ronan recognized him immediately and greeted him. "Murchad, welcome."

The young man joined the crowd at the grave site and stood silently as the priest continued with the prayers. After the grave was filled and stones placed over the mounded earth, the warriors each offered condolence to Deirdre and the children, then left for Ceann Coradh.

As Deirdre was walking back to the rath with her children, she put her hand on her belly and said quietly, "What will the world hold for you?"

Murchad waited until the grave was covered and Ronan left with the other warriors. He found Deirdre, alone, standing on the bridge and staring out over the wildflowers covering the hillside. He approached her, "Laoghaire was more than a great warrior," he said. "He was a great man. He stood by my father, Brian, when they fought the Limerick Norse and every battle since then. He helped train the young warriors of the Dal gCais and now, he leaves behind a family. My father has ordered this purse be given to you," he said as he handed it to Deirdre, "to help sustain you till your son and daughter are grown and you will be taken care of as long as you live."

Deirdre accepted the purse, smiled and thanked Murchad, "Tell your father, Brian, this is appreciated, and the children of Laoghaire will grow tall and strong." She placed her hand on her swollen belly again and said, "All of his children."

*　*　*

Part Four

CONALL

36

978 AD Munster, Éirinn
an mac tíre feargach … An Angry Wolf

December, 978 was a cold and wet month in western Éirinn. A rare light snow falling overnight had dusted the trees and covered the ground. The morning sun rose, changing the falling snow to rain, and melting that already on the ground, leaving it wet and muddy. A gathering of dark clouds moving across the sky dropped a sleeting rain into an inconsistent wind, pelting the walls and roofs of huts and roundhouses sheltering people and animals.

Cnoc Gorm was a farm of almost 30 acres, it surrounded a small rise where a circular rath of stone and heavy log pickets enclosed several round houses and a few animal pens. The walls of the main roundhouse were in need of repair and the winds carried freezing drops of rain through openings left by missing daub. Inside, deer hides hung from the roof beams, along the outside walls, cutting most of the wind and rain that penetrated the wattle perimeter. A small fire pit in the middle of the single round room warmed a woman and her two children as the storm raged outside.

Deirdre, ripe with child, laying on a bed of straw and hides close to the fire pit, was feeling the pains of her child's attempt to birth. She was a strong and wise woman. Her husband, Laoghaire, was carried home on a horse-drawn cart four months prior, following the Battle of Bealach Lechta. He had been a Dal gCais warrior, close to Brian mac Cennetig for more than fourteen years. Their victory at Bealach Lechta had cost Laoghaire his life and given the crown of Munster to Brian. The new King had depended on his friend, his comrade in battle, many times before and knowing Laoghaire left a widow and two children, he sent his young son, Murchad, with a purse of gold, silver and copper coins to sustain Deirdre.

She used the wealth wisely, spending the money in the purse only when necessary and now, as she lay on her bed of straw and hides, she could see another use for a few of the coins. She would hire someone to rethatch the roof and she could replace the missing daub in the walls herself.

Muirin, now in her ninth year, served as her nurse. She had been present when her brother Earnan was born four years earlier and she had accompanied her mother to help others in their tribe with the birthing process on six occasions, learning a little something new from each. Now it was her mother's time to deliver a baby and Muirin was alone with her mother and brother. She had no fear, no reservation, "We've done it before, Mam," she said with a confident smile, "this time'll be no different."

Muirin placed another small log on the fire and the three stayed close to the pit, keeping warm. A hearty people, the women of this time needed little help in birthing a child, but this baby was different. It was large; bigger than her first two and in these final days, active as a playful hound. Deirdre felt the pains coming closer together and called to her daughter, "Muirin, I'm close to the time, feed Earnan and be sure the gate is properly closed, this may take a while to finish."

Muirin handed her little brother a bowl of cooked meat and turnips, then hurried outside to check the gate. She hefted a pole into place across the closed doors and knotted a short length of rope around the supports, pulling it tight. Having done as her mother asked, she hurried back inside the roundhouse, checked the cauldron of water and collected clean bedding and blankets for the new baby. She looked in Earnan's bowl, gave him another piece of meat and said, "Be a good boy now, and we'll play a game when Mam is done with the birthin'."

The little boy was happy with his food and content to watch as his sister fussed over their mother. He watched but didn't understand what was about to happen.

"Do you have a feeling, Mam? Could it be a girl or another boy?" Muirin asked, trying to ease her mother's discomfort with conversation.

"I've no way of knowin', girl. But this one is big as an ox and I'll be glad when the birthin' is done," replied Deirdre.

Muirin smiled at her brother, "Do you know what's happenin', little brother?"

Earnan looked up at his sister, "Is Mam feelin' sick?"

Muirin thought for a moment, "Not really sick, Earnan, she's about to let the new baby come out and join us."

Earnan didn't understand, but he smiled and returned to his bowl of food.

"Are you feelin' more of the pains, Mam?" asked Muirin.

"That I am, and they're closer together now. Be ready, girl, with the knife in case I have to be cut," replied Deirdre.

It had been snowing or raining since the sun left the sky and a new day had begun. Deirdre's labor had lasted through the dark and as the baby's head began to appear, the storm outside continued. Deirdre delivered her third child, a large, well developed and loud boy who screamed his way into the world as lightning flashed and a wolf howled in the distance. Muirin took the baby, cut and tied the cord then washed and dried him. She wrapped him in a clean, coarse blanket and handed the screaming bundle to his mother.

"What name have you chosen for this one?" asked Muirin as she washed her mother and dried her off.

"He howls like *'an mac tíre feargach'*, an angry wolf," replied Deirdre, "He'll be called Conall. Conall mac Laoghaire. His father would've been proud to see this one." Deirdre held her new son close and fed him. When he finished feeding, she looked at her daughter, "I'm tired, girl. Take your new brother and let me sleep a while."

Muirin took the baby and laid him on a clean blanket, then covered her mother and watched the two of them fall asleep. She watched and quietly played with Earnan while the storm continued to rage outside.

*　*　*

The winter warmed and the gentle spring rains began. Life returned to many plants and the hills on both sides of the path from the main road leading to the gate in the rath bloomed with blue wildflowers.

The rath wall was old, originally made with a field stone base surrounding timber pickets embedded in the ground. A dry moat was dug around the outside of the picket wall, the dirt being used to raise and level the interior of the rath. The pickets initially reached a height of eight feet above the inside ground. As the years passed, each repair to the wall used larger and taller pickets. The wall now reached a height of nearly twelve feet above the ground inside the rath and an interior walkway was added on the perimeter wall, seven feet above grade. Standing on the walking platform, a man could look over the wall and twenty feet down into the moat, now several feet deep and over ten feet wide. This served as protection for the inhabitants from a casual intruder, both human and animal. The main opening in the wall was the gated doorway, large enough for a horse drawn cart to pass through.

The gate, two heavy wooden panels, sturdy enough to contain the stock of horses and cattle, and solid enough to keep wolves from entering, but not much protection against a determined human intruder, was secured with a wooden bar on the inside. Originally the bar was a heavy wooden beam, about 4 inches square, now it was a wooden pole about 2 inches in diameter that Muirin could lift and set in place. A second opening in the perimeter resulted from two of the large new pickets coming loose and easily moved. Earnan had discovered this secret passage to the fields when he was six and used it to surprise his mother when she thought him to be on the other side of the wall.

The buildings and animal pens were spaced around an open yard. Toward the middle of the yard were a large stone lined fire pit, a well, trough, a few worktables and stretching racks. The main roundhouse was vented at the peak, allowing a small fire pit inside, and the walls had several openings covered with shutters, allowing a flow of air when desired and closure against the cold, wind, and rain.

The farm had been in Laoghaire's family for several generations, and each had aided in the construction, improvement or expansion of the walls and defenses. Laoghaire had completed work on a tunnel below the house that led to the barn in the summer before he left for Bealach Lechta, and he intended to strengthen the main gate upon his return. "Always something to repair or build anew," he had laughed as he left on his last journey to Ceann Coradh.

The tunnel was a simple passage with one open area where several people could hide if necessary. Laoghaire used the space to store valuables that were not in normal use, including Deirdre's treasured books and scraps of writings. She had a few gold and silver pieces, but her most prized possessions were the books, scrolls and scraps of paper, Laoghaire had brought home over the years. The tunnel also had a place for the weapons of Laoghaire's father and grandfather. Following his burial, Deirdre had Laoghaire's axe placed in the tunnel along with a dagger which had been Ceara's, his great grandmother's, seventy-five years earlier.

Deirdre, a tall, strong woman, with long dark hair and bright blue eyes in her twenty-sixth year was now left with three children and a farm much larger than she could manage on her own. Laoghaire's brother, Tanai, helped in caring for the farm as much as he could. He had his own farm and family to tend to and Cnoc Gorm was often a second thought. Deirdre cared for her children, worked a few acres of vegetables and tended the animals as best she could, using coins from the purse sparingly, wisely.

She hired help only when necessary and was able to maintain the farm as her children grew. There was little profit in the crops she harvested, needing most of them for the family and she was skilled with the bow, able to bring home an occasional deer. As the children matured and could help with chores, the family became more independent and self-sustaining. Muirin and Earnan were useful in the fields and Conall would soon join them. Life was not easy, but not impossible either.

The rath, the buildings and the pens were in constant need of attention, maintenance or repair. Deirdre could patch the walls with daub over wattle, but thatching a roof proved beyond her reach and keeping the pickets straight, beyond her strength. When Tanai was not available, she paid a neighbor from her purse to tend to the roof of the house and left a number of minor repairs forever put off 'till the morrow' that never seemed to come.

The family's stock of one horse, six sheep, four goats and two head of cattle were let out in the morning through the gate to fields where they could graze the day away. The same collection was herded back inside the rath before the sun set over the rolling hills to the west in the evening. About thirty chickens ran loose in the yard and two dogs completed the animal count. There was plenty of grass for grazing in the fields outside the gate and a series of stone fences and wattle fencing kept the entire domesticated menagerie from wandering off.

Storms end, time passes, and wounds heal. Deirdre taught the children what she could about farming, and they all stayed busy from dawn to dusk. She was a religious woman, praying every day and attending mass whenever a priest was celebrating nearby. She shared her religion with her children and taught them to read and write. Each evening, she would read to them from her collection of books, scrolls or scraps of parchment she had acquired over the years. Laoghaire knew how she enjoyed reading in both Irish and Latin and during his campaigns with Brian mac Cennetig and others, he was constantly on the lookout for anything written that he could take home to his wife. The years of Norse plundering of the monasteries in Éirinn had spread the booty from those raids around the island and Laoghaire made it known to his fellows that he would trade for such treasures.

Several years of bargaining and trading by both husband and wife had resulted in a personal library that was modestly extensive. The bits and pieces from numerous documents and scriptures might fit well with other collections held in monasteries. Deirdre enjoyed reading and trying to understand the writings in her collection. Conversations with traveling priests and monks about an interpretation of scripture or a bit of history were enjoyable sessions she anticipated, and she brought her children into her circle of learning, teaching them to read, write and think about the words scratched on parchment and vellum.

Over time, her collection changed and grew as she traded with the visiting monks and scholars passing through. Always on the lookout for something new to bring his wife, Laoghaire came across a cláirseach, a small Irish harp during an expedition into Meath. Deirdre was excited about stroking the strings and eventually forming little tunes. A bit of advice from a friend and a few hints from a monk who also was familiar with the harp, had Deirdre playing pleasant little tunes and singing to her family.

* * *

37

987 AD Munster, Éirinn
An buachaill … The Boy

Deirdre and her three children lived a basic life as the youngest grew to his ninth year from a screaming bundle to a tall lanky boy. He grew quickly, seeming to be taller and thinner in starts and stops then filling out to a well-muscled young man before growing taller again. Earnan and Conall were four years apart in age, both big-boned and broad-shouldered. They shared the look of their father, sandy hair, dark blue eyes and a square jaw. They were brothers of a special kind. They were close, seeming to be of the same mind, one knowing what the other was thinking and able to finish each other's thoughts and sentences.

The difference was in their temperament. Earnan was calm, even tempered, very little could shake him. Conall was different, in normal activity with his family, he was calm like his older brother. He could wrestle with Earnan and laugh as one or the other gained an upper hand. No matter what the hold or hit, Conall and Earnan never lost patience or became angry with each other. It was with those he didn't know where Conall could lose that calm when slighted, or upon seeing his mother or sister threatened. It was then he showed signs of rage that terrified everyone around him.

Conall's life had been one of family, farming and play until late in the summer of 987. They had cleared a large patch of cabbages and turnips on the farm and took them to a local market. Deirdre was known as the widow of Laoghaire, a woman raising three children on her own and people favored her goods at the market. Her prices were fair and her vegetables as good as any others. Muirin, now a grown woman, helped her mother at the market and the two drew the attention of many men, both young and old.

The boys were young and playful. Neither had been schooled in warfare, as most young boys their age had been. They had no father to guide them. Their mother taught them what she knew of farming and hunting. She educated them with the scrolls and scraps of writing Laoghaire had brought home after raids on Norse settlements and campaigns into the territory of those who had raided the Irish monasteries over the previous hundred years or more.

She displayed her collection to monks and priests passing through the nearby villages and soon came to trade for new and different writings.

Deirdre knew little of the sword and felt she had given enough to the warrior culture. Her dream for her sons was to become learned men and farmers where they could live peacefully and productively.

The crops the family grew were more than they could use, and Deirdre made an occasional trip to the marketplace in a nearby village where she sold or traded her little harvest and visited with friends. The journey from farm to market was no more than a little stretch of the leg and the family made the trip several times each year. They approached from the east with the sun at their backs. The road led to a short bridge and a gate in a rath wall that stood on top of a brief rise in the ground, surrounded by a dry moat, similar to their own farm, but larger, much larger.

Each of the four entrances into the village had a similar bridge and gate, large enough for a horse-drawn cart. The rath wall was fieldstone and earth topped with log pickets reaching to a height of nearly twice that of a man. The rath was circular, nearly 300 paces across with four main gates and a bridge at each gate. Inside the rath, the roads all ended with a circular road that paralleled the outer wall less than fifty paces inside each gate.

The market was an open space in the middle of all with carts, tents and horses in no specific arrangement. The vendors set up where they found an opening, arranged a display and sang out their products. There were leathers fashioned into belts, boots and coats. Metals shaped as tools and weapons. Fabrics, yarns and sewing implements. Fruits and vegetables and still more. The village smithy was busy as people brought in their tools and weapons for repair and looked for new and different items.

Deirdre and Muirin found a vacant spot, set up their cart and Muirin led the horse out to a pasture to graze the afternoon away. Earnan and Conall were drawn to a gathering of youths as a game of hurling was being organized. They were prepared, each having brought his caman in the vegetable cart. The match was to be between the village closest to their farm and another village several miles distant. The rules of the game were not well defined and the objective of getting the sliotar, a small ball or stone, between a set of posts using a caman, seemed simple enough.

The sides were set, and the game began. The players were all boys between the ages of eight and eighteen, give or take a year or two and the number of players was, 'Whoever wants to join in.' The rules, well the rules were vague. Several men from the two villages served as referees and the confusion began. There were nearly twenty boys on each side and the initial play appeared to resemble a game. Less than five minutes into the game, the play appeared more like a battle fought by young, short warriors. Camans were used to hit opponents and the sliotar was often less important than knocking someone to the ground. Earnan and Conall both enjoyed running about banging into others and chasing the sliotar. As the game progressed, one of the boys was hit across his face and a gash opened. He fell to the ground and an official helped him from the field without stopping play. That was the impetus for the level of play to change to a more combative posture on both sides. Conall was struck on his leg by a bigger boy from the opposing team and he responded with laughter and a solid strike to the boy's arm. A fight ensued. The bigger boy attacked Conall with his stick and Conall reacted with another strike and no smile. The bigger boy was hit hard in his chest. He regained his posture and came at Conall again. As this fight was developing, several boys from each side paused to watch. The boys from the opposing team began to cheer Conall's rival, "Ruarc, Ruarc!"

Ruarc took this as a signal to go into full attack mode and charged Conall. He raised his stick above his head and began a downward movement. Conall watched, his eyes narrowed, his teeth bared, and a low growl began in his gut. As Ruarc charged, Conall suddenly stepped to his right and swung his stick, catching Ruarc's back and forcing him to the ground. Ruarc floundered and rolled over. Conall's low growl rose to a fierce, thunderous roar as he swung his stick once more striking Ruarc in his chest, causing him to recoil in pain. Conall's eyes opened wide, his teeth clenched, his breathing slowed, and he moved closer to Ruarc. He raised his stick as if to strike Ruarc again when Earnan called his name.

"Conall, enough. He has had enough," he said as he approached his brother.

Conall froze, then looked at Earnan. The expression on his face was one of anger, hate. A look of savagery about to strike. He scared several other boys who backed away and Earnan walked up to his brother. "I think this game may be over for us, little brother."

Conall relaxed, his arm dropped and his caman touched the ground. "He should not have attacked me, this is a game, not war." The two walked off the field, dragging their camans behind and sought out their mother and her vegetable cart.

Ruarc was carried from the field and his father opened his shirt, looking at the bruises and cuts on his son's back and chest. "There are bones broken in his chest," growled his father, Ogan. "Who was that boy who hurt my son?"

Ogan learned the boy's name was Conall and asked, "Where is he?" Conall was pointed out to Ogan and he stormed across the open field after him, "You, Conall, you hurt my son! You must answer for that!"

As Ogan approached Conall, reaching to grab him, a tall powerful man stepped in front of him. "This was a dispute between boys. Let's leave it at that."

Ogan looked at the man and replied, "Deaglan, you know this boy?"

"No, old friend, I know Ruarc. He attacked this boy, and the boy had the better of him. It's over, leave it be."

Ogan relaxed, "I wish no dispute with you, Deaglan. But my son is hurt."

"Then go to your son and tend to him. I'll see to this other boy," said Deaglan.

Ogan walked away, unhappy, but in no mood to argue with his good friend, this tall, strong warrior, Deaglan.

Deaglan turned to see Conall and Earnan staring up at him. Earnan spoke, "We need no help from you, but thank you anyway."

Deaglan was about to speak when a tall girl with dark hair and brilliant blue eyes stepped toward him, "And I thank you, sir. My brothers and I wish no trouble here."

Again, Deaglan was about to speak, and the girl interrupted him, "I am Muirin, these are my brothers, Earnan and Conall. We're here to sell our little harvest of vegetables with our mother."

As Muirin spoke, Deidre approached, "I heard something, a boy was injured, broken ribs," she stopped and looked at Conall, "And my son, Conall broke them." She turned toward Conall with a questioning look.

"Yes Mam, I did it," said Conall, standing tall.

"Conall mac Laoghaire, could you explain this to me?"

Deaglan looked at Deirdre, "mac Laoghaire? I knew a man named Laoghaire. A great man, a great warrior."

Deirdre held her head high as she said with pride, "My husband was a warrior, he died at Bealach Lechta."

Deaglan breathed deeply, "It's my honor to meet you. Laoghaire was a very good man. I was a young warrior at Bealach Lechta, but I remember him." As he spoke, others around them heard him and some stepped closer. "Our king, Brian, ordered several warriors to carry him home. I would have been honored to have been chosen, but that honor went to the best of us." He looked at the boys, then at Deirdre and continued, "Brian spoke of him often after that day. Laoghaire was a man to be followed. A man to emulate." He looked at Deirdre, "I would consider it an honor to see you and your family safely home, although I see that may not be necessary. These two boys stand very tall and need no help from me." He looked at Muirin, "Muirin is a beautiful name. I like the sound of it. May I walk with you a while?"

Muirin was now in her eighteenth year and did not need her mother's approval, but she looked to Deirdre none the less.

"Go, walk with him if you wish. I'll be here for a while, after I see to the damage done by your brother," said Deirdre with a smile. Her little girl was now a woman and even though many boys and young men had noticed Muirin, it was about time she showed an interest in one of them.

Deaglan and Muirin walked the fairgrounds together and Deirdre told the boys to tend to the vegetables while she checked on the injured boy. As she approached a small crowd someone recognized her and said, "Here comes Deirdre, she knows of these things, deep cuts and broken bones."

"I'm Deirdre, my son is Conall. I've come to help this boy if I can."

Ogan stood and looked at Deirdre, "I don't know what to do. He's hurt and cannot breathe deeply."

Deirdre knelt next to the boy and as she gently touched his chest, "What is your name, boy?"

He winced and tightened his chest, making the pain even greater, "Ruarc," he answered just above a whisper.

Deirdre smiled as she continued to move her hand about his chest, then, "The pain is here?" she asked and pressed gently.

Ruarc winced again and nodded.

Deirdre continued to move her hand around the boy's chest, pausing and gently applying pressure and asking the same question. Finally, she stood, turned to Ogan, "He has two broken ribs. They will heal, but it will take time." She pulled Ogan closer to his son, "Look here, the break is in these two ribs," she said putting her hand near Ruarc's chest but not touching him. "As long as he remains calm and still, he will heal." She looked at Ogan and repeated her words, "Calm and still. Do you understand?"

Ogan saw a woman who had dealt with injuries before. Serious injuries. He also recognized she was the widow of Laoghaire. He remained silent and nodded his head.

Deirdre again knelt next to Ruarc, "You must not move more than necessary and try not to breathe deeply. In a few days these bones will begin to heal, and you will feel better. Better, and you will be tempted to do more than you should. You must give them time to heal all the way through," she said in a commanding voice.

Ruarc nodded again. Deirdre stood and turned to Ogan, "My son did this. He is a very strong boy, stronger than his years should allow. When he fights, he fights hard, and when he plays this game of hurling, apparently, he plays just as hard. The wolf in him does not allow for gentle combat or half-measures in games. He, like his father, has a temper that no man should see."

Ogan was confused, Conall had hurt his son and Deirdre had helped his son. He thought about Deaglan's words, *I know Ruarc,* and he said, "My son also plays hard, perhaps they are both too strong for this game."

Deirdre smiled and looked Ogan in the eye, "Calm and still. At least a full turn of the moon. Perhaps longer." She turned and walked back to her sons and the vegetables.

A short while later Muirin returned, "His name was Deaglan. His farm is only a brief ride from here on horse," she said as she danced about. The boys helped Deirdre load their cart for the journey home and Deirdre remembered her first meeting with Laoghaire nearly twenty years before. She smiled as she remembered how he made her feel, then when the cart was loaded, she rode on top with her daughter and the boys walked behind, teasing, and testing each other, occasionally asking Muirin a question about Deaglan.

* * *

38

989 AD Munster, Éirinn
An chuairt … The Visit

Muirin continued her dancing every day for a week. When clouds filled the sky, all she saw was the single ray of sunshine beaming through. As she smiled even at the darkest of moments, the spirits of all around her were lifted and on a Sunday morning when the tall warrior rode up to their gate, she almost made the spring flowers bloom. Earnan and Conall were returning from the pasture where the animals were put out to graze the day away, "Good mornin' to you, tall man," said Earnan. "Have you come to help us with the chores?" he laughed.

Deaglan dismounted and looked at the two brothers with a smile, "No boys, 'tis your sister has brought me to your gate." He walked his horse through to a watering trough, "Would you be kind and tell her I'm here?"

Earnan was about to answer when Conall interrupted, "And just what is your interest in our little sister?"

Before Deaglan could respond Earnan spoke, "Pay him no mind, Deaglan, we have yet to teach the boy manners." He led Deaglan toward the roundhouse and Conall followed. "Wait here," said Earnan, "and I'll tell her you've arrived."

Conall stood in front of Deaglan and looked up at him. "You're a fine tall man, Deaglan. I know you'll be kind to my sister."

Muirin came out of the roundhouse and approached the two. "Conall, please be nice, Deaglan is here to walk with me this mornin'." She turned toward Deaglan, "The priest is in the village to celebrate a mass today, Mother and I would like to be there."

Deaglan looked at Muirin and said, "Then call your mother and we'll be on our way." He looked at the boys, "Will the boys be joinin' us?"

Muirin giggled and said, "The good lord knows they need it."

* * *

Earnan was the older and taller of the two boys, heavier and well-muscled. Conall was not far behind, his shoulders were as broad as his brother's and his hands as big, but he was more bone than muscle. They were both strong and worked the fields together, tended the animals together and constantly pushed each other in racing and wrestling. As the oldest, Earnan never hurt his younger brother. As they grew, they became much closer in size and strength and as their wrestling bouts became more evenly matched, the boys learned when to stop and avoid hurting one another.

They shared the daily tasks of the farm and were soon carrying the workload with little coaxing from their mother. In the evenings, or on rainy days Deirdre would read to her children and show them the written words. They listened and learned all she could teach them about reading in the Irish, Latin and a little Greek.

She also taught them to hunt. Meat was an important food and the red deer that populated the farm and surroundings were an excellent source. Deirdre was a capable archer and taught all three of her children how to make and use a bow, how to hunt and how to make the best use of the animal killed; not just the meat, but the bone, hide, antlers, sinew, every bit had a use somewhere.

As the years rolled by, the boys were doing more of the work in the fields, cutting the firewood and bringing home the occasional prized deer. Life on the farm was routine to the four of them and they fared well.

While still youthful and striking as she neared her fortieth year, Deirdre was intent on facing the future solus. She drew the attention of many men, but none seemed to match her memory of Laoghaire. She had her two sons, who grew more like their father every day and her daughter whose dark blue eyes were undeniably the same as Laoghaire's. Deirdre had her children, her religion, her pieces of writings and her memories. These filled her life, and she sought no more than that.

* * *

The air was warm, the breeze cool and the trees seemed to be full of birds engaged in gossip. The five left and walked to the village two miles away. They attended the mass and had small conversations with a number of people afterward. Deirdre enjoyed these Sunday visits with others, and she was making the most of it. Deaglan and Muirin walked around, talking mostly to each other and occasionally to others. Earnan and Conall met other young boys and when the suggestion to start a game of hurling was made, they were both eager to join in.

"This'll be a friendly game," suggested Earnan, as he looked at Conall, "We don't want to break any ribs today, little brother."

Conall grinned in response and said, "A friendly game."

As the day wore on, Deirdre had visited with practically everyone in the village. Deaglan and Muirin were drifting closer to the gate and the boys had played enough to be completely covered in dirt and sweat without engaging in even a single small fight. It was obvious the other boys had no desire to scrap with Conall.

Deirdre saw Ogan and approached him, "Ogan, how is your son? His ribs should be feeling better by now."

Ogan was not smiling, "He stood yesterday, and the pain came back even greater. He is not healing."

"I told you, and him as well, 'Still and calm'," said Deirdre. "It has been but a few days, these things need much longer to heal. Now, he may need even more time." She glared at Ogan, "If he tries to do too much too soon, the ribs will not heal, and he could be all the worse for it. A full turn of the moon, no less."

Ogan was not happy. His son was injured and couldn't help with the chores around their farm and certainly couldn't carry on as the other boys his age were. Unhappy, but accepting Deirdre's words, he replied, "I'll make him sit and wait. Then perhaps you could look again and see if he has healed."

"That I'll do, Ogan. When the moon is as it is now, bring him to the market and find me. I'll be here and we'll look at Ruarc's ribs together." She looked about for her sons and saw them coming in her direction. She waved to Ogan as she turned to walk toward her sons. "We should be goin' home, 'tis time to start the dinner fire and bring in the animals." She scanned the fairgrounds, "Where is your sister?"

"She's walkin' with the tall man again, Mam," replied Earnan as Conall smiled broadly.

Deaglan was easily spotted. He stood taller than most men and a wave and a whistle brought him and Muirin closer. The five left the market grounds and walked back to Gorm Cnoc, Earnan and Conall in the lead followed by Deirdre with Muirin and Deaglan far behind.

* * *

Muirin was as taken with Deaglan as he was with her. He was tall and rugged, like her brothers, and looked as strong as her memory of her father, Laoghaire. Deaglan was a farmer and a warrior, as Muirin's father had been. And just like Laoghaire, he was ready to take up the sword and shield when needed to defend his home, friend, neighbor and tribe.

As he courted Muirin, Deaglan spent time helping her mother with various chores and repairs around their farm. "The roof thatch could use a little work," he proclaimed one fine summer day.

"That it could," returned Deirdre. "I've enough left in my purse to hire someone to do the work before the summer is done." She pointed toward the barn, "Laoghaire had a store of thatch and some poles cut and ready. They're in the barn."

Deaglan smiled, "I have a few days free, if these two boys are willin' to lift and carry, we might be able to have it done by Sunday, if we have enough thatch and poles."

Muirin looked at Deaglan, "You've thatched a roof before?"

"I have," he returned. "More than one."

Deirdre knew the work had to be done, "I can pay you…"

Deaglan cut her off, "A drink of water, a smile on your face and a twinkle in her eyes," he said looking at Muirin, "and I'm well paid."

Deirdre said, "This'll not be a small piece of work. Laoghaire had Tanai with him last time, perhaps he could come again."

"You've two fine strong boys here," said Deaglan, "and it's time they learned to do the thatch."

Deirdre called to her sons. "This fine tall man is going to help us fix the thatch on the roof. You two boys keep your eyes open, watch what he does and help him when he asks."

The boys were curious, they had never worked on thatch before and asked Deaglan what they should do.

"Well now, it'd be a poor job indeed if we didn't check the poles and cross pieces inside first and find any in need of replacing," he said.

They went inside and looked up at the roof poles. Conall wondered how they were set in place and if his father replaced any when he last worked on the roof. "Mam, did Da put any of those poles up in our roof?"

Deirdre smiled remembering Laoghaire climbing a ladder and setting several poles and cross pieces, "He did, perhaps ten poles and all the cross pieces between as I remember. See those there," she said pointing out three poles with two black marks near the wall. "He marked the ones he replaced, you'll see if you walk around and look."

The boys each counted the poles with markings, "Yes, mam, "said Earnan, "Just ten poles have the marks."

Conall stood next to his brother, "Yes mam, ten." He looked questioningly at the roof, "How long did it take to do all that?' he wondered aloud.

Deirdre looked at Deaglan, "we sheltered in the barn while he did the work," she said, "it took him several days to get all the poles and cross pieces ready. He had collected thatch over the years and stored it in the barn, there's probably enough there now to do this bit of work." She looked to the sky, "The rain stayed in the clouds 'til he was done, we can hope for the same luck this time."

Deaglan looked at Deirdre, "Well, the sun is shining now, no better time to get started." He looked at the boys, "First we make sure we have enough thatch for the roof. Are we repairing weak spots or are we replacing the lot?"

The boys looked at the roof and puzzled for a moment when Deirdre stepped closer, "Your Da replaced the thatch the year before you were born, Conall." She looked at Earnan, "And you were only three, so you may not remember." She looked at Deaglan, "I think there are two or three spots where it could use replacing," she turned and pointed to a section of roof, "There, and a little more on the back side toward the barn."

Deaglan looked at the boys, "Well then, do we have enough thatch?"

Earnan started toward the barn, "That we do, in the barn."

Conall hurried to catch his brother and the two laughed and shoved each other as they raced toward the barn.

"You've raised two fine boys," said Deaglan as he and Deirdre watched them disappear into the barn. "I'll teach them all I can, if you'll allow me." He looked at Deirdre, "Laoghaire was a great warrior and a wise man. He taught me a number of things and now, perhaps I can return the favor."

The boys returned, Earnan pulling a hand cart filled with straw neatly bundled and Conall, carrying three poles ready to be used. "Now what do we do?" asked Earnan.

The work went smoothly as Deaglan showed the boys how to remove old thatch and set new in its place. The day's work done, Muirin placed her hand on Deaglan's shoulder, "If you'll wash the dirt and dust off, I'll bring you and your helpers some food and water, or maybe a little honey and milk."

Deaglan would teach the boys more of the ways of living in this rural place. He began with the thatch and as time passed, taught them more about tending animals, plowing fields, repairing buildings, and mending fences. Replacing the daub on the wattle walls and thatching the roof of the roundhouse and barn were tasks that needed tending as soon as they presented themselves. The boys listened, watched, and learned, but always showed an interest in the weapons Deaglan kept close at hand.

Two months into their relationship, Deaglan told Muirin he had a gift for each of her brothers. "What are you givin' my brothers, tall man?" she asked. He showed her and she approved.

Deaglan called Earnan and Conall, "You've both shown interest in the weapons I carry. Weapons you might someday be needing to protect yourselves and your family." He drew his sword from his belt and held it at arms-length, "You're both big, strong boys. This sword I wear may be too large for either of you today, but soon it will fit your hand." He set his sword down and took a bundle from his horses back. He unwrapped the blanket covering two wooden swords, "You learn to use these and when the time is right, a sword of steel will take its place."

"And what of this?" quizzed Conall with his hand on Deaglan's axe. "I would like to learn this as well."

"And so, you shall, boy. One weapon at a time. This axe is very much like the one your father used. He told me where it was made, and I found the armorer who made it when I was in Ceann Coradh a few years ago. He made it to fit my hand and my skill. The axe head is steel and heavy, so when it strikes its target, it strikes hard. The blade is wide and curved, so it can cover more area and cut deep. The tip is sharpened steel to allow a forward thrust. The back side is like a hammer, broad and flat so it will not be lodged in its target. The staff is as long as I am tall, so I can swing it far out, beyond the reach of most others. From top to bottom it is the same height as me. The oak shaft is thick enough to be strong and thin enough to be light, then covered with a wrapping of leather so it will not slip from my hand. Yes, Conall, it is a beautiful weapon, but one that requires a strong hand. The sword and shield will be first, then, when you have mastered them, the axe. But never put one aside in favor of the other. The day will come when you'll need both."

The boys accepted their new wooden weapons eagerly and began to challenge each other. Deirdre, Muirin and Deaglan watched the boys chase each other around the yard and bang their swords in mock battle. They were both eager to learn, both eager to pick up a steel sword, both looking forward to real combat with a live enemy.

"Be very careful, boys," cautioned Deaglan, "A real man with a real sword can kill you in one thrust. You have to choose your battles; know the man you face and be ready for him to be good or to be lucky. It makes little difference if he strikes with skill or luck, if you're not prepared, if you act rashly, you could easily be defeated."

The boys calmed and listened to Deaglan. "Battle is very serious; you win by killing your opponent. There is no second chance, if you fall, you will be killed." The boys listened intently as Deaglan continued, "The axe I carry can cut a man in two. More often my opponent is cut open and I follow with a strike to his neck, sometimes removing his head or a lunge with the pike."

"Deaglan," said Earnan, "why take his head if you have cut him and made him fall?"

"A man is dead when you know he can no longer breathe, much less wield a sword. You put him down and be sure he is dead. A strike with this axe at his neck will usually be enough."

"Should a warrior kill his opponent, then kill him again?" asked Conall.

Deaglan put his hands on the boy's shoulders, "Some warriors will strike their enemy many times after he has fallen. Sometimes because he may not be dead, other times because the victor is angry and sometimes because he is crazed."

Conall looked up at Deaglan, "Do you strike each man again and again?"

"A wise warrior is sure his enemy is dead, then wastes no more time on him. Remember, there is always another looking for an opening, looking to strike at you. Kill, be sure and then look where you cannot see."

The boys were wide-eyed and breathing heavily, listening to Deaglan, "Enough of this talk for one day," said the tall man, "Your first lesson of the sword begins now." He handed each boy a small shield made of wood. "The sword is only half of the weapon. The shield is just as important." Deaglan drew his sword and touched Earnan on his arm near the shoulder. "Your sword is in your right hand and your left is open, thus the shield." He pulled back his sword and said, "As a man attacks you, you must be able to block a thrust, a lunge and a slash." He raised his sword, "Now, Earnan, look at me and think what I may do, I may slash, or I may thrust. What'll you do in response?"

Earnan thought for a second, assumed a position of defense with sword and shield at the ready. "I'll protect myself and be ready to attack."

Deaglan grinned and gently swung his sword toward Earnan's shoulder. Earnan quickly blocked the slash with his shield and stepped in toward Deaglan with his wooden sword ready to strike the tall man in his belly.

"Good, boy," said Deaglan. "Now the two of you practice blocking the slash. Start slow, and as you get used to the movements, move faster." He turned and faced Deirdre and Muirin. "They're fine young boys and I'll teach them as I was taught, if you'll allow it."

Deirdre half smiled, "I know they should learn these things, I know they want to learn—they want to be as their father was, a warrior of the Dal gCais."

"I'll teach them as I was taught by the Dal gCais warriors. I'll teach them as the greatest of the Dal gCais would, if he could be here today." He looked closely at Deirdre, "I was taught by the best of them, I was taught by Laoghaire."

The boys practiced every day after finishing the morning chores and bumps and bruises became a more common occurrence. Deirdre and Muirin often watched, knowing that someday this would not be play, but real. Deirdre knew that day would come far too soon, and the boys would need to be ready.

Deaglan visited frequently, showing the boys more and more each time. After several weeks, he visited with a pair of horses dragging a large log. It was about twelve feet long and more than a foot thick. "Now we will have an enemy, but this one does not fight back," said Deaglan. He led the team of horses to the middle of the yard. The old practice posts were gone, and Deaglan saw where the ground had accepted the old posts, "Boys, dig a hole in the ground, here, as deep as I am tall." He smiled as the boys took shovels and began to dig.

Muirin stood next to him and said with a smile, "Are you plantin' a tree, tall man?"

"No girl, it's to be their constant enemy. I'll teach them how to strike and they can attack this wooden man, not each other." They watched as the boys dug the hole to a depth of six feet. Deaglan then guided the horses, allowing one end of the log to drop into the hole. He turned the horses around and pulled the tree trunk to an upright position. "Now boys, find some rocks and begin to fill in the hole." They dropped rocks and clay in the opening and tamped it down then added water. They drove more rocks into the opening. Again, clay, tamping and water, then more and larger rocks, clay and water until they had filled the hole around the post. "Here boys, this is your opponent. Show me how you would attack, as if he were alive and held a sword bigger than yours."

The boys were tired, but Earnan moved first, slowly approaching the post. Then in a burst, he slashed at the mid-section and quickly stood off to the side and began a second attack to the head. He made five passes at the post striking each time in a different location. "Any one of those blows could have fallen a man, Earnan," said Deaglan. "Now be aware, there's always another man behind you, fresh and ready to attack. You move well, but never stop. And always look where you cannot see. Conall, let's see how you'd fare."

Conall attacked casually, slowly moving his wooden sword to several positions and from each, he lunged or slashed, slowly. Then again, this time quicker and the blows landed with a louder thud. A third time and Conall swung the wooden sword at the head of his wooden opponent. He didn't pause but moved in a circle looking everywhere and again assaulted the post with strikes that nearly broke his sword.

Deaglan put his arms on both the boys and said, "You two are my army, if ever I see combat again, I want you at my side." The three laughed and Deaglan said, "Now if I may, 'tis your sister I've come to see. You two practice, I'll see you tomorrow."

*   *   *

The boys practiced with their wooden weapons, listened and learned from Deaglan and as the seasons flowed past, they grew ever taller, stronger and better with the sword and shield. Both boys were becoming adept with the sword and practice with Deaglan was a serious business. He would move slower than he did in actual battle, but as the boys practiced and improved, Deaglan moved faster and struck harder. These sessions occurred several times each week and each session left bruises and cuts on all three.

Deaglan arrived on a horse drawn cart one day and after a brief visit with Muirin and Deirdre, he approached the boys as they finished their morning chores. "Let's have a match, the two of you attack me, and be aware boys, I'll defend myself." The session was brief, the boys had each landed hits on Deaglan with their wooden swords and he on each of them. "Enough for one day," said Deaglan. "You boys are ready to take another step," he proclaimed as he tended to his arm after their match. He went to his cart and pulled back a blanket. "I took this from a man two years ago in battle. He fought well and I was lucky to defeat him. His sword should be used by another worthy warrior." He handed it to Earnan, "You are the oldest, and the first to earn a real sword." He looked at Conall, "You are the youngest, but fight like a true warrior. Allow your brother the honor of being your elder, and the first. Your sword is already set aside for you, and you'll have it in one week."

Earnan was already moving the new weapon in different positions and striking the wooden post. "I like the feel of this sword," he said. "It's not as heavy as I thought it would be, and it cuts through the air with such ease." He continued to strike at the post as Deaglan and Conall watched.

Conall turned toward Deaglan, "You've honored my brother, and I can wait for my sword as long as you think I should."

"Yes Conall, but while you wait, I have something else for you to try. It's not a sword, but you may find it to be an equal." He moved the blanket on his cart and uncovered a long, wooden staff with iron weights on each end. "This is a staff, you carry it with you wherever you go, move it about from hand to hand, toss it in the air and catch it. Get used to its feel, its weight. Use it to do everything it can, it is an extension of your arms, your hands."

Conall took the staff and looked puzzled, "How will I fight with this stick?"

"It's not the stick, it will be the axe that comes after that you will use. This staff will get you used to the weight, the length, the feel of the axe when the time is right. This will teach you to know the axe without cutting everything around you to pieces."

Conall started to move the staff about and said, "It feels strange, uncomfortable. Are you sure this is what I should do?"

Deaglan took the staff from Conall and said, "Watch and learn." He threw the staff from hand to hand, then suddenly spun it around and tossed it up in the air and caught it without looking. He mimicked a slash, a lunge and a parry as if being attacked. Then he touched Conall's shoulder with the end of the staff and spun it around his back and touched Conall's other shoulder. He handed the staff back to Conall and said, "I learned to use this staff before I learned the axe, my teacher would have it no other way."

As Deaglan spoke, Deirdre came out of the roundhouse. She walked over to Conall and touched the staff Deaglan had given him with a knowing smile. She looked at Deaglan.

Deaglan said, "He gave it to me, taught me how to use it and now I give it to Conall."

Deirdre said, "He went everywhere with this staff, always moving it around, and then when he would practice with his axe, he would spin the axe, toss it in the air and catch it, just like this staff."

This'll break if you strike the post so practice the movement and stop your strike before it breaks. Learn to move with it, to parry a slash and thrust from a sword, learn when to strike and when to thrust. We'll work together with this staff 'til you're ready for an axe of steel."

The boys were thrilled with these gifts and practice seemed to take on a new energy. Their work was completed earlier each day and their practice session lasted longer. "I believe my sons are more warriors than farmers," Deirdre said to Colman, a priest visiting one day as they watched the boys practice. "I fear for their future. Will they live to see their own sons grow to men? I can only hope."

"Deirdre, this land is constantly at war," said Colman. "Your sons are better prepared than most of the men I know to defend their country, their family and their farm." He took Deirdre's hand and continued, "They may march into battle one day and, God willing, they will march home again. I know they live the role of the farmer today, but they will someday be warriors and they must be ready."

Deirdre watched her sons hone their skills and saw their father in them. She was proud of her boys, but still worried for their safety.

* * *

On a bright summer day, Muirin was in the fields checking on the cabbages and Conall was collecting stones to reinforce the rath walls. Muirin wandered close to the edge of the field, near a stand of trees. As she leaned to inspect a cabbage, a wolf crept out of the wood and moved to within 100 feet of Muirin. She saw movement out the corner of her eye and turned to see the wolf moving quicker in her direction. She screamed and Conall turned to see the wolf only 50 feet from his sister. He stood tall and called her name, "Muirin, don't move." He held a stone in each hand as he bellowed at the wolf and charged from near the same distance from Muirin as the wolf. The wolf saw Conall but continued toward Muirin. Conall hurried his pace and raced to intercept the animal before it could reach Muirin. At a mere five feet from Muirin, Conall crashed into the fully grown wolf and the two rolled on the ground. The wolf regained his feet and faced Conall with his head lowered, hackles raised, teeth bared and drool dripping from his mouth. The wolf growled as Conall raised to a position of one knee and one hand on the ground. The wolf stepped toward Conall, gnashing his teeth and Conall responded with a low roar building in his gut. His head slightly lowered, his eyes burning the air between him and the wolf, Conall waited until the wolf leapt toward him. He then came up hard and fast with his hands grabbing the wolf's throat and again the two rolled on the ground. He squeezed the wolf's throat as hard as he could, and the wolf thrashed and kicked at Conall's torso. The fight lasted only a few seconds and the wolf fell limp. Conall raised himself to one knee and continued to hold the wolf's throat. He shook the corpse and let it fall to the ground and stood.

Muirin, still shaking from the attack stepped to her brother, "Conall, you're bleeding, the wolf has…" she paused, and a look of fear crossed her face as she looked past Conall toward the wood.

Conall turned and saw three more wolves slowly emerge from the wood. He turned to fully face them, then leaned down and grabbed the dead wolf's legs, stood and spun around, tossing the dead animal at the three. The dead wolf bounced on the ground in front of the others and Conall picked up the two rocks he had in his hands earlier and started toward the wolves. The animals hesitated then began growling and lowering their heads. Conall was now only twenty feet from the closest wolf, and he hurled one of the stones, striking the wolf on its left shoulder with a loud cracking sound followed by a yelp from the injured animal. A second wolf started to charge and Conall threw the second rock, catching it hard on its right eye. Another telling sound and an accompanying yelp, and the three wolves began to back away.

Muirin's scream had alerted Earnan, and he was fast coming across the open field with a pair of short swords in hand. He saw Conall's injuries and the wolves near the edge of the wood. "Conall," as he handed his brother one of the swords, "Are there more than the three?"

Muirin responded, "One lies dead there, two of those may not live out the day and I've only seen the one other."

Conall began to relax, his face calmed, his breathing slowed, and he looked at Muirin, "Are you alright?"

"I am, 'tis you that needs to be cleaned and bandaged," she said touching the gashes on her brother's chest and pulling him toward the gate. She looked at Earnan, "We should go inside the wall before they find more of their kind and return."

"He what?" exclaimed Deirdre as they walked into the roundhouse. "Wolves? I haven't seen a wolf around here in years." She walked to her son, "Conall let me see these wounds."

*　*　*

Time passed, the story of the wolves was told over and over, eventually deviating from the truth and claiming Conall as a slayer of many beasts. He grew tired of the tale and began denying it ever happened, "I threw a rock at a wolf and scared it. That's all."

Deirdre grew older, her daughter, now a woman, grew ever closer to Deaglan and her sons grew into men. Muirin's wedding to Deaglan took place at the farm after the fall harvest in 990. They moved to Deaglan's home several miles away, close enough to allow frequent visits. The farm was now a lot quieter, Muirin was missed, but they were happy for her. A year after they wed,

Muirin and Deaglan visited Deirdre with news. Muirin took her mother aside and said, "Mam, come this spring, I will call you Seanmháthair."

* * *

39

Earnan was in his seventeenth year and Conall his thirteenth. The two had grown to men, Earnan standing over six feet in height and Conall only a few inches behind. The work in the fields, the constant practice with their wooden weapons and the food prepared by their mother had resulted in two very tall, strong, healthy, young men. Muirin had a daughter, Tuathla, a healthy girl, with the dark hair of her father and his eyes, but the look of her grandmother, Deirdre.

As the boys learned to handle the sword, and the axe, the wooden post in the yard was beaten to splinters and was replaced several times. Earnan had earned his steel sword and practice with Deaglan became a very serious endeavor. A misstep now meant a cut, not just a bruise. Conall also practiced with a steel sword on the post, continuing his practice using his wooden weapons with Earnan and Deaglan.

Deaglan noted how adept Conall was with his wooden axe and one day he handed Conall his weapon of steel and oak, "When the day comes that I have a son, I hope he learns as well as you have. This axe has served me well, but you look to be better than I with it in your hand. It's now yours. Be careful as you use it and we'll continue to practice together with the wood. Use the steel on the post, and never give up on the sword." Conall practiced with the axe every day and the post in the yard lost so many bites to his exercise, it quickly became little more than firewood and required frequent replacement.

Deirdre watched her sons as they grew and learned. They tended the fields, the animals, took care of repairs and practiced at the post. She felt pride in her sons, they worked hard and practiced harder. She also feared the day they would use those skills and she prayed that day was far off. Watching the boys practice one day, Deirdre noticed the supply of firewood was low. She opened the door and called to Conall, "We need more firewood, take your axe to the wood and fell me a tree, boy."

Conall laughed at his mother's words and returned, "Will one tree do, mam, or shall I slay two?"

"One, buachaill, and bring me the larger pieces of the wooden man in the yard."

Conall found humor in his mother's chiding and gladly cut firewood when asked but returned to the post as often as he could.

*   *   *

Roaming bands of outlaws, including Vikings, Celts, Scots and other Irish were not uncommon. Towns and villages were safer than rural outposts and farmers had to be prepared to defend their homes at all times, sometimes by themselves. The boys practiced and planned meeting groups of two, or more intruders. They fought well and Deaglan taught them how to fight as a team, protecting each other's back. They played at combat, learning to complement each other in their efforts. They also established a set of code words for different situations. If Earnan said "right," he would step to his right and Conall could move with him without looking. The words and meanings at times made little sense to anyone but the brothers. Deaglan watched them for several weeks and finally joined in their dance. The three men learned to fight as one unit, moving together, complementing each other and protecting each other's backs. They learned and practiced fighting alone, then with one other and finally as three together.

The desire to do battle in the minds of young inexperienced boys was very compelling. The boys looked forward to the day when all their skills would be tested. What they did not envision was losing a contest. This Deaglan could see in both. "Let us pray you never need to defend your home, boys, but if you do, I know you'll do it well."

Late in October a band of eleven horsemen, riding east, paused at the base of the rise leading to the rath. Two of them slowly rode up the path toward the bridge as the others waited on the road. Earnan and Conall were both in the fields, not far from the house. They saw the riders approaching the bridge and went immediately toward the rath.

"We should go through the loose pickets," said Earnan. "Deaglan may need our help and our weapons are in the house."

The two boys went around the rear of the rath to the loose pickets and clambered through. "It used to be easier, climbing through this hole," complained Conall.

"You're no longer a little boy, brother," said Earnan. "I'm surprised you could fit through at all."

As the boys were coming through the opening in the picket wall, Deaglan, looking through an open door, saw the first rider approach the bridge. He immediately moved to the door and saw a second rider coming up the rise. He lifted his shield, put his hand on his sword and stepped out through the door. Standing outside the roundhouse, Deaglan could see beyond the first and second riders. There were several other horsemen at the bottom of the rise, probably on the road. He turned toward the open door and said, "Muirin, bar the door and take Tuathla to the cave below, then he turned and faced the first rider.

He looked at the man at the gate, the one riding nearer and the others in the distance riding slowly toward him, still several hundred feet away. He moved slowly toward the first man as the two boys crossed the yard to the rear of the roundhouse and in through a back door. Muirin was moving Tuathla to the cave entrance and worriedly said, "Earnan, we have visitors. Deaglan has gone out to meet them."

"Yes, we saw them," returned Earnan.

Deaglan immediately faced the horseman nearest him as Deirdre pushed the door closed and lowered the bar, then she went to the window to close the shutters and watched as Deaglan stopped in front of the horseman.

The rider spoke in the Irish tongue, but poorly. He asked if he and his friends could water their horses and rest a while inside the rath. "This country is full of robbers," he said to Deaglan, "it is not safe to close your eyes and sleep. We would stay the night behind your fine wall and thank you in the morning as we continue on our way to Dubh Linn."

"You are more than enough men to travel safely and rest anywhere you please without fear of an attack," returned Deaglan.

The rider looked about and saw movement in the roundhouse, "a woman is hiding in your house," he said.

You may have water for you and your horses," said Deaglan, "then you should be on your way."

The man strained to see inside the window of the round house, "you should bring the woman out and let us see her," he said with a leering grin.

"Perhaps you should leave now," said Deaglan.

"Or perhaps we will not," said the rider. "I think we will see your woman, she could bring us food and drink," he laughed then drew his sword holding it in a threatening posture. Deaglan reacted quickly as he hefted his shield, grabbed his sword and walked toward the horseman. The man spurred his horse toward Deaglan, raised his sword, and brought it down hard toward Deaglan's head. Deaglan turned his shield, causing the sword to glance to his left, then delivered a return slash to the man's mid-section. His blade didn't penetrate the man's mail but pushed it deep into his ribs.

Deaglan saw a splash of blood as the rider belched a cry of agony and fell to the ground. A second slash to the downed rider's neck finished the match and Deaglan turned his attention to the second rider as he dismounted and charged across the bridge into the open yard on foot.

Earnan looked at Conall "Now we may see if all the training has made us true warriors." They hefted their weapons and moved to the door.

"Buachailli, this is not a game," said Deirdre.

"And today we are no longer boys," replied Earnan as the two gripped their weapons, unbarred the door and moved out into the yard.

Deaglan met the second rider with two vicious blows to his shield and a third in an upper cut that caught the man by surprise and broke his jaw. Before the man could cry out, Deaglan pushed his sword through the man's neck and readied himself for the next attacker to come up the rise and cross the bridge.

"Why are these men attacking our home?" wondered Conall aloud, as the two boys entered the yard.

Deirdre closed the door and set the bar again. Muirin peered out through the partially opened shutter, and they had both strung a bow each and had several arrows at the ready.

All nine of the remaining riders had dismounted and were approaching the bridge. They crossed slowly, carefully passing through the gate and saw both their companions lying in the dirt. They saw Deaglan holding a bloodied sword and began to move toward him, cursing in their tongue, curses Deaglan had heard before.

Earnan and Conall moved out into the yard and went to either side of Deaglan. Earnan moved quickly to Deaglan's left flank where he appeared weakest. Deirdre, watching through the shutter with Muirin, shivered, drew a deep breath, and in prayer quietly said, "Laoghaire, your sons follow your steps," she bowed her head, "Please guide them."

The two boys moved to stand with Deaglan, and he said, "Remember what you have learned." As he had taught the boys, Deaglan looked beyond his two kills and watched as the nine others entered the rath. They walked slowly across the open yard, Deaglan and Earnan, each with a short sword and shield, and Conall with a long-handled axe.

The nine invaders spread out to face the trio. Two men drifted far to the right, away from the others and turned toward the roundhouse. Deaglan quickly scanned the other seven. None were near him or the brothers in size and they all looked old and tired. He gave them no time to consider how to attack. He charged the smallest of the three men directly opposite him, wildly crashing down on the man's shield, stunning him and forcing him a step backward. The man was no match in strength for Deaglan, who immediately spun to his left with a similar blow to another man with no teeth, then turned back to the small man. Another man to the right of the small man had stepped closer and was bringing his sword in a downward motion toward Deaglan's head. Deaglan adjusted his movement and met this man's sword in a loud clash of steel above their heads and quickly continued his sword down on the attacker's shoulder, opening a wound at his neck. The man fell backward, screaming in pain and Deaglan turned his attention to the small man again.

As Deaglan was attacking the first man, Earnan had stepped to his left, turned in on the invader wearing a red shirt at the end of the row of seven, and Conall swung his heavy axe at the other end, breaking a man's shield and sending him to the ground. As Deaglan met the sword over his head, Conall drove the bottom end of his long-handled axe into his first opponent's throat and turned wildly to face a second man with a savage swing of his axe. His aim was high, and he caught the tip of the man's helmet, taking off his head and sending it across the yard.

Deaglan's first opponent, the smaller man, still stunned by the initial charge, stepped cautiously toward Deaglan and received another violent blow to his shield. He again stumbled backward, and Deaglan quickly turned on the second man, meeting his sword with his shield and bringing his sword across the man's thigh. Blood spurted out and the man screamed as he went to his knees allowing Deaglan an open slash at his neck.

Conall reversed the swing of his axe and caught his second opponent between elbow and shoulder to the sound of cracking bone beneath his coat of mail. The man cried out in agony and Conall delivered a killing blow to the man's helmetless head. Earnan had driven red shirt into another man in a green vest, and as the man stumbled, Earnan thrust his sword into the red-shirted gut. A painful groan and the man vomited as he fell forward. Earnan pushed his shield farther forward, blocking a lunge from green vest as he pulled his sword from red shirts gut. His sword came free of red shirt allowing Earnan to tilt his shield and swing his sword at green vest's knee. The cracking of bone and spatter of blood sent green vest to ground cursing and spitting. As he tried to regain footing, green vest slipped on the blood and vomit-soaked ground and Earnan found an opening to his head. A hard swing of Earnan's short sword at green vest's left ear ended his pain. The toothless man had fallen backward from Deaglan's slash and was able to clumsily swing his sword at Earnan, striking him on his leg with the flat of the sword. Earnan fell and Deaglan wasted no time in turning on the toothless man.

As their friends were being killed, the two men who had moved off to the right of their fellows, continued toward the house.

Earnan was regaining his feet, Deaglan turned and looked toward the two men approaching the house. Conall turned toward the house as the door flew open and one of the raiders started to run at the door. He would be through the door before any of the three could reach him and Conall cursed as he began to run at the door. As suddenly as he began his charge, the raider stopped. He could not cry out, nor could he draw another breath with an arrow through his throat. The man was dead before he hit the ground. Just as quickly a second arrow flew from the door and the other man staggered as the missile pierced his coat of mail. He stayed on his feet, stunned and stared at the open door, not seeing Deirdre notch another arrow and draw the bow the full length of her arrow. Conall arrived as the first man fell. He looked at the arrow in the man's throat, then at the second man as the next arrow arrived. Conall was about to dispatch the second man when Deirdre's third arrow struck, and the man fell. Deirdre had already notched another arrow, ready to take down another raider if necessary. Muirin stood next to the door with a sword in one hand and an arrow in the other. Conall smiled at his mother and sister, then turned back toward the scene of his first battle.

The encounter was over. All eleven men attacking the farm were dead. The brothers had scratches, bruises and cuts, but no serious wounds. Deaglan was bleeding through his vest and Muirin rushed to him. As Muirin tended to Deaglan's back and Deirdre cleaned Earnan's leg wound, Conall went out into the yard, stripped the bodies of all but their tunics, putting everything in a pile next to the fire pit and loading the bodies on a cart. As he led the horse drawn cart out through the gate, then down the rise to a small ravine about 100 paces beyond the road, he muttered to himself, "Why do they attack? Why did we have to kill them? He continued to mutter and curse as he off loaded the bodies and left them at the bottom of the ravine.

The clothing and blankets were dirty and smelled worse than an old battlefield. He wanted to burn everything but thought Deirdre or Deaglan might find use for some their things. He left it all in a pile and went back into the round house, "I made a pile of weapons and filthy clothes in the yard," he said to his family, "If any of it is useful, we may keep it, the rest we should burn." He stood looking confused, then turned and went back out to the watering trough. He was feeling an ache in his back and right shoulder as he raised a bucket over his head allowing a rush of cold water to wash over his body taking away dirt and drying blood.

Muirin approached, "Brother, you've a wound in your back. Come in the house and I'll clean it." Conall was tired, still trying to understand what had just happened. They walked into the house, "Why did those men attack us?" he muttered.

Muirin answered, "They look for coin, for weapons, for anything they can carry."

Deaglan added, "They take what they want from those who cannot defend themselves. Here, they may have seen two boys working in the field and no one else. We looked an easy target for them, so they came in and when we stood in their way, they attacked."

Conall sat on a bench and Muirin cleaned his wound saying, "This is deep and will need a stitch or more to keep it closed."

Conall sat still as Muirin pulled the stitches closed on his back. He didn't move, he sat silently and finally said, "They could've asked for food or water, and we would've fed them. They could've worked our fields and we might have paid them. They wanted to take and not give. Now, they're all dead. He sat quietly staring at the door, thinking. This was Conall's first real battle and the glory he had imagined as he grew and practiced was now replaced with the grim reality of battle, blood and death. Senseless death.

* * *

Three weeks later, Conall and Earnan were again in their fields checking their crops when a horseman approached. Earnan nudged his brother and said, "Go to the barn little brother, and I will meet this man at our gate. You have both our swords and shields at the ready."

Conall slowly turned and walked toward the loose pickets behind the barn and did as his brother asked. Earnan walked slowly toward the horseman allowing time for Conall to get through to their weapons.

The man called out to Earnan, "You there, are you the man of this house?"

Earnan replied, "That I am. And who might you be?"

The man wore iron mail covering his head down to his knees. Under the mail was a tunic, over, a leather vest and belt with a sword and a dagger. "Your name, be it Deaglan?" The man spoke with the accent of a north man, a Viking.

"No," replied Earnan, "Tis not."

Conall came back through the gate with his battle axe in one hand, and Earnan's shield and sword in the other. He stopped next to his older brother handed him his shield and sword and looked at the man on horse.

The man spoke again looking at Conall, "You, are you Deaglan?"

Conall smiled, "No your majesty, he's more handsome than am I, and taller."

The man hesitated, "There was a group of men through here three weeks back, traveling from Corcaigh to my home in Dubh Linn. They've disappeared and several people suggested they may be here. They say I should speak to Deaglan."

"I would be happy to go find Deaglan," said Conall, "But I've work that needs doing here."

"Where's he to be found?" asked the man.

Earnan looked at Conall then back at the man, "Well, he's not here."

The man was getting angry and looked back down the path to the property line. Four more horsemen approached. The man turned back toward the two boys, "I'll ask you again, where is this, Deaglan?"

"Are these friends of yours?" asked Conall.

"Answer my question, you insolent bastard," yelled the man.

"Ah, you should watch your tongue, your worship," said Conall. "It's my mother you're now insulting. You may say what you wish about me, but my mother is a saint in my eyes. Now ask me again nicely and I'll allow you to leave sitting up on your horse."

The yelling brought Deirdre to the door of the round house. The man saw her and roared, "Woman, I seek Deaglan, where is he?"

Conall stepped closer to the horseman and pointed the pike end of his axe at the man's face. The smile was now gone, and his voice was deeper, "I've told you to be nice and you are not listening."

The man drew his sword and as he raised it toward Conall, Conall spun to his left putting the axe in a round motion that landed a blow with the hammer side on the man's back, unhorsing him. The man regained his feet, stood feeling the spot on his back where the hammer made contact. He picked up his sword and faced Conall. "Do I have to kill you to find my friends?"

One of the four new arrivals rode through the gate and into the yard. He guided his horse close to the fenced enclosure where twelve horses were kept. He peered over the fence and said, "Inimar, there is Starkad's saddle and blanket. They were here."

The man, Inimar, turned again toward Conall, "Where are they?"

Conall turned his head, smiled again, and in the same deep voice replied, "Well, your lordship, they may be sleeping in the ravine over there." He pointed across road toward a grove of trees and a ravine.

Two other men rode to the ravine. As they approached the crest, Earnan and Conall readied themselves. The five men had separated themselves. One inside the rath, near the horses, over fifty feet from Inimar, two others, near three hundred paces away at the ravine and Inimar with the last of them only a few feet away.

One of the men at the ravine yelled, "They're here. Dead and rotting in the dirt."

Inimar and his companion turned to see Conall and Earnan armed and ready. Inimar charged at Conall and Earnan intercepted him with a blow to his shield. Inimar hesitated and Conall moved his axe to cut down the last man. Earnan delivered a second blow to Inimar's shield, driving him to the ground, and finished him with a final slash to his throat.

The two at the ravine turned their horses and charged toward the gate and the two boys. The man at the coral charged from inside the gate. The two men from the ravine rode close together as they covered the distance to the two boys in seconds. Earnan and Conall charged toward the horsemen on foot and as they were about fifteen feet away, Earnan stepped to his left and Conall to his right. The horseman nearest Earnan had to sit up straight and try to guide his horse toward Earnan. He raised his sword, opening his chest to Earnan. The man brought his sword down as hard as he could and Earnan met the blow with his shield and a return slash to the man's middle.

The horseman to the left of the attackers held his weapon in his right hand and was trying to turn his horse to attack Conall when Conall's axe found the man's left leg and touched the horse's ribs. "Sorry, horse," roared Conall as the man bellowed in pain and reached for a leg that was no longer there.

The brothers now faced the last of the Vikings coming out through the gate. He thought better of further conflict, reined in his horse turned and rode off.

Earnan walked over to Conall as he turned to the man who had remained astride his wounded horse. Conall looked at the man as blood drained from what remained of his left leg and his face showed confusion and shock. As his leg flowed blood, his face paled and life seemed to slowly leave his body. "I meant your horse no harm. Fall here and I'll tend to the animal. Ride off and you'll both die."

The man's eyes closed and opened again; his shield and sword had fallen. He had paled grey, almost white and he groaned, breathed deeply and fell to the ground. Conall walked to the horse, took the reins and led it away, looking at Earnan, "Is that one dead now also?"

Earnan looked at the man, then pushed his sword through the man's neck and said, "Yes."

They dragged the four bodies to the ravine and stripped them of weapon, mail, armor and leather. Deirdre collected the horses and led them to the pen. There were now fifteen bodies. Conall had lined them up next to each other and now began to think about covering them with dirt and rocks. "These bodies stink and have drawn crows and other critters. Perhaps we should load them on carts and carry them farther afield beyond our land where no crops grow. Put them there in the rocks and let God and his creatures devour them."

Earnan nodded in agreement, "We should burn their clothing, put all the horses in the pasture, then hide their weapons and armor."

Deirdre came out of the rath and walked to the wounded horse, stroked the beast's neck and said, "This one needs some attention and perhaps a stitch."

Earnan took their weapons into the barn and brought out a cart, hitched a horse and the brothers walked over to the ravine. They loaded the dead men on the cart and tied them down.

"Mam," said Earnan, "We'll take these men over the far hill and leave them in the rocks. No one ever goes there, and they will be no more than bones soon enough."

Deirdre said, "Take their horses as well and release them in the pasture to graze, they may bring a fair price at the market. I'll stack the rest of their weapons in the barn and start a fire in the yard to burn their blankets and clothes. When you return, we'll finish cleaning this mess and wash away the blood."

The boys led the horses north and east, away from the rath, toward a series of rocky hills. They passed a ridge about a mile from the rath and turned toward the east. Another mile and they were in an area that was covered with large boulders and twisting paths. They unloaded their cargo in the rocks, well away from pathways.

The last of their enemy unloaded and out of sight, Earnan said, "Enough for one day, eh little brother?"

Conall, still quiet, looked at Earnan and said, "When the first of these men came to our farm, I thought they'd leave. I didn't think they'd fight. I didn't want to fight, but at the same time, I did." He looked around the countryside, "Today, they angered me. I remember the fight, but it's not clear to me, I was angry, and I killed them. It was easy, I could have killed two times that number."

They started toward home and Earnan said, "It bothers you little brother, the men you killed?"

"Yes, and no, they attacked us, we had to defend ourselves and we did." They walked on, back up over the ridge and down toward the rath.

As the boys crested the last rise leading to the farm, they could see smoke from the fire-pit in the yard of the rath. They crossed the bridge and walked through the gate where they saw the fire burning the raider's clothes and blankets still smoldering. Smoke filled the sky and as they neared the fire pit, the hearth fire in the house was obvious through the half open door. They walked across the open yard and saw their mother lying in the dirt on the far side of the fire pit, in front of the roundhouse.

"Mam," screamed Earnan. They rushed to her side, but her neck had been cut halfway through.

They both fell to their knees at her side, Earnan reaching for her head, moving it to close the gaping wound in her neck. Conall stared at his mother, her wound, her eyes and he touched her hand. She had been dead since her sons had reached the rocks where the raiders were left and blood had stopped flowing from her wound. Her sword lay in the dirt, bloodied and still in her grasp.

Conall felt a chill in his back and across his shoulders. He stood, fighting back his emotions, his arms tensed, his eyes narrowed, and he scanned the enclosed yard, the barn, the house, the horse pen that now held three horses. He bent to his brother, "Three new horses in the pen, brother. They probably wait in the house or barn."

Earnan, kneeling in a stunned state, noticed a shadow move inside the door to the roundhouse. He turned his head back toward his mother, "the house, little brother," he whispered, "go to the barn and enter from the rear. I'll wait till you're about to open the back door and I'll enter through the front, with this," he took the sword from Deirdre's hand, "our mother's little sword."

Without hesitation Conall stood and walked slowly to the barn, his gut churning and his anger rising. Once inside, he moved quickly through to the door leading to the roundhouse, picked up a sword and shield and quietly crept to the roundhouse. He opened the rear door suddenly and burst into the house. Two men with drawn swords were standing on either side of the front door waiting for the boys to enter and the third lay on the floor, dead. "Earnan," he yelled, "Two are at the door, one is dead. On your left." Conall charged the man on his left with shield up and sword at the ready. Earnan crashed through the door and turned toward the man on his left. Without hesitation the two young men waded into the two Viking warriors fighting as they had practiced, back-to-back, only this was not practice, this was not battle, this was anger and hatred venting itself on the two intruders.

One of the Northmen was close to the door and quickly backed through it. Conall pursued and caught the man before he could reach a horse. Conall's sword opened a gash in the man's back and he fell to the ground trying to cry out. Conall did not hesitate, he brought his sword down on the man's head, crushing his skull and silencing the scream ready to erupt. He turned as the second man came out through the door with Earnan close behind. Conall stood in the man's way and swung his sword hard at the man's shield slowing him enough for Earnan to bring his sword down across the man's back. He fell, still alive, and tried to crawl away. Conall again did not hesitate but brought his sword down hard on the man's neck, almost separating his head from his body.

Conall stood over the man with sword in hand, breathing hard and staring at the nearly decapitated body. He didn't speak; he stared.

Earnan approached his brother, "Conall, he's dead." He looked about the yard, out through the gate. "I see no other intruders." He walked to the gate and pulled it closed, dropped the bar in place and returned to Deirdre's side. "We should take Mam inside." He turned toward his mother and pushed his sword into the ground, "Conall, help me."

Conall looked at his brother, then at his mother, shook his head, dropped his sword in the dirt and walked over to his mother. "Why did they do this? Why kill a woman who was no threat to them?" He looked lost, like a child in a strange place. "They should have taken what they wanted and gone, left her alone," he paused then knelt and moved her head, holding it in place as Earnan lifted her and they carried her into the house. They laid her down on a table. Conall moved her head, closing the wound in her neck. Earnan placed the little sword in her hand again and looked at his brother. "You stay here; I'll get Muirin. We've work to do."

Earnan left on one of the raiders horses and Conall stood next to his mother in silence. She was gone, murdered and a piece of Conall's life had died with her. That morning she was alive, the raiders who attacked their home had been killed and she should have been safe inside their rath. His mind saw the three new raiders attacking the gate, he saw Deirdre take up her little sword and stand in their way. He saw them attack her and he saw her slash at them, killing one. Then he saw the other two descend on her. He turned his head up and roared like a wounded lion, "I should have been here with her." He dropped to his knees and lowered his head. He felt anger, sadness, confusion and a constant wonder, "Why did they kill her?"

He stood, touched his mother's hand one more time and looked about the roundhouse. He looked at the dead raider on the floor, grabbed his arm and dragged him outside. He picked the body up, threw it on the cart still standing in the open yard and added the other two dead raiders. With sword in hand and his axe on the cart, Conall led the horse to the same place the others had been left.

As he returned to the rath gate, he hoped more raiders would be waiting for him and he held his axe in one hand as he crossed the little bridge. The yard was empty, the fire still burning slowly and no new horses in the pen, the air was still, no birds singing or bees buzzing. It was quiet, deathly quiet.

He threw the remaining bits and pieces of the raider's possessions into the fire pit on top of the burning blankets and added more wood. Then he went back into the house and sat with his mother for the rest of the time it took for Earnan to return with Muirin and her family. As he waited, he talked to his mother and prayed for her, looking up and asking why her God had allowed her to be killed this way. Finally, he dropped to his knees as his eyes moistened.

Muirin entered the house, saw Conall standing next to Deirdre's body and walked to her brother. He put his arms around her and held her as she looked at their mother and cried. Then, as Deaglan and Tuathla came in all three stepped closer to Deirdre.

Muirin knelt at Deirdre's side, took her hand, then bowed her head and prayed. She stayed next to her mother as Tuathla and Deaglan joined her. Finally, after a while she stood, "I have to wash her and dress her in her finest. Then," she looked at Conall, "we'll prepare a place to bury her next to our father."

Earnan and Conall left the roundhouse and as Earnan took another horse from the pen, he looked at his brother, "I'll go to Fearghal and her brothers, then find the priest." He mounted the horse, leaned down and touched Conall's shoulder, I'll be back soon, little brother," and he urged his horse forward.

Conall picked up his mother's sword, placed its blade in the fire, then walked out to the place on the hillside where Laoghaire had been buried years prior. He began to dig the grave for his mother next to Laoghaire's. He paused, looked at the markers for his father, his grandparents and great grandparents, and wondered about the things Deirdre taught him about her God and heaven. It gave him little peace, thinking she might be in a place where no one could ever hurt her again. He continued to dig, then, when the grave was dug, he found stones to line and cover it.

Finished this task, he went back into the house, took her sword from the fire and bent the blade, quenched the hot metal and cleaned it until it shone. Muirin had washed Deirdre's body, closed the wound on her neck and dressed her in her finest gown. Then she wrapped her in gauze and set aside a blanket to be placed in the grave for her to lay on.

Earnan returned with Deirdre's father, Fearghal and one of her brothers, Tuama, with his wife, Siomha. They went to her side and knelt in prayer. Then, Fearghal went to Muirin and said, "Her other two brothers will know of this soon, if not already and will be here as quickly as they can."

Earnan approached the family, "I saw a priest in the village, he will be here before mid-day tomorrow. Others will be here also, friends, she had many friends."

Deaglan walked to the grave site where Conall stood in silence. "Conall, there are no words that could ease the pain of this. I can only say Muirin and I are here and feel her loss."

Conall turned to his friend, "Deaglan, you taught me to fight, to kill with the sword and axe, to kill an armed man who would kill me if he could, but not a woman who offers no threat." He turned back to the open grave, "Why did they do this? Why?"

"Not all men think as you do, Conall. To some, killing is a way of life. It matters not who stands before them, man, woman or child. Some men kill who they may and take what they want. When those men attacked us weeks ago, they were here to take whatever sparkled or would fill their bellies. Those few who came later tried to avenge their deaths. Now they are all dead."

Conall turned and looked at Deaglan, "Will I now become such a man?" He paused, then turned toward the rath and the two men walked back in silence.

*   *   *

The sun broke the morning clouds and warmed the air. Birds flew silently by as a procession, led by a priest, made its way to the hillside where Deirdre's grave had been prepared. Her body had been placed on a small cart and was pulled to the grave site by her sons. The priest said several prayers in Latin, then he repeated the same prayers in the Irish. Deirdre was laid in the grave on a blanket and the crowd was silent. Muirin placed Deirdre's sword in her hand, then she folded the blanket over her, and the earth was slowly spread over her body. When the earth was mounded high enough over her, Conall placed large, flat stones over the grave and her family knelt at her side. The three had all been very close to their mother and they all felt anger along with sorrow. As they knelt and prayed, Muirin heard her youngest brother mutter, "I want to kill them all, all Northmen."

The day passed with friends stopping to express sympathy to the three siblings. The consensus was that Deirdre was a good woman who had helped her neighbors in times of need and never spoke an unkind word. She would be missed by more than just her immediate family. After the sun set over the hills to the west and the family went back into the roundhouse, Muirin and Siomha prepared food for the family and Muirin placed some in front of her brothers. "Eat brothers, our mother has been killed, but we are to live. Now eat."

Conall repeated his thought, "All Norse should die."

Muirin touched her brother's shoulder, "Conall, there is Norse blood in many of us. They are not an evil people, some of their sons are, but not all. Be careful, brother, when you curse the men who killed our mam, you do not curse who you are."

Earnan stood, "I am also angry, and I want to kill Northmen, but our sister is right, Conall. We have that blood in our veins as well. The men who killed her now rot on the rocks north of here. We should leave it at that."

"I hear your words, Earnan," replied Muirin as she walked over to Deaglan. "I know you will avenge her death, and I will always be there to stitch you together and wipe your wounds as long as I live but remember what I say. Their blood is in our blood too."

*   *   *

40

As the year passed, the pain of Deirdre's death eased but life on the farm was no longer the same. Earnan and Conall both found themselves practicing with their weapons more and farming less. There were more and more places on the walls of the roundhouse where wattle was exposed, the shutters seemed to remain closed, and the roof once again needed re-thatching.

Muirin visited her brothers and her mother's grave frequently and stayed only as long as Deaglan and her brothers worked on their skills with the sword and the axe. She busied herself cleaning the house, preparing food for her brothers and reminding them of the needed repairs to the daub and roof thatch.

The brothers grew bigger and stronger with each visit. They were both young, but better trained than most men and had proven capable of battle when they defended the farm the year prior. The contest had been difficult, and their success demonstrated their readiness to face the trials of full combat. They talked about going to Ceann Coradh with Deaglan to join Brian and his forces and now they planned the trip, readied their weapons and decided they would turn their livestock over to their uncle, Tanai when the time came.

Time and the practices continued and as Conall passed into his sixteenth year, he had grown to a height of six feet and two inches. Both of the brothers were now very well trained in a number of weapons, particularly the sword and the axe. They both practiced regularly, almost religiously, constantly honing their skills, never satisfied with the progress, they constantly improved under Deaglan's tutelage. Deaglan knew they were ready, more than ready, he thought, they might be better prepared than he was himself.

The spring of 993 brought Deaglan to prepare to leave and rejoin Brian. He took Muirin aside and told her he could not hold either Earnan or Conall back any longer, "Earnan is very good with his sword and Conall has shown much of his father in himself. They are no longer boys; they are men and among the best I have ever seen with their weapons. They have both come to me and asked if they could go with me to Ceann Coradh. I think they're ready."

"I know, Deaglan," replied Muirin, "But they are still my little brothers, and I cannot help but to worry."

* * *

Conall visited his mother's grave regularly and often grew quiet; sullen, after a short while below the oaks. Occasionally, he would walk off toward the hills nearby and stare at the river in the valley below. Sometimes he would walk for half the day, going nowhere and then return home.

Muirin and Deaglan were visiting and Conall asked his mentor, "Those men who attacked our home, do you think they had homes like ours? Or a family, a mother or a brother? Could they have had sisters or little Tuathlas? Could they have had friends like you?"

Deaglan paused, "Conall, does it still trouble you that you killed those men who attacked your home?"

Conall thought and replied, "It troubles me that men kill men over little things. If a man wants the coins in another's purse, he could ask and the other may share the coins with him. If he's hungry he could ask for food or ask for work so that he can earn a meal. Why kill people and take from them? I don't understand. It's not my right to take what isn't mine, even if I could kill the man holding it."

Muirin found the two talking and brought them back into the house. "What are you two talking about, you look so serious?"

Deaglan touched Muirin on the shoulder, "Your little brother asks questions that even kings can't answer. These questions trouble him."

Muirin looked at her young brother, "Conall, what bothers you?"

He began to pace the floor, then he answered his sister, "You're my sister, Tuathla is your daughter, I'd stand against anyone who would pose harm to either of you. Earnan is my brother and Deaglan is part brother and part father to me. You all are my family and I'd face any army that would pose to harm you, but I don't understand why men fight and steal from others. These men would have killed us all just to see if there was anything of value here for them to take." He paused, looked at his sister and continued, "Whatever I give to my family, I'll grow in my fields or make with my hands or earn in labor for another, but I'll not fight to take from others."

"Would you fight if our chieftain, our king, called us to war?" asked Muirin.

"For Brian, I would fight. He honored our father and gave money to help our mother after our father was killed. I'd march with his army against any who would try to take his kingship." He again paced the floor, "Brian may be our king, but he is also family."

*   *   *

When Brian mac Cennetig sailed up the Shannon River to Connacht, later that year, then to Breifne, Ulster and Meath, Deaglan and Earnan were prepared to go and Conall saw an opportunity to serve the man, the king who had been kind to his mother. His size, his strength belied the fact that he was only in his sixteenth year. He stood an impressive six feet and almost two inches more and looked both Earnan and Deaglan straight in the eye. He was growing and gaining muscle every day. He tipped the scales at over sixteen stone and was as hard as a rock. So it was, the three men left their homes and made their way to Ceann Coradh where they joined Brian's army.

*   *   *

Deaglan managed to have Conall and Earnan both assigned to his command. The battles, or more accurately, skirmishes, in which this group would be involved, might match them against opposing groups of twenty to a hundred or more men. Each skirmish was going to be a learning experience for this new warrior. He found himself eager to see battle, anxious to use his axe as he had practiced for so many years, but still questioning why it was necessary. He had seen the consequence of a battle with a few men who came to steal - to plunder. Now he was to see the consequence of armed men, more than a few, perhaps as many as a hundred or a thousand on each side, clashing in a battle that would leave more than half of them dead, hacked apart with swords and axes, and more wounded and dying. He was at once ready to fight and at the same time questioning why men had to treat each other this way. In all his wonder, he didn't think of himself as the possible vanquished, rather he envisioned himself as the victor, unscarred, standing amongst dozens of dead men. He didn't see the blood, the mutilated corpses, the parts of human beings scattered about. He only saw a battlefield, a bright sun in the sky and his enemy scattered about as if asleep, unbloodied.

In the first skirmish, Conall remembered his mother. He could see her nearly severed head and as the conflict began, his anger rose, his axe flew harder and the men who stood before him met an awful end. Heads, arms or legs were slashed, and some cut off with nearly every swing of his axe. Men fell and died as he advanced through his enemy's wall of shields. "Strike, kill and move on," Deaglan had taught the brothers in years prior. There, on the battlefield, Conall saw other warriors take time to desecrate the dead. The fallen were often butchered and Conall remembered more of Deaglan's words, "There is always another man ready to attack you."

He didn't waste time in over-killing his enemy. He moved on quickly to another, often leaving the wounded to the swords, pikes and axes of those following him. The scene was a savage bloody affair. The ground ran red with sticky fluid draining from the dead, the limbless, the decapitated. Conall moved forward, getting angrier as he killed, finally getting to the end of the battle fully enraged. He paused, scanned the field, saw an enemy still living and brought his axe down on the man's head, splitting his skull and spattering red and grey matter everywhere. He stood in the midst of the carnage, looking around as he slowly calmed and changed from the giant slayer of his enemy to the tortured soul trying to understand why he had to kill and why he stood the victor.

The battle was done, and men were gathering to search the field for wounded friends and still living enemies. Conall saw several of the enemy on their knees, cowering before three Dal gCais warriors. The prisoners were suddenly and viciously butchered. Their heads severed and kicked into the mud. Now, he saw the reality of his deed. He saw other men, not unlike himself, being slaughtered, cut to pieces by angry and laughing warriors. He stood silently watching the warriors desecrate what was left of their enemy. He stood, stared, and wondered if this was how he had envisioned it. The glory of battle was not glorious. It was bloody, and it was ugly.

* * *

The king, Brian, had been engaged in the battle and had seen some of it from a high point above the field. He had noticed the large, young warrior, stripped to the waist with no battle paint, his sand-colored hair flowing behind him as he waded through the enemy's lines, cutting down everything in front of him. He asked one of his guards to find out who the young warrior was, "I want to know who he is, where he came from, there is something about him I can't place," said Brian.

Shortly after the battle, the guard found Brian and reported, "His name is Conall, he joined us at Ceann Coradh just a few days ago, he and two others."

"Who came with him?" asked Brian.

"Deaglan mac Aodh, and another, Earnan mac Laoghaire," replied the guard.

"Laoghaire," Brian stood and said, "An old friend. Laoghaire had a son; I think his name was Earnan. Bring these men here, I wish to speak to them."

The guard left and returned with the three warriors. He entered Brian's tent and urged the three forward. Deaglan entered first, "Brian, you asked for us?"

"Deaglan, you have been with me for a number of years now and have fought well," said the battle tested king, "who do you bring with you today?"

"Brothers-in-law, Brian. This is Earnan, son of Laoghaire who fell at Bealach Lechta," he said putting his hand on Earnan's shoulder.

Brian stood and stepped closer to Earnan, "I knew your father, he was a good friend, and a great warrior. I knew he had a son; you have the look of him, and his size." Brian placed his hands on Earnan's shoulders, "I am proud to have you with us." He stepped back and looked at Conall, "And who is this giant of a young man?"

Conall stepped forward and answered, "My mother has named me Conall, I am also the son of Laoghaire."

Brian stood as tall as he could, looked up and said, "Laoghaire had two sons, I didn't know. I knew he had a daughter and one son, and your name, Conall, it is a name known in my family."

Deaglan said, "Yes, Brian. Laoghaire's daughter, Muirin is now my wife, and these are her brothers."

Brian smiled broadly and placed his hands on Conall's upper arms, "Your father was an even better man than I knew."

Conall looked down at the ground, "I never knew him, and he never knew me. I was born in the winter after he was killed." He stood tall and continued, "And you honored him, and our mother, Deirdre. Now we come to stand in his place."

Brian stood between the two brothers and said, "You will come to my tent this evening after you have washed the battle off and join me for our dinner."

The dinner was a feast of different meats and vegetables. The mead flowed freely and the more he drank, the friendlier Conall became. He asked Liamhain, a serving girl, for more venison and she brought it to him. He asked her for more mead, and she brought it to him. When the evening was passing into the next day, Conall asked her to help him find his tent. He staggered to his feet, and she tried to hold him up, but he was near three times her size and two fellow warriors came to her aid.

"He's drunk, Liamhain," said one of the two men. "Where should we lead him?"

"This way," said the little woman, as she walked toward a small hut near the open square. She pulled aside a worn deer hide and pointed at the pile of straw and blankets. "There, he'll rest there till his head clears.

The two warriors made their way back across the open yard, laughing and pushing each other, "A pretty little thing, that one," said one man.

"And himself, too damn drunk to know what sleeps next to him," said the other.

The morning came with a misting rain and a cool breeze. Conall woke and felt the drink from the night before pounding in his head. Liamhain rose to her knees and leaned in close to Conall's face, "You drank more than you should have and now you pay the price.

Conall blinked his eyes and looked at Liamhain, "Where am I?"

"I brought you home with me, or you would have slept in a puddle of your own making," she returned. "Do you feel well enough to stand and maybe even walk?" she giggled.

"Are you mocking me, little girl?" he said as he grasped her arm and gently pulled her to him.

Liamhain smiled, allowed herself to fall nearer and said, "I am, you great ox, and you make a terrible noise when you sleep."

"Then it's a good thing the sleepin's done," he said as he drew her even closer.

The day passed with rain starting and stopping several times and several times thunder and lightning filled the sky. Near day's end, Conall stood and washed himself off with a rain-soaked rag and looked at his tunic, "It's clean," he mumbled.

"That it is," said Liamhain as she stood and wrapped a blanket about herself. "I had to do something while you growled through the night."

The next week was spent in Ceann Coradh, eating, drinking, and enjoying the company of friends. Liamhain and Conall spent several nights together, once more in a drunken stupor and a few more times without mead and a very clear head.

Conall lifted her so her face touched his, "You're a very pretty girl when I've had too much to drink, and even prettier when I've not."

The nights brought more rain and cool air, but they didn't notice. They kept each other warm and unaware of the distant thunder.

*　*　*

Days turned to weeks, then months and years. Conall reached his nineteenth year as Brian achieved rule over Leth Moga, the southern half of Éirinn. When Brian's army began to move once again, Deaglan was given a command of forty-four men including four, more experienced warriors. His company was divided into five smaller groups of nine, each with him or one of the experienced warriors as a leader. The company was to move east of the main force, then parallel their march north and be ready to protect the right flank if an enemy was encountered. They maintained contact with runners and stayed no more than a mile apart as they marched. They met a number of smaller forces, some less in number than their own and some larger. The smaller forces were attacked and destroyed; the latter approached more carefully.

Each battle - every skirmish in which they engaged saw Conall become more confident in his axe. Each encounter gave him more confidence in himself and his fellows. Every day he seemed to grow taller, stand stronger and fight angrier. His comrades took care to stay out of range of his axe and would often push an enemy into his path.

Conall's anger was only quelled when a battle was over and Earnan, Deaglan or another trusted friend approached him. His anger and his temper had earned him a reputation as a madman. A man to be far away from in battle.

A man the enemy would hear about and view as a champion, one to be challenged in single combat, if you had the courage.

The smaller battles were becoming less exciting and Conall seemed to relax, lose his concentration on the force before him, but his anger never calmed as long as he saw an enemy. He attacked with the same ferocity, going straight on at an opposing shield wall with powerful swings of his axe. He disliked attacking a foe from cover always wanting to face his enemy and allow them to test their skills. He was proud of his ability with the axe and in combat, he justified his pride.

Earnan and Deaglan both saw the changes starting in Conall. They worried that his disregard for his own safety would be the death of him. As he engaged in struggles with other men, he took chances, often leaving his back uncovered, open to the last efforts of those he defeated and stepped over, depending on the men following him to finish a kill. He fought with great abandon, not seeming to care if he lived or died. As a result, he was frequently wounded on his blind side or back. He walked away from every encounter, often cut and bruised, but always the victor, never the vanquished. Fortunately, the wounds were small, but the scars mounted. The aches and pains of healing and living with a body cut and battered on a regular basis, grew daily.

Still, Conall fought with a ferocity greater than any other man, but his wounds forced him to rest more frequently as he took longer to recover.

Taken to a physician for treatment, Conall protested, "I did not come here to hide in a tent," he said to his brother, "I want to be in the battle, not on a pallet."

* * *

Deaglan led his warriors parallel to the main force. At times the distance between them grew and at other times fell to less than the intended mile. As they approached a river crossing, a ford was found east of their position. This would take them near a half mile farther away from the main force.

"Take half our number to the ford and cross," Deaglan said to Earnan, "Then come back to that position," he said pointing across the river. "Once you are secure there, the rest of us will follow."

Earnan took two of Deaglan's lead warriors and their men, including Conall, and did as Deaglan ordered. When in position they signaled to the remaining force south of the river. Deaglan then led the second half of the force to the crossing. As the northern half of the force was waiting for their fellows, scouts moved out ahead and returned with news that the main force was having difficulty crossing the river and less than half their number had completed the ford. The second scout returned with news that there was an enemy force of about two hundred men marching south, directly toward them. Deaglan and his contingent were still in the fording process, so Earnan sent a runner to the main army asking for another band to help meet this enemy force. He also sent a runner to Deaglan to tell him what he was doing. The first runner returned saying that the main force was also facing a threat and they could only spare fifty men. Earnan decided to establish a defensive position where they could quietly wait for Deaglan. He had a total of seventy-one men, including himself. He sent a runner to Deaglan with the message, "We have formed a line across an opening and will draw the Norse in toward us. If you move north before coming west to our position, you will find their backs to you and our backs to the river. Wait until they attack us and are committed to our direction, then attack their rear with your twenty."

Earnan and Conall moved to the middle of their line and with thirty on each side, they waited. "Sit and rest, drink some water and check your weapons. These Norse outnumber us and we need every advantage we can gain. They should be tired marching through this heavy brush, we will be rested."

Deaglan heard the runner and hurried his men. "We are running to a fight, but we run quietly." His force completed the crossing and hurried to the north as Earnan suggested and turned west. Soon they neared the Norse as they moved south. Deaglan cautioned his men, "Quiet men, they pass near us. We will wait until they have positioned themselves to attack Earnan. Be ready to take their rear. Javelins and slings first, then the sword."

As Earnan waited, a runner came from Deaglan's force, "Our men are behind the Norse. We are ready."

"We wait here until they have committed their forces straight ahead," said Earnan. Once they begin to move ahead in an attack, it will be difficult to turn and fight on two sides. We'll have them."

Conall listened and stood in the middle of their line. "We should try to look as if we are less than 70. Let us move half our number into the clearing ten paces. The rest will stay hidden here and let them see us. Then we step backwards as if in retreat and encourage them to attack before they rest."

Earnan told half the men to lay low in the trees and half to stand and move into the opening. "Now we look about thirty, hardly a threat to their two hundred. When they see us, we will move back."

Conall grinned, "Let them come, brother, I will drop to one knee 'til they are closer. Let them come." He moved forward and knelt on one knee with his axe on the ground next to him. He would be visible to the approaching force as they entered the clearing.

Deaglan's group rested and waited for the Norse to pass and begin their attack. "They will pass by near enough to hear us if we speak, we must remain silent."

The Norse reached the clearing and saw the kneeling Conall and several of the Dal gCais. They stopped and waited for a decision from their leader. It didn't take long, the Irish were turning and heading into the wood. Immediately the Norse began a charge across the open field.

The few Dal gCais retreated a few steps toward the wood and the forming Norse shield wall broke apart as they began to move quicker across the clearing in pursuit. As the Norse front line crossed the clearing in a run and their rear ranks joined in the attack, Earnan and the others in his force of thirty stepped out of the wood and faced the Norse. Then, as the first of the Norse came into range, the Irish loosed their javelins and stood ready with sword and shield. Immediately, the rest of the Irish under Deaglan charged from the wood, attacking the Norse rear, throwing their javelins and casting darts and stones. The Norse were not in their controlled attack formation and the Irish were in their element causing mass confusion.

Conall stood with axe in hand and a short sword in his belt less than thirty feet from the first of the attacking Norse as Deaglan and his twenty men broke from cover. The clash of swords in the meadow and Conall coming to his full height in the middle of his line slowed the charge of the Norse. He attacked the middle of the Norse line with his axe, breaking a shield and sending a man to the ground. The pike end finished the man and Conall brought his weapon up in a round motion, connecting with another shield. This man was as tall as Conall, and strong. He blocked the axe and followed with a slash of his sword. Conall rotated, parrying the sword with the handle of his axe and a blow from the dull end to the man's head. Then, a turn and the axe found the man's right shoulder, pushing his mail into his chest in a great splash of blood.

Earnan had engaged one Norseman, and another attacked him on his left. He blocked the second man with his shield and stepped back to avoid a slash from the first. Ronan had picked up a javelin when he saw the first man begin another move toward Earnan's open side. He was close enough and heaved the javelin into Earnan's attacker and again drew his sword to face another.

Conall was at the center of their line and was given a wide berth. He caught two men completely unaware and then faced another large sword-wielding man. The Norseman brought his sword down hard on the oak and steel shaft, splintering the wood and bending the steel shaft. Conall returned the slash with a wide and clumsy swing of his damaged axe. It was of little use in its current condition, and he moved his left hand up to the axe head, drew a sword with his right hand and met the large man's second slash with his sword. A swing of the broken axe at the Norseman's belly snagged a clump of mail and pulled the man to his right. Conall then swung his sword at the man's open chest and brought him to his knees, bleeding profusely.

The engagement was in Deaglan's favor as six more Norsemen fell to the ground. The battle was all but over and Conall was getting angrier with each minute. He hacked at another man with his sword and delivered a final blow to the man's head after he was dead. He turned, looking for another challenge, and seeing a wounded Norseman starting to rise, he swung his sword as hard as he could, severing the man's head, and sending it ten feet away.

The battle saw near forty of the Norse fall from javelins and stones before the first swords clashed and another twenty or more before the first of the Irish fell. As Conall's axe took a man's arm off at the shoulder, the battle was turning in their favor. The leader of the Norse was on horse and very visible to all. A young warrior saw him and killed him with an arrow through his neck. The loss of the leader disheartened most of the Norse and though they fought, they fought poorly. In the end there were twenty-four Norse prisoners and near one-hundred-eighty dead Norsemen. The Irish losses were sixteen dead and ten more wounded.

"Conall, we are done, this day is now won," said Earnan.

"When they are all dead," replied Conall as he turned looking for another living Norse.

Conall looked around and saw the bodies of stabbed, slashed and hacked apart dead. He also saw his comrades, his friends, standing and screaming their praises. "We have won, we are invincible."

Deaglan came through talking to the men. They were told they could take anything they wanted from the dead enemy. "Find a better sword, shield or spear. They no longer need their purses or their daggers. Take anything. But remember, whatever you take, you must carry."

Conall saw nothing he wanted and turned to walk away when Deaglan called to him, "Conall, here take this purse. It holds copper coins you can use."

"Steal from the dead? I didn't come to steal. I came here to kill." He started away again.

"Conall these men would have killed you and taken everything you have. That's how this works. You win, you take what you want. You lose, and all you have will be taken or go to rot."

Conall listened and hung his head as he walked away. He went to the center of the main battle and found Earnan. "Brother, how did you fare?"

Earnan looked up and saw his younger brother covered in blood and carrying his broken axe, "Conall, are you alright, were you injured?"

Conall looked at his arms and seeing the blood he replied, "Not my blood brother, I am well." He reached out for Earnan's hand, "Let's make a camp and clean the blood and bits of our enemy from our backs."

Earnan laughed, "Yes, did you take anything from the field, brother?"

"Like another man's purse?", he quizzed. "No, I want nothing to do with taking from those I kill."

Earnan moved three purses to his other hand and the two walked to the river where they washed the blood and dirt from their bodies. Conall was quiet as the two found their way to their camp. Deaglan was there with Ronan talking about the day.

Deaglan saw the brothers approach, "Earnan, Conall, your group fought well today. We lost only sixteen men and have killed all of the Norse. It's a good day."

Conall had calmed and replied, "Sixteen of ours and two hundred of theirs. Dead. All dead." He walked away with his head down, muttering, "That is a good day. Why?"

* * *

The agreement between Brian and his old rival, Máel Sechnaill, wherein they decided that Máel Sechnaill would retain the title of Ard Ri and rule over the north half of Éirinn and Brian would be given rule over the southern half of the island would not last. The next few years saw a rise in tension between Brian and the kings of Dubh Linn and Leinster. The rebellious kings raised armies as they conspired against Brian and the High King, Máel Sechnaill.

* * *

41

999 AD Leinster, Éirinn
Cath Ghleann Mama … Battle of Glen Mama

Conall continued to grow and by his twenty-first year he had reached a height of six and a half feet and balanced the scales at nearly twenty stone. Heavily muscled with broad shoulders, thick arms and legs and a narrow waist, he stood like something carved out of stone. His long sandy hair reached his shoulders, and his dark blue eyes were set deep below a heavy brow. His hands were large, gnarled and powerful, and he wielded his sword and axe as if they were twigs. Neither his good friend, Deaglan, nor his brother, Earnan, stood as tall or as broad. Though his arms and back were covered with scars from battles fought over the last five years, none of the wounds had been deep enough to keep him from battle. His apparent continued attitude of not caring if he lived or died had probably served him well, rather than poorly. He freely swung his axe and sword in battle, finding flesh and bone more than steel or wood and men fell before him like so much wheat at harvest. Killing became a matter of ease with Conall. He waded through shield walls and masses of enemy foes leaving blood, severed limbs and corpses in his wake. In the end, he killed the enemy still living, but he rarely desecrated a body. "They fought and died for what they believed," he said, "I will leave it at that."

He had been to Westmeath with Brian in 996, Clonfert in 997 and now in the summer of 999 he again joined the assembly at Ceann Coradh. Life was relatively easy, time was wasted simply sitting about, eating, drinking, telling stories of past battles and growing soft. Earnan, Conall, Deaglan and several other warriors took up their wooden swords to practice their craft less and less. "We haven't seen real battle in too long a time," complained Earnan, as he poked Deaglan with his wooden sword. "We have won in days past because we were prepared, ready for hard challenges."Deaglan looked at his two constant companions, "You think we are not ready to meet real warriors in battle?"

"I think we should train harder, as if we were about to meet our greatest enemy," returned Earnan.

"Then I have taught you well, Earnan and now you teach me," said Deaglan.

"What say you, Conall," said Earnan.

"As we have done before, we should practice every day," he returned with a smile. "The little aches and pains become more as we do nothing and less as we do more."

Earnan looked at his brother, "I think I understand …"

Deaglan laughed, "I've taught you both well."

The practice sessions began with some great huffing and puffing as all three became more aware of their need to exercise their craft. "Simple things first," said Deaglan, "as they found their wooden weapons and began to test each other.

Deaglan and Conall were moving in slow motion, testing their ability to cover an exposed side as they looked for an opening on their opponent. Conall raised his sword to come down on Deaglan and Deaglan raised his shield in defense. Earnan watched as Conall struck Deaglan's shield when a voice behind him said, "You've left your side open to his sword," The tall warrior stepped closer, "Bring your sword around to your right and open his chest or meet his sword before he strikes you."

"Well said, Murchad," said Deaglan as he lowered his shield and stood to greet an old friend. "I heard you have a new son. Has he a name?"

Murchad extended his hand to Deaglan's shoulder, "I do, Deaglan and his name is Tiordelbach." They both turned toward Conall and Murchad said, "And these are the sons of Laoghaire; Earnan or Conall, I presume."

Conall stepped forward with a knowing look on his face, "You stand next to my brother, Earnan and I am Conall" he said lowering his wooden sword to his side. "And you are Brian's son. I've seen you but we've never met."

"No, Conall, you and I have never met, but this one, Earnan I met over twenty years ago. My father had given me a gift to bring to your mother, I remember a girl and a little boy standing next to her. I assume that boy was you."

"It was," returned Earnan, "And the girl, Muirin is now Deaglan's wife."

Murchad turned to Earnan, "You've grown well, I have heard stories of you and your brother. Some from my father." He picked up one of the wooden swords, "May I join you three in this exercise?"

Deaglan handed him a shield and said, "You're more than welcome. We move slowly, learning the movements at first then as we know what we should do, we move faster."

Murchad touched Deaglan's shoulder and said, "The movement you just did, allow me to show you what I meant."

Conall stepped back and placed his sword on his shoulder. Deaglan stood in front of Murchad, and he began by raising his sword over his head. Immediately Deaglan raised his shield in a defensive movement and Murchad began to bring his sword down slowly toward Deaglan's shield. Then, suddenly he changed direction, circling Deaglan's shield and slashing across toward Deaglan's mid-section. His wooden sword touched Deaglan just below his ribs and Murchad stepped to his right out of range of Deaglan's sword.

Earnan said, "I think you should step to your right as you change direction with your sword," He looked at Murchad.

Murchad thought for a moment and said to Deaglan, "Again." This time he did as Earnan suggested and as his wooden sword touched Deaglan's ribs, Murchad smiled, "Faster this time."

The session went on as the men made little adjustments to their movements and soon all four were grinning as they sat and looked at each other. "A good session," said Conall.

"What can we try next?" asked Deaglan.

Murchad picked up his two short swords and felt the movement in his hands, I have a problem with a long sword against these two shorter swords."

All four again picked up their wooden swords and examined their movements, again more corrections as they moved faster and faster. They continued until the sun passed behind a distant mountain to the west and they walked back to their tents.

* * *

The summer passed in uneventful fashion and as the leaves on the trees began to change color and fall from their branches, word reached Ceann Coradh of the rising unrest in the east. The two kings, Sigtrygg Olafsson, and Máel Morda, prepared to lead their assembled army in rebellion against Brian and Máel Sechnaill.

The response from Brian was quick. He called his army together and marched nearly 100 miles across the island toward Dubh Linn. In late December, the two forces approached each other in the narrow valley of Ghleann Mama.

* * *

Conall's hatred for the Norse continued to inspire him to fight and his disregard for living made him look death fearlessly in the face. He fought what stood before him, not behind. As he carved his way through a battle, others followed his lead and protected his back. The dead from his axe were often mutilated by his following and anyone still alive in his wake was hacked to pieces.

He met more Irish in combat than Norsemen, but he still fought with the ferocity and abandon that had earned him a reputation as a great warrior; an angry man who was merciless in battle and cared little for his own safety. He repaired his axe with new oak and had a smith wrap iron bands around the oak, giving the axe greater weight and greater strength against damage. He completed the repair by wrapping the handle in leather strapping to better fit his hand. In battle, he used the axe more than the sword, but he remembered Deaglan's words from years before, "Never put one aside in favor of the other. The day will come when you will need both."

As Brian's army approached Dubh Linn, they met the combined forces of the Leinsterman, Máel Morda and the Norse king of Dubh Linn, Sigtrygg Olafsson. The two opposing forces faced each other across a small open area. While still far apart, the warriors on each side prepared to join in battle. Shields were checked, mail secured, helmets strapped on, and swords raised.

While preparing for the battle, Deaglan offered Conall paint to decorate his face and body, "It will scare them to see you painted like a wild beast."

Conall sat calmly and said in a quiet, but deep voice that resembled distant thunder, "I am a wild beast, my friend. I don't want to frighten them away; I want them to come closer so I can kill them. All of them." He stood, removed his shirt, took his axe in hand and walked toward the front line moving the axe in exaggerated motions, testing his grip on the new leather strapping.

Two walls of shields formed, and insulting jeers drew the two forces closer together until the kerns saw the rear lines of their opponents were in range.

Javelins, darts and stones were hurled by the kerns aimed at the rear ranks beyond the shield walls. The warriors in the front lines were close enough to reach out with spears and jab at the other's shields. The insults and savage screaming reached an apex and as shield touched shield the battle began in earnest. Spears poked between shields and swords crashed down on metal, wood and flesh. The heavy axe in Conall's hands swung hard at a Norse shield, splitting it in two, leaving the man behind exposed to a forward thrust. Conall quickly pulled the pike from the dead man's heart and stepped through the gap created by the fallen man. He swung the axe at shoulder height and caught two men peering over their shields. An expression of calm on his face belied the rage inside and Conall stepped again into the mass of Norse warriors. Earnan, fighting to Conall's right saw the opening in the shield wall and followed his brother through the line, yelling to his brother, letting him know where he stood. As when they were boys practicing with Deaglan, the two fought back-to-back. The gap widened, more Dal gCais poured through and the battle favored Brian's army. The fighting raged on and men, now slashed open, some armless or headless fell on both sides. Deaglan was twenty yards to the left of Conall and Earnan and surrounded by Norse. Conall stood above most men and could see Deaglan's fight going poorly. He yelled to Earnan, and both moved in unison toward Deaglan shouting their coded words back and forth as they continued to hack at the enemy. Now only ten feet apart, Conall yelled to Deaglan and the brothers turned together cutting through the last of the Norse between them and Deaglan. Together, the three immediately spun into position of protecting each other's back and resumed their assault on the Norse surrounding them. They had not practiced the strategy in a few years, but the three fought in a triangle as if they did it every day.

The shield wall of the Norse and Leinstermen shattered, and they split their defenses into three groups. Each group tried to retreat to safety but were cut down in the rout as they approached the river.

Once again, Conall fought with the abandon and ferocity that left him cut and bruised at the end of the day, but very much alive. As the battle waned, Conall continued to show no mercy. He only stopped when no enemy would come near him. As the wounded were being helped and dead were being collected to be taken home, Conall continued his search for any living enemy whom he could kill.

"Conall, the battle is done," said Deaglan, "We have won, and it is time to celebrate."

Conall, still covered in blood and dirt, turned toward his friend, "Brother, drink the mead for me and sing the praises of today's heroes, I will finish what I started and prepare for the next battle."

"Conall, you have done more than any other in this victory. You should come with me, show yourself, allow our fellows to hear of your deeds," said Deaglan.

Conall relaxed his eyes and approached his mentor, "My friend, I don't do this for the praise of others." He smiled, patted his friend on the shoulder and walked back to the camp and a trough of water.

Deaglan walked with him and stood as Conall lifted a pail of water over his head and washed it over his face. Then another over each shoulder. "You are cut," said Deaglan, "Your wounds should be cleaned and bandaged."

Conall poured more water over his body until the blood and dirt were washed away. "I'll see the physician after he tends to those more seriously wounded. I'll live 'til then, my friend."

Deaglan laughed and said, "Let's find Earnan and maybe he can talk you into a bandage and a stitch."

They wandered about the camp looking for Earnan. They paused, asked one of their fellows and he pointed them toward a physician's tent. They entered and found Earnan being tended to by an old man. His wound looked serious, but not life threatening. As the physician worked on him, Earnan bellowed, and cursed the little old man.

"The pain will go away slowly, my big friend and perhaps you will not curse me anymore," laughed the little man. He turned and saw Conall and Deaglan. "Ah, two more?"

"No," replied Conall. "It's my brother you treat, and we've come to see. I see he still has a voice."

"Yes," said the little man, "and his life. Though I fear his days as a warrior may be through."

Standing nearby was another man, Ronan. Deaglan recognized him and asked, "What happened to Earnan?"

"After the three of you cleared the field about you, Earnan moved in my direction. He fought well and kept me alive with a swing of his sword. We were on the left flank, separated from our group by only a few feet, but enough to be attacked from two sides." Ronan looked at Conall, "Your brother cut down an enemy about to remove my head, and for that I'm grateful." He looked at Earnan, "These people will help him with stitches and bandages, but, as the physician said, his wound is deep, and he may not be able to join us in battle again."

Deaglan looked at Earnan, then back at Ronan, "How did it happen, Ronan?"

"We were regaining our hold on the flank, Earnan had two men in front of him and I was on his right side with one other. My man wielded a hammer, and I went down from a hard strike. I was stunned and the man had his hammer about to crush my head when Earnan turned, charged and pushed the man aside, then as he finished him, another struck Earnan from the left, cutting deep into his leg and yet another caught him with the flat of his sword on the side of his head. I was still on the ground and able to slash at Earnan's assailant, taking his leg and finishing him with a second stroke." Ronan paused, "Earnan's wounds to his arm and leg wound are deep and he cannot walk as yet, but the stroke to his head only dazed him and thank God made him appear dead. His other wounds are small in comparison, but I fear our season is over. Earnan may not be able to walk again without a crutch, and I will help take him home."

Conall went over to his brother, "Earnan, this physician thinks you will live to see another day, but your fight is done. You're going home to our farm where you can raise cabbages, turnips and chickens."

Earnan was awake, groggy, and in great pain and struggled to say, "We won this day, brother and you are well?"

"A cut here and a bruise there, but well, brother," he replied. "Now rest and ready yourself for the journey home." Conall turned to leave with Ronan and Deaglan when the old man, stopped him.

"You are Conall, I've heard men talk about you. You are a great warrior, but these wounds on your back must be cleaned and bandaged. Come with me." He led Conall across the tent where he inspected the deeper cuts and placed a stitch where needed and bandaged the wounds. "It's my honor to help a warrior like you, Conall. Stay well and I'll put clean bandages on these wounds tomorrow. You must do that each day until they heal." The old man reached up and patted Conall on his shoulder, "Your brother will live, but he'll find walking difficult. He will need a crutch for a while, but perhaps he'll be able throw it away one day. He is also a great warrior, you two have fought with bravery and honor. Stay well, my giant friend."

The next day, Brian's army took Dubh Linn with no effort and began a sack of the city. Conall and Earnan decided to prepare for the trip home and Deaglan was looking forward to seeing Muirin.

Over the next three days Conall had his wounds checked and his bandages replaced daily. Earnan was finally able to sit up and talk in spite of the pains in his leg, his arm and the bandage around his head.

"They tell me that I may have trouble walking or holding a sword for a while, brother, and riding a horse is out of the question until this leg heals. If I am to go home, it will be in an ox cart, on my back."

Deaglan, laughed, "I've already found a cart and a horse to pull it, or us. One horse, one cart, four men." He stood, picked up his weapons and turned toward the others, "The day is young, whenever you're ready, we can leave."

Earnan was stretched out in the bed of the cart, Conall sat with him, and Ronan sat with Deaglan up top with the reins. The four warriors left the camp moving south and west toward home.

Conall and Earnan arrived at the farm and the roundhouse was quickly rearranged to allow Earnan a place to rest near the small fire pit. Deaglan and Ronan headed to Deaglan's home where he would explain the situation to Muirin, knowing she would want to travel back to see her brother. Ronan's home was a short walk from Deaglan's, and he left the horse and cart for Deaglan, Muirin, and their children to go back to see Earnan and Conall.

Muirin was happy to see her husband and pleased that her brothers were both safe at home. She was concerned about Earnan and insisted on a trip back to see him as soon as possible. "I'll see my brother and be sure the physician has done his work as he should," she said with authority.

Deaglan watered the horse and wiped it down, "We'll wait while the horse rests, then we'll go."

*   *   *

Arrival at their home was met with the stark realization that the farm needed tending and the winter would not be spent resting. Conall set about immediately patching the openings in the walls and collecting firewood for the pit inside. Earnan was restricted to his bed as Conall busied himself cleaning and arranging the house.

"Sure, and if I don't clean the place our little sister will complain from dawn 'til dusk," said Conall. "I've faced many a hard man in battle, but I have no desire to argue with Muirin."

Earnan laughed, "I understand, little brother. I wouldn't want her to be scolding me either. She may just boil some soup and say we're on our own and leave."

Conall paused, "No brother, she'll fuss over your wounds 'til you're back workin' the fields and thatchin' the roof. Then she'll go home and feel good about it."

Soon, Muirin was walking in through the door with Tuathla and Ciaran close behind, "Well now, what have we here?" She looked at Conall, touched his arm, then the bandage on his back and looked at Earnan. "Brother are you feeling pain?" She walked toward Earnan.

"Muirin, I'll trust your judgment more than the physician's that bandaged me," said Earnan with a forced smile. "But first look at our little brother, he's been cut and battered as much as I and he's still walkin' about."

Conall grinned as Muirin took a look at his arms. "Those bandages are filthy," she said, "We'll change them, but first, there's not enough wood for a decent fire." She looked at her husband, "if you don't mind." As Deaglan went out to the yard, Muirin inspected the few iron pots in the house and handed one to Conall, "Would you please clean this out and get me some fresh water, little brother?" She then went to Earnan and sat beside him. "I'll look at these wounds now, brother."

Conall took the pot and went out to the well. Deaglan was coming back with an armful of cut firewood. As they passed, Deaglan said, "Tis good to be home again, Conall."

"It is that," replied the quiet giant, "it is that."

*   *   *

42

1001 AD Munster, Éirinn
Athruithe … Changes

As the winter passed, Earnan improved each day. He knew he would never recover completely, but he was determined to regain as much mobility as possible. He walked with a definite limp, at times with a crutch, and his right arm was constantly in pain, severely restricted in movement. He tried daily to hold a sword again, but the strength needed to grip the sword firmly was gone. Finally, Earnan resigned himself to the fact that he was now going to be a farmer, not a warrior.

The coming of spring was announced with lush green growth on the trees, blue flowers blooming on the rise outside the rath and birds courting mates. Conall had spent his time over the winter with farm repairs, rest and constant exercise with his weapons. He frequently visited the hillside below the oak trees where the graves of his family kept vigil over the stream and fields below. There he would quietly talk to his mother and look to the clouds, as if waiting for answers to his many questions.

The old post in the yard was replaced and beaten to splinters twice before the spring rains stirred the blossoms. Conall felt the aches and pains of older wounds with slight twinges in his shoulders and more time required to stand full upright in the morning. He learned to exercise every day to keep his arms limber and strong.

"You've not lost a step, brother," said Earnan as he watched Conall move about the post. "But now you will have to train someone else to fight at your back," he said leaning on his cane. "My days as a warrior are done, brother."

"Earnan, watch me as I move," said Conall, "Tell me if I could do better." He moved around the post as if in battle and struck the post with several hard blows.

Earnan watched and noticed Conall moved in a way that left his right side open for a moment. "Brother," he yelled, "I could strike your ribs as you finish that arc with the axe. Your arm is high, and your side is open."

Conall stopped and repeated the last movements slowly.

"There," yelled Earnan, "there you are open."

Conall repeated the movement several times, each time lowering his arm a little until Earnan said, "Yes, now you are not open."

The brothers worked together with Earnan watching and correcting movements, helping Conall improve. The work they did each day gave Earnan the feeling of still being an effective warrior and Conall's skills grew with each session.

As Conall made the final preparations to travel to Ceann Coradh, Deaglan and Muirin arrived. The children were now old enough to travel on foot and the trek from their home to their uncle's was an adventure for both. This visit brought another, a close friend of Muirin's. Her name was Grian, a small woman, with bright green eyes and flaming red hair. Her slight figure was misleading as she had carried Cianan on her back a good portion of the trip and hadn't missed a step.

Conall had prepared his weapons and was sitting with his brother. "I've cut the ground and seed can be sewn any time now." This was to be the first time Conall would leave without his brother. "I'll miss you, brother, your teaching and your sword. When I return, we'll make more plans for the farm and talk about what the future holds for us both."

"Brothers," said Muirin, "I see the fields are plowed and the stock out to pasture. You have been busy, and now I have less to do," laughed Muirin. She again touched Conall on his arm, smiled and went to Earnan. "Your leg, Earnan, does it hurt today?"

Battered and now crippled, Earnan was not about to admit defeat. "I can stand and walk, little sister," he replied like a true warrior, "I walk out in the yard every day as Conall practices at the post," he said, rising to his full height. "But I fear my life will be contained on this little farm. The battles of yesterday are that, yesterday. Today and tomorrow will be spent tending sheep and crops." He walked to the door and turned toward his sister, "I can walk, not run. I can lift, not carry. I will do well enough with help from a cart and a cane." He turned again and walked out to the yard.

Muirin followed Earnan and caught him at the watering trough, and she could see he was feeling the desire to go with Conall and Deaglan. To march with the warriors and see battle again. "Earnan, you have stood tall all your life, you are no less a man today because of your wounds."

Earnan turned toward his sister and caught her eye, "I know what I am, and what I have done. I also know I am more a warrior than a farmer, but a broken warrior, restricted to the tasks of the farm."

Conall and Deaglan had come out of the house and the children raced behind them with Grian close behind. Muirin started after the children and Grian said, "I'll tend to the children, Muirin. You stay with your brothers," and she was fast behind them, laughing and playing.

Earnan breathed deeply, looked at the children and said, "Who's the girl? She's not much older than the little ones."

"Grian, a friend, and all of 18 years. She loves the children and was happy to make the trip today, knowin' I'd need a hand with a few chores."

Earnan looked closer at the red-haired girl, and relaxed. "I wish I could move as easily as she."

Deaglan and Conall were ready to leave for Ceann Coradh and said their goodbyes. The children hugged their father and uncle then ran off again with Grian close behind. Earnan stood with Muirin watching as the two warriors rode off to the north.

"Now, brother, we've seed to sew and animals to tend." She started to walk toward the barn and Earnan said, "I've got the cart ready, and the seed loaded. All I need do is hitch the horse and I'm ready to begin." He walked to the gate and saw the horse across the pasture.

"I'll get him for you," said Muirin.

"No need, little sister, he'll come quick enough," said Earnan as he held a piece of fruit for the horse to see. The animal slowly plodded across the field and Earnan fed him the fruit, then led him to the cart and put the collar over the horse's head.

"'Tis a clever man, you are," said Grian as she rounded the fence with the two children in tow. "Have you all you need for the plantin' now?" she asked.

"I do," replied Earnan as he sat on the back of the cart with the reins over his shoulders.

The children ran toward Muirin as she came out of the house and Grian continued, "Would you let me lead the horse as you scatter the seed?"

Earnan thought for a moment and replied, "If you'd like, it may make this easier."

Grian smiled broadly and took the reins, walked to the horse's head and said, "Where would you like to begin, Earnan?"

"The field out the gate and on the right, we just follow the furrows plowed by Conall and I'll drop the seed as we go."

* * *

The summer passed with Muirin and Grian making several visits with the children. Each visit seemed to bring Earnan and Grian closer together and on a warm summer day, Earnan let the animals out to pasture save the horse, which was hitched to the cart and traveled to his sister's home. "I've come to visit and see the little ones."

Muirin noticed he was looking around and she surmised he was looking for Grian. "Can you stay for dinner, brother?"

"That I can, Muirin," he smiled, "my cooking isn't near as good as yours."

They walked from the house toward the village only a few hundred feet away and met Grian returning from the market. "Well now, I see the brother has come to visit," said Grian. "'Tis always a pleasure to see you," she smiled at Earnan.

Muirin looked about quickly and said, "Will you two excuse me, I have to talk to Fionuir, and I see her there." She quickly walked across the square and began talking to another woman.

"She's a clever girl, your sister," said Grian. "And how are you this beautiful day?" she continued, looking up at Earnan.

* * *

The summer spent at Ceann Coradh had Deaglan and Conall training warriors. Discussions with Murchad and other warrior leaders began to elevate Conall in the eyes of his peers. He was a great warrior, no man could imagine engaging in single combat with the violent giant. In training sessions, Conall was occasionally struck with a sword, drawing blood. On the first of these accidents, fear raced across the face of the inflictor. He was sure he would be killed by this man who had so often shown great anger in battle, complete rage at his opponent. But to the surprise of all, Conall bellowed then laughed, saying to his training opponent, "Good, you are learning, and it appears I also need the practice." He held his sword at his side and touched the bleeding gash, "In battle, this could have been the end of me. Think, all of you, what did I do wrong? How was this man able to put his sword into my side? Learn from this." He went to a physician and had several stitches placed along his ribs and returned to the training posts.

That evening, the conversation centered around Sigtrygg Olafsson. He had been soundly defeated at Ghleann Mama and was chased from Dubh Linn as the town was sacked and burned. Sigtrygg went to several places on the island seeking refuge and was roundly denied. He returned to face Brian, negotiated a peace, ended up back in Dubh Linn with a new bride and unbeknownst to him, a handful of Brian's spies to keep watch over him.

At summer's end and a week into the fall, Conall and Deaglan returned from their visit to Ceann Coradh. When Conall arrived at the farm, Earnan was outside walking from the front of the roundhouse to the barn and back without his crutch. Standing at the front door was the little red-haired woman, Grian.

"Earnan," called Conall, "you're doing well, I see."

"I am, I am," replied Earnan with a broad smile and open arms for his brother. "I didn't expect you for another month or more. Was there no battle to be fought, no Vikings to chase from our shores?"

"No, brother," replied Conall as the two hugged. "We're home for the winter. We talked about a campaign next spring and Deaglan and I demonstrated some of our fighting skills to the younger warriors. Imagine, brother, I am now a teacher as Deaglan taught us."

Earnan smiled and said, "Muirin is here," he looked at Deaglan, "she's inside with the children, you should go to her."

Deaglan looked concerned and Earnan smiled, "Go to her." He looked at Conall as Deaglan went into the house and asked, "What did you do over the summer besides teach young warriors?"

"Well, I met some new friends, taught the younger men things we learned in battle. We all ate and drank too much. I read two books and had several conversations with some scholars Brian has brought to Ceann Coradh."

"And what about the women? I know there are women there, young and beautiful women."

"I did spend some time with one, her name is Eithne. She was nice enough but turned very quiet one day and I haven't seen her since."

Deaglan returned with Muirin walking beside him. He looked at Conall and said, "I'm to be a father again."

* * *

43

1002 AD Munster, Éirinn
Atogail … Reconstruction

Three winter nights, several weeks apart brought snow that melted as soon as the sun rose the following day. The rains came nearly every other day and Earnan had replaced most of the missing daub on the walls of the roundhouse during the summer months. The winter winds brought little rain into the house and the brothers were comfortable enough. The summer crop of wheat was harvested and traded for flour, the hives drained of honey, the cabbages and turnips were harvested and divided between home and the marketplace. They traded for yeast, apples, salt and other staples. Meat was plentiful as deer roamed the farm freely, and Muirin was as skilled with a bow as her brothers.

Earnan wanted to travel to see Muirin and the children on those weeks when she and her family stayed home. "'Tis more the seein' of Grian than the little ones," laughed Muirin to her husband. "I'm glad he has taken to her; I know she's taken with him."

Deaglan was amused at his wife's meddling in her brother's life, "So much the better for him," said Deaglan. "She's a fine woman and a good cook." The two were pleased Earnan had moved beyond his affliction and might be starting a family.

"Now if we could find a match for Conall," said Muirin.

Deaglan hesitated, "I don't think he's ready to take a wife and start a family, girl. He's a gentle man when here at home, but a raging beast on the battlefield. The weight he carries on his shoulders, going into battle with no hesitation and then questioning everything he has done afterwards takes him away from us all. It sometimes takes days for him to ease his mind enough to talk to brother and friend. A great warrior, but a tortured man at the same time."

The visits back and forth between Muirin and Earnan became a regular weekly event. Muirin made sure she included Grian on these trips to Earnan's home to "help her with the children," and she was always available when he traveled to see her family. In the month of June, Earnan met Grian's family and was warmly accepted. His visits hence included a visit to her family and the inevitable wedding was planned for the late autumn month of November.

* * *

Conall sailed with Brian up the Shannon to Meath, Breifne and beyond. The battles were small and often a mere positioning in front of another force was enough to claim victory. Brian's kingdom started to settle down and it did not always require an armed conflict. Peace was found more often and the opportunity to improve the country was seized. Brian began a campaign of building roads and rebuilding destroyed monasteries. Munster was his first concern. The work began there, reaching out to the distant parts of Éirinn. He sent people abroad to other civilized lands buying and trading for books and treasures to replace those taken over the years by the Norse invaders in hundreds of plundering raids.

The force under Brian increased in size when an expedition was planned and only a few warriors remained at Ceann Coradh during those lax times between campaigns. Both Conall and Deaglan chose to stay at Ceann Coradh for three or four weeks at a time and journey home for a week or two, when time allowed before making the journey back.

Conall was restless during these quiet times and soothed when he found another scroll or scrap of paper to read. "My mother was fond of the writings of others," he announced, "And now I see why. There is much to learn from these scratchings." Sitting in an open room with a scroll, Conall noticed a woman looking at him. "Have you a question for me, girl?"

"I see you read the scrolls," she smiled. "Could you teach me to read as well?"

"I might, but first, I have to hear your name," said Conall.

"'Tis Ainnir," she replied, "and you are Conall mac Laoghaire, I know."

The two spent days together, days that rolled into weeks and soon the reading of the scrolls went from the main reason to be together to only one of several reasons. Ainnir was a strong girl, not one to allow someone else to lift and carry that which she could. She showed interest in Conall's weapons, and he taught her how to use a sword. In practice sessions, Ainnir was no match for the giant warrior, but she never backed away from a crashing of their wooden swords. He respected her and when the swords and scrolls were put aside, they found a gentler way of enjoying the evening and night times.

* * *

Conall traded with other warriors for the prized books and scrolls that he and Ainnir enjoyed. His friends teased him, calling him "Conall, the scholar", and he laughed with them. He enjoyed bringing new scraps of writing to Ainnir and she learned quickly to read and engage in discussion on almost every topic.

As time passed with fewer and lesser battles to fight, many warriors became complacent. They slept more, ate and drank more and started to fatten. Conall noticed the changes in their quickness to respond when a battle presence was required, or a show of strength was needed. He noticed himself, moving slower and with less force. Thinking of his earlier years, Conall wandered into the woods with his axe in hand and found a clearing near a stream. "Perfect," he muttered and began to look about the edge of the woods for a proper tree.

He found an oak tree that was as big around as he was and the branches began over ten feet above the ground. He cleared the brush and smaller trees around this oak, giving him room to move and practice as he did years before. As he was clearing the space, Deaglan approached and noticed the tree.

"Are you plantin' a tree, tall man?" asked Deaglan, remembering his wife's same question from years gone by.

Conall looked at Deaglan, thought for a moment and smiled, "No girl," he jested, "'tis a constant enemy that I found here." The two men laughed, and Deaglan helped Conall finish clearing brush about the tree. They sat on another log and looked at their work. "A fair piece of work for two young boys," said Conall.

"That it is, my friend," replied Deaglan. "Now to the practice. I think we both need it and the others also." He stood, drew his sword and as he approached the tree he paused, "Clearin' the ground around this trunk was a day's work in itself, my friend." He looked at Conall, lowered his sword and continued, "I don't want to kill it too quickly and have to find another."

Conall laughed, "Then 'tis the little wooden swords you made for Earnan and me that we need."

"Perhaps a little bigger wooden sword than the ones I carved back then," said Deaglan. "Those were made for two boys, and what we need today should test everything we have. They should be bigger than the swords we carry and the axe you use so well."

Conall stood and looked around the clearing, picked up his axe and walked into the woods to a small grove of young trees. He found one about two inches in diameter and straight for over eight feet. He cut it down with a few well-placed swings of his axe and dragged it back into the clearing. "This one'll do for me," he said looking at Deaglan. "Just a little carving and it'll fit my hand."

Deaglan looked at Conall's tree and said, "Might I borrow the axe I gave you and find a tree for myself?"

Conall set the tree across a large fallen trunk and cut it to a length he wanted, looked at the staff and handed the axe to Deaglan, "I'll be here, with my knife, turnin' this into a weapon."

Deaglan took the axe and went to the grove where Conall found his tree. "I'll be back in a few minutes," he said as he hefted the axe.

The two warriors spent the afternoon sitting on the fallen tree, laughing and carving their new "weapons".

"This tree should have a name," said Conall.

"I agree," said Deaglan. "We could call it Olaf, Olaf the Slow."

"Because it doesn't move?" laughed Conall.

"That too," laughed Deaglan, "and after we have killed Olaf enough, we may have to find two or three of his brothers and set them in the clearing, as we did at Cnoc Gorm."

"Maybe we find a bigger log, like the one we're sitting on, and call him Olaf the Fat," said Conall.

"He may live longer than his slow brother," laughed Deaglan.

* * *

The next day the two men lifted their wooden weapons and walked to the clearing. "Remember what you taught me, years ago," said Conall. "Move and strike, strike again and move, always seeing what is ahead and behind. Move, don't stand still."

"Yes," replied Deaglan, "And the part of that which you seem to forget is looking behind you, where you have been."

Conall paused and looked at the ground, "I wish to live, my friend. I have no urge to die, but when I fight, the men in front of me draw me closer and those behind are dead to me."

"Not all dead," responded Deaglan. "Most, yes, they're dead or so wounded they can't fight anymore. But you don't watch your back and the men who follow you through the shield walls have often finished what you have started. It is in great measure that they have kept you alive in many battles."

Conall smiled, "Then I thank them for saving me from a sword or an axe," and held his wooden axe at arms-length, "Watch me, Deaglan and tell me when I should change my movements."

The two began their practice and kept it up through the afternoon. As the sun began to wander farther west and touch the tops of the trees, Conall set his axe against the fallen log. "Enough for one day, my friend," and he waded into the nearby stream until he was in water to his waist. He turned toward Deaglan and spread his arms, closed his eyes, smiled, and fell backward into the water. He stayed under for a minute then stood, shaking his head, and walked out of the stream. "I'll be dry by the time we get back to our camp," he said.

"You no longer go to Ainnir." said Deaglan as he walked into the water.

"I do, but she has grown quiet, so less than before," replied Conall. "I think she has had enough of me." He shook his head in a thoughtful, unknowing way. "She no longer wants to read the scrolls with me or practice with the sword and is unhappy when I talk about seeing battle again."

Deaglan walked out of the water and the two went back to the ringed fort where they had camped. The next day as they were heading to the clearing, Ronan asked where they were going.

"To slay Olaf, again," replied Deaglan.

"Yes," added Conall, "And if you had a wooden weapon like ours, you could help us."

Ronan looked confused, "Olaf?"

Conall put his arm around Ronan's shoulders and pulled him along with them. The two tall men took Ronan through the wood to the clearing and 'Olaf'. "There he is," said Deaglan pointing to a tree with most of the bark gone from a foot to six feet above the ground. "Now we must kill him."

Ronan looked at the two warriors and shyly stepped backwards. Conall hefted his wooden axe and started to move around the bark-less tree and strike it with the heavy blows. Deaglan swung his wooden sword a few times, loosening his arms and went to the opposite side of the tree and started to move and strike. As the two warriors worked through the movements they would repeat in battle, Ronan understood and watched intently. Conall paused, leaned on his axe, and said, "The axe I use here," he leaned the wooden axe toward Ronan, "Is heavier than the one I use in battle. When the time comes to use my axe of steel, it will be lighter and easier to move, my arms will be stronger and Olaf," he pointed the axe at the post, "Olaf will die again."

Deaglan walked over to Ronan, handed Conall's steel axe to him and said, "The grove there," pointing to the two stumps in the woods, "Is where we found these weapons. See if you can find one to fit your hand and join us."

* * *

As the days passed and the call to battle dwindled, Deaglan, Conall and their fellow warriors practiced on several 'Olafs', and Conall slowly drifted farther away from Ainnir. She didn't pursue him but stayed in her small hut and Conall was a warrior once again. He practiced with his fellows and as they found more time to return home to their families, so did he. The visits were shorter in the spring and summer and longer in the fall and winter. As the winter of 1002 approached, Conall and Deaglan journeyed home for the winter and found a few changes.

Earnan and Grian were going to wed, and they would live at Cnoc Gorm. There was more than enough house and farm for the two brothers to share and not be in each other's way.

The wedding day was planned for after Conall and Deaglan returned from Ceann Coradh and as the leaves began to fall from the trees, the two were wed. Conall was very pleased for his brother and his new bride. He took them outside the roundhouse and to the gate. There he looked at his older brother, placed his hands on both their shoulders and said, "Brother, I'll fix the loose pickets behind the house and replace the thatch where it's thin. Then I'll be on my way, the farm, brother, and little lady, is yours."

"No, Conall, we can all stay here. There's no need for you to leave," said Earnan.

Grian looked up at the giant and said, "Conall, this is your home, I see no reason for you to leave."

"I'll be going back to Ceann Coradh in the spring and the good lord knows what will follow. No, you two have the farm. Live here and raise cows, chickens, and children. I'll find my own way."

The three stood near the gate and looked out over the pastures where the animals grazed. The air was cool, and a hint of rain came from the grey sky. As lightning flashed over the mountains to the west and thunder rolled in the distance, Grian leaned into Earnan. Conall turned to go back into the house and Earnan said, "We'll stand here and watch the lightning for a minute or two and be inside before the heavy rains come."

The skies rumbled through the night and in the morning as the sun pushed its way into the meadows and pastures, Conall was busy securing the pickets behind the house. Earnan found Conall and handed him a cup with warm milk and honey, "You rise early, little brother."

Conall eagerly accepted the drink and said, "I want to finish these little chores before I leave and there are no clouds in today's sky."

Earnan understood. Conall was a warrior, not a farmer. His life was the battlefield and confining him to the farm would be like putting him in chains. "Where will you go, little brother?"

"There are places on this island I've not seen. In the spring, I'll march with Brian wherever he goes. The others we face on the battlefield of late have little desire to engage in real fighting and we win as often with our name as with our swords. 'Tis a strange way to fight a battle, eh, brother?"

The two men laughed and Conall finished securing the pickets and they walked back to the house.

*   *   *

As Conall was preparing to leave Cnoc Gorm, Grian led the large horse, out from the stables. "You call this one 'Capall', Conall," she smiled, "He eats too much, and doesn't like me at all." She smiled, you'd be doin' me a great favor if you'd take this beast with you and let the king feed him in his pastures." She handed the reins to Conall, "Perhaps he will like the grass in the fields about Ceann Coradh."

Conall said, "But this one can pull the plow and the cart when fully loaded. I can take the other horse, the smaller one." He looked at Grian and knew he would not change her mind.

Grian folded her arms, cocked her head, lifted her chin, and said, "This horse can carry your bulk and your weapons, the mare would drop dead under your weight before you were halfway to Ceann Coradh."

There would be no debate, no discussion, Conall would take the larger horse. He appreciated her thoughts and knew again his brother was a lucky man.

Earnan came out of the roundhouse, carrying a large brown bear skin, he handed it to Conall, "Remember this, little brother? One of the raiders left this here ten years ago. It's the biggest fur we have and might cover you on a cold night." He looked at the horse. "Yes, this is a horse that will stay under you and carry you a long way, little brother."

Grian looked at her man, "You agree, this is a proper horse for Conall."

"Yes, girl, I do."

"Then it's done," she said with a smile and a twinkle in her eye.

Conall had his weapons, a horse and saddle, a bear skin, and provisions for the ride to Ceann Coradh. "I'll be this way again in the fall," he said, "But only for a visit, then I'll be off again to see what I have not yet seen." He mounted the large horse, looked down at his brother, nodded and rode off to meet Deaglan.

* * *

Deaglan was ready to leave when Conall arrived. They paused for Muirin to say a brief prayer for her husband and her brother, give the two warriors a bag of food and kiss them both. They rode through half the morning toward Ceann Coradh when they met an old friend, Brogan. He traveled light, carrying no weapons and riding a small horse.

"Brogan, good friend," called Deaglan, "I haven't seen you in years. How have you been?"

Brogan smiled broadly as he neared the two warriors. "Deaglan, do you travel to Ceann Coradh?"

"We do, old friend," replied Deaglan. "Conall and I will see what adventure Brian has for us this year." The three men dismounted and led their horses to a stream to drink, they opened their bags of food and settled in for a brief meal before continuing their journey.

Brogan looked at Conall, "So this is the great Conall mac Laoghaire. I am honored to meet you."

"Not so great, my friend, and the honor is mine. I have heard your name when Deaglan and some of the others talk of the days in the hills of Tipperary. You lived a hard life then and knew my father."

Brogan smiled, "Ah, yes, the great axe man. He was the best of us, and you look like him, but bigger."

The men talked away, telling Conall stories of Laoghaire and his deeds and the words he passed on to the young warriors around him. "He was a teacher as well as a warrior. He made us practice with a tree as our enemy."

Deaglan and Conall laughed, "So it was my father who taught you about the post in the ground," said Conall slapping Deaglan on his shoulder.

"Yes, your father and mine, they both made me kill many a tree." said Deaglan.

Conall noticed again the lack of weapons on Brogan's horse. "You travel light, Brogan. No weapons."

Brogan looked about, then in a low voice, "I can no longer hold a sword or a shield as I once could. Today, I fight a new kind of battle, with my ears." He took a drink of water and continued in his low voice. "Brian needs to know the 'weather' in Dubh Linn. Will it rain, will it snow? He needs to know which way Sigtrygg will turn in the morning." He took another drink, "I watch, I listen and when I learn something, I send word to him." He leaned back and added, "I am no threat to anybody. So, nobody pays attention to what I do or where I go."

"It is a dangerous thing you do, Brogan," said Deaglan. "If they knew you were a spy, they would not hesitate to kill you."

"I can no longer stand with you and Conall in battle, but I can do this thing. I'm old and not a threat to the 'foreigners' in Dubh Linn. They know me as a merchant, not a warrior and talk freely in front of me. This is my way of fighting, keeping Brian informed as best I can. This is my battle."

The three men rode together toward Ceann Coradh. When they were a few miles south of the Shannon, Brogan slowed, "You two go ahead, I must go another way and try not to be seen." He touched Deaglan's shoulder and said, "It was good to see you again," he turned toward Conall, "And you, Conall." He looked around again and said, "Tell no one of our meeting. I am a forgotten man and that I must remain." He waved and turned his horse to the east and rode slowly away.

"Brogan's war," said Conall, "He's a brave man, walking into Sigtrygg's camp."

"Yes," agreed Deaglan, "a very brave man."

* * *

They arrived at Ceann Coradh, went to their campsite, and met with old friends. The next day, as they were wandering about an open area, Murchad approached. "Deaglan, good to see you again," he turned, "and Conall. My father asked me to find the two of you and join him. He waits in a garden, I'll take you."

They went into a large open garden and saw Brian sitting on a bench in the middle, talking to several warriors. As the three men approached, the warriors went away in different directions, looking behind bushes and trees. Then they stopped and stood as guards, far enough away that they could not hear the conversation, but close enough to protect Brian if necessary.

Brian welcomed the two men and all four sat around a small fire pit. Brian spoke, "You two met an old friend on the road here yesterday."

Both Deaglan and Conall knew what was about to be said and Deaglan began, "An old friend that we will not talk about. A man who stood with you in battle many times and now stands alone."

Conall added, "We will not speak his name, here or anywhere we may be."

"Good," said Brian, "His life depends on it." He stood, breathed deeply and said, "Tonight we dine in the hall, you will join us." He gestured to his guard, and they left the garden.

Murchad added, "There will be more talk tonight, after we have dined, and people begin to sleep. Keep a clear head and be ready to talk." He nodded to both men and hurried off after his father.

Evening came, Deaglan and Conall enjoyed their meal, and they noticed Brian and Murchad having conversation with various chieftains and minor kings, both together and separately. These sessions kept Brian busy most of the evening, allowing little time to enjoy the food and very little drink.

As the new day began and moon was high in the sky, Murchad approached and took Deaglan aside for a private word. When Deaglan returned, he told Conall to "drink less and keep a clear head," then he quietly said, "We've been touched to do some work for Brian, and we will talk with him soon."

*　*　*

Time passed, the crowd thinned and Murchad again touched Deaglan on his shoulder, "It's time to talk, bring Conall back to the garden. Himself will be there, waiting."

Deaglan and Conall went to the garden where Murchad took up one of the sentry positions and the two warriors again met with Brian near the fire pit. "Deaglan," said Brian in a low voice, "we cannot be heard if we keep our voices low."

The three men sat around the small fire and leaned in close. "The man you met on the road, my old and trusted friend?" The two warriors nodded. Brian continued, "He often has news for me, but I cannot go to meet with him as I wish, there are too many eyes and ears that try to follow my every move." He paused, looked about the garden and saw Murchad standing near the gate to the garden. He caught Murchad's eye and the two nodded to each other. "My son would be my first choice, but of course he too is watched. He is also more the warrior and less the inconspicuous courier. I need a few men I can trust. Men who can carry a message and walk in the shadows. The watchers know this and will follow anyone who visits with me. You two are not what they expect to be spies. No, you two giants couldn't sneak up on a dead man." He stirred the fire. "But that may be exactly what I need. I trust the two of you.

You could probably boldly march on the road from here to Dubh Linn and the watchers would assume you're just two warriors looking for a battle. But they would not think you to be carrying a message."

Brian poked the embers with a stick, "There is much to know about Sigtrygg and his friends in Dubh Linn. They talk and some day they will act on their words. That day could come tomorrow or in a year, perhaps more, but it will come, and I want to be ready. Brogan gains little bits and pieces of information that all added together with other bits and pieces, tell us a story." He paused and looked about again, then continued, "We have a number of spies watching and listening all over the island and some in other countries. They all are important, but Brogan has given us very dependable news and his information is most important." Brian sat up straight, "I must hear what he has to say, how he sees the 'weather' in Dubh Linn. I must hear and I need someone I trust to meet with him and bring me word. The two of you are trustworthy and can do me a great service." He paused again, nodded at Murchad and continued, "Brogan sells his leather goods at the market in Clondalkin as often as he does in Dubh Linn. I ask you two to meet him and bring his news to me."

"How will we know when he will be there?" asked Deaglan.

"Perhaps two or three times each week, Brogan makes the trip. He will go to the tower and walk past. If he knows he is followed, he will not stop, but continue. If he is sure there is no one watching, he will stop and rest on the tower's west side."

Conall was about to ask about the tower when Deaglan spoke, 'The old monastery, yes, I know the place. We've been there before, Brian." He nodded, "Yes, it's been years, but I remember it."

Brian smiled, "Good, try to meet him every few weeks, at first light, on the west side of the tower." He kept looking around and nodding at Murchad, then back to the conversation. "Meet with him, in secret. Hear all he has to say, then come back here, find Murchad and he will bring you to me. Then we will talk again." He looked at Deaglan then at Conall, "I knew your father well, Conall and I know your mother taught you to read and write. These are important skills my friends and here is where you may use them. I need as much information as I can gather and be ready to protect our tribe, our island." He paused again and then continued, "Remember, Brogan is now a merchant, a dealer in leather goods. If he is not at the tower, go to the market in Clondalkin and find him. Try to buy a belt or boots from him, anything that will give you the opportunity to talk to him. If he refuses to bargain with you, it means he is being watched and you should move on to another vendor. We do not want you to be suspect to unfriendly eyes and ears."

Murchad approached, nodded and smiled, "There you are, father. The sun will soon light the day and we have much to do."

Brian understood Murchad's words and muttered to Deaglan, "We've been seen, you two should leave quietly. There are many spies here in Ceann Coradh, just as we have in Dubh Linn."

Deaglan and Conall remained seated as Brian walked to Murchad and the two left the garden. They waited at the fire pit, looking at the smoldering embers and finally Deaglan said, "The bush to your left, Conall. There stands a man trying not to be seen. A pair of eyes from Dubh Linn perhaps."

They remained seated, talking quietly until Conall noticed a shadow move near the bush, "I think he leaves us."

"Yes, he moves like an ox. I could watch him with my closed eyes," said Deaglan. "We can leave now."

The morning came with a misting rain and a cool breeze. The two warriors continued to conduct practice sessions at the Olaf trees and their audience increased each day. Brian had heard of the sessions, discussed them with Murchad and instructed his personal guard to join.

After a week had passed, Deaglan and Conall prepared to journey home, or so it appeared. They made preparations as they always did and left on the same road they usually traveled.

Several miles south of Ceann Coradh, the two stopped, hid behind a thick grove of trees, and watched the road as their horses drank from a stream. Within a few minutes a pair of horsemen approached and casually passed without noticing the two warriors hidden in the trees.

"Are we followed?" asked Conall, looking at Deaglan.

"It is a common road, they may be traveling just as we were, or were supposed to be. We don't know," replied Deaglan.

"If we continue, we'll soon reach the road to Dubh Linn," said Conall. "I think we should go now, keep a look out and avoid these men if we can."

"Look at us, two warriors avoiding a fight." said Conall.

"No, two very large spies trying stay unseen, in the shadows," said Deaglan as he slapped him on the shoulder.

The two laughed as they led their horses back to the road.

* * *

44

The walls about Dubh Linn had been breached by Brian's forces a dozen years before and the King, Sigtrygg Olafsson had escaped. The town was entered, sacked and parts were burned. Brian and his forces carried off gold, silver, gems and other valuables. He returned to Ceann Coradh wealthier and in a forgiving mood. Sigtrygg fled north and was not welcomed, he turned west and was not welcomed there either. He soon had no other options and he returned to submit to Brian. An exchange of promises, a marriage to Brian's daughter and a marriage of Brian and Sigtrygg's mother, Gormflaith, coupled with Sigtrygg's armed force now under Brian's control, brought about a period of peace between Brian and the Dubh Linn Norse for several years.

There were of course several other conditions and adjustments. Among them, the unannounced installation of several men in Dubh Linn in the guise of normal citizens who watched and listened. Brogan was one of these spies. He had been with Brian in the early days in the hills of Tipperary and now, older, and partially disabled, he continued his service to his old friend and king, Brian.

Brogan had appeared in Dubh Linn when Sigtrygg was in the north trying to find refuge and his presence was never noticed as unusual. When Sigtrygg returned to Dubh Linn, Brogan was already established as a trader in leather goods, and he moved about freely.

Deaglan and Conall made the journey to Clondalkin as time permitted and established a routine with Brogan. They would try to be there on the first day of every month. Their meetings were brief, often centered around the purchase of a belt or boots and the information he provided was delivered to Brian or Murchad. Then in 1012, the meetings were a little more tense and the information more troubling. As the years had passed, Sigtrygg had grown less and less content and began plotting against Brian, perhaps with an eye toward the crown of all Éirinn. His mother, Gormflaith returned to Dubh Linn after her brief marriage to Brian and may have supported Sigtrygg's thoughts of rebellion. When the King of Leinster, Máel Morda, rose in revolt, Sigtrygg joined with the Leinsterman and others. They had battle with and defeated

Máel Sechnaill somewhere north of Dubh Linn and Sigtrygg also dispatched a naval force south to Corcaigh and Cape Clear where they inflicted damage on Brian's fleet and burned parts of Corcaigh.

As Sigtrygg continued to plot against Brian, his discussions were no longer as secret as they should have been, and Brogan plied more information from his numerous contacts. A word from one, a word from another, in apparent casual conversation added up to Brogan learning of Sigtrygg's journey to visit Sigurd, Earl of Orkney and Brodir of the Isle of Man. As Sigtrygg gained new allies in his planned revolt against Brian, Brogan readied himself for his regular visit with Deaglan and Conall.

The message Brogan was preparing for Brian was partially written in a code and he prepared to have the men memorize other parts of his message. He set out for his usual trip to the marketplace in Clondalkin. His cart was laden with goods to sell, but his mind was on the message for Brian. Brogan had been a strong and dependable warrior in his younger days, but now, older, and unable to hold a sword, he was defenseless, vulnerable to assault from another. The message was important, and he hurried to finish his preparations. Then, riding in his cart toward Clondalkin, he felt a pain in his chest and his arm. He now worried more, the message was not complete without the spoken word, and he might not live long enough to pass it on.

It was the morning of the first day of the month and Brogan was not seen in the marketplace. Deaglan and Conall walked the grounds calmly, looking at various vendors' wares, laughing and enjoying the day. As mid-day arrived, the two warriors began to worry. "We have not seen our friend," said Deaglan. "I worry that he may be in trouble."

"He could be on the road, coming this way, and just late in arriving. It could be nothing that should cause concern," replied Conall.

"Then, again," said Deaglan, "He may be in trouble. I feel one of us should travel the road back toward Dubh Linn. The other would stay and hope to see him."

Conall looked at Deaglan, "He has never missed one of these meetings, he would be here if at all possible. I'll start on the Dubh Linn road, if you wait here a while and then leave in the same direction, you should be able to catch me before I reach Dubh Linn."

"You may encounter an enemy, someone who would do you harm if they could. Someone who may have done harm to Brogan," said Deaglan.

Conall thought for a moment, "I think you may be right. If our friend has learned something that Sigtrygg wouldn't like made known to Brian, he may have paid a price."

Deaglan returned, "Remember, we're not warriors, we're spies and have to act like spies. You be careful."

"I will," said Conall. "I will be very careful."

Conall rode east on the Dubh Linn Road for less than a mile when he saw a horse, attached to a cart, grazing off the road. He knew it was Brogan's horse and cart, but he did not see Brogan. He dismounted and moved closer. As he approached the cart, four men came out of the wood with swords drawn and surrounded Conall.

"Stop where you are," commanded one of the four. "Who are you? And what is your business with this man?" he said pointing his sword towards the ground near the cart."

Conall ignored the command and stepped closer to the cart, saw Brogan on the ground and turned toward the man who had spoken. "What have you done to him?" he demanded.

"We've done nothing," replied another of the four. "Nothing, yet."

Conall noticed Brogan move, "How did he come to be on the ground?"

The four men moved closer to Conall and one spoke, "He seems to have fallen from his cart and we happened to see him. We'll help him back to Dubh Linn and you can be on your way."

Conall had one short sword in his belt and a dagger, he surveyed the four men, "How do you know he was on his way to Dubh Linn? He may have been going to Clondalkin as I was. Perhaps we should ask him."

The man spoke again, "There is no need to ask him anything, we will take him to Dubh Linn, and you will take the road to Clondalkin."

Conall moved closer to Brogan and the four men moved closer to Conall. He looked down at Brogan and said, "Where are you going, old man?"

Brogan was still in considerable pain and half whispered, "To Clondalkin, I must get to Clondalkin."

Conall turned suddenly to the four strangers, "There you have it, I can help him and you four may be on your way,"

As he spoke, Conall noticed one of the men grip his sword and the others grow tense. He placed his hands on his hips, touching his sword and was ready to do battle if necessary.

Then another of the four spoke, "This man is a spy, he was on his way to meet someone to pass along information and we were following him. Perhaps you are the one we should take back to Dubh Linn."

Conall feigned surprise, "A spy, you say. Are you sure of this? He's just an old man," said Conall, surveying the cart and Brogan's wares. "He is trying to sell belts, coats and boots what makes you think him a spy?"

"Yes, a spy," came a quick response. "He was seen listening to conversations he should not have heard. Now we watch him to see who he will meet, and who comes to help him."

"Are you the one he goes to meet?" demanded one of the four. "I think Sigtrygg would like to ask you a few questions." The four men took another step toward Conall.

"I have nothing to tell Sigtrygg or any of you, said Conall, "and this man is no spy, he is a merchant on his way to a market. Now, I'll help him, and you'll not stop me."

"He's the one," yelled one of the four as he charged Conall drawing his sword. Conall quickly drew his sword, met the attacking man with a block of the man's sword, then Conall turned and avoided another sword aimed at his back as he slashed at the first attacker, cutting through his neck. He suddenly exploded with anger and a savage roar as he swung his sword at the second attacker's arm.

The man fell to the ground, his right arm nearly severed and Conall turned again, facing the other two men. He looked at them, paused and suddenly stepped toward them slashing with his short sword. The one closest was driven to the ground and the other turned to run. Conall looked at the man on the ground, raised his short sword and crushed the man's skull. He turned, saw the last of the four running away. He knew he couldn't catch him and quickly surveyed the field. Brogan was still alive, obviously in pain and not able to stand. Conall lifted him into his cart and laid him on a bed of leather boots and coats. He looked at both horses and decided to release Brogan's horse and use his larger animal to pull the cart. As soon as he had stripped Brogan's horse of all his reins and bridles, he pushed him away and led his horse back to the road. He mounted the cart and began the trek back toward Clondalkin. When he looked behind, he saw Brogan's horse lazily clopping along behind the cart.

After a little while, Deaglan appeared on the road. Conall told him to turn around and they would talk as they continued west. He told Deaglan of the four men and the one that got away, "He would need some time to get to Dubh Linn, more to gather some help and more again to get back here. I think we have an advantage of perhaps half the day before they find us."

A while later they stopped, several miles west of Clondalkin on another road leading to Ceann Coradh and Limerick beyond. Conall looked at his friend, "Deaglan, if that man gets back to Dubh Linn and they decide to pursue us, they will most likely think we would have taken the northern road to Ceann Coradh. So, I think I should take the longer, southerly route. Then if you go ahead to Ceann Coradh, gather a few men, and come back along that southern road with help, we should be safe."

Deaglan looked at Conall, smiled and said, "Now you think like a spy." He dismounted and the two went to check on Brogan.

"I've seen this before," said Deaglan. "It's his heart. It pains him and he may not live out the day. He needs rest and a physician. We should be very careful; the ride must not be as bumpy as it has been. You will have to go slower and keep him calm, quiet. Then hope for the best."

Conall was about to remove some of the heavier items from the cart when Brogan spoke, "No, no Conall. I have hidden information in one of the coats, we need it." He breathed deeply and lay back on the pile.

Deaglan said, "I guess you're now a leather merchant. When you move the cart to the south road, I'll wipe out your tracks and I'll see you as soon as I can turn around at Ceann Coradh and bring help."

The two men nodded and started their journeys, Conall to the south and Deaglan to the north. Deaglan rode as hard as his horse would allow and made the trip in less than two days. When he arrived, he told Murchad of the events and Murchad immediately dispatched twelve hard warriors to accompany Deaglan on the southern road with two sets of horses. They stopped for a rest only four times and finally saw Conall and Brogan in the cart when they were a good day's ride from Ceann Coradh. Brogan was sitting up and talking as Conall drove the cart.

Brogan tried to tell Conall everything, "If Sigtrygg's men catch us, it's most important to get this information to Brian. If we're attacked, leave me in the cart and take the fastest horse we have."

"I don't plan on leaving you anywhere but in the palace at Ceann Coradh, old friend," replied Conall as Deaglan and his friends arrived.

The twelve warriors surrounded the cart and Deaglan said, "Well, good friend a nice day for a ride through the countryside." All the men laughed, and Deaglan looked to two of them, "See if we are in any danger from the rear, I'd guess a mile's ride would be good enough."

The two men left at an easy gallop, and he continued, "We should move quickly, no time for resting yet."

"Agreed," said Conall as he urged the horse forward again.

Several miles more down the road, the two scouts returned to the others. "A few miles behind us, but they are coming, pushing their horses harder than they should. There may be as many as thirty men."

Conall looked at Deaglan, "How long till we reach Ceann Coradh?"

"At this pace, we'll be there by nightfall. If we can stay ahead of these 'foreigners', we may not need to engage them," he replied.

Conall frowned, "We need a little diversion." He walked back and forth for a moment looking at the trees and the pathway through a wooded area where the road narrowed, then at the woods beyond. He walked through the passage, surveyed the open field and the rest of the landscape beyond and then looked at the twelve warriors, "What weapons do we have?"

Each of the twelve carried a short sword, daggers, a sling, and a javelin. Five of the men also had bows and over a dozen arrows.

Conall thought for a moment then turned to Deaglan, "You take Brogan to Ceann Coradh and Brian. The rest of us will slow them down."

Deaglan frowned, "Conall, I don't want to leave you out here. I can stay as well."

"No, my friend," said Conall. "You must speak to Brian; he trusts you and will listen. If Brogan dies on this trip, you have to tell Brian everything." He didn't wait for a reply, he turned to the other warriors and said, "You five with bows will stand behind trees on either side of this narrow passage and wait. When these people are in range, you will strike. Each of you take out one man and quietly get to your horses. They will likely stop and seek cover in the trees. The rest of us will be out of sight, ready to attack if necessary, or quietly leave them cowering behind trees and bushes. It may take them a while to remount and come after us again. If we can reduce their number by four or five, then fall back two or three miles and get ready for them again with another surprise, we may do this without losing any men."

Deaglan knew his friend, his student, was not to be dissuaded. Conall would remain and fight and he would take Brogan to Brian. He took the reins of the cart and urged the horse forward.

One of the warriors said, "Conall, why not stand and fight them all here. We are better than they are and could easily defeat them."

Conall walked over to the warrior, "Yes, my friend. We may well defeat them here. But our task is not to kill them, it is rather to assure Brogan gets to Ceann Coradh. If one gets by us and catches Brogan then all this is for naught. Brogan has information he must deliver to Brian, that is all that matters. So, we will strike from cover and run away. Then strike again, and again. Each time we hit them, they slow. Each time we strike, they will lose another one or more of their number and seek cover. All of this takes time. Time that Deaglan will use to get Brogan to Brian."

He walked the path a short distance and said, "Here, the 'foreigners will pass through one at a time. They will be very vulnerable at this point." He looked at the group of warriors, "Who has the fastest horse?"

A young warrior said with a smile, "I think I am the fastest of all these old fat men. And I think you need someone to be the bait for this trap."

Conall held the young warrior's reins, "Don't get too close to them, let them see you and stay well ahead of them." He looked at the others, "As he passes our position, we strike at the first five to come through." He then pointed to positions where each archer might stand. "After you have loosed your arrow, move quickly and quietly to your horses and ride to the next position. Someone will be there to point out where we will do this again."

Conall looked at the remaining warriors. "You two, ride ahead two or three miles. It would be best if the foreigner's horses were tired when they reached our next trap position. Find another place like this and be ready." He looked at the remaining five men, "Each of you stand ready at the rear, we may yet have a battle here where we stand."

Everybody reached their position and Conall turned to look at the road from the east. As he was about to speak, the young warrior came into view, riding hard and laughing, "They're right behind me."

The archers readied their bows and waited. As the first of the foreigners passed through the narrow passage and came into view, the first archer loosed his arrow. The first rider was struck in the throat and was dead in his saddle as his horse continued across the open field. The second archer immediately took his man as the first archer crept to his horse and moved out. Then the third archer loosed his arrow. The first three archers were mounted and moving as the fourth and fifth each took an enemy. The foreigners did as Conall had hoped, they stopped at the edge of the clearing, dismounted and sought cover. All five archers reached the main group, and each loosed another arrow in the direction of their pursuers. The foreigners didn't know if they were still under an attack and remained under cover as Conall and his group slipped away farther east to the next trap.

The same ruse worked again where several fallen trees partially blocked the road, and the pursuing band was reduced to about twenty riders. "This time the running away may not work as well," said Conall. "We will strike and lie in wait for them to begin to move and hit them again, immediately."

The number of pursuers was again reduced and Conall looked at the sun. "The day is near done and Deaglan has enough of a start, we should follow. These foreigners may not have the stomach to continue after us anymore."

The Irish warriors quietly crept from their positions back to their horses and slipped away. They covered another ten miles to the east toward Ceann Coradh when another group of warriors approached from the west. Their leader stopped, facing Conall, "Deaglan said you may want company on your ride back to Ceann Coradh."

Now with nearly thirty riders, Conall and his group paused, he thought for a moment, looked up at the rider, "Do I Know you?"

The tall warrior dismounted and approached Conall. He looked at Conall with a grin and said, "Shall we play a game of hurling?"

Conall hesitated, "Ruarc, how are your ribs?"

The two men laughed as the others looked confused. "It has been a long time," said Conall. "Perhaps we can talk when we are back in Ceann Coradh." He paced about, thinking, then walked over to Ruarc. "Has Deaglan delivered his message?"

"Yes, Conall," replied Ruarc. "And the man with him lives."

"Then let's go back to Ceann Coradh, there is much to do, and we will need all the men we can muster for what is to come."

* * *

45

1013 AD Munster, Éirinn

an Trodaire adh … The Silent Warrior

Brogan awoke in the morning with a slight pain in his chest and feeling like he had wrestled every warrior in Ceann Coradh and lost each match. He was exhausted and excited at the same time. The court physician saw him stir and told him to stay on his back, to rest, "You have had a meeting with the woman of the barrows, and you'll not fare as well a second time, now lie down and relax."

As Brogan was about to speak, Deaglan and Conall appeared to check on their friend. "He's awake," said Deaglan, pointing at Brogan.

The physician bravely stepped in front of the two tall warriors, looked up and said, "Yes, he is awake. And if we want him to wake again tomorrow, you will allow him to rest. Now, out of here, the both of you."

Brogan sat up and said, "Deaglan, have we delivered the message?"

The physician whispered to Deaglan, "Tell him all is well, then leave and allow him to rest."

Conall calmly brushed past the physician and stood in front of Brogan, "You have done more than many others, my friend. Now Brian needs you to heal and come back in good health. There will be no more adventures on the road, you will sit in council and advise our leaders. The information you provided this time is of great interest and we will act on it. Now rest and we will come to visit you again soon."

The physician nodded to Conall as the two warriors left the room and went in search of Murchad.

"Brogan's information is very important," said Murchad. "My father hastens to increase our force and I am also to meet with several tribal leaders with the same purpose. You two should rejoin your troops and increase the training. We must be prepared to march at any time."

Conall stood silently, listening to Murchad's words, then when walking back to their campsite he said to Deaglan, "Brogan told me many things as we rode together. His message to Brian was disturbing."

Deaglan nodded, "He also told me many things in case he died before getting to Brian. Things that Brian would need to know."

Conall paused, looked around and saw they were alone, then said, "Why does Sigtrygg oppose Brian?"

"I think he wants the crown for himself," said Deaglan, "And remember, his mother probably encourages him to overthrow her old husband, I think that woman's hatred may move an entire nation."

Conall looked down at the ground as they again walked, "But Brian is the king, and a good king. He has brought more peace to this land than we have seen in years, he builds roads, fills libraries, what would Sigtrygg do if he wore the crown?"

"Conall, we are warriors, we fight and keep Brian on the throne. He is our king." Deaglan stopped, looked at Conall, "I think we would fight as well for Sigtrygg if we had been born in Dubh Linn or fight for Máel Morda if we were born in Leinster."

The two men walked in silence for a while, then Deaglan said, "When you were younger and the raiders came to Cnoc Gorm, you asked why men try to take from others that which is not theirs. Now you ask why Sigtrygg and Máel Morda oppose Brian." He stopped and looked at Conall, "These are good questions, and I don't have answers that would satisfy you."

Conall said, "I fight for Brian because he helped my mother and I think he has done good things for Éirinn." He paused, looked at Deaglan, "He has been kind to you, Earnan and me, to our family, and I'll continue to stand with him."

Deaglan listened to his friend, his student, and heard the undertone of discontent. "You still puzzle over why these men do as they do? Why do the foreigners come to our land and try to conquer us?" He looked at Conall and continued, "That I can't answer. You're a great warrior, Conall. Your skill with the axe and the sword is not matched in any contest we've had. I go into battle with you at my side and I don't fear our enemy, I almost pity them." He noticed Conall looking off into the distance. "You are a warrior who loves peace, a contradiction to be sure. But you're more than a warrior, you're a symbol to so many who go into battle with you. They fight with more energy, more strength because you are there. You lead because they want to follow you and you're great because you and those who follow you are victorious and live to fight again."

Conall paused and looked up to the sky as a gentle rain began to fall, "My mother prayed to a God in the heavens. Many men do the same and I look to the sky and wonder why a God would allow his creatures to fight and kill each other as we do." He looked at Deaglan, "A few years ago, we fought a battle at Glenmama with the people of Dubh Linn. Then, later, we marched into another battle and the man standing next to me was my enemy from that earlier battle, this time he was my comrade. Now, if he still lives, he may be my enemy again."

The rain fell and Conall lifted his face to the clouds and quietly said, "Wash me, wash away the blood and dirt of every battle and give me peace. You made me, gave me these arms, these hands, this size and allow my anger to rule my sword, my axe. You allow those others to stand before me and I kill them. Have I done good, or will I burn in fire forever?" He stood quietly as the rain increased and Deaglan stood next to him.

The two warriors arrived at their camp and Deaglan gathered several other group leaders, "We should make ready to march. Clean our swords, hone the edges, and exercise our arms. Battle is not far off, and we should be ready."

Within a period of three weeks, Deaglan led his unit into a skirmish outside the town of Kilmainham. The town was sacked and burned, and they marched on toward Dubh Linn only a few miles east. They arrived at a field south of the River Liffy, outside Dubh Linn where the larger part of Brian's Army had established a camp. Another band of warriors had sacked and burned Clondalkin, and a third group was wading into Munster. It was September and the siege of Dubh Linn had already begun.

There was not much for Conall to do, and he found himself wandering the nearby woods and neighboring settlements. As he wandered, he eventually found his way to Clondalkin and the tower. It stood in spite of the sack and burning of the town by Brian's troops. There he sat on a rock, remembering his meetings with Brogan and his few years as a spy. Laughing to himself, he wandered through the old marketplace and found his way to the inn where he and Deaglan had found food and shelter several times. The inn had not burned and as a gentle rain began to fall, he entered and found a quiet corner. He ate and drank, finally falling asleep only to be awakened by a young serving girl. His mind immediately wandered away from battles and politics and settled on a softer and more pleasant subject.

Three days later Conall wandered back into the encampment outside Dubh Linn and found his comrades. The banging of wooden swords meant Deaglan was probably teaching his contingent of fighting men some new maneuver or honing their skills on that which they already knew.

"Ah, Conall," said Deaglan, "Now we can delve deeper into this practice." He tossed Conall a wooden sword and continued, "You remember our last session?" he said as he began an overhead slash toward Conall's head.

Conall laughed as he moved to block the overhead movement with his sword and laughed louder as Deaglan changed direction of his sword, striking Conall just above his right hip.

"What's this?" exclaimed Deaglan, "I've delivered a killing slash to the giant's belly."

Conall backed up with his eyes wide open and a look of confusion on his face. "I think I've been killed," he laughed as he dropped his wooden sword and leaned against a tree. "Now that I am dead," he said, "May I lie down and rest?"

Deaglan stood looking at Conall with his hands on his hips, "It's a woman. You've found another woman and that's where you've been these last few days."

Conall shrugged and started to say something when Deaglan cut him off, "This is very serious and we have to be ready for combat at any time, in a week, in a day, now!" He threw his wooden sword to the ground and turned to walk away.

"Yes, Deaglan, I met a woman," said Conall, "And I allowed myself to relax." He stood and walked to Deaglan, "I know what we must do, so let us be about our business of battle and killing."

Deaglan looked at Conall, "It's not just you. These men look to you for leadership, for inspiration, we should not laugh at the mistakes we make. Those little errors can cost a man his head. We have to train them better and save the laughter for after the battle."

"You're right, old friend. Let's do this over again and make each of them repeat it till it's done without thought."

The session continued and the men were all exhausted and not laughing. "These things you teach us," said one of the men, "It makes us better?"

"Yes," replied Deaglan. "But always remember, if you relax as Conall did, you may never have another chance to defend yourself." He looked at Conall, "To the river and a quick wash before we rest for the night."

As the two men walked across the open field to the river's edge, Deaglan said, "So, it was a woman, anybody I know?"

"I don't think so. She's a serving girl in the Inn in Clondalkin where we stayed a year ago. I don't think she was there then."

"Well, perhaps it's time you thought about taking a wife and raising a few children. Is this someone who could make you think more of farming and less of battle?"

"Ah," replied Conall, "She's a very nice girl, but we're just good friends, no more than that."

* * *

The siege of Dubh Linn continued until December. As supplies dwindled and Brian tired of the long battle, the decision to back away and return to Ceann Coradh was made. The army slogged their way back across the cold terrain, happy to have an end to the struggle, unhappy to come home empty handed.

Brogan had healed as much as he would by the time the army returned to Ceann Coradh. He was saddled with reduced use of his left arm and a limp, but he eagerly greeted his friends upon their return.

"I've heard again from one of my sources. Someone who is no more enamored with Sigtrygg than any of us here," said Brogan.

"Have you told Brian of this?" asked Deaglan.

"I want to be sure of what I report." Brogan hobbled to a bench and sat down, "But, I cannot travel as I used to."

Conall leaned forward, "Are you asking us to be the spies again and go to Dubh Linn, or Clondalkin?"

Brogan sat as straight as he could, "I am." He looked about cautiously, "But this time it will be our secret, there are too many ears here and we cannot take any chances." He shuffled on the bench and continued quietly, "His name is Ainle, and you'll find him near the tower. He will carry a red scarf that he will say is his wife's. Tell him you have looked for such a scarf and would pay a high price for it, if you had the coins."

Conall spoke softly, "What news could he have?"

"Perhaps nothing, then again, perhaps the word that could keep us all safe, I don't know what he will have., but I do know he has something."

Conall looked at Deaglan, "Are you ready for another trek through the shadows?"

Brogan continued, "I think only one of you should go. You Conall, you spent some time in Clondalkin recently and would not raise suspicion if you returned."

Conall and Deaglan looked at each other, "How do you know about my visit to Clondalkin?"

Brogan grinned, "I'm a spy, I have my sources."

The three men laughed, and Brogan added, "You are very noticeable when you walk about, my large friend. But you have reason to be in Clondalkin, your friend, Blathin."

Conall looked at Brogan, "You had someone watching me?"

Brogan laughed, "No my friend, the report I received was that there was a great large warrior from Brian's army in the town, spending time with a young lady. The description could be none other than you."

"So, you want me to return to…"

"To the tower," said Brogan. "And Ainle will see you. You will tell him about the scarf and when he asks if you know me, you say no."

"When?"

"In five days' time, that will be this coming Saturday and the marketplace will be busier than usual."

Deaglan said, "I would go with you, but…"

Brogan again interrupted, "Yes, go as far as you can without entering the town, then when Conall leaves Clondalkin, the two of you ride together back here."

Deaglan and Conall prepared for their trip the next morning. It was a cold and rainy day, and they were not seen or at least not followed as they left Ceann Coradh. The journey to Clondalkin took three days in the rain and over muddy roads. They arrived at a cave, two miles outside of Clondalkin where Deaglan had stayed years before with Conall's father and several other warriors.

"I remember this place," said Deaglan. "There were near twenty of us then, and Laoghaire was leading us." He looked around the cave and continued, "this was our base, we went out in smaller groups looking for Donnuban."

"Here, in Clondalkin?" puzzled Conall.

"We were looking toward Dubh Linn, then, when we received word that he was south of here, we rejoined our main force and marched toward Corcaigh."

They sat and spent the remainder of the day talking about the battle at Cathair Cuan.

Saturday morning, Conall made his way into the town and Deaglan remained at the cave. Conall walked about the market, looking at various belts, boots and colored scarves. There were few vendors on this cold and damp morning, but Conall spotted a man near the tower carrying a red scarf.

"Tis a fine-looking scarf you have there," said Conall, "I'd pay a high price for such a scarf."

The man looked at Conall and replied, "Well now, would you be knowing a man by the name of Brogan?"

"Brogan, no, can't say as I do," returned Conall.

"Well," said Ainle, "Let me write down the name of the vendor that sold the scarf to me." He took a folded piece of paper from his shirt, scribbled a note and said, "You should hurry to see him, he may not be there long." He handed the paper to Conall, hesitated and added, "There are two pieces of paper in your hand, Conall. Secret the one back to Brogan and the other, on which I wrote, that one you may surrender to Sigtrygg's people if necessary." He looked around again and continued, "Brogan is an old friend. He and I traveled the roads of this island many times together." He looked about and added, "Tell him I remember it took eight trips to reach the mountain and four more to return." He smiled and said, "Now go, quickly."

Conall looked at Ainle, a little confused and immediately left the marketplace, regained his horse and rode out to meet Deaglan at the cave. "I've been given a scrap of folded paper. The little man said I should hurry, so let's leave now and make the most of the remaining daylight."

As the two were about to leave, a group of four men approached. Deaglan looked at Conall, "I don't like the look of this, stand ready."

The horsemen halted facing the two warriors, "You there, you were just in Clondalkin talking to a little man near the tower. I know he gave you something and I want it."

Conall reached inside his shirt and produced the scrap of paper on which Ainle had written a name. "Tis just the name of a vendor where I could buy a scarf for my lovely wife."

"We know who you are, Conall mac Laoghaire," said the leader of the four. "And you have no wife. You met with a spy in Clondalkin and you're taking a message from him to Brian."

"See for yourself," said Conall, "Tis just a name of a man who will sell me a scarf for my lovely bride."

Deaglan added, "And a beauty she is."

The Dubh Linn man took the scrap of paper, looked at it and said, "You've no wife, you were spending nights with a whore in Clondalkin and now I want the paper Ainle gave you." He put his hand on his sword as did the other three.

Conall's eyes narrowed, "The lady is no whore," he said in a deep voice that did not hide his rising anger. "She is a good woman and I'll not hear you say otherwise."

The men from Dubh Linn slowly dismounted and all drew their swords. Conall stood rigid as they all stepped closer. "Give me the paper from Ainle, now," said the leader.

Deaglan stepped to Conall's left side and drew his sword, "We were about to leave. Is that a problem for you?" he said to the Dubh Linn men.

"You'll go nowhere. We came for that paper and now if we have to, we'll kill you to get it."

The anger within Conall was about to explode, "The little man, did you hurt him?"

"He wouldn't talk, so we split his skull and hung him by his ankles as an example to the rest of his kind," replied the Dubh Linn man. "Now hand over the paper."

Conall drew his swords and immediately attacked the man on his right with a single blow to his shield, sending him backward two steps, then turned on the leader with a series of four hard blows that sent him to the ground. Conall didn't waste time and turned on the first man he attacked. The contest was no contest. Deaglan dispatched his two opponents and Conall killed the first of his attackers.

Conall turned toward the leader as he tried to stand. "You should have stayed in Dubh Linn," he said as he knocked the man's sword out of the way. "Deaglan, I see one of these fools has a rope on his horse. I have a use for it."

Deaglan and Conall mounted their horses, and each took a second and third horse in tow. The four men were left hanging upside down from a tree, stripped naked and sliced open at the belly and their heads split in two.

Deaglan and Conall rode back to Ceann Coradh, pushing their horses to the limit.

* * *

Brogan opened the folded paper brought by Conall and read the script. "Did you try to read the paper?" he asked, curiously.

"No," said Conall. "I wanted to get it back here as quickly as possible and took no time to read it."

"Just as well," said Brogan. He opened the paper and scanned the writing, "It's mostly written in Latin and some parts are in Greek."

Conall smiled, "My mother taught us all to read and write in the Irish, Latin and Greek, but it's been a long while since I've had either the Latin or Greek to keep me up on it."

"Well, it says here that Ainle may have told you something additional, did he?"

Conall lowered his head, "Yes, he said it took him eight trips to reach the mountain and four more to return." Conall twisted his face and added, "I'm not sure what that means, but I assume you do."

Brogan smiled, "Yes good friend, I do." He turned to walk away, then stopped and said, "Was there anything else."

Conall looked at Brogan, "Ainle, they killed him. They followed me out of town to where I met Deaglan and demanded the paper."

Brogan lowered his head, "Ainle, yes we walked many roads together," He looked at Conall, "Those who followed?"

"All dead," replied Deaglan.

Brogan paused for a moment, "He knew it could end badly, now we'll see what he died for. I have to translate it into something readable to pass on to Brian."

Deaglan and Conall looked at each other and left.

*   *   *

46

1014 AD Leinster, Éirinn
Cluain Tarbh … The Meadow of the Bull

Brogan sat at a table with a quill and ink and made note after note, constantly remembering the phrase Ainle had uttered to Conall. The message finally complete, Brogan rose to his feet, placed his completed writing under his bad arm and with the aid of a crutch, hobbled off to find Brian.

Brogan entered the meeting room where Brian and several of his battle commanders were discussing the current state of the nation. "Sigtrygg hides behind his wall of Dubh Linn and casts stones and insults," stated one of the commanders. "He cries for his mother and listens to her curse the high king."

Brian rolled his eyes and said, "Sigtryyg is a very dangerous man. He holds the city of Dubh Linn and together with Máel Morda and his Leinster contingent, they are a formidable force."

Brogan stood quietly in the back of the room until Brian saw him and halted the conversation. "Gentlemen, I need a few minutes with Brogan. Please excuse us."

The five commanders walked out of the room recognizing Brogan and greeting him as they left. Brogan hobbled over to Brian and half out of breath started to talk.

"Brogan, you're in no condition to be running around, now sit, relax and we'll talk," said Brian.

Brogan sat, relaxed, and began, "The information we have can be expanded." He paused, caught his breath, and continued, "Sigtrygg has about 2,000 men that he could deploy, but the sense is that he will hold as many as half that number to stand on the walls."

Brian nodded, "I assumed he would leave some force in the town remembering the Battle at Sulcoit and our taking of Limerick."

Brogan shuffled his notes, "Máel Morda may have 2,500 to 3,000 men from Leinster, that's more than we assumed last week."

Again, Brian nodded, "Yes, and it is possible he may rally more by summer if this is not stopped soon."

Brogan continued, "Sigtrygg has sent emissaries to Alba, Man and beyond. We don't know how many men will be coming from those requests, but he is making promises he cannot keep to attract Brodir and Sigurd."

"What of Ospak?" asked Brian.

Brogan held out his hands in an unknowing gesture, "I'm not certain, he seems not willing to oppose you, but I would advise we assume he will be involved."

The two men talked for a while and Brian finally said, "Now to count our troops I must call my commanders back to join us."

*   *   *

"We leave Ceann Coradh in the morning," said Deaglan. "The march to Dubh Linn may take ten days, depending on the weather."

Conall laughed, "Ten days if we walk in the sunshine, maybe eleven if it rains," He looked around at the men gathered and added, "Three or four more if we trudge through snow."

"We haven't seen snow in five years," said one of the warriors. "We'll be in Dubh Linn in less than ten days."

Morning came and the men prepared for the trek east. "The last time we did this, we were gone for four months," said a grizzled veteran. "But there are more of us this time and Brian grows impatient with these foreigners." The sentiment among most of the warriors was the same, this time there would be a battle and they would be home in a turn of the moon.

"We are more than 1,000 Dal gCais," said Deaglan, "More by three or four hundred. Murchad leads another larger group of men from Munster. Malachi has 1,500 men from Meath, and I am told the Connaught clansmen number near 1,500." He looked at Conall, "We also have a contingent of Manx Vikings and some mercenaries, maybe 500, maybe more."

"How does that balance with Sigtrygg's army?" asked Conall.

"I don't know, but if we see Brogan, we may ask him."

* * *

The march across the middle of Éirinn was blessed with sunshine and cursed with rain. The army arrived at Kilmainham in five days and established a base camp.

"Do we siege the walls again?" asked Conall with a hint of disgust.

"No," replied Murchad, "This day we send troops to Fine Gall and Howth to the north and others to south of Dubh Linn." He sat with his old friends and shared a drink of mead. "We will draw them out of Dubh Linn and defeat them in the open plain."

As the men continued their conversation, a boy approached Murchad, "Your father asks that you come to his camp immediately."

Murchad rose and said, "What is at issue, boy?"

"Tis not for me to say, but I believe the foreigners are boarding their ships, they seem to be running away."

"Ha," said Murchad. "A victory without a single bloodied sword."

Conall and Deaglan looked at each other and laughed, "We may be home in no time at all." They poured more mead and saluted Murchad as he hurried off to Brian's tent.

"A good night's rest, a warm meal in the morning and perhaps we sit through a day or two of negotiations, then we march home," said Deaglan, "I'd call that a great victory."

Shortly, the boy returned and said, "King Brian wishes you to join the forces returning from Howth. They're assembling near the beach."

"What's happening, boy?" asked Deaglan.

"King Sigtrygg has sent a force out from Dubh Linn's walls to meet our forces and the Northmen that ran away yesterday, have returned. They're coming ashore as we speak."

* * *

The morning air was cool, dew covered the grass and wet the leaves on nearby trees. As the sun rose to cast light upon the low land near the water, word spread that the Norse had sailed out of the harbor and turned around in the night, landing near the weir of Cluain Tarbh, joining Sigtrygg's forces and moving to meet the Irish troops returning from Howth.

Battle lines were beginning to form. Brian had sent his Dal gCais to the left flank near the water. Deaglan and Conall hurried to join their comrades. They approached from the rear, stretching, flexing, loosening their limbs and testing their weapons.

Murchad was moving amongst his warriors from Munster when he saw Conall approaching the Dal gCais from the rear. He found Deaglan and said, "Conall appears to be going to join the left flank."

"He still carries his hatred for the Norse and sees more of them there than here," replied Deaglan. "He needs no direction; he will charge ahead and destroy everything in his path."

The gap between the opposing armies was near two hundred feet, warriors on both sides could see their breath as they stood in wait. A slight breeze wafted in the smell of the sea and hardened warriors began to wonder if this was the last of their days on this earth. Men shivered from the chilled air and some from the thought of swords sharp edges, lances pointed ends and heavy rocks raining down on their ranks. Most of the men assembled on the fields were veterans of more than one battle, but that did not prevent the level of fear from rising in their bellies. The officers, leaders in charge of different groups, began to inspire their troops with shouts of victory over the opposing side and the hurling of insults across the open field.

Plaitt, a Northman known to be a ferocious warrior, singled out one of Brian's Scottish allies, Domnaill mac Eimin. The insults and curses finally drew the two men to a low patch of open field where they continued to curse the other, spit at their opponent and to move in wide circles. The Northman with his helmet and mail-covered body against a bare-chested man from Alba. Even these men felt the uncertainty of their future and with screams and cheers from the crowds, the two men engaged. Sword crashing upon shield, back and forth the two men pounded each other until Domnaill saw an opening and thrust his sword at Plaitt's chest. Mail slows a sword but does not always stop the incoming thrust. The man stabbed returned the thrust and both men slowed as both were deep wounded. In a final burst of energy, Domnaill pushed his sword deeper into Plaitt's chest and as he pushed, he also followed and Plaitt's sword sunk deeper into his chest. They both stopped, fell to their knees and in a final grabbing at their opponent, died with sword driven into each other and their hands reaching for the other's throat.

The crowds again roared with insults and Murchad, Brian's son, met a challenge to single combat in the open field. He met, fought and slew the man. Other challenges were issued from both sides and after another bout of single warriors, a man in full armor guided a horse slowly out of the Norse ranks and halfway down the slope near the water's edge to the middle of the open field. "Is the man called Conall mac Laoghaire among you," he shouted to the opposing crowd. There was no answer and the man again shouted, "I seek the coward called Conall mac Laoghaire, the murderer of women, children and old men. I challenge him to individual combat." Again, there was no answer. The level of taunting rose from the crowd behind the armored warrior. "Coward," shouted several men. "Murderer," shouted others.

The force assembled on the north side of the glen was quiet, then a murmur seemed to rise from the rear of the Dal gCais troops. The crowd began to open a path for someone coming forward. At first the Norse man saw the head of an axe with a curved blade move through the crowd. It was half a man higher than the tallest of the crowd. As it neared the crest of the hill, the crowd opened wide to allow the man carrying the axe through. He was six and a half feet in height. His shoulders were bare, and his long sandy colored hair flowed to his shoulders. The man's arms were bigger than most men's legs and his scarred face had the look of a battle-hardened warrior. He walked down the slope to the middle of the open field and turned toward the armored man. In a quiet, but deep, commanding voice he said, "Who is it you seek?"

"I have called out Conall mac Laoghaire. He is a coward and a murderer of innocents. I have come for his head."

The large man tilted his head, showing no expression on his face as he stared at the armored man. "And who are you to call this Conall out?"

The man spurred his horse forward to the bottom of the slope and approached the large man. "I am Ringard, Son of Olaf and I am here to slay this Conall."

The large man lifted his head, straightened his back, came to his full height, and said, "And take his head?"

The crowd on the north slope roared in approval as the large man stepped closer to the man on the horse. "My name is Conall mac Laoghaire, but I do not slay women and children and I think I will keep my head. If you want it, come at me now or go back to your camp and bother me no more."

The two men were about thirty feet apart, Ringard drew his sword in his right hand and gripped his shield in his left. He spurred his steed toward Conall, guiding his horse to Conall's right side. When the horse had reached a full gallop, Conall spun to his left and stepped to his right moving his axe in a wide arc and connecting with Ringard in the small of his back as his horse carried him past Conall. Ringard was off balance, lost his sword and fell from his horse. Conall took four steps, raised his axe high above his head and brought it down on Ringard's skull.

Conall pulled his axe from the other man's corpse, wiped the red and grey on Ringard's cloak and started back to his comrades. A second man wanted to challenge Conall. This man stepped into the field and called to Conall. He challenged, then cursed him and spit on the ground.

Conall heard the challenge and insults as he casually turned, walked back through the crowd and onto the open field. As he stepped through the front line, he could again be seen by all. His great size and battle axe identified him, and the crowd fell still. Conall stepped out from the front ranks, stood at his full height, gazed at the crowd, and said, "Now, who calls my name?"

The man across the opening stepped closer and replied, "I do, Ragnar, son of Meldun. I challenge you to single combat."

Conall looked at the man. He was a large man, over six feet in height, in full battle gear, chain mail, armor, helmet, shield and sword. He moved closer to Conall who stood in the field stripped to the waist and holding his battle axe on a long staff.

The man looked at Conall and said, "Ready yourself for battle."

Conall returned the stare and replied, "I stand ready, little man. You made a great noise and now here I am." He started across the open field. The men were about fifty feet apart when Ragnar started toward Conall.

Conall carried his axe at his side as he stepped toward Ragnar and brought it to both hands as the two men came to ten feet apart. Ragnar raised his sword above his head and charged, taking two full steps as Conall casually stepped to his left, raised his axe to shoulder height and began an arc down toward Ragnar's legs. The Viking's sword came down, missing Conall's right shoulder as the axe severed Ragnar's leg above the knee. Ragnar fell to the ground, screaming in pain, and Conall drove the sharpened tip of his axe through the Northman's throat.

Another from the Norse crowd called Conall's name and pushed his way through the crowd. This man was less encumbered with heavy armor and moved with greater agility. He stood as tall as Ragnar and showed no fear. "This is your day to die, Irish. And I am here to send you to hell."

"I wouldn't be welcome there," replied Conall. "I've sent far too many of your kind to burn in those fires and I'd only increase their pain."

The man began to run toward Conall. At a distance of fifteen feet, Conall stepped to his right and began to swing the axe in the same direction. When the man had covered the next nine feet, the axe was there to meet him, crashing solidly on the man's shield. He staggered slightly and as he regained his balance, Conall continued the movement of the axe in a circular motion up over his head and brought it in a downward motion. The man saw the axe as it struck his helmet and glanced off striking his left shoulder, cutting through his collar bone and removing his arm. He lay on the ground, dead. The axe had broken his neck.

Conall turned to walk back to his front line when a fourth voice called his name. Another warrior from the Norse camp guided his horse down to the flat plain and called out to Conall, "You killed my friend, now I will kill you."

"You need not do this thing," said Conall.

The man said, "If I killed your friend, would you not want to kill me?"

Conall paused, turned toward the man, "No, I have no friends."

Again, the crowd roared with laughter. The man dismounted, drew his sword and approached Conall. He was a large man, near Conall's height, but not as massive. He raised his sword in an attack posture. Conall waited for the man to close the distance between them to about ten feet. Then he swung his axe at its full length and struck the man's shield, sending him to the ground.

"Stay there if you like, little man, and you may live," said Conall as he began to walk away.

The man regained his feet and saw a chance to strike at Conall's back. Conall heard him, turned, and parried a blow from the man's sword. He pushed hard and knocked the man to the ground again, then raised his axe high above his head and paused, "You should have stayed down."

The man was now beaten, if Conall had not paused, the man would be dead like his friend. He rolled to his right, regained his feet, and looked at Conall over his shoulder as he ran back through his fellows to the woods.

Conall walked back into his front line and met Deaglan, "Will the rest be that easy, old friend?"

Deaglan and the men around him laughed, "We can only hope."

Conall moved away from the front line toward the rear and saw Laisren talking to Ciaran and another young warrior. "Who's your friend?" he asked.

Ciaran replied, "This is Meallan, he comes from Ceann Coradh and wants to stand with us today."

Conall looked at the young man, tall with broad boney shoulders, yellow hair and dark blue eyes. "You remind me of my brother, Earnan. He's a great warrior."

"Is he here with us today?" asked the young man with a deep voice.

"No," replied Conall. "He was hard wounded at Ghleann Mama and can no longer stand in battle, as much as he wants to, and would if allowed." He looked at Meallan and was about to ask a question when he heard his name called.

"Conall, it begins," yelled Ronan from the front line.

Conall looked at Ciaran, "Remember what I have taught you. Fight well my friends and this day will be ours." He turned and hurried back to the front line with axe in hand.

Deaglan stood with the contingent of Dal gCais on the left flank. Ronan and Faolin joined him, each in command of a group of nine warriors. Laisren and Ciaran were in Faolin's group and Meallan was in Ronan's group. Conall was supposed to be in Deaglan's group but found his way to the frontline between the clansmen from Connaught and warriors from Munster. He was now in the center of the Irish line, directly across from the Vikings from Orkney. This was where Conall wanted to be. He still carried the hatred for Northmen, and he didn't wait for an alarm. The two sides had been inching closer by the minute. Another challenge had been called out and two other men had moved to the center. Four more challenges and four more dead men littered the field. Insults from the shield walls crossed the remaining open space and javelins were thrown over the front-line troops. The sides were now close enough to jab with spears and as the open space disappeared, the clash of steel on steel, wood and flesh rose in a fanatical, bloody symphony. Conall stepped through the front line and charged the Norse line. As he was about to deliver the first blow with his axe, something grazed his left arm above his elbow. His axe never slowed, rather it gained speed and split a Northman's shield, stopping halfway through the man's head.

The battle was now full on. Screams began as arms and legs were severed, and heads rolled freely on the muddy ground. Conall was jabbed by a lance in his ribs and cut by two different swords on his arms. The wounds were not serious and as his anger rose, his temper flared, and his axe killed another man almost immediately. The battle raged on and the gaps between living, fighting warriors grew as the dead began to pile up on the ground and the dew-soaked grass now ran with blood. The mixture of dirt, sweat and blood covered the warriors still standing on both sides. Screams and cries of the dying and the groans of the wounded filled the ears of the combatants. The stench of death, defecation and vomit warming as the sun rose in the sky filled their nostrils. The older, experienced warriors had seen and smelled this before and ignored the noise and odors as much as possible. The younger warriors experiencing battle for the first or second time often paused, coughed, choked, or turned away only to fall victim to the blade of an enemy.

Conall was cut, bleeding and bruised, but he fought on as if none of these impediments existed. He wasted little time on individuals, delivering two or three blows to an opponent, then driving him to the ground with a killing blow and moving on to another. If the man went down before him was not dead, the others who fought with Conall, following him through battle, delivered a death blow to the fallen enemy warrior.

As the middle of the day approached, the two sides were exhausted and backed away in a mutual pause. The break was brief, as men tried to rest and drink, the fronts again reformed and moved toward each other. A call to single combat was issued from the ranks of the Norse. Two brave souls stepped into middle ground. They were both already bloodied and battered, and the clashing of their swords brought the rest of the warriors into the fray. It was as if there had been no break. Again, the screams and cries of men being hacked apart filled the air and the spray of blood was everywhere. Large stones, darts and javelins again filled the air crossing in both directions. The axe in Conall's hands found flesh and bone as often as wooden shields and the steel of the Northmen's long swords. Men fell in front of him as he waded through the weakened and broken shield wall and mangled bodies of men. The dust and dirt kicked up in a storm of twisting bodies mixed with the splashing blood from sword and axe slashes and the sweat on every man's body, caking the warriors in layers of blood-soaked dirt and sweat. The battle raged and again both sides backed away from the field. Those left on the field were dead or near death. Soldiers from both sides reached out to pull still-living comrades from the carnage. This temporary truce allowed the two sides a longer rest than the first pause. Some rested, some tended to wounds and others counted their dead. As Conall cleaned the dark sticky coating of blood from his axe handle, the battle began again.

Again, warriors issued challenges. Again, men met in the middle and again, half of them died. A call to Conall to stand in single combat was met with an angry roar and Conall stepped into the open field. He hesitated for less than a second, and before the man could repeat his insults, Conall charged what was left of the Viking shield wall, taking the heads of two men in one huge swing of his axe. He continued into the ranks of the Vikings, clearing a path with his axe. Others followed his charge and the break in the wall was widened. The Dal gCais warriors poured through the opening and a rout began. After a while, the fighting slowed, and the two sides retreated. Some wounded were carried from the field, some were killed where they lay. Warriors on both sides drank, some ate, and they returned to the original battle lines of the day.

Battle resumed and again, men hacked each other apart. The day passed slowly and soon the sides again pulled back. The bodies of the dead and wounded littering the field were again scouted for those worth saving. With little hesitation, the third engagement of the day began and lasted less than the two previous engagements. The tide swung in favor of Brian's army. The remains of the Norse were driven from the field, they scattered, ran to the weir and toward their ships. The Leinstermen made for the bridge to Dubh Linn. Each group was pursued and as they were caught, the fleeing Norse and Irish were slaughtered.

Conall stood atop a small rise, watching the Norse retreat. He didn't run after them, although others did. He stood alone with axe in hand looking over the battlefield. His thoughts began to drift to the questions he always felt after a battle. *Why did this have to happen? Was there another way to solve the problem? What was the problem?*

His breathing eased, his muscles relaxed and several cuts and bruises from the day's battle began to announce themselves. He picked up a piece of a dead man's shirt and began to clean the slick of blood and grey matter from his axe handle and as the sky darkened and a cool breeze drifted across the meadow, Conall saw a man moving in his direction, a large man with a long sword and a battered shield. A Northman. He was tall and broad. He wore a metal vest over chain mail, an unadorned helmet, dented and dirty. His beard was soaked in blood and dirt, and he moved between the dead and wounded without looking at them, continuing toward Conall.

A gentle rain began to fall, washing the dirt and blood from Conall's back. He felt a chill, from the rain or from the approaching Northman. He stood still, his muscles beginning to tighten, the little aches disappearing, his head lowered, and he stared at the stranger. He felt the heft of his axe at his side and waited, wondering what the man was going to do.

The man stopped twenty feet from Conall and touched his sword to the ground. "You, Irish," he said in a deep voice, "this day is not yet done as long as we both stand."

Conall looked at the man and felt the chill come over him again. It wasn't from fear, it was more like listening to thunder roll through the clouds and watching lightning strike the ground. He stood and remarked, "This day is ours. Your friends are running for their ships, and you stand here alone."

The man casually glanced over his shoulder at the harbor beyond the river, then looked back at Conall, "You don't chase them," he said. "You still seek those who remain to fight, and I did not come here to run away when there is still a warrior on the field to challenge."

"What is your name, Northman?" asked Conall.

"My name is not important," said the large man, "but for you, it is Leif, son of Rodmar." He looked at Conall, "Your name?"

"I am Conall mac Laoghaire."

"As I thought, names mean very little now. When this day is done, one of us will be dead, perhaps both," said Leif. He lifted his sword and stepped toward Conall.

"You don't have to do this," said Conall. "You may walk to your ship and leave; I will not pursue."

"No, I think you would not run, either after me or from me." Leif paused, "I think you are a true warrior. I have had my day; I have had many battles and I have never run. I will not run today." He took another step toward Conall and raised his sword in a salute, then another step and raised his sword ready to attack.

Conall felt chilled again and looked at the ground around him. Bodies and parts of the slain were everywhere, the field was soaked with a black, red ooze of blood, rain, and earth. He moved his axe to both hands, looked up and stood ready to meet the Leif's slow charge. As Leif neared, Conall could better see his face; old, scarred and twisted. His hands, large, gnarled and covered with the marks of battle. His huge arms were thick, strong, marked and stained, and his eyes, his eyes had stared at death many times.

Leif's long sword came down in a hard slash. Conall blocked it with his axe handle and the two men stood for a second frozen in place. Great strength had met great strength and the two men were only inches apart looking into each other's eyes. Both men were prepared to fight, both to die. Each was equal to the other. Leif was older and his strength might not last as long as Conall's. Conall was younger and his disadvantage was inexperience. The two pushed apart and Leif swung another slash at waist height. Conall moved back but Leif's sword caught Conall's axe handle, knocking it loose from one hand. Conall stumbled backward and regained his feet. Leif stepped closer with his sword raised. Conall moved to his right, away from Leif's sword hand and brought his axe in a round swing, striking Leif's shield.

Leif's arm absorbed the blow and he muttered, "That's better," then stepped again toward Conall. His sword raised above his head, Leif swung hard at Conall's head. The sword struck the axe head and Conall brought the bottom of the handle up hard to Leif's chin, standing him up straight and opening Leif's chest to a downward strike of the axe.

Leif was cut below the mail, and he roared and brought his sword down towards Conall's neck. The axe handle again slowed the sword but did not stop it completely. They pushed apart, both men now wounded and bleeding. Leif grinned and moved slowly to an attack position. "You are good, Irish, but I do not die easily." He stepped again toward Conall with a lunge. Conall moved backward and swung his axe hard at Leif's head. Leif raised his shield, catching the axe and stopping the blow. He swung the great sword again, catching Conall's thigh with the tip, opening a shallow cut. He was again open and

Conall brought the axe head down hard on Leif's shoulder near the first cut and broke the collar bone.

The large Viking fell to his knees as blood spurted from his neck and shoulder. He looked at Conall, smiled and said, "You fight well Conall. Live another day." As his eyes closed and opened slowly and his breathing slowed, he reached for his dagger and raised it in an attack posture, "Finish the battle," he tried to reach Conall with the small blade.

Conall understood, lifted his axe, and placed the pike at Leif's throat, "Sleep well my friend," and pushed the point through the Northman's neck.

Two other warriors approached, "His purse, take his purse."

Conall looked at them and said, "Don't touch this one. He was a great warrior and should not be dishonored."

The two backed away as Conall placed Leif's sword on his chest and his shield next to his left arm. He put the dagger back in Leif's right hand, stood and looked around again, then walked away with his axe.

* * *

The battle was over, and the battlefield was being closely checked. Any from the north still alive were being summarily dispatched and those from Brian's army were pointed out to be helped. As the victors scoured the battlefield, valuables, weapons and leather were taken and the collection of copper, silver and gold mounted in the purses of the victors.

Deaglan and Ronan seized their fair share of the booty and more. They took mostly coins and precious stones. Things that were easy to carry. When they returned home, the coins and jewels would be divided evenly and Conall's share was to be secreted at Cnoc Gorm, in the cave below the round house. The two men talked about telling Conall about the cache, "Yes, but not today," they agreed.

Conall wandered to a physician's tent and asked if they would bandage his shoulder and thigh. As he was being stitched, Deaglan found him and said, "Conall, are you hurt, that cut on your chest, is it bad, will you be alright?"

"Relax, Deaglan, I am well taken care of and you? Are you alright, and the others? What of Ronan, Faolin, Laisren, Ciaran and their new friend?"

"All are well, you seem to have had the worst of it." Deaglan watched as the physician finished stitching and bandaging Conall's wounds, "Let's go find Brian, he'll have heard by now, and we should celebrate this great victory."

Conall looked at him as they walked out of the physician's tent and across the field, "What have we won, good friend? Look at these men, hacked and slain. The price we paid is great." He turned again looking at the field covered with blood and bodies, and up on the rise where Leif rested, then he turned to Deaglan, "Yes, let's find Brian."

*   *   *

The High King Brian mac Cennetig was a great warrior in his younger days. But now past his seventieth year and a very religious man, he had given command to his son, Murchad and he remained behind the lines. He may have been praying in his tent, he may have been asleep, he could have been getting ready to come out and celebrate the victory when a band of retreating Norse stumbled upon his tent. Brian's guard proved no match for the fleeing Vikings. They were quickly killed, and Brian was found. The king may have reached for his sword, but not quickly enough to prevent a killing blow from a Norse sword.

Brian, the High King of Éirinn was dead. The battle won and the king is killed. An end to a man who had risen to the position of Ard Ri by his own sword, now slain by the last remnants of a retreating, defeated foe. The group of Norse quickly moved away from Brian's tent and toward the river, not toward their ships. They were trying to escape the slaughter being done on their comrades. They had turned inland, perhaps to hide, perhaps they were lost. They were trying to escape this land where most of their fellows had fallen. They ran, but not far enough, not long enough.

The group of Dal gCais warriors hurrying to be with Brian to revel in this victory, found their king dead. They quickly called an alarm and men moved out in all directions looking for the murderers. The band of Norse running toward the River Liffy was seen and the Dal gCais ran after them. The Norse were caught in a wooded area and brutally killed. The last of these men to be killed, their leader, was stood against a tree, his gut split open, and his entrails drawn out. He died a very slow and painful death.

"There, Brian is avenged," proclaimed one of the Dal gCais warriors.

"No, he is just dead," said Conall. "Dead and no longer able to rule this great mixture of tribes and nations." He started to walk away, "Now who will pick up his sword and continue his work. Murchad is dead, killed today as were his son Toirdelbach and too many others. Is there a man big enough and wise enough to rule?"

* * *

Deaglan, Ciaran and Meallan gathered at their camp after finding Brian. As Ronan and Conall approached, Meallan started to move toward Conall, and Deaglan stopped him. "Now is no time to talk to Conall. After a battle he needs time to rest his mind and come to peace with all he has done today." Deaglan started to walk away, turned and added, "I heard we will take Brian's body to Swords in the morning. Then on to Armagh. This day is done, but not the task."

Meallan looked confused, he was thinking about Conall, "He was magnificent. Everybody says he was. He must have killed a hundred enemy."

"No boy, Conall may have killed more than you and me together," said Deaglan. "But not a hundred. The songs and poems of the battle you hear after this day may claim that number, but never say it to him."

Again, Meallan was confused, as was Ciaran. They both looked at Deaglan with questions in their eyes and Deaglan held up his hand. "When he was younger, a wolf attacked his sister, my wife. He killed the beast with his hands, just his hands. The stories that came out of that incident called him a great slayer of beasts. That angered him. He had killed a single wolf, nothing more. He has never wanted praise for things he had not done."

Conall walked over to the fire, looked at the others and nodded, "You are all well." Then without pause he picked up a bucket and walked away toward the river. There he stood and poured water over his head, washing away the dirt and blood of battle. Soaked, but clean, he knelt and washed his axe.

The battle was over, the day was won, and King Brian was dead. His body was taken to Armagh where he was honored for twelve days before being interred in a stone coffin in the Cathedral. After the interment, Conall and the remaining Dal gCais followed Donnchad in a return march to Ceann Coradh. They met minor opposition on the road from several groups, but each group relented and allowed the Dal gCais passage.

On the march Deaglan took the two young warriors aside and said, "Conall is a great warrior. That everyone knows and sees. He has fought in a number of battles, and it is always the same. He prepares for battle; he knows what he must do and he does it very well. He does it but he does not like it. He kills but notice he does not mutilate. He kills and moves on, often leaving wounded men behind who can still fight. We follow him and finish what he does not. When the day is done, he may kill the enemy still living with a single blow from his axe, not ten. Usually, he leaves the execution of prisoners to others"

Ciaran looked at Deaglan, "What troubles him?"

"He doesn't understand why men attack other men. Why do these raiders try to take what is not theirs? Why one man will kill another man for silver or gold? These things trouble him and yet he continues because he is a warrior, he fights for what he thinks is right and good. He fought for Brian, our king because Brian was good to his father and mother. When his mind is settled and he is again calm, then we can talk of this with him, but not yet."

Conall was now unsure of his responsibility to Brian. "Deaglan, I wonder why I should I stay with the army here in Ceann Coradh and pledge my axe to Donnchad, or to Tadc? I think rather that my service to the king is over?"

"I wish the answer was easy Conall, but it isn't. You've served honorably and any debt to Brian and his crown you have felt, has been paid. Any continuation on your part will be entirely your choice." Deaglan paused and turned toward Conall, "I'll go home to my family. I'm in my forty-seventh year, I'm tired and now it is time for me to raise crops and children. My service is done."

"Deaglan, how did Ciaran fare in battle today?" asked Conall as he touched the wound on his thigh.

"As you should expect, he fought well. After all, he is my son, and I taught him as I taught you," he replied with a smile.

"I recall years ago, you handed me this axe," said Conall as he held it out to Deaglan. "You said someday your son might learn its worth and its use. Perhaps that time is now."

Deaglan took the axe and with his head slightly bowed, he thought for a moment, "He will be honored to use the axe of the great warrior, Conall."

Conall put his hand on Deaglan's shoulder, "As I was honored years ago by my teacher."

* * *

47

1014 AD Munster, Éirinn
an Deantoir Claiomh … The Sword Maker

The year after the fields of Clauin Tarbh, Conall was in the palace at Ceann Coradh, meeting with a number of chieftains who had been talking about banding together to form a nation that could bring all of Éirinn together. The conversation became contentious and nearly resulted in battle itself as these men could not agree on leadership.

Disappointed again, but not surprised by the discord, Conall left the gathering, found a tavern, and opened his purse to count his money. "Enough for food and drink for another day," he muttered to himself. He entered the tavern and found a quiet corner to sit and decide on his next move. He bought a piece of meat, a fresh loaf of bread and a drink of milk and honey. As he began to eat an old man approached him with a curious eye.

"I know you, big man," he slurred as he stumbled toward Conall. "You were at the bull's meadow, Clauin Tarbh. I saw you take three challenges that day and sent them all to hell." The old man sat at the table and looked at Conall. You are a big, powerful man and a great warrior." The old man drew a breath, "You fought with an axe, an axe I know."

Conall stared at the man and asked, "How is it that you know my axe?"

The old man smiled, "I made that axe years ago for a tall, strong warrior. His name was Deaglan." The old man drank again, then leaned forward and stared at Conall, "How did you come to have this axe?" He looked at Conall, demanding an answer, "Deaglan, do you know him?"

"What do you want old man?" quizzed Conall.

"Did you kill Deaglan and take the axe?" asked the old man.

"No, Deaglan is my sister's husband and my teacher. He taught me to use the axe and gave it to me."

"Ah, yes. And a wise gift it was. You use it well." The old man drank again and continued, "But I know what you need." He paused, drank, and continued,

"A sword, as well as an axe. A large sword that would fit a man of your size, your strength," he sputtered. "And perhaps a bigger axe."

Conall leaned back, looked at the drunken old man and said, "And where would I find such weapons?"

"I am a blacksmith, an armorer," said the old man, as he lifted his head. "I have watched men fight for years and wondered if I could make a better sword, a better axe, something that would make a man a better warrior." The old man lifted his cup and drank deeply. "I made the axe for Deaglan, and I would make a sword that you alone could use. A sword too large for a normal man, even too large for a very strong man. But you, you're a giant, and need a giant's weapons. You're a skilled warrior and a sword that I could make for you would make you even better." The old man leaned back against the wall and again stared at Conall.

Conall was interested in the man's words and grinned as he asked, "Why not make the weapons for yourself, and you use them in battle?"

The old man smiled, "I have. Years ago, I was at Sulcoit with Mathgamain and Brian. I was very young and not much help, but we won and went on to Limerick. As we looted the city, I found a smithy and took a pair of tongs and a hammer. These tools I learned to use and use well."

"What's your name, armorer?"

"I am Aodhan."

"Aodhan, I'm not a rich man, I have a few copper pieces that will buy my meal today and perhaps a place to sleep the night, but no money to pay an armorer for a new weapon."

"Allow me to show you my workshop, show you some of my weapons. Then we'll discuss the price."

"What are you suggesting, old man?" asked Conall.

"I suggest you allow me to make you a sword that matches your strength and size," offered the old man.

"And again, what will this sword cost me, blacksmith?"

"Tell the world where the sword came from and pay me for the metals that I would use in its construction. Not all men ply their trade for money, some of us do what we do because we can—and want to."

"You assume that I'll be alive to sing your praises after a battle using this weapon."

"I know you'll be alive, your size, your skill and this sword will assure it."

"You assume there will be battles to fight. We have had years of peace."

The old man coughed and again leaned toward Conall, "Peace, yes peace. Then again there was Clauin Tarbh." He leaned back against the wall, "Oh yes, my large friend, I know my countrymen all too well, there will be more battles to fight."

Conall thought and emptied his purse on a table, "I've only these few pieces of silver and copper, old man. What can I buy with that?"

The old man counted the pennies and said, "The money isn't important. I'll make the sword, you'll use it, and you'll come back to pay me more as you win in battle."

"A bargain," said Conall, "How much time do you need to craft this sword?"

"Come back with me to my smithy, see my weapons and let me collect the measure of you. Then return in three, maybe four weeks' time and it'll be ready."

Conall finished his food, and the two men went to Aodhan's workshop where Conall looked at weapons of various sizes and shapes Aodhan had made. There were axes, swords, clubs, maces, daggers, and dozens of arrowheads. He took hold of several swords and tried the balance and weight in his hand, "These swords are not special, they are just swords."

The old man smiled, handed Conall a large piece of metal. "This is iron," he said as he handed Conall a second piece of metal, "And this is steel, steel is the son of iron. It is iron with a few other things blended in, if it is properly done, the steel is stronger, better for weapons. If it is heated, cooled and hammered properly, it is even stronger and the stronger the blade, the smaller and lighter it may be, or the longer and sharper it may be."

Aodhan smiled as he retrieved the two pieces of metal, "One of these could make a fine weapon for you, my large friend." He walked over to his furnace and moved the bellows, exciting the fire burning inside. "We will measure you and test your strength, not only your ability to lift the sword, but the ability to hold it in combat as long as you need. The size, the weight and the strength all must be measured and blended into the crafting of the weapon." He looked at Conall, "Are you ready to begin?"

"Where do we begin, old man?"

"First, let us see your strength." He put his hand on a long bar of steel, "Lift this piece of metal and hold it out as you might a sword or an axe."

Conall casually put his hand on the metal bar and tried to lift it. His hand slipped and he looked at Aodhan, then, with two hands he lifted the bar and securing his grip with his right hand, he held it out at arm's length with just his right arm. It was heavier than he initially thought, and he strained to keep his arm extended.

"That bar is the same in weight as a full-grown man with armor," said Aodhan, "And few men could lift it with one hand, much less hold it out at arm's length." He put his hand on Conall's arm and pulled down.

Conall was straining but didn't yield to Aodhan's extra weight. "It weighs as much as a man?" quizzed the giant.

"Yes," replied the old man. "Now move it about as if it were a sword, and you are attacked."

Conall moved the bar through several positions, slashes and thrusts. As he moved, Aodhan noticed his movements were slow, strained and Conall began to tire. Finally, Conall let the bar touch the floor and Aodhan smiled as he said, "Now I can slay you."

Conall took two deep breaths as he looked at Aodhan, this is too heavy for a long battle, I should use a smaller weapon."

"Yes, my giant, but how much smaller?" He dragged a second bar close to Conall, "Try this little piece of steel."

Conall breathed deeply, then put his hand on the end of the bar and lifted it up with little strain, "Much better, old man, much better."

Aodhan watched Conall move the piece of metal with ease and said, "Perhaps too light." He walked across the room and rummaged through his several metal bars and finally pulled one from the pile. "Try this one, Conall."

Conall set the one piece down and took the piece offered by Aodhan. It was a little heavier, but still moved with ease and fluidity. Aodhan watched and studied Conall's movements. Then went back to his pile and brought out another steel bar, "Now, this one my friend."

Again, Conall's movements were fluid and quick. Aodhan smiled, "Yes, we have the right one." He made Conall stand in several poses and measured his arms, his height, his stride. "There's more to battle than warriors," he said. "If my weapons do not do as the warrior wishes, he dies. Then, we both lose." He went to another table and began to lay out several pieces of steel and returned to Conall. This will take some time; full turn of the moon should be enough."

Conall was rummaging through bits and pieces of steel and leather picking up different items and testing them. "What's this," asked Conall as he held a piece of leather with metal bars stitched into it?

Aodhan walked over to him and took it from his hand. "This is not big enough for you. Look at your arm. You hold a sword in this arm and swing it at your enemy. He too has a sword and swings it at you. This is placed on your forearm and the steel bars give you some protection from a sharp edge that may miss your sword and strike your arm."

Conall held out his arms and showed Aodhan the scars he had from many such a blow. "I know what you mean, Aodhan."

"Now, you go away. I have work to do and you'll be in my way."

"A turn of the moon," said Conall.

"Yes," Aodhan paused, "That and perhaps a few more days."

*　*　*

Conall returned to Aodhan's smithy in the prescribed time and the old man presented him with a sword that was over six feet from pommel to point and weighed nearly twelve pounds. Conall could raise it with one hand, but it was made to be used with two. The double-edged blade had been hammered and folded then hammered again to an edge and a finish that shone in the light of the fire. The edges were then sharpened with a stone.

"This blade in the hands of the right man can take down small trees in a single hit," said Aodhan, "or separate a man into two halves without slowing down."

Conall took the sword in one hand and held it straight before him. The blade had been fashioned with a thicker than normal grip, wrapped in leather and a fuller on both sides of the blade. The taper began about halfway from the cross guard to the well-sharpened point. The blade carried no decorative designs, or encrusted jewels. The grip fit his large hands and as Conall began to move the blade about, he found it necessary to step out of the smithy to give him sufficient room to swing it in a full arc.

"This is a fine weapon," said Conall as he continued to swing it in arc after arc. He paused and looked closely at the blade.

The old man said, "You've no need of flowers or birds on your blade, Conall. This is a warrior's sword, made for combat, not something to make you pretty."

"I like this sword, old man, but I cannot use it close in. I need an open field."

"Yes, and these," said Aodhan as he produced a pair of shorter swords, "these are its companions, for close in, as you say."

The pair of swords were shorter, and each made for one hand. The blades were wide and slightly curved. Each had one sharpened edge and large a rounded cross guard. The blades were unadorned, with but a fuller on each side.

"These blades may be used to cut down trees or men. They are too heavy for a smaller man, but like their large companion, either of them can cut a man in two with one great swing."

Conall took the smaller weapons and held one in each hand. "The weight is not that much," he said. "I like the feel of them."

"Conall, there stands a tree," Aodhan gestured toward a small grove, "see how easily each sword cuts the branches and its trunk."

Conall walked over to the grove, moving the smaller sword as if in battle, then suddenly he attacked the tree, lopping off the branches and with four swipes at the trunk, felling the entire tree. He paused, looking at the blade and turned toward Aodhan.

"This blade is well made, armorer. Now we will discuss the price."

"First, another piece." Aodhan produced a pair of leather forearm wraps with a half glove at one end that was large enough for Conall's hand and arm. He showed Conall the inside. "I have lined it with sheep's wool and cloth. Not for comfort, but to take the shock of a direct strike." He showed Conall how to put it on his hand and arm and buckled it firmly in place, "Now hold your sword and swing it."

Three steel bars were stitched into the arm guard protecting the arm away from the body. It was not comfortable, but Conall could judge the value by the number of scars the guard now covered.

"Aodhan, these are fine weapons, but again I tell you, I do not have enough to pay you what they are worth."

"One final weapon," said Aodhan as he turned to go back inside his smithy. He returned immediately with a long-handled axe, longer than the one Conall had used before and heavier but looking almost exactly the same as Deaglan's.

Aodhan smiled, "And as I told you, tell the world who I am and when you have a few extra pennies, then you can pay me more. I am not concerned about the money, Conall. I wanted to make these weapons."

* * *

48

The years following the Battle of Clauin Tarbh found Conall looking for a place where he could fit in. He was a warrior, not a farmer. He roamed the countryside, living off the land and joining in every pursuit of outlaw bands or raiding parties that presented itself. The continued incursions by renegade bands of Norse and others (including some of his fellow countrymen) had him engaging in lesser battles and skirmishes across southern Éirinn from Dubh Linn, south to Corcaigh and around north again to Limerick. These were mostly small conflicts, usually involving bands of ten or less in opposition. The enemy he encountered were not as well armed, sophisticated or coordinated as the armies he had faced. These were easy conquests, defeating robbers and outlaws rather than warriors in large battles. He used his short swords more than his axe or long sword and when a battle was done there were often prisoners. Prisoners of Norse and Irish origin. He left their disposition to those he had helped. Killing was a consequence of battle, he didn't hesitate to cut an armed man in two as they fought, but he had no want to take their heads as they knelt in defeat. He fought to protect his people and was at peace with his actions when all was done.

Killing was not important to him, defeating the outlaw or raider, preventing him from continuing on a raid was his objective. He rarely lost himself to anger, but rather swung his sword and axe with an ease that showed him to be a man first and a warrior second. His conquests were satisfying in themselves, and he derived as much satisfaction from a group of outlaws turning and running away as he did in killing the raiders. He roamed through the countryside on his horse making it known to small pockets of people that he was available to combat the outlaw bands of men that preyed on their villages. He spent most of his time along the coast because he loved the smell of the sea and the warm winds that came ashore from the southwest. The coast was also the most dangerous, where raiders would begin an attack, going inland and making a circular route, then escaping by the sea. They might start and end in Éirinn or come across from Alba, Scotland or even from a distant northern port. Raiders seemed mostly interested in silver and gold, but would take anything they could carry and occasionally, prisoners, especially young girls, to be sold as slaves.

The spring and summer of each year could yield four or five raids. Each year was different, depending primarily on the weather. If the seas were calm, the number of raids from Alba and the north might be greater and storms were a small deterrent. The raiders usually sent several men ahead to acquire horses and one or two to scout the countryside. The main raiding party arrived several days later numbering from twenty to as many as seventy men.

Conall had given his axe to Ciaran and was thankful to Aodhan for having made a new one. He used his new swords, becoming very adept at clearing a wide arc with the long sword and exchanging it for the smaller one when combat was close in. The arm protectors proved valuable on more than one occasion and as he returned to Aodhan for repairs on each visit he left a few more copper or silver pieces in payment for his weapons.

In mid-summer 1016, Conall passed through a small village that had been attacked by a party of foreign raiders, some thirty men strong. He learned they were moving to the north and west when last seen and he reasoned the time passing should have the raiding party beginning to circle back toward the coast. He covered the few miles to a village he knew could be in their path and subject to attack in the next few days. Upon arrival, he found his friend Ronan tending to his horses and told him of the raiding party.

"Ronan, good friend, I've come with some news that may require us to gather several men to defend your village." He told Ronan about the other village the previous day and the raiding party could be coming this way.

"Conall," said Ronan, "you realize that the raiders could just as easily go a few miles north of here and attack Faolin's village."

"I haven't been there yet," replied Conall. "If you're prepared here, I'll go north and warn Faolin." Conall mounted his horse and turned again to Ronan, "The shortest way to Faolin?"

Ronan pointed to the north and a little west and said, "There, you'll cross a small stream in about five miles, then turn left and follow the road to his home."

"If they don't come his way, I'll return here," said Conall and he urged his horse northward. He arrived at a cluster of several round houses, surrounded with a single broken rath. The wall was in very poor condition, obviously in the process of being repaired and it would not serve as much protection as it currently stood. He approached a small gathering of several men where he found his old friend, Faolin near the main gate to this little village. He greeted him saying, "I've come from Ronan with a warning of a raiding party possibly coming this way."

"We've heard," replied Faolin, "A man, living west of here was hurrying back to his home to get his family to safety. He said we should hide our children and fortunes, now!" The two men walked to a small rise and looked off in the distance, "They'll be coming from that direction," said Faolin as he scanned the eastern horizon. He shaded his eyes and said, "Something comes this way."

Conall looked, saw the cloud of dust, and turned to survey the area where they might meet this band. "Faolin, how many men can stand and fight?"

"A few," he replied. "But we also have boys and women who will stand and fight."

Conall saw several boys and three women begin to cross the dry moat. "No," he said raising his hands, "Stay behind the wall. Any of these raiders that present you a target, kill. Use your bows and slings from the protection of the moat and what wall there is." He looked at Faolin, "We will stand and meet them here." He led his horse to the bridge across the moat and urged him through the gate. "Did your friend know how many would be coming?"

"He said there may be more than twenty, maybe twice that number." Faolin looked at his small village and back at Conall, "I'll go call the others."

Conall drew his great sword, stabbed it into the ground and checked his short swords and daggers. He pulled on his leather gloves and arm protectors, threw off his shirt and as he again touched his great sword the raiding party entered the far end of the clearing outside the village. Faolin returned with two other men and said, "The others are being found and will be here soon."

"Good," said Conall as he finished a rough count. "We are going to need more than the four of us for this lot. I count about twenty-four of them." He hefted his great sword on his shoulder and said, "Friends, give me a wide space. This blade does not know friend from foe, nor man from beast. It will slay all in its path."

The group of four spread out before the gate and as they stood ready, six more men of the village joined them. Another group of women and younger boys gathered behind the wall with bows, javelins, and slings. The village was as ready as it would be.

The raiding party slowed, scanned the people standing in opposition, talked amongst themselves, then turned and charged. They saw a chance to break through the gate and concentrated their charge in that direction. Conall was in the middle of the defenders, directly in front of the path over the moat to the gate.

The first two men on horse charging the gate were going to have to get past Conall. He waited with the point of his sword touching the ground until they were too close to change direction, then he feinted to his left, stopped and moved quickly to his right, bringing his sword up in a hard arc to the bottom of a rider's shield. The shield flew up over the rider's head and Conall continued the arc in a hard and slashing move across the riders back. The blow was stunning, unhorsing the man and leaving him on the ground with a broken back.

The second man had passed Conall and was halfway across the moat when a javelin thrown from the wall stopped him. He fell into the dry moat, unable to rise to his feet.

The remaining twenty or more attackers dismounted and charged the ten defenders. Conall did not wait for them to come to him, he charged them and cut down two men as they hesitated in surprise. The reach and powerful swing of Conall's sword was more than either could deflect. The first fell after an initial blow and died looking at the anger rising on Conall's face. His eyes were wide and his roar loud as he brought his sword down on the man's head. Without any pause, Conall spun to his right, meeting the second man on foot with a slash of his sword against the attacker's sword. Conall's movement went through, pushing the man's sword back into his face and a third slash found the man's neck.

Faolin had stopped one man and was struck on his arm by another. Conall moved to stop another strike to Faolin, and another raider came at him on his right. Stumbling and off balance, Conall managed a parrying movement and regained his feet. He stepped into the raider's path and a hard swing of the large sword took the man's head. Faolin was down, severely wounded. The other eight defenders were being beaten. They had taken three raiders and lost five of their number. Conall raged into a group of four raiders, swinging wildly and destroying two shields. One of the defenders finished a shieldless raider and moved in on the other as Conall turned toward two more. Again wild, savage swings of the great sword were more than the raiders could defend. Conall drove one man to the ground and finished him with a blow to his skull. The second shieldless raider was now down and a villager drove his sword through the raider's throat. Conall had another man backed up against the moat and a javelin from the wall finished him. As Conall was turning to find another, he was slashed across his back. The raider's sword was not sharp, and the cut was not deep, but painful. Conall roared again turning full on his attacker and a series of five blows to the man's shield was followed with a killing slash to the man's chest, splitting the mail and cutting through his ribs.

Another attacker was felled with an arrow from the wall and two others with javelin throws. More arrows flew from the wall and another attacker fell. Five of the remaining attackers charged Conall. He swung his great sword catching one man's shield and knocking him backward. Another of the defenders finished him with a slash across his back. Five other attackers were backing up toward their horses and four were surrounding Conall. He stabbed his great sword in the ground and drew the short swords from his belt. One of the five joined the four men attacking Conall. They moved forward cautiously and Conall chose the tallest to strike first. He lunged at the man, slashing with both short swords at the man's shield. The man staggered backward and Conall pressed harder. The man went down and Conall drove his sword into the man's gut.

He had to put his foot on this corpse to pull his blade free. The opportunity was open for the others, and they all managed to draw blood from Conall as he spun and bellowed with both swords in hand. He closed on one man who stumbled backward and saw his last glimpse of the sky as Conall's blade found his forehead. He again turned and moved toward another when a third made a weak thrust at Conall's back. The wound was not deep, and the pain was more angering than disabling. Conall finished the second man with a slashing blow that splintered the man's shield and cut deep into the side of his head. Conall turned and now faced two remaining men. The myriad cuts across his back were taking their toll and Conall felt unsteady as he stepped toward the two. Not knowing how badly wounded he was, the two decided to run rather than fight this angry giant. Conall watched them run, then turned to survey the field and saw a group of ten or more riders coming at a gallop. It was Ronan and men from his village. Conall, breathing heavily, fell to his knees and stabbed his swords in the ground.

As the riders with Ronan approached, the last of the raiders were vaulting onto their horses and trying to escape. The men from the village still able, mounted horses and together with Ronan's men, pursued the raiders.

Conall was wounded, more seriously than he knew. He was weak and stayed on his knees, breathing deeply, and beginning to feel the pain of the cuts and slashes to his body. Then, a young girl from the village he had just defended walked through the gate, pausing at each man who had fallen in the defense of their little village. She paused longer at one fallen warrior, Faolin, and bowed her head. A moment later she was on her feet, walking toward Conall. She stopped, looking at Conall's back, then touched a clean damp cloth to his wound.

Conall turned his head and with a strained voice he said, "Enough girl, I'll tend to my own wounds."

She stood straight and backed up a step, then as suddenly she glared into his eyes, stepped forward and said in a firm voice, "You'll not, you great large man. You're cut, bleeding and bruised. If someone doesn't tend to these wounds now, you'll be dead before the sun rises in the morn. Now get on your feet, I can't lift you, and follow me." She turned and began to walk away, then looked at Conall, "Well, on your feet and be quick about it, you're not the only one with a wound that needs tending."

Conall stood, somehow shocked into action by the stern words from this little person, accepting that she was probably right. He followed her to a roundhouse. They entered and she told him to sit on a bench in the middle of the room. "Sit there and take off what's left of your tunic."

"But I," Conall hesitated.

"It doesn't require your talking, you great ox, now off with that filthy thing."

Conall timidly stood and removed his belt, and what was left of his tunic, "Can I ask, what is your name?"

She straightened, raised her head, and replied, "M'name is Tressa, my father is Faolin. He is lying out there, killed by these raiders today." She gathered several clean cloths and dipped one in a pot of boiling water, then approached Conall, "be still and let me do what I can for your wounds."

Conall was surprised at her words, then with an obvious sadness in his voice he said, "I came here to warn Faolin and help him if I could, but..." he hesitated, then, "I have never met his family. He's a good friend, and I came to stand with him one more time. More than once did we fight, protecting each other back-to-back."

"Yes, you are Conall mac Laoghaire," said Tressa. "He spoke of you often. You, the fields of Clauin Tarbh and the weir," she said with her head down. She paused, then continued, "Now he's gone, killed." She breathed deeply, lifted her head, stood tall and looked at him with a strength that made Conall wait for her next words. "Now, you sit still, I'll clean your wounds and stitch them closed."

As they stared each other down, Conall could read determination, grief and confidence in her steel blue eyes. He sat and she washed the dirt and blood off his body. When she had cleaned the greater wounds, she handed him a fresh tunic that had been her father's. "I'll close these wounds and stitch and bandage the ones needing it." She continued to clean his back and shoulders.

"Your father was a good man," started Conall.

"I know who my father was, Conall, and I know who you are. You are a great warrior, and our village owes you a debt for being here to protect us. But now forgive me for being less than friendly. I'll bury my father in the morning and then try to think about the next day. Perhaps I'll go to my uncle's house to live."

"Your mother?" asked Conall.

"She died two years ago, and my brother just before that." She approached him with her needle and thread. "Grit your teeth large man, my needle is small, but my eyes are tired, my hand not steady and this is going to hurt."

Before Conall could respond she drove the needle into his shoulder and began to pull one of his wounds closed. She finished sewing the last of the wounds needing a stitch and, wiped it down with a hot cloth then tied a bandage in place. Conall had lost a great deal of blood and was very tired.

Tressa could see him close his eyes as he sat waiting her next command, "No sleep yet, Conall. First, you'll eat what I put before you and drink what I pour. Then you may sleep 'til the morn."

* * *

The following day Conall woke to the sound of Tressa walking out her door, dragging a shovel behind her. He could see the strength in her and knew that she was about to dig a grave for her father. He rose, felt a twinge of pain in his shoulder and slowly moved his arm, testing his range of motion. He walked out the door and saw Tressa halfway up a slight hill, standing below a large oak tree. She was looking east away from the rath, at the sun rising in the sky. The ground in front of her sloped slowly down and away.

Conall approached and saw three graves marked with stones, all facing the rising sun. He stood next to Tressa, silently and watched birds fly across the sky and the sun illuminate the rolling hills to the west. He looked down the hill to a small river flowing north and west, "Where does the river take you?" he asked.

"To the Shannon and the great ocean beyond," she replied. "He would talk about taking a boat from here to the ocean and who knows where it could take us."

As she spoke, Conall saw tears slowly move down her cheek. He reached out and took the shovel from her hand.

"I must dig my father's grave," she said standing tall again.

"You'll allow me. This was one battle where I didn't stand at his back well enough. It would be my honor to dig this for you and him," he replied.

"Your shoulder, the wound will open again."

"Your stitchs'll hold," he said and pointed at the ground, "Is this where you wish the grave to be?"

Tressa looked again at the river and said, "He would often sit here and tell me stories of the battles he fought, and after my mother died, he would talk of her. My mother lies there," she said pointing at one of the graves behind her. "Yes, this is a good place for him to rest. Next to my mother."

Conall took the measure of the plot and began to dig. Faolin would lie next to his wife, below this oak. Tressa walked about picking up stones and brought them back to cover the grave. He watched her as she walked and saw something in her he wanted to know better. It confused him, he had never looked at a woman that way and when his eyes rested on her he felt none of the aches and pains from the previous day's battle.

The following morning found Conall tending to Tressa's horses and cattle in a pasture. He saw her come out of the roundhouse and scatter feed for the chickens in the yard, then carry water back into the house. "I could get used to this," he muttered to himself and returned to his task.

"Conall, come, I have made bread and warmed meat from yesterday's meal."

He went into the house and as the two sat and ate they both caught themselves looking at the other. "Where do you go from here?" she finally asked.

"I have no plans. I might stay somewhere for a day, a week, a month, then move on. I'm a warrior constantly seeking a battle."

"You'll need more time to allow that wound to heal. You should stay several more days at least."

"I don't wish to be in your way, and you said you may go to your uncle's house to live. Perhaps I could take you there when it's safe to travel."

Tressa looked at Conall, "eat while it's still warm." She walked across the room, stood at the door looking up the hill toward her father's grave with a pained expression. "I don't know what I should do. This is my home."

Conall stood and walked over to her, put his massive arm around her shoulder and pulled her close. "Tressa, allow the day to pass. Allow the sun to warm your face and breathe the fresh air. Time heals many wounds and tomorrow and the next day will be easier than today. You will never forget your family, but you can still smile and live your own life. Nobody can take that from you." She leaned into him, and they stood in the doorway looking out for a long time.

* * *

The few days passed, and his wound was healing as Tressa had predicted. Her eyes still moistened when she looked out at her father's grave, and Conall was anxious for her mourning to pass. In the brief time they had together he had seen hints of a happier person and wanted to see her true self surface. "How do you feel this morning, Tressa?" he asked.

She looked up at him, "You're a savage beast, a ferocious warrior Conall, and the world knows it. You're also a man with a heart, and I know it. There's good in there," she said poking her finger at his chest, "I've seen it, and felt it and I thank you for it." She turned and went to her hearth, ladled some broth into a bowl, picked up a loaf of fresh bread and returned to the table where Conall stood. "Now sit and eat, you're not done healing yet."

He sat, ate and pondered her words. She joined him and they both ate in silence. Conall spoke first, "Your uncle, would he be your father's brother?"

"My mother's," she replied, "but I'm growing less inclined to run to him. I want to stay here, but I have to change this house." She got up from the table and walked around the house. "There are too many memories of both my mother and father in here. I'm thinking about what changes I could make." She paced the floor in thought.

Conall rose, walked out of the roundhouse over to the gate and out on the open yard. To the south there was a low cliff that reached a height of about fifty feet and ran a distance of several hundred feet before blending into the ground on either side. The ground in front of the cliff was slightly higher at its base and a heavy grouping of bushes grew in the first ten to fifteen feet, then a sloping, grassy plain back to the roundhouse. Conall started to approach the cliff when Tressa walked up behind him.

"There's a cave in that cliff, behind the bushes. My father used it to store his weapons and other things that he valued."

"A cave?" Puzzled Conall.

"Yes, would you like to see it?"

"I see no opening. Where?"

"Come, I'll show you," she said with a smile as she tugged at his good arm.

Conall looked at her face and noticed her eyes, large and blue as the sky. Her hair, long, dark, and falling to her waist, and her smile made him want to say yes to anything she suggested.

"Come on, I can't carry you," she said as she hurried in front of him. She wasn't as young as he had thought, she was a woman, not a girl and his eyes took in her entire body as she led him to the cave's entrance.

"See here," she said pushing aside a bush, "The opening is this way." She stepped toward a gap in the rocks, turned to her right and disappeared into the wall. Conall followed. The separation was enough to allow a man of his size to walk into the cave fully upright even if carrying a load of firewood.

"We should get a lamp and see what's farther in," Conall began.

"Here," said Tressa as she scratched a flint on rock and brought a torch to life. "Father has several torches and lamps here." She turned and said, "See, 'tis high enough even for you to walk about."

Conall looked around him and saw the floor was nearly flat and sloping away as the cave went deeper into the cliff. The ceiling was about ten feet high at its low point and went to about fifteen feet at the high point. The floor stretched some twenty feet to the right and a little more to the left. Directly in front of him, the floor dropped gradually as did the ceiling and the opening disappeared in darkness ahead.

"There is a spring down there" said Tressa, pointing ahead, "and Father found this spot was best for a fire," she said standing below the high point in the ceiling. "There's an opening up there that allows smoke to find its way out to the cliff."

Conall walked about looking at the ceiling and down at the floor. He walked to the wall on the right of the entrance and saw an opening in the wall that led to another room. "What's this?" he asked.

"That," Tressa said, "Is where Father put his weapons. It's not as big as this room and when I was little, I wasn't allowed in there."

"Now you're not little, perhaps it's time for you to learn how to use those weapons."

"He started to teach me the sword," she replied, "when I was fifteen."

Conall looked at her and said, "And how old are you now?"

"This is my nineteenth year," she said, standing tall and holding a sword at her side, "And I'm now quite good at wielding this blade, great large man."

"Perhaps I can show you more of its use, when time allows."

"I would like that," she replied, smiling, and quietly repeating, "I would like that."

* * *

Conall's wounds continued to heal as the days passed, and soon he was once again able to wield his great sword. As he practiced his movements over several days in the cave, out of sight of any onlookers, his arms began to regain their strength and he thought more about his place here in Tressa's house.

She frequently came into the cave and watched him exercise and knew soon, he would be able to leave and continue his life. At first, this was the objective, Conall would heal and leave. Now, after coming to see other sides of this giant, Tressa was not sure what she wanted. She was leaning against the entry for a few minutes before he noticed her.

"I've warmed food, come and we'll eat," she said as she turned and walked outside.

Conall sensed something was wrong and immediately followed her outside. "Tressa, wait. I'm coming."

As she crossed the open yard between the house and the cliff, she quickened her pace and said, "The clouds are gathering, it'll rain soon, and I wish to be inside."

In the house, they sat at the table and began to eat. Outside, the rain started, and thunder rolled across the heavens. Tressa cowered in her chair as lightning flashed and the thunder shook the walls of the roundhouse.

"You don't like the lightning?" quizzed Conall.

"No," she replied, "I don't understand it and it terrifies me. I've seen trees, houses and cattle that had been struck and three years ago a man carrying a spear was burned to death by lightning."

Conall stood and took her hand. She sat rigidly and he said, "stand with me by the door," she relaxed, stood and he led her across the room. He opened the door, put his arm around her and they stood inside looking out the door as the storm raged. "I don't understand the lightning either," he said, "Nor do I fear it. I have come to respect it and stay out of its way. If there is a God and he casts lightning about, I'll not tempt him by standing out there in a storm."

Each bolt of lightning and each clap of thunder drew her closer to him and as the storm began to calm, Tressa stayed close, burying herself in his chest.

"You think me a silly girl, Conall?" She stepped away and back to the table. She sat and continued to eat.

"No, Tressa, I think you a good and strong woman who does not like the thunder." He looked at her and he wanted to hold her again. She was a woman and he a man. He looked at her differently than he had viewed Liamhain, Eithne, Ainnir or Blathin. They were all wonderful and they enjoyed each other when they were together, but they were as easy to leave. Now, his thoughts were clouded in his mind, and he thought he should walk away from her before he made himself look foolish in her eyes. She was the daughter of his friend, Faolin; she was weakened by his death; she was kind to him because he fought off the raiders; she was a girl; and he was a grizzled warrior. He had no claim to her, and his feelings should have been those of a father toward a daughter. But his feelings for her were those of a man for a woman. He wanted to protect her and at the same time he wanted to feel her against his chest.

"Tressa, my wounds are healed, and my arms are strong again." He said as he finished eating. "You've been very kind to me, and I should impose no more on you."

"You don't impose, Conall. We have shared my house for a month, and you've helped me gather my life back. If you're of a mind to leave, the door is there," she said pointing at the still open door, "you can pass through it whenever you wish."

Conall looked at her and said, "Tressa, it's not what I wish, but I want to know what you wish. What I should do is leave. I'm a warrior, not a tender of sheep and chickens. The day will come when a battle will need my attention and I'll be gone, perhaps forever. I fight and win because I don't care if I live or die and one day, I will die. That is who I am."

Tressa looked at him, stood tall and straight in front of him and said, "I have buried my brother, mother and now my father. I know death and live with it. It does not scare me and if you leave today to fight as you did when you came here, I would hope you would return."

"I don't know what to say, Tressa. I want to be here with you more than I want to fight another battle. This is the first time I can remember that I've felt this way."

Tressa looked briefly at Conall and turned away as her face reddened. "I've chores to do," she said and hurried out of the roundhouse into the mist that hung over the yard.

He stood there wondering if he had hurt her or scared her. "It's time for me to go," he muttered to himself and began to gather up his weapons.

Tressa came back into the roundhouse and stood in front of Conall. "I don't want you to leave, I want you to stay here with me. I don't know what I'm feeling but you make me feel safe, and I find myself smiling more when you're with me. You're a great, large, rough man, Conall mac Laoghaire. But a man with a good heart and I find myself wanting to be close to you." She stood straight, drew another deep breath and continued, "There, I've said what I feel. The door is not barred," she said as she waved in its direction, "I'll not stand in your way." She stood aside, head held high and hands together behind her back.

Conall put his arms around her and pulled her close. "Tomorrow, I'll take you to meet my family."

*　*　*

49

1016 ADMunster, Éirinn
Cnoc Toirneach … Thunder Hill

The journey to Muirin's home took a full day by horse and the time was spent talking about building a new roundhouse, raising a few more sheep and planting one of the fields that had been fallow for two years. They arrived finding Deaglan herding cattle into a pasture.

"Conall, welcome, it's good to see you," said Deaglan. "What brings you this way?"

"Deaglan, you remember Faolin, our friend and brother in many a battle?" asked Conall.

"I do," he replied, "I remember him well, he's a good man, and a good friend," said Deaglan.

"This is his daughter, Tressa," said Conall.

Deaglan looked back to the road, "Does he come with you?"

Conall dismounted, as did Tressa. She spoke first, "Deaglan, my father spoke of you often and had many kind words to say about you. I'm honored to meet you."

"How is your father?" asked Deaglan.

Conall spoke, "Their village was attacked by raiders and Faolin was killed."

Deaglan looked at Tressa, "He will be missed, he was a good man."

Tressa said, "Thank you, I'm at peace with it now and he'll be remembered."

Deaglan looked at Conall, "You look tired, come into the house and rest, Muirin and Tuathla will be back soon and happy to see you."

"Tuathla, is Laisren here also?" asked Conall.

"No, she's here with Deirbhile. Laisren is working in the fields today," Deaglan returned, "and her little one is in her fifth year already."

The three sat and talked until Muirin came in with her daughter. "Conall, you visit and there is no wound for me to stitch? How rare, and who is this traveling with you?"

Conall stood and put his arms around his sister, "I have come because Tressa and I are going to wed."

Muirin stepped away from her brother and looked at Tressa, "You're welcome in our home. This great large man is my little brother, and his family is my family." She stepped to Tressa and hugged her.

"How long have you been planning this marriage, brother?"

Tressa spoke before Conall could respond, "Your brother and my father were friends and Conall came to our village about a month ago to help us fight off a raiding band of outlaws. He drove them off and was wounded. I patched him up and he stayed with me as he healed. Now we wish to stay together."

Muirin said, "So you know what sort of man he is?"

"Yes, I do. And I'll be proud to stand next to him before a priest," Tressa said standing closer to Conall.

Muirin seemed to think for a minute then said, "Then it's good. She has the look of a strong woman, brother. Fortune is smiling on you this day."

Tuathla hugged her uncle, took Tressa's hand and led her outside. "My uncle is a great man, Tressa. He has done many things for other people both in war and in peace. I want to wish you both a long and happy life and tell you that our home is open to you any time."

The two walked quietly for a few minutes, then Tuathla continued, "He is a warrior. Maybe the greatest warrior ever to have lived, at least he is in my mind. My mother patches his wounds and stitches them closed whenever he returns home from battle." She bowed her head, "Someday, he will not return. As great as he is, there will be a day when he can no longer win."

Tressa touched Tuathla's shoulder, "I know, and as much as I know the day will come, I cannot let that keep me from him."

The two young women sat near the well and continued talking through the evening.

* * *

Conall was happy, living the life of an ordinary man, tending sheep and scratching the ground to grow crops. A life made so much greater with Tressa at his side. He gradually set his great sword aside along with his other weapons and allowed them to gather dust in the cave.

A new roundhouse was first in Conall's mind, and he set about gathering large stones, some requiring a horse, and set them close to the cliff with the cave. They decided to build the house in a half round configuration with the cliff forming a straight wall and the opening into the cave in the middle of that wall. The largest stones he could find would form the base of the outer wall in a half round pattern reaching over twenty feet from the opening in the cliff to each of the two ends, with the door at the mid-point. Logs near a half foot in diameter were cut from the nearby oak trees and would stand as pickets around the half circle wall forming the upper half of the outer wall. A door and two shuttered windows were built into the wall and a traditional thatched roof would extend out from the cliff to the pickets. The door in the front wall was formed of heavy oak planks and was large enough for Conall to pass through standing fully upright.

Conall then built a large chair, big enough for both he and Tressa and placed it in front of the hearth. Many an evening was spent sitting in this great chair talking before the fire. The two were very happy together and the day Tressa announced Conall was to be a father, he felt a pride greater than in any battle and he thanked the God of his mother for his great good fortune.

Inside the cave they arranged a store of firewood, and his weapons found their way into the small room, out of sight and almost out of mind. He had hung a large woven rug over the cave entrance and placed a chest in front of the rug, hiding the entrance. They could still go into the cave, but it required moving the rug and walking behind it.

* * *

Spring of the following year brought rain, wind and their first son, Olcan. He was born during a storm, just as Conall had been and Tressa held Conall's hand as their son drew his first breath. The two had been happy together before Olcan and even happier after. Tressa sang and danced as she worked in the fields, cleaned their house and tended to their baby. Conall worked on the property, removing rocks from the fields and using them in the construction of a rath. The walls were similar to those of Cnoc Gorm, stone base and picket fencing. When he finished the rough construction, he stood back to admire and criticize his work.

"Is it worthy of a name yet," asked Tressa.

"The namin'll be for you to choose, girl," he replied.

"I think of the day it rained and the thunder frightened me," said Tressa. "T'was that day you put your arm around m'shoulders and made me feel safe." She hesitated, looked at Conall, smiled and said, "I'll call this place Thunder Hill, Cnoc Toirneach."

A year later, in 1020, Tressa delivered another boy. They named him Torcan. "Two sons," marveled Conall, "how lucky can I be, a beautiful wife and two healthy sons. I can't wait to see what tomorrow brings.

Tomorrow came a year later when their third son, Seanan was born and, in another year, Conall was the father of a beautiful baby girl, Fiona. Their lives had been peaceful for several years, but that was about to change.

* * *

50

1022 AD Munster, Éirinn
Labhair Siochana … Talk of Peace

In September of 1022, an emissary of Brian's son, Tadc came to visit Conall. "I told Tadc I knew you, old friend," said Ronan. "There may be trouble brewing between him and Donnchad. Trouble that your axe or your sword might help in settling."

"You're suggesting that I take up arms for one son of Brian to fight another? No, my friend, I will not battle either of Brian's sons. If they have a problem, they must settle it themselves." He looked over the landscape before them and continued, "I stood with Brian because he honored both my father and mother, I'll not dishonor him now by taking the side of one of his sons against another." Conall led Ronan out to the pasture where vegetables grew, and Tressa was busy with the boys and the harvest. "I am now a farmer, Ronan. I haven't used my sword in over a year." He paused again, then, "If we were attacked by the foreigners again, I would again stand with my friends, but I have no wish to see battle ever again."

Ronan watched the woman working in the fields as three little boys ran around her, and a baby lay in a basket. "You've found that peace you sought years ago, my friend?"

"That I have Ronan, and I've no want to take up the sword again." They turned back toward the gate, "My brother and I are very lucky, because of his wounds, he found Grian and because I came here a few years ago, I met this woman."

As the two men walked back to the open yard, Olcan, the oldest of Conall's sons ran up to them. He was approaching his fifth year but was tall and bony. "Da, Mam wants to know if your friend'll have dinner with us tonight. She said we've a fine deer that you brought home yesterday."

Conall smiled at his son, looked at Ronan, "Well man, answer the boy, we've a fine deer and the best vegetables this side of Cnoc Gorm. Will you join us this night?"

When morning came and Ronan saddled his horse for the ride back to Ceann Coradh, Conall brought him a sack of food for his trip, "The same question came from Donnchad's man last week," said Conall, "and I gave him the same answer. I hope I'm done with the fighting and killing. 'Tis time for me to raise these four children and keep a smile on Tressa's face. Tell Tadc, I said he should talk to his brother, not fight with him and I wish the both of them the best."

"That I'll do, Conall. Perhaps the next time we meet, it'll be to talk of our sons with another fine deer on the table." He mounted his horse, "I'll be passing Earnan's home on m'way back to Tadc. I'll see how the vegetables compare."

With a laugh and a slap on the horse's hind, Conall watched his old friend leave.

"He's a nice man, husband," said Tressa, "is he the last of them to come ask you to lift that big sword again?"

"I don't know girl, but I do know what I'll say if they do."

*　*　*

As the summer passed Conall heard of several conflicts between the sons of Brian. "Why don't they just talk to each other?" He wondered aloud. "What about the peace that had been built by Brian and was now falling apart?" He was tempted to go to Ceann Coradh, not to fight, but to talk. "Do you think they would listen to me?" he asked Tressa.

"T'would be a pack of fools to not listen," she replied. "You're the greatest warrior they've had in years. Your voice should be heard."

"Then I'll go to Ceann Coradh. I'll talk to both of them, and maybe we can all lay down our swords and live in peace."

Conall prepared to make the trip to Ceann Coradh. He left and headed to Cnoc Gorm. Earnan would be a strong ally in this arena that Conall was not accustomed to. Here he would speak, here the words that he had might not carry the weight of his sword and here he was concerned.

"Conall, little brother, you are the biggest man most have ever seen. You are a warrior that no man wants to face, even with his best friends at his side. And when you choose to speak, there is no man who does not listen." Earnan leaned on his cane, "Yes I'll go with you and be proud to stand next to you as

345

you speak." Earnan sat down, "You are my little brother, whom I have looked up to for a long time."

Grian hitched Conall's horse to the cart and prepared a sack of food. "When you return, I'll have baked loaves and cakes, I'll pick the finest vegetables and I'll see about a deer. This may be the greatest victory the two of you have ever shared."

The trek to Ceann Coradh was spent with long discussions about the political situation in Éirinn. Brian mac Cennetig had brought the island together with the sword and intimidation. The peace that followed allowed the construction of roads, the restoration of monasteries and the return of treasures stolen over the past centuries. The country was ripe for advancement into a peaceful society without the constant threat of warfare with neighbor or invader. The two warriors who had made their way with sword and axe now talked of peace. A peace for all of Éirinn, like the one they had tasted over the last few years before Clauin Tarbh. When they arrived at Ceann Coradh, the news that Tadc been assassinated changed everything.

*   *   *

The brothers met with a number of old friends at the palace. The air about the palace was one of uncertainty, "We are still a country of tribes constantly at war with each other," said one of their old friends. "Donnchada is now the king of Munster, and he has a large task ahead of himself."

"How did the killing of Tadc happen?" asked Conall.

"Who can say?" was the response. "It is not something we will talk about here at Ceann Coradh." The nobles began to leave. They all needed to be at their own homes, within their own tribes. Earnan and Conall sadly returned to Cnoc Gorm, and the talk of peace faded.

*   *   *

The winter of 1023 passed with the uncertainty of rule still haunting the countryside. The spring brought several raids by outlaw bands of Norse in the far eastern counties and the north. Munster was quiet for the time being, but the people knew sooner or later, they would come. The family had gathered at Cnoc Gorm in April of the following year and the conversations drifted from concerns of the farm to concerns about raiders roaming the countryside.

Deaglan, Earnan and Conall had faced and defeated raiders in the past and they now discussed plans to protect their homes again.

"We are now more and stronger," said Earnan. "Now we have Laisren, Ciaran and Tola."

"Yes," said Conall, "and good friends like Ronan nearby."

"We should talk to our nearest neighbors," said Earnan, "and be ready to band together. Alone, we are easy targets. Together, we are more difficult for these raiders."

"Agreed," said Ronan. "If our numbers are enough, we will be left alone. A strong show of force may be enough, and battle may not be necessary."

Another said, "We have Conall, what more do we need?"

Conall listened and remained quiet. Deaglan went to Conall and quietly asked, "You are strangely quiet my giant friend, what do you think of all this discussion?"

Conall stood, looked at his friend, put his hand on Deaglan's shoulder and turned toward the room of men and women, "My friends, you all know who I am and what I have done. I have seen battle at its ugliest and have lived through it all. I have lived, but many, far too many good friends have not." He walked to the middle of the room, standing taller than any other man, "When I was young, I dreamt of battle. Dreamt of standing in bright sunlight with hundreds of slain enemy about me." He paused and looked at the crowd, "Hundreds, and when the reality of battle showed its face to me, there were indeed hundreds of dead. But near half of them were our people, and the sun was not shining."

Earnan looked at Grian and said, "I know what he is saying."

Conall continued, "If we wish to protect our homes, our families, we must not only show a mighty force, we must be a mighty force." He looked around the room, "I have slain many men in battle and could do it again, but one day a sword, an axe, a spear, an arrow will find me, and I will die just like any other man. Others must be there to continue the battle, to keep the mighty force together."

"What do you propose, Conall?" asked Ronan.

Conall looked at each man and said, "You have a sword, an axe or a sling. I think we should come together in one place and learn to fight as one, not as many."

Earnan moved his cane and leaned on it, rising to his feet, "My little brother is perhaps the greatest warrior I have ever known. And he knows battle, he knows the closeness of hacking another man to pieces as he tries to kill you. Both he and I marched with Brian mac Cennetig and we learned much. We learned that we are more effective if we work together, practice our skills together and learn to help each other in battle."

Deaglan stood, "Conall, we should have the lessons of the post, the sessions with Olaf."

"Yes, the slow and the fat," the two warriors, laughed. "Allow me to explain," said Conall.

As the session went on, Deaglan, Earnan and Conall talked about the training exercises they went through years ago. Men and women talked about the defense of their homes, rath walls, moats, the use of swords, axes, slings, javelins and bows.

Muirin stood, "My mother could bring down a deer with her bow, and I remember well the day she used that bow in defense of our home. We should all be able to help in our own defense."

Another woman stood, "We know how to hunt. I can use a bow as well as any man. What we haven't done in the past is work together in battle. My husband talked of Brian and how he taught his warriors to fight as one. We should do as the brothers suggest, learn to fight the same way so we can better protect ourselves."

Earnan stood, leaned on his cane, and said, "We all have homes that have to be protected. Rath walls that have stood for years and all need repair. I know the work is hard, lifting stone and setting picket logs is difficult, and I could not do it alone. Fortunately, I have two very large and strong sons who can do the heavy work. I think that we would do well to gather and go to one rath, repair it and move on to another. If we help each other, the work is easier and may get done before another raid."

Another man stood and said, "Points well stated, my friends. If I bring down a deer this week and prepare a feast at my rath, could I entice some of you to come help me with my walls?"

Earnan stood again, "An excellent suggestion, my friend, and the week after perhaps someone else will prepare another feast for us after we repair another wall."

Conall said aloud, "A feast each week. We should also bring our weapons and learn more of cooperating in battle."

"And bring the wooden swords for our children to practice as Earnan and Conall did years ago," offered another.

Deaglan added, "Learn and practice. The post, we each will have a post."

Muirin smiled at her husband, "With age comes wisdom, eh tall man."

"We hope, we truly hope," said Deaglan.

* * *

51

The wind cut quickly across the open plain in front of Conall. His horse, a large draft animal stood like a rock as the blown rain pelted both beast and rider. "Home, horse," rumbled the giant on its back, "Home, to a green pasture for you and a warm meal for me." He eased the animal to his right toward the river down a small hill.

The rebuilding of several raths had begun in the summer and now in the autumn, Conall, Deaglan and several of their friends had taken it upon themselves to patrol the countryside in hopes of finding raiding parties before they could do their damage to the inhabitants. Their few encounters were minor, and as they passed south and west of Corcaigh, they noticed a stretch of land that jutted out into the ocean. They followed the shore south and west to an open view of the ocean atop a cliff. The blue expanse on their left and the sea pounding the rocky beach a hundred feet below drew their attention and wonder.

"A beautiful view," said Conall, "I could stand here, breathe the air and listen to the water pound the beach below for the rest of the day." He looked to his right, south along the coast. The land turned into the ocean and seemed to disappear a few miles away. "We will go a little farther south," he said. "This is not a place to come ashore, and the cliff seems to extend as far as I can see."

The group turned south and followed the coast as closely as they could. Soon they came to a wood that filled the land from the cliff's edge and south. Off in the distance, to the west, the trees could be seen continuing west and north again. They followed the forest edge, looking for an opening, or a way through to continue south. As they rode, a worn path in the grass became apparent. It led them south, into an open area heading toward a wall of trees.

Deaglan said, "We may have to go around this wood, it appears to be from the edge of the cliff behind us, around this open plain and back north again, over there." He pointed at the wood, west of where they stood.

Conall smiled, "We'll follow this path some more and see where it takes us, then we will turn north again, and perhaps another mile or two west, then, home." As they rode along the path, Conall continued, "The ocean, I like the feel of the wind on my face and the smell of the salty water." He paused, "Perhaps there is a break in the trees which may lead us back to the shore, or we will find it again beyond this wood."

Another mile on the path brought the group closer to the south end of the clearing. Then in the distance they saw the roof of a small roundhouse at the edge of the wood.

"Now we will know more, if anyone is in the roundhouse ahead," said Deaglan. He sat up in his saddle and said, "I think I see someone outside the roundhouse, sitting on a log." He turned toward Conall, "What do you notice, old friend?"

Conall put his hand on his short sword, "No defenses. No rath, no wall of any kind and the roof of the house needs repair. The ground is high with grass, no animals grazing, no fields are planted, and the man does not move."

The man sitting on the log outside the roundhouse did not stir as the horsemen approached. When they were close, he finally looked up at Conall, squinted and thought for a moment. then said, "I know who you are, Conall the Giant. You were at Clauin Tarbh, as was I and my two sons." He slowly got to his feet and Conall dismounted. The old man continued, "What brings you to my home, Conall?"

"We look for raiders, or signs of raiders," said Conall as he studied the man's face. "I don't recognize you, old man. You say you were at Clauin Tarbh, who was your leader?"

"I was with the Dal gCais under Murchad in the middle. My sons were ahead of me on the front line about twenty feet to your right. I was in the back casting stones and darts."

"What is your name old man?"

"I am Glaisne," he replied.

"Well then Glaisne, have you seen any raiders pass this way?"

"Not of late. A month ago, there were some. And what will you do with them if you find them, big man?"

"We have a small force with us. If we could, we would challenge them. Mostly we want them to be discouraged from coming here at all. So Glaisne, have you seen anyone we would like to meet?"

"Not in a long time, my friend, and there is nothing here of any value to a raider." Glaisne turned, extended his arm toward the forest to the south, "There is oak, so much oak on the island, it is difficult to walk a straight line." He turned back toward Conall, "Do you wish to build a ship? If so, there is the wood. All you need do is cut it and carry it down to the beach below." He laughed and continued, "Come, I will show you."

They walked a short distance into the wood and Glaisne said, "See, look there," pointing at an opening in the trees. "There is the end of the land and a drop of some distance to the beach below," he laughed again. "The thing I have of great value would not be taken easily by a raider, and I have nothing else."

Conall looked over the edge of the cliff and then east and north out over the ocean. He breathed in the salt air, turned toward the old man and said, "Where is this island you mentioned?"

"Ha," said Glaisne, "not really an island, big man, but for a narrow strip of land to where we stand."

"Can you show me?" asked Conall.

"No," said Glaisne, "I can no longer walk through the wood that far, but you may if you wish." He laughed again and added, "Just be careful where you step, if you go over the edge, you will never come back up."

Conall looked at Deaglan, "A walk in the wood?"

Glaisne said, "Leave everything here you don't need, the walk through this wood is difficult enough without all that metal."

Conall put everything on his horse except one of his short swords. "This will clear a path where there is none."

Deaglan also took a short sword and the others remained with the horses as Conall and Deaglan stepped into the wood.

Glaisne looked at the other riders and said, "You may as well sit and be comfortable, they will be gone for a while."

*　*　*

The two warriors waded through the wood, staying close to the edge on their left. They came to a clearing and saw the other side of the land on their right was only a few hundred feet away. Ahead was open ground for another few hundred feet and the thick wood began again.

"I see the island," said Deaglan. "This land bridge is all that ties it to where we stand."

"Yes," said Conall. "How big do you think the island may be?"

"I can't tell, it seems to widen out farther away. We'll know more when we cross this clearing and the land bridge," replied Deaglan.

As the two started toward the island, the land bridge narrowed, rose and fell. They walked several hundred yards and as the bridge dropped, the rise in the distance looked like a break in the bridge with the south side several feet higher than the north side where they stood. The break in the bridge had been dug out about four feet deeper and the stones and earth had been piled up on the south side. The resulting difference left the north side almost ten feet lower than the south.

"Should we cross?" asked Deaglan.

"I would like to see more, but the day is near done and the old man probably knows much more than he has spoken."

"I think this old man may be touched in his head," said Deaglan.

"Yes, I thought the same," said Conall. "We should return."

"First a look at the other side of this narrow strip," said Deaglan.

The two warriors walked across the open field and looked out over the great ocean to the west. They stood and gazed as the southern wind gently blew warm air up over the cliff that dropped a hundred feet to the waves crashing on rock.

By the time the two returned to the little roundhouse, the sun had left the sky and the others had already made camp around the old man's fire pit.

"I have meat to cook for a meal, Conall and mead to drink as we talk about what you have seen," said Glaisne with a smile. He went into the roundhouse and returned with a bag of meat cut to pieces suitable for cooking on sticks over the fire. He turned to go back inside and looked at his guests, "You there," he said to a tall young man. "You come help me carry something."

A minute later the young man came out carrying an earthen jug and the old man followed with several cups. "Now we eat," said Glaisne, and everyone skewered a piece of meat and held it over the fire.

Bellies full and their cups emptied several times, the group sat and lazed about the fire. Conall looked at Deaglan and asked Glaisne, "How did the trench come to be?"

"Ah," said Glaisne, "there was a gap between the two sides, and we began to dig out what we could in between, twenty years ago, maybe more. Then my sons were young and strong. We planned on building a wall across the narrow on the south side and a roundhouse beyond. There is game on the island and fresh water from all the rain. It would have been a good place to live, and my sons could raise families." He bowed his head and grew silent.

"Your sons," said Deaglan, "where are they?"

Glaisne stared at the ground, "I don't know anymore. We went to Clauin Tarbh with Brian, and they were both killed." He paused again, "I brought them home and buried them on the other side of the trench," he again bowed his head. "Their mother was so sad; she died a year later, and I buried her with them." He paused for a moment and sat up straight, "We were going to build a new home, a safe home, with a wall. Then Brian defeated the Northmen at Clauin Tarbh, and we should have been safe." He sat silent for a moment, then continued, "Over the years, raiding parties have come this way several times and taken what little there was to have. I have always managed to go deep enough into the wood that they never pursued me." He looked around at the group, poured another cup of mead and after a drink said, "I thought you were raiders when you came across the meadow. But I no longer care. I was sure I was going to die this time. Die and be with my family." He finished his cup of mead and bowed his head again.

The morning found the group making ready to continue their journey around the southern part of Éirinn another twenty miles and then head north and home. Glaisne had put more pieces of meat in a sack and handed it to the tall man who carried the jug. Then he walked over to Deaglan and Conall.

"You are welcome here any day. You may even choose to finish the trench and build a roundhouse or two on the other side." He laughed, "That would be very nice."

Conall looked at him and replied, "I do like the ocean, and the land is perfect for a home and farm, but I have a wife and four children already in a very nice place. But I will be back here again, my friend. If just to breathe the ocean air."

*   *   *

52

1024 AD Munster, Éirinn

ionsaí ar a bhaile … An Attack on His Home

The trek home took the group south to another river and then north toward Limerick and home. A fork in the road gave the group a few choices and Conall opted to try the left fork with two men while Deaglan with the others went to the right. As Conall and his friends came to the bottom of a small rise, an unnatural movement in the bushes at the river's edge gained Conall's attention. Not a threat, perhaps a small animal taking water or hiding from the horse and rider. Then a muffled cry from a child. Conall halted, looked at the bush, saw the color of flesh and the brownish red of dried blood. He dismounted, walked to the source of the sound and found a boy, perhaps six or seven years of age, crouching and now crying.

"Here boy, you've not to fear me." His large, rough hand reached down and lifted the boy from the bush. "You're hurt, and you're cold." He unrolled the bear skin he wore in bad weather and wrapped the boy. "How did you come to be hurt?" he asked.

The boy cowered below the bear skin, shivering, and said, "they came before the sun left the sky."

Conall could see blood and looked at a cut on the boy's back. His eyes widened, "You've been cut with a sword or a knife. Tell me boy, what happened to you?"

The boy seemed to relax, this man spoke in Irish and seemed to be comforting him. "We were attacked, they killed my father and mother. We ran to the woods to hide, and they chased us."

"Who did this, boy?" asked Conall in a thunderous voice.

The boy shrank in fear of this loud and scarred giant and said, "I don't know, they didn't talk like us, I think they killed my brother and sister as we ran away. Will you kill me now?"

"No, boy, I don't kill children," said Conall. "Where is your father's farm?" he asked, "and the rest of your people?"

The boy looked up stream of the river, "That way, there," he said pointing east and north. "Our farm is there."

"How far is it?" asked Conall.

"I don't know, I've never been this far. I just ran and hid, then ran again, I don't know how far."

Conall saw tears form in the little boy's eyes, he lifted the boy and mounted his horse.

"Where are you taking me?" asked the boy.

"Home, buachaill, home." Conall scanned the horizon as they set out. His massive arm held the boy securely and the boy wrapped his arms around Conall's. As they rode the boy seemed to calm, "What's your name?" asked Conall.

"Liam, my name is Liam," replied the boy. "What is your name?"

"Conall."

The boy looked closely at the bear skin, then up at Conall, "I think I have heard about you, and the wolf. Is this the skin of a wolf?"

"No, 'tis a bear's skin."

The boy nodded knowingly, "Yes, another beast," he muttered.

Conall smiled, the only time he found comfort in being thought of as a killer of wild beasts.

They rode for a while and came to a small village. There had been seven roundhouses, now three remained standing and four were in ashes, still smoldering. A young girl saw Conall and the boy and stood staring at them. She looked angry and happy at the same time. Conall halted his horse and dismounted, still holding the boy.

"Is this your village, Liam?"

The girl answered, "That it is, and who are you holding my little brother?" She stepped closer, still hesitant, even though the large man spoke in the Irish tongue, he had the look of a Northman.

"We found him hiding by the river. He's hurt and needs attention." Conall set the boy on the ground and Liam ran to his sister.

The girl hurried toward her brother and hugged him, "Liam, where are you hurt?"

As the girl checked the boy's injuries, Conall demanded, "What happened here?"

The girl looked defiant as she hugged her little brother and stared at Conall, "You don't know? We were attacked by raiders, Northmen mostly, I think." She kept her little brother close as she turned and hurried him away. "Now, I have to take care of Liam. He's cut, cold and hungry."

"These raiders, which way did they go?" asked Conall as the girl hurried away with Liam.

"They went east," responded a man's voice.

Conall turned to see an older man who had been wounded seriously and was leaning on a crutch but still had a sword in his hand. "How many and when?"

The man staggered closer and said, "I know you." He scratched his chin, "You're Conall, son of Laoghaire. I was at Ghleann Mama with you and your brother and the one who came here earlier today," he said, "His name is Deaglan." He looked about and turned toward Conall, "I was with you and that one again at Clauin Tarbh."

Conall looked at the man and seemed to recognize him, "Yes, you look familiar. Tell me, what happened here?"

The man moved to a log and sat down, allowing his sword to fall to the ground. "It was a raiding party. I think they came from the coast, or at least beyond Limerick. There were too many of them to fight off and we lost a number of people, both men and women. They also killed children, as many children as they could catch." He hung his head.

Conall stood straight, and in a quiet voice asked, "When?"

"It was yesterday, late, not long before the sun set. Then Deaglan and ten men from your villages came through here this morning on their way home. They were not enough to go after and fight the raiders, so they went north and east to join the villages there and be ready for the raiders to return to the river."

Conall moved to his horse and began to mount.

"They may be heading upriver or inland, away from the river," said a woman. "There are several farms and villages that way, more east than north. If these men are looking to rob and murder, that is where they would go."

The old man agreed, "Deaglan thought it best to go inland."

Conall nodded and prodded his horse in that direction. He rode to the first settlement; there he spoke to another old man. Deaglan had been there and informed them of the raiding party. Then he had gone to another village farther on. They had not come that way, yet, but Conall knew they probably would on their return to their point of entry. As he approached a third village, a rider, the tribal chieftain, Riordan, from the first village caught up to him on the road.

"Conall, we feel the raiders may be stopped before they reach this next village. We have near fifty men coming this way and the next village is only a few minutes' ride away. They will add another twenty people or more to increase our numbers."

"Are they all warriors?" asked Conall.

"Some are, some not." He bowed his head, "Boys and older men who can no longer wield a sword. Some are archers, Conall, most are good with the bow, and some can throw a javelin as well as any other man," replied Riordan.

"Well you have my sword as well, Riordan. This fight is not yours alone."

"You're more than welcome Conall," said Riordan. "Our numbers are not that small, but your sword is most welcome. Your name alone may frighten some of them to the edge of death." He smiled and continued, "I have sent riders out in different directions to find our visitors."

"From which direction will the raiders approach this next village?" asked Conall.

"We should know soon after we get there. I think if they have gone north along the river, they would return this way through the wood and the meadow just east of us."

They rode on, arriving at the next village. Deaglan was there talking to several men and women. Soon, Riordan's band arrived on horse and in carts. As they talked with the new members of the force, one of Riordan's scouts arrived. He went straight to Riordan and said, "They come this way. We should see them soon."

"Do you know their numbers, and are they burdened yet with plunder?" asked Ronan.

"Their number was put at fifty to sixty men, and they seem to have come for silver this time," answered Riordan.

"Which way do they come?" asked Conall.

"From the north and east," replied Riordan. "Through the wood and the meadow."

Conall reached for his horse, "Let's see the ground they will cover, and the wood."

The men moved to the south and out away from the village. "There," said Riordan, "they will come through the wood there to the north and east."

"Then they will cross the meadow," said Conall. They will be riding into the afternoon sun."

Conall sat on his horse, looking about the open field in front of them. "We should wait there for them," he said pointing at a narrow opening in the forest on the west side of the meadow. "They would want to go there to continue to the river and these three villages."

"Do you expect they will come up to you and ask politely for passage?" asked Riordan.

"No," returned Conall, "if they see but a handful of us, they will attack."

Riordan looked about at the small, combined army of about seventy-two men and noted Conall's band of eleven. "Our numbers are greater than theirs, I am not concerned."

"Riordan, let's try not to lose any men in today's fight. I suggest that we divide our force into three groups. The first would stay here, those with heavy horse and lance. An even number of archers on either side in the wood, concealed with lighter horse and swordsmen on their far flank. As the band enters the meadow before us, the lighter horse will close off the rear and maintain distance. The archers will have their bows at the ready and on a signal, loose two or three volleys quickly into their midst. These men then pick up their swords and shields and move slowly to the middle. If the winds are fair and the archers aim is favorable, there will be fewer for us to face, and we may all go home after a brief encounter." Conall again surveyed the open field and waited for Riordan's reply.

"I defer to you Conall," said Riordan, "You have seen more battle than I ever hope to and a warm meal in my belly tonight is more appealing than cold steel."

"Good, send a man on a fast horse out to spot the band and get back here without being seen," Conall ordered.

Riordan heard Conall and sent a young man, or more like a boy, out to look for the raiders. The eighty-three men and boys were thus divided, and all took up stations as agreed. Conall and Riordan with ten heavy horses waited at the far end of the meadow as if they were the only opposition to the raiders. There were about twenty archers on either side and ten light horses. Time passed and the people were becoming restless in the woods. Conall, Riordan and the ten lancers had dismounted and were resting when the young scout came across the meadow at a full gallop.

"Riordan, they are less than a mile away. Riding at an easy lope," said the boy.

"How many are there?" asked Riordan.

"I counted forty-two," replied the boy.

"Good," said Riordan, "now, go join your brothers in the wood, there," he continued pointing to the left side of the meadow.

Conall stood, "To horse, my friends and if there is a God, let him give us a short task this day."

The men remounted and took up their lances. The group formed a line across the opening leading out of the meadow and waited with their lances down. Within a few minutes the band of outlaws entered the meadow on the east side and seeing the twelve men at the far end drew to a slow pace. They conversed amongst themselves and as suddenly as they had slowed, they spurred their horses to a gallop. Conall allowed the riders to cross the first hundred yards of the meadow and then raised his great sword. The lancers all raised their lances and that being the signal, the archers loosed the first volley of arrows. The second volley was loosed before the first had reached the riders and the third came quickly after. The arrows took nearly half of the riders and the men pressing in from the rear on horse had an easy time with another ten, leaving only nine men to face the heavy horse in front of them, or the sixty people pressing in from both sides of the meadow.

It was not a battle; it was a killing of some forty men without any casualties to Riordan or Conall's people. Conall watched as a surviving raider was brought in front of him and pushed to the ground.

Ronan placed his sword at the man's throat and said, "Where are the others, where are the rest of your band of thieves and murderers?"

The man did not speak but spat on the ground. Conall dismounted, put his great sword in a sheath tied to his saddle and took out a small knife. "Ronan, this man does not wish to speak, so be it. Let us skin him now and leave him for the wolves."

Ronan hid a smile, "But, Conall, what if he were to tell us where the others are?"

Riordan looked at the man, noted his features and said, "You're not a Viking, you're from our own soil. Do you know who this giant is, fool?"

The man cast a glance at Conall as he approached with a knife in hand.

Ronan spoke, "This man is Conall mac Laoghaire, do you know that name?"

Fear came across the man's face as he tried to speak, "No, he's dead," said the man.

"No," roared Conall, "I am very much alive. Now where are the others?"

The man shrank from Conall's words and began to babble. "They went north," he stammered.

"How many?" demanded Riordan as he waved his short sword in the man's face.

The kneeling man knew he might not live through the day. He hoped for mercy and spat out what he knew. It became apparent the rest of his raiding party had split off and was taking the plunder thus far gained back to the river near Limerick.

Riordan looked at Conall, knowing that his home was now in their path to the north. Conall also knew and he had to move fast, he offered no explanation, but hurried to his horse and started off.

Riordan drew his sword, looked at the kneeling man, cursed him for raiding and killing his own people, then as he started to walk away, he turned and swung his sword toward the kneeling man's head, striking him mid-ear.

"Leave him for the crows," he said as he wiped the mess off his blade across the man's tunic. "Conall gave us a great victory today, now his home is in danger. I ride to help him, who goes with me?"

A dozen men raised their weapons with a shout and were ready to join Riordan. One man tucked his short sword in a belt ring, picked up a longer sword left by one of the raiders and tested its feel with a swing and mock battle thrust. He looked at Riordan, "I'll find a shield and a stout horse and be with you as well."

Another roar from the men and several others also found better weapons and horses. Riordan smiled at his band of near forty men, armed and mounted. He looked at the remaining older men and boys, "Load everything of worth in the carts and return to the village. Stand ready, there could be more trouble coming your way." He turned his horse to the north and with another shout led his band out of the meadow.

Riordan's band was behind Conall and arriving at his home, saw him standing beneath a large oak tree on a slight hill overlooking the river that flowed to the Shannon. Two men were digging graves and several others were gathering stones to cover them.

"What has happened here?" asked Riordan of an old woman.

"They came slowly, one at first, then two or three at a time and finally all thirty or forty were inside the gate. They began to take things from people, then said they came looking for gold and silver. Conall's wife, Tressa hid the children in a cave behind the house and stood outside her door with sword in hand. One of the Northmen raised his sword and threatened her. He demanded her silver and any precious stones she might have. She said she had none and stood her ground."

The old woman turned and looked at Conall as he led his children away toward the hill sloping to the river. She looked back at Riordan and continued, "The leader of the outlaws shouted out to the man standing in front of Tressa that he should kill her and sack the house."

The woman looked at Conall again and continued, "He started toward her, and she raised her sword. He raised his, spun around and killed her where she stood. Several men ran into the house and found very little. Then they set fire to her house and left as quickly as they had come. They never found the cave, or the children."

Deaglan approached Riordan, "We're too late to stop the attack. Five people killed, including Tressa and one little boy. A number of wounded and we're still trying to find the rest of the people who ran into the woods when the killing began."

Riordan looked about the settlement and asked, "What will Conall, do now?"

"He stands on the hill, there," replied Deaglan, pointing toward the oak tree where Tressa had buried her father, "with his children." "They were safe in the cave behind their house, and we brought them out as soon as we could get to them. Now Conall will bury Tressa with her father, mother, and brother on that hill. He and his children are now alone." The old woman started to walk away, and Riordan said, "These men, which way did they go?"

"They went that way," said the old woman, pointing north and east. "That way to the river or the sea."

Riordan sent three of his fastest riders after them and walked to stand next to Deaglan. "I have sent men to find these murderers. What will Conall do?"

Deaglan sighed deeply, "The gates of hell are about to open. I have known this man for years and have been with him in battle. The men who did this, have no idea what's coming."

"What should we do?" asked Riordan.

"Ronan and I will stay with him," said Deaglan, "If you would divide the others, send them to our villages and farms, stand ready to protect them."

Riordan said, "I'll send five people to each of your villages until you return. The rest will come with me as we ride with you in pursuit of the raiders."

They stood silently as Conall stared out over the river.

"He looks calm," said Riordan.

"That is what frightens me the most," replied Ronan.

* * *

53

1024 AD Munster, Éirinn
Dioltas … Revenge

Conall lifted Tressa's body, turned toward the ashes that were their home, looked at Deaglan and quietly said, "I need Muirin's hand to do this right." His voice was deep, like thunder far away. His eyes were dark and angry, and his hands moved gently as he carried Tressa into the cave. Deaglan cleared everything from his path and Conall held her for a moment then gently laid her body on a long table. He stood next to her with his hand on her wound. His eyes narrowed, his breath deepened, and he said, "Deaglan, I need your help."

Deaglan stepped closer to Conall, "I've sent someone to get Muirin and bring her here. They'll pass Cnoc Gorm on the way and bring Earnan as well."

"Thank you, friend, brother."

Deaglan could sense the trouble in Conall's mind and knew the man would stay with his wife until she was buried. The question in Deaglan's mind was, *what would Conall do then?*

Muirin and Grian would care for Conall's young sons and daughter and there was a small army of warriors ready to follow him into battle with the raiding party. Deaglan watched Conall for a minute and noticed no tears, no outward emotion at all. Only a stone giant standing next to his murdered wife with his head bowed and a storm brewing inside him. This woman had brought peace and happiness to this great and ferocious warrior, she was the mother to his four children, his closest companion, his trusted ally and his lover. She was more to Conall than anyone knew and now she had been slain, protecting their children. The storm he might unleash could frighten Scathach herself and every warrior she had ever trained.

* * *

The three men sent ahead rode hard and eventually found the raiders. Osgar was the youngest and he took fastest horse to ride back to tell Deaglan or Riordan where the raiders were. He would lead them back to that place and if the raiders were still there, they would wait for Conall.

The band of raiders began to move again and the two men watching them, followed. When the raiding party finally stopped for the night and started to make camp. Scannal and Niall crept as close as they could and counted at least sixteen men. "I'll keep them in view, and you come back here with the others as soon as you can," said Niall.

Osgar arrived at Conall's farm just after dark and found Riordan. "Niall and Scannal have them in sight and one of them will meet us where we parted. We could leave before first light and be close by mid-day. Then the other two will lead us closer."

Riordan told the young man to get some sleep, "And get some food in your belly. We will do as you suggest and leave early in the morning."

Well before first light, Conall was pacing outside the rath wall and Riordan approached, "Have you slept," he asked looking at Conall.

"No, I wait for my brother and sister to arrive. I'll attend to Tressa first, other things will wait 'til she is in heaven."

Riordan said, "We will leave soon and find these men. We will keep them in view until you arrive, if it takes several days, so be it, we will wait for you."

"I will need the day when Muirin arrives and perhaps one more. Then I will join you."

Osgar approached the two men, "Riordan, we can leave at any time. We will walk leading our horses until the sun breaks day and then we can ride."

"Yes, take the lead with as many men are ready and we will follow as soon as Conall is free. It may be two days before that happens, but we will bring extra horses and will ride fast. Leave someone every few miles and we will catch you as soon as we can."

Osgar left with thirty people walking into the darkness before dawn. As the sun appeared over the eastern mountains, the group mounted and rode to meet Scannal and Niall. They met Scannal as planned and continued on to find Niall.

"Niall is staying close to them," said Scannal. "He'll leave a mark in the ground to show us where to go."

As morning broke the darkness, Earnan arrived with Muirin, Grian and their children. Grian immediately took all the children, including Conall's, to the field behind the barn and played games with them. Muirin went to Tressa and looked at her, then at Conall. "Brother, she was a beautiful, wonderful woman, and she loved you."

"She died protecting our children, Muirin. We will bury her with her sword, just as we buried our mother."

Earnan took the sword from Tressa's hand and placed the blade in a fire. When it was hot enough, he took it out and bent it across a stone then quenched it in water. He took the sword to a large log, sat down and began to clean the blade.

Six young men, led by Laisren, rode into the yard outside the rath wall. The young warrior Conall had met at Clauin Tarbh, Meallan, now nine years older and looking more like Conall and Earnan, was among them. They dismounted and approached the brothers.

"Conall," said Laisren, "we are here to offer our condolences for your wife and go with you to find her murderers."

"I thank you for the kind words and your offer to ride with me, but that isn't necessary."

Meallan stepped forward, "We'll talk of this when we've finished our task, Conall," he stated, "until then, this is Lonan," he said pointing to another young warrior. "And this," he continued, "is Maolan," pointing at yet another young man.

"You three look like brothers," said Earnan, "are you?"

Meallan answered, "We'll talk of this later, Earnan. Not now." The others nodded in agreement.

The group was rounded out with two of Deaglan's sons, Ciaran, and Tola. The young men then walked away from the rest of the people and talked amongst themselves. At a distance they appeared to be long lost friends just finding each other again.

Deaglan found a large flat stone and, along with two other men, carried it near to the grave. Then a small man approached, "Deaglan, I've my hammer and chisel and I'll carve a small cross on your stone to mark the lady's grave."

Deaglan touched the man's shoulder and said, "That would be very nice, old friend, and Conall would appreciate it."

The old man sat next to the stone and scratched a design with his chisel, then began to carve with very gentle strokes, eventually forming a cross with round and triangular knots in each arm.

The interment was simple. Just as Conall and his siblings had buried their mother, they now buried Tressa. The carved stone was laid over the grave and other stones were laid around its perimeter.

A priest said prayers in Latin and Irish and Conall stood next to the grave until all was done. "She is now with her family," said the priest, touching Conall's arm. "God will welcome her, and she will welcome you when it is your time."

"I should have been here to protect her," said Conall, "I am the warrior, it is I that should live or die by the sword, not a woman protecting her young." He turned and slowly walked away from the large oak tree toward the river. As he stood looking over the flowing water, he saw three deer come out of a wood and begin to feed in the open field. His mind drifted through many memories, and he thought of Tressa working in the fields, smiling in the sunshine and quivering during a storm. He remembered her laughter and her voice, a voice that could stop him and hold him with one word. A smile that could drain pain from his battered body, and a touch that he would no longer feel. He bowed his head and quietly asked Tressa if she could forgive him for not being there to protect her, as he should have been. His face was without expression, his eyes looked at nothing and his breathing slowed and a tear finally leaked from his eye and rolled down his cheek.

The family and friends gathered to see Tressa for the last time, all walked back to the gate in the rath wall and Conall stood alone on the slope toward the river. Earnan hobbled up the rise to the oak tree, paused at Tressa's grave, then continued to his brother. The two men stood together for a few minutes and Earnan said, "When you are ready, we will pursue these raiders."

Conall looked at Earnan, touched his shoulder with a slight nod and turned toward the rath. The two started toward the gate at a slow pace. Then, as Conall crossed the open yard, his bowed head slowly rose, his eyes dark and cold, his hands opened and closed into fists and when he reached the scorched ground where the roundhouse stood, he gathered his weapons and turned toward his brother. "My children, will Muirin and Grian watch them?"

"'Til we return, brother."

Conall looked at his brother, "Thank you, brother, I'm not thinking as a warrior now. I'm thinking as a very angry man. When our mother was killed, I felt hatred, no fear, just hatred. Now the hatred is much greater and still there is no fear. I want to kill these men and kill them again. Their deaths will not bring Tressa back to me, they will not right the wrong done here and may not help her rest in peace. I'll kill them for me. I'll kill to satisfy my anger and I'll kill them again, I'll destroy them, completely."

Earnan heard his brother's words and understood. When their mother was killed, they both felt the hurt, the insult, both had wanted revenge. Now Conall had been insulted again and his anger was even greater. "I will stand with you, Conall."

"Brother, your sword no longer has the strength it had years ago, but your words, your counsel will guide me just as it has since we were boys."

Earnan stood a little taller hearing that from one of Éirinn's greatest warriors. "Brother, you will always have me with you."

The day still had light as the sun was halfway from noon to dusk. Conall placed his weapons in a cart along with food and other supplies. "Earnan will ride with me in the cart," he said as the brothers prepared to leave, and my horse will follow. The others were ready and the group of fifteen left the farm heading out toward the west and the coast.

*　*　*

The small band of fifteen traveled till a lone rider approached. It was Osgar. "I left Scannal a few miles west. The raiders are traveling along the river and staying well hidden. Niall is staying closer and will keep Scannal informed about their movements. Scannal will meet us ahead on this path."

Conall looked at Earnan and said, "I will take a horse and ride ahead. I will see you soon." He untied his mount from the back of the cart and rode out with Osgar and six men. Earnan and the remainder of the group continued.

The sun was halfway to mid-day when Conall reached Scannal. As they were talking, Niall returned to the camp site. "They make ready to leave," he told Conall.

"Can we get there before they move out?" asked Conall.

"They are probably moving now," responded Niall, "but they have only one direction to go, and they are laden with their booty."

Scannal said, "If we leave now and quickly go around them, we can lay in wait between them and the river."

"A good suggestion," said Conall. "We will leave two men here with everything we don't need. When Earnan arrives with the rest of our number, fill the cart and follow their path to where we will meet them." He hesitated, looked at Riordan and said, "As we did the other day, we will leave archers in the wood, on their left. The river will be on their right and more of us will be ahead of them. Those following will have the rear."

Riordan smiled and said, "Again friend, we do battle and may not lose a single man."

The men in the band looked at each other, unburdened themselves of everything not needed for battle and took to horse. They hurried off to secret themselves around the raiding party and set up an ambush by a clearing near the river.

Conall moved to the center of the force at the far end of the clearing and dismounted. He drew his great sword and checked his short swords. His sleeves in place, he walked out of the wood and stood as if alone in the clearing, waiting.

Earnan arrived at the site where Osgar waited, they talked, then loaded everything into the cart. One of the women stayed with Earnan on the cart, the others mounted their horses and followed the raiders trail along the river. The trap was slowly being set.

Conall pushed his great sword into the ground and leaned on it looking toward the wood where the raiders would come. He was partially hidden by a bush, and he crouched down to let them come fully into the open. Soon, they began to appear. They traveled with pack animals loaded with booty and a few captives; young girls to be sold into slavery. There were forty-three men with more than twenty pack horses and their progress was slow. Conall waited for the last of them to come into the open and he stood, walking toward them dragging his sword. The leader saw Conall and called two of his men to charge forward and kill him. Conall paused, brought his sword around in both hands and waited. The two men on horse were fifty feet away when Conall raised his sword. That was the signal to loose a volley of arrows into the front of the raiders.

In the last fifty feet of their charge, the two riders both raised their swords to hack at Conall. He feinted left and stepped right as he brought the big sword in a full arc. The horseman who had been on his right was now on his left and the great sword connected with him just above his saddle. The man was cut in half and tumbled from his horse. At the same time the first volley of arrows from the archers, found their marks and six raiders fell. Two horses were seriously wounded and falling took their riders to ground with them. Conall turned to see the second charging man turn his horse and attack again. Conall stood motionless until the rider was too close to make any corrections and he brought his sword up over his head and a downward slash, split the rider's shield and knocked him off his horse. The man hit the ground with a cracking sound of bone breaking and Conall swung his sword again at the man's neck. The man's head rolled in the dirt in front of Conall and he kicked it back toward the man's falling body. Two more swings of his sword removed one arm and split the man's body open from shoulder to heart.

The second volley of arrows took another seven men and another horse fell. The warriors in the wood now charged the raiders killing the three on the ground and moved toward the remaining twenty-six still living. Before the warriors could reach the raiders another volley of arrows took four more and the rear was closed off by the warriors following the raiders. Three raiders turned and tried to retreat only to find six women with bows in their path. The women each struck a target and two of them loosed a second volley. The three were dead and the women each notched another arrow, waiting for another to retreat.

Conall strode towards the remaining raiders and Laisren and his friends came even with him. The line of warriors marched into the remaining twenty-four outlaws and sword met shield and metal. Two of the young warriors used an axe and used it well. Lonan took one raider's head and Maolan severed a man's arm, then brought his axe down on the man's head, splitting it in half. Another arrow found a man's leg and a warrior quickly slashed his throat.

Conall noticed a man who appeared to be the leader of this band of raiders and moved in his direction. The man was large and well scarred. He had obviously seen many battles and did not shrink as Conall approached.

"Do I know you big Irish?" asked the raider.

"You killed my wife, and now…"

"Ha, the little woman with a sword. Yes, I killed her. Now you will die," yelled the man.

Conall was silent. His mind saw Tressa standing defiantly in front of this filthy raider. He saw her raise her small sword and stand her ground. He stood still as the raider stepped closer and raised his sword. His face without expression, Conall stabbed his great sword into the ground and drew his short swords. A sudden burst of six hard blows to the Northman's shield had him stumbling backwards and falling to one knee. Conall again saw Tressa being pushed back and he again delivered a crushing blow to the raider's shield, splintering the wood and breaking its bindings. The raider's shield was coming apart and his arm was stunned when Conall struck him over top of the shield, cutting deep into the man's shoulder. A second blow to the same spot cut through the flesh and some of the mail. The man's arm was nearly severed inside his mail and Conall swung at the other arm. Three slashes took the second arm, and the man was quickly losing blood and life. Conall's face showed nothing; not hate, not anger, not weariness—no expression as he drove his sword down through the man's skull to his neck. A second slash across the man's neck severed both halves of his head and Conall followed with six more hacks at the man's torso.

The bloody mass in front of him was in a number of pieces and Conall stepped on the man's head as he moved forward toward another raider. There were now twenty men remaining and they dropped their weapons, begging for mercy. Conall walked over to the prisoners, and again with no expression on his face, he hacked two of them apart. A third fell to his knees and cried for mercy when Conall's sword removed his head. He kicked the man's head aside and without hesitation killed two more with vicious slashes to their shoulders and heads.

Twelve of the remaining raiders were wounded and Conall nodded to Riordan who immediately stabbed his sword into one and looked to Meallan. The other eleven were summarily executed.

Conall looked at the last three able raiders standing motionless. He turned to Deaglan and said, "Give each a sword," he pointed at the three, "and stand aside."

The three were each given a sword and the crowd moved back away. Conall stepped over to Meallan, put his hand on the young man's axe and

Meallan surrendered it to Conall. He turned, faced the three men and stepped toward them. The three were terrified of this huge warrior who had just slaughtered several of their comrades and they backed away. Conall moved quicker, swung his axe connecting with a sword and sending the man wielding it back a step. Immediately the other two tried to move in and Conall spun around stretching his arms out to the fullest and took one man's head. The sudden gush of blood on the ground near the headless torso, made footing more difficult and Conall slipped as his axe tried to reach another of the three. A laugh from the intended victim and he charged Conall thinking he had an advantage.

Conall rolled to his right and full up on his feet with his axe at the ready. He roared, stretched his arms full out and high with the axe in his right hand and began a slash that finished with both hands on the axe handle and its blade finding the soft flesh of the charging man's belly. A cry of disbelief and sudden realization he was about to die, the man screamed more in fear than pain as the axe came down on his head, splitting his skull.

The third man slashed at Conall's back as his axe sliced through the charging man's head. The man landed a shallow cut on Conall's back. Immediately Conall roared, turned and with one crashing blow from the hammer side of his axe, he shattered the man's skull.

All the raiders were dead. Conall stood motionless, holding his axe, the look of a crazed beast still on his face. Earnan slowly put his hand on the axe and said, "it's done brother. It's done."

Conall was wounded, but none of his other fighters were seriously hurt. Earnan signaled to a young woman on a cart. She brought the cart as close to Conall as she could, leapt down, went to Conall and looked at his wound. "He needs to be treated, put him in the cart on his belly and bring me some clean water."

Conall looked down at the young woman and his arms began to relax, the tension left his shoulders and his face changed from a frightening dark through a confused grey and to an accepting color of flesh. He touched the woman's shoulder, nodded and accepted a hand up getting into the cart. He lay on his belly as the woman wet a clean cloth and began to clean his wound. "This may hurt, my friend," said the woman. "But this wound must be cleaned."

Conall remained silent and showed no pain as she cleaned the wound, placed a few stitches and wrapped it. He sat up, then stood and gently flexed his arm, felt the pain of the wound and looked at the woman with a slight smile and a quiet "thank you."

"It'll take time, my large friend," she said, "give it a few days before you lift anything heavy."

Conall paused, looked at the woman, "Thank you, I will do as you say." He forced a smile and walked over to Deaglan and Earnan. "The things taken from the people should be returned to them. They have lost enough. Men, women and children were killed, and homes looted and burned."

Earnan looked at Deaglan, "I agree, this should all go back."

Deaglan nodded, "You're right, I'll tell the others."

The young warriors approached Conall and Earnan, "We'll take all this booty back and distribute it," said Meallan. "Then we will come to your farm, and we can talk."

* * * * *

54

1024 AD Munster, Éirinn
Fásann an teaghlach … The Family Grows

The loss of Tressa was going to take Conall a long time to get past. His redemption lived in the children they had raised together, three sons and a daughter. He could see her in each one of them, though the boys were undeniably his. They were big, strong boys; broad-shouldered, with sandy colored hair, deep, dark, blue eyes and they were as active as the playful hound Deirdre had seen in Conall that many years ago. The girl was definitely Tressa's daughter. The hair, the eyes, and her smile melted Conall each time he looked at her.

Their house was burned, the rath wall damaged and their animals scattered. Rebuilding the roundhouse was going to be the first task and establishing better defenses was also a priority. Conall had been in many battles and fighting in another battle did not frighten him. The fear in him was for his family, his children, his brother, sister and their families. He paced the ground outside the cave late into the night thinking about several possibilities he wanted to explore more completely. One would be to rebuild this farm with higher and stronger walls. Another would be to gather his brother, sister, and their families into one defensible rath. Still another would be to move to a location inaccessible to a raiding party, such as up a steep hill. He thought of the narrow spit of land south of Corcaigh and the land beyond. Practically an island, big enough for his entire family and more. The idea appealed to him, only the decision to leave the graves of Laoghaire, Deirdre, and Tressa behind rankled.

Earnan was awake and noticed Conall outside, sitting on what was left of the rock wall that was their home. "You look deep in thought, little brother. What troubles you?"

"We have defeated the Norse, yet they still come and raid. I built a better rath than the one that was here and still they came, killing Tressa and burning the house. If they knew the children were in the cave, they would have killed them also." He stood and paced again. "I think we should move to a place safer than this." He looked at Earnan, "I think we should all move, together, to a place where we could feel safe and be able to defend our homes, our families."

"I'm also nervous about more raiders and protecting my family," said Earnan. "There is not enough room to put us all here or at Cnoc Gorm. It would have to be some other place."

"Yes, brother, and I think I know such a place."

"The island, or whatever it is called?"

"Yes. Deaglan and I looked at some of it and now it is time to see the rest more closely," said Conall.

"I am willing to look, and I know Grian will be also. We should have a family discussion, to see who would be receptive to this idea, and who would not."

When the sun broke the night and a gentle rain began to fall, they gathered in the cave around a small fire and Earnan said, "We have had a tragedy this week and lost six of our own. Tressa was a wonderful woman, and we cannot allow another loss like that again. Conall and I have talked, and he has some thoughts to share with everybody." Earnan sat down and Conall stood.

"I have been a warrior all my life and seen many battles. I have no fear of battle, no fear of death. My fear is the loss of another of my family. You are all my family and each one of you is important to me." He paused and paced as he had the previous night, "When Deaglan and I were away a week ago, we came across a place like none other I have ever seen. It is some distance south of Corcaigh, on the coast." He paused again and then continued, "There is a narrow spit of land that reaches out into the sea and a place that is almost an island. We have not explored all of this yet and would like to go back and look at more of it."

Earnan said, "Grian and I share Conall's concern about defending our home against raiders. I can no longer fight as I once could, and our sons are still young. I would like to see them grow old. This place might allow us to do that."

Laisren said, "Our children are also young and should be allowed to grow old." He paused, "Is this place defensible?"

"Yes, very easily defended with a proper wall and only a few men with bows, javelins and slings."

"Men and women," added Tuathla to a round of laughter.

"Yes, women," said Muirin, thinking of her mother and her bow.

Ciaran looked at Deaglan and said, "If my father thinks this a good idea, then I want to know more. I am about to take a wife and we want a safe place to raise our family."

"As would I," said Tola.

Muirin stood, "I would like to know more of this place." She looked at Deaglan, "You say it reaches out into the sea?"

"Yes, the narrow bridge of land is less than a mile long, then the island is a few miles long and near as wide."

Muirin thought for a moment, "Water, is there fresh water?"

"We don't know, but the old man said there is from the rains."

Grian said, "May I ask a question?"

Earnan smiled and Conall said, "We are here to discuss this idea, anyone with a question or a concern should speak." He looked at Grian and said, "Your question?"

Grian smiled, "The ocean, is there access to the ocean?"

Deaglan looked at Grian, "So the old man told us. He said he keeps a boat on the north side to catch fish, but we didn't see it."

"Then you'll go back and see more of this place, yes?" said Grian.

"Yes," said Muirin, "and I'd like to go also."

Tola stood, "We should all go, if the place is pleasing, we can begin work immediately."

Conall said, "We'll take enough provisions to allow us to spend time there, see the entire place, and stay if we choose."

Flann was now in her sixteenth year and still a little shy about speaking in front of her uncles. She turned to her mother and said, "Does that include me as well, Mam?"

"That it does, girl," replied Grian. "Everybody means everybody, including the children, but you are now a woman and have a voice here."

Conall looked at his niece, "Flann, tell me what you think of this."

Flann looked at her uncle and said, "It's an adventure; the sea, a new home, it might be wonderful."

* * *

The family began at once to make preparations for the journey south. Earnan and Grian went back to Cnoc Gorm and packed all the necessary things for an extended trip in three separate carts and set out with Earnan in the lead cart, Amhra in the middle cart and Siollan in the third.

Deaglan and Muirin also loaded two carts as did Laisren and Tuathla. Ciaran and Tola rode in one cart while Muirin and Deaglan rode in another.

The family met at Conall's farm to begin their trip. Conall loaded two carts and allowed Olcan to drive the second cart. He was in his fifth year, but like his father was years prior, he was bigger and seemed older than his young age. As the family readied the carts and animals, the five young warriors returned from their mission returning goods to the victims of the last raid. "We returned as much as we could, Earnan," said Ciaran to his uncle. "Some of the booty must be from places we did not go, and we brought it here. The coin, silver, copper and gold, we gave more to some than the raiders took from them." He shrugged and sat down.

Meallan held out a sword to Earnan and said, "The swords and daggers of some of the raiders were encrusted with stones like these." He handed a long sword to Earnan. "Nobody wanted their swords or daggers, and we brought them here."

Earnan looked closely at the sword and then at Deaglan, then back at Meallan, "How many swords like this are there?"

"Maybe forty swords and as many daggers," replied Meallan.

Earnan placed the sword on a table and with a dagger, pried a stone from the sword's handle. He looked at the stone and back at the young men, "Bring all the swords and daggers here to me," he said.

A few minutes later there were near one hundred assorted blades dropped at Earnan's feet. He surveyed the pile and noted most of the weapons were decorated with jewels. "Everybody, take a sword or dagger and pry loose the stones. I want them all in a pile on this table."

Some blades had one stone, some had as many as eight or more. When all was done, there were over three hundred stones on the table. "We've found a treasure," said Lonan.

Deaglan and Earnan laughed, "Perhaps a small treasure, boys. These outlaws put the lesser stones in their weapons, not the finest jewels," said Earnan. Now we should fix these weapons so they may be more to our friends liking."

Deaglan held a long sword and moved it about, "We should all try to use these as well as our own weapons. Conall and I learned a long time ago, practice all you can and never be left with an unfamiliar weapon."

As the swords were being collected, Conall came out of the cave and over to Earnan. "What's going on?" he asked.

"Just a little cleaning and dividing," he replied. "Look at this pile of jewels, brother. These were taken from the swords and daggers of the raiders."

Conall brushed his hand through the pile and picked up a red jewel, "Not the finest, eh brother?"

Earnan smiled and said, "No, but perhaps worth enough to help some of our friends after this series of attacks.

Conall looked around the open yard, "These young men have distributed the booty from the raiders?"

"Yes, and they had coins left over and went back to give them all away," said Deaglan.

Conall looked at the three young men and said to Deaglan, "Those three, they look very much like Earnan."

"That's true," said Deaglan, "and Earnan looks very much like you."

Earnan laughed and Conall said, "yes, we are brothers."

The three men looked at Meallan, Lonan and Moalan, then at each other. Earnan said, "Conall, what have you not told me?"

Conall looked puzzled. "You think I'm…I mean…" He looked back at the three young men. "Meallan, come here."

Meallan walked over and looked at the three men, "Well, have you figured it out?" He turned and called Lonan and Moalan over, then looked back at

Conall. "Yes, we are brothers. We have the same father, but different mothers." He paused and continued, "The three of you spent time in Ceann Coradh over the years?"

"Yes," said Earnan, "we were part of Brian's army."

Meallan looked at Conall, "And you knew a woman named Liamhain."

Conall thought for a moment, "Yes, I did. She was very nice, and an attractive woman. She helped me several times when I had too much to drink."

"Yes," said Meallan, "she was my mother."

Conall knew immediately, "Was?"

"Yes, she died twelve years ago," said Meallan.

"I didn't know about her, or you," said Conall.

"And I didn't know about you until my father, the man who raised me, said that I was already in my second year when he met my mother." He waited for that to sink in and continued, "He died this last year, a good man and a great warrior in my eyes. I learned of you just after Clauin Tarbh, when my father came home, wounded. We didn't know if he would live. It was then, he told me about you. My mother didn't hide the fact that you were my real father from him, and he told me when I was seventeen." Meallan smiled, "Then, he fooled the physicians and lived another eight years."

Conall was still absorbing this news when Lonan stood. "You also knew my mother."

Conall looked at Lonan, then he said, "What is her name?"

"She is Eithne."

Conall looks embarrassed, "I didn't know."

"Well now you do."

"Is she well?"

"Yes, she is alive and well, living with her husband and my little brothers and sisters in Ceann Coradh," said Lonan. He laughed, "She told me about you a long time ago but asked me to keep it a secret." He paused and continued, "After all, who would believe my father was the greatest warrior in all of Éirinn?"

Conall looked stunned again and he saw Moalan stand. "What is your mother's name?" he asked Moalan.

"Ainnir, father," he replied with a grin.

Conall sits quietly thinking, "Are there more?"

"Yes," said Meallan there is at least one more we are aware of, her name is Neamhain, and her mother is Blathin.

Conall stood, "I have another daughter?"

* * *

55

The procession of carts, men on horse and animals in tow began their trek south. Three days of travel had the party at the southern coast just below Corcaigh. They traveled west along the coast until they reached the small peninsula leading to Glaisne's house and the island. When they arrived at the old man's house, they found him, as before, sitting on a log and not moving. Conall approached him and thought he might be dead. He was asleep, not dead.

"Glaisne, old friend, I have returned for another look at your island."

"Ah, Conall," said Glaisne, stirring from another drunken stupor, "and you have brought your family?"

"Yes," replied Conall, "we would make camp here tonight and look at the island tomorrow."

"Look at all the children, where did you find children?" asked the old man with wide eyes and a big smile.

"We are very lucky men, Glaisne," replied Earnan, "Our children have children, and we are all here."

Glaisne's smile faded as he remembered his sons. He lifted a jug to his mouth, drank deeply and slumped over, asleep again.

"I believe the man is drunk," said Muirin.

"Yes," said Deaglan, "he lost his two sons at Clauin Tarbh and his wife shortly thereafter."

Muirin walked over to the old man, touched his shoulder and said, "Take the jug and cover the man, we should allow him to sleep."

They made camp away from Glaisne's house and brought wood in from the forest for the fire. Muirin and Tuathla began a pot of soup and cut meat to be roasted over the fire. "When he wakes, the old man can eat with us," said Tuathla.

"Yes, daughter, he should," replied Muirin.

Tents were pitched and the animals were herded out to graze. Tola and Lonan went to watch over the small mixed herd of horses and cattle as the others gathered around the fire to eat. Glaisne woke, a little more sober than before and reached for his jug.

"First, you will eat, my friend, then you may look for your jug and the drink inside," said Muirin.

Glaisne looked at Muirin and smiled, took the cup of soup she offered him and said, "Conall, you have come back, and with your family." He drank from the cup of soup and looked around at the gathering of new friends. "Tomorrow we will go deeper into the island, across the trench and see the open plain beyond the south wood."

Earnan looked at Conall, "You didn't tell me about an open plain."

Glaisne smiled, "It is not easily seen. First you must cross the trench, then the open plain and into the south wood. The open plain beyond the wood is where I was going to build my house for my family." He paused, looked at nothing and sighed deeply.

Muirin said, "Glaisne, is there space for more than one house?"

Glaisne looked at the gathering and said, "Yes, there is room for many houses." He stood, cleared his throat and said, "A good night's rest and we will go to the south plain tomorrow," he paused, looked around again and added, "and, if we have time, perhaps we will see some of the caves."

Conall looked at Deaglan and then Earnan, "Caves, I didn't know about the caves."

"Tomorrow we will see more," said Glaisne, "Now 'tis time for sleep." He walked into his round house muttering something about his jug.

*   *   *

The morning came with a bright sun, a warm breeze out of the south and the smell of food warming over the fire. Conall was up, walking out away from the camp, looking intently at the tree line both east and west. Earnan approached and said, "Did you sleep, little brother?"

"Yes, and well," replied Conall. "I woke just a short while ago and wondered about other people in the area. I see deer out, feeding with no hesitation, birds flying about calmly. I don't sense any other people nearby."

Earnan looked out to the west and said, "Is that Meallan out with the cattle?"

"Yes," returned Conall, "he and Maolan relieved Tola and Lonan before I was awake. Their stirring probably woke me." He turned and looked at Earnan, "The walk through the wood is difficult enough for me, you may wish to wait until we have cut a path."

"I would like to go with you, but I will wait for the path. I don't think Grian will wait with me, she's excited about the caves and wants to go now."

The two men laughed as they walked back to the tent area and the fire pit. They arrived as Muirin, Grian and Flann were passing around cups of soup to everyone. Glaisne was sipping on a cup and squinted as Conall sat next to him.

"I asked the lovely lady if she has seen my jug and she said it seems to have wandered away," said Glaisne.

Conall smiled, "A clear head today my friend, and perhaps we will find your jug when we return."

*   *   *

56

1024 AD Munster, Éirinn
Draighean Cnoc … Blackthorn Hill

The walk through the wood to the meadow before the trench took longer than expected. Glaisne led the group through the wood on a path that had nearly disappeared from disuse as Conall and Deaglan cut enough brush away to allow the cart to pass. Siollan, Amhra, Ciaran and Grian cleared the smaller brush still in the path.

"'Tis a tunnel through the wood," said Grian.

"Are you sure a cart can pass through this tunnel?" asked Ciaran.

Conall laughed and said, "If not you may have to come back and make it bigger."

When they reached the first clearing, they were stunned at the wide open plain in front of them. It was over a thousand feet from east to west where the land dropped off over cliffs over a hundred feet above the ocean on both sides. The open land rose to a crest two-hundred feet ahead of them and fell away again continuing the open plain another few hundred feet to a narrow strip about one-hundred feet wide. The narrow strip led to another, larger open plain atop a mesa with a small mountain in the middle. The open land in front of the mount bordered on a thick growth of trees, covering the small mount.

Partway across the narrow strip there was a trench running east and west and the beginnings of a stone and picket wall. The ground was higher on the south side of the trench and the top of the wall was about twenty feet higher than the ground on the north side.

Glaisne started toward the east end of the trench, turned to Conall, and said, "This way, we can still go around the trench and not over it." He led the group to the cliff overlooking the ocean and moved a pile of brush, exposing a narrow path down along the side of the cliff and around the end of the trench. The path came back up about fifty feet from the trench and they were back on the open plain. They continued to the south wood and Glaisne paused, looking at the trees. "There's an opening in the trees, I haven't come this way in a few years, but I know it's here somewhere." He stumbled through the first few feet of the wood and after a few minutes, shouted, "Here! I found the old path."

The group followed and waded through another two-hundred yards of thick forest, keeping to the east side of the mount. Soon they saw the sun passing easily through the trees ahead and finally broke out onto another open plain. This plain seemed to reach out at least a mile in all directions in front of them. They started walking south again and Glaisne said, "This is where I wanted to build my house, this is where I wanted to plant my fields and raise fences for my cattle and horses."

They walked to the south end of the land and looked out over the ocean on three sides, seeing land several miles away to the east and north. As they walked westward, they saw land even farther to the west and north. At the three edges of the plain, the cliff dropped to surf pounding against rocks more than a hundred feet below. The group walked around the open plain for a while and Conall looked at Glaisne, "Water, where do we find fresh water?"

Glaisne said, "Look back at the wood. What do you see?"

"Trees, I see the trees," puzzled Conall.

"Yes, and in the midst of the trees there is a little mountain rising up and from the mount there is a stream flowing to the edge over there," he said pointing near the tree line at the western-most point. "There it falls down to the sea, down the cliff."

They walked toward the waterfall and Glaisne said, "I thought about digging out a small pond and building a dam at the edge to catch the water for the animals to drink." He seemed to drift off again, thinking or remembering.

Deaglan turned to Conall, "He seems to have a number of ideas well thought out, but no longer a reason to act on them." He stepped over to Glaisne, put his hand on the old man's shoulder, "That's a good idea, I think we have a few strong young men who could make it happen."

Glaisne lifted his head, smiled and thought maybe this was a good thing, this family coming here to his island. Maybe they would stay and build roundhouses and raise their families. Maybe he had found a new family.

Grian scurried about looking at everything, almost falling over the cliff at the waterfall and dancing about the open plain. "I love this place, but where are the caves you talked about?" she asked looking at Glaisne.

"Caves, did I tell you about the caves?" he asked the group, shook his head and looked at Conall.

"You said there were caves, but no more than that," said Conall.

"Well then, you should see the caves, at least the ones I have found thus far." He started to walk toward the east side, turned to the group, "This way, come this way."

He led them down a narrow pathway similar to the one at the trench. This one sloped down almost a hundred feet and stopped about twenty feet below the top of the cliff. He went ahead and at the end, turned into the face of the cliff and disappeared. Grian was close behind him and also disappeared, then Deaglan, Conall and the three young men.

"You can see a short distance from here," said Glaisne, "But to go much farther, we would need torches. I had one here somewhere," he said as he fumbled in the half dark. "Ah, here," he struck a flint and lit some tinder then the torch. "This will not last long, so stay close and we will go in a bit more."

The cave was deeper than even Glaisne knew and branches went in several directions. It was a project for another day, decided Conall and the group returned to the surface.

"We have time to get back to our camp," said Deaglan, "And tomorrow, again we can begin to move through the first wood."

They cut more brush as they walked back, making the passageway more to Ciaran's liking. "Now, I am sure our carts will pass," he said.

* * *

The next week passed moving the carts into and through the north wood and establishing a new camp at the trench. Timbers were cut and a bridge across the trench was built. Then, the carts were once again moved, and camp set up at the next wood. The animals were all moved to the south side of the trench and fences were put up to contain them and work began on the trench and wall. At the same time, a path was cut through the south wood to the open south plain.

Earnan studied the south plain and suggested the group decide on several common concerns before the construction of any of the new roundhouses began. "We should have a common area with the houses built around it, or a wide road with houses on either side." He looked around to make sure everyone seemed to be in agreement, and he continued, "Glaisne suggested digging a pond for collecting water for the animals and for us. I think we should pitch our tents in a middle area around a fire pit and the pond and dam should be our next task."

Conall sat quietly as his brother spoke and seemed to drift away in thought. When it was time to cut timber or dig in the trench, Conall worked as hard as any of the others, remaining quiet and staying at the task from early morning until after dark. The wall took two weeks to complete with help from Meallan and his newfound brothers, the work progressed quickly. The final touch was a walkway on the south side of the wall and a gateway with a tower above at the bridge. The temporary bridge over the trench was reconfigured to be lifted with ropes and provide closure in the gateway. The walkway was five feet below the top of the wall, over fifteen feet above the ground on the north side of the trench.

Conall and Earnan walked the length of the wall on the walkway and agreed it made a good defensible fortress. "A dozen of us could fight off a hundred Norse from here, little brother," said Earnan.

"Conall smiled, "Yes, and such a wall at Cnoc Toirneach might have protected Tressa and the others that day." He looked over the wall to the north, "We will post a guard here every day and every night."

"Perhaps two or three to keep each other awake at night," said Earnan.

Conall looked at his brother, "Earnan, think of a band of raiders right now there," he pointed toward the north wood. "You are on guard and see them, what do you do?"

Earnan looked at the wood, then at Conall, "I call for help."

Conall looked south toward the south wood, "And everyone is in their house on the south plain. They will not hear, and they will not arrive in time to defend the wall." He paused, looked north and south, then north again. "We need a plan where we can respond to an attack quickly."

Earnan also looked back and forth from north to south and thought for a few moments. "If some of us slept there," he said pointing to the ground immediately behind the gateway, "we could respond quickly."

"Yes, but none would want to build their house here. I would not with four young children. I think we need a small roundhouse where you pointed to serve as a place for those taking a turn at the wall. They will all have a house on the south plain, but each will take a watch here at the wall and be ready."

"You would make us all soldiers?" said Earnan with a smile.

"Yes brother, soldiers who would see their families every day and fight only if we need to fight."

*　*　*

The family all gathered at the wall to see it finished and hear Conall and Earnan speak. "We have discussed this and decided several things," said Conall. The wall alone will not stop raiders, we must man it and be able to defend it. It is a magnificent wall and from the north side seems a great barrier."

The people walked across the bridge and faced the wall, saw its advantages and Earnan called to them from the walkway above the gateway, "See where I am, I have an advantage over you, but just my face will not keep you out. We must all be able to fight from this position on the wall."

"How do we fight from there?" asked one of the young men.

Conall said, "From there, my sword is useless, but a bow, a javelin, a sling may each serve as an effective weapon."

"From the wall, even I can use my bow," said Grian.

"As can we all," added Muirin.

"Yes," said Conall, "and we should all learn to use those weapons effectively from the wall."

Deaglan said, "We will set up a number of straw targets outside the wall and there will be regular practice sessions for everybody with bows and javelins." He looked around and continued, "The arrows and javelins we use will be collected and used again and again on the targets." He stood at the north edge of the trench and paced off ten steps to the north, "Set the first line of targets here, and space them from east to west at twenty paces." He stepped off another ten paces and turned to the people, "Another row of targets at this distance and halfway between the first row." He stepped another ten paces and added, "This will be another row and when we can hit all these targets, we will move them farther out until we find the limit of our range."

Earnan spoke up, "We will keep a good supply of all weapons, bows, javelins, and slings to be used from the wall, here under the walkway."

"Don't forget the arrows and stones," added Meallan.

Earnan spoke, "Yes, any weapon which can be used from the wall should be stored and used in practice every day and all arrows are to be collected at day's end and put back below the walkway."

Everyone listened and heard. There had been too much death and destruction of late to not listen. Earnan looked at Conall and said, "Little brother, the horns, we should tell them about the horns."

Conall looked at the people around him and said, "We have horns, horns to be used as signaling devices when the wall is approached from the north. When you are on the wall and someone approaches, the horn should be sounded so that it is heard on the south plain. If they be friend, a single blast, then three more on the horn; if foe, two then two again and a third time." He looked at Earnan, "And everyone will practice on the horns," he added.

Earnan stood and paced before all the family and friend gathered. "We need one more thing. We need a chieftain. One who will lead us through the next years. I will follow my little brother wherever he leads this family. He has proven himself a great warrior and I have seen the wisdom in his everyday life." He put his hand on Conall's shoulder, "Conall, my brother, my chieftain."

*   *   *

As the people were walking back to their tents, Muirin and Tuathla were talking to Grian and Flann, "I feel safe here," said Muirin.

"As do I," added Tuathla.

"And I too feel the comfort of this little island," said Flann.

Grian looked at the others, "What name do you think those tall men give this place?" she asked. "If it were up to me, I'd say something about an island."

Muirin thought and said "Flann, what do you think?"

Flann said, "I don't know. I've never been anywhere but Cnoc Gorm and my own home. The blue flowers on the hillsides gave us its name there. This place has the white flowers of the Blackthorn, not the blue flowers, so we might say Blackthorn Hill, Draighean Cnoc.

Tuathla smiled and said, "I like what Flann said—Draighean Cnoc."

*　　*　　*

57

1024 AD Munster, Éirinn
Tógáil A Sráidbhaile … Building A Village

As the family members traveled back to their former homes to gather belongings, others became aware of Draighean Cnoc. Deaglan's brother and sister joined the new village as did Ronan and his family. Riordan visited and was impressed with the wall, and the open land.

"It looks a pleasant place to live and raise a family," said Riordan, "I should think about moving here myself. Ah, perhaps next year, after we harvest our crops."

Two families from a farm near Gorm Cnoc joined the village and the number of roundhouses being built grew to a dozen, with a population of nearly fifty people.

The people of Conall's small village began their practice sessions with bows, javelins and slings from atop the wall. The straw targets were set up as Deaglan had directed, at different distances from the face of the wall. Conall began the first session, "Not everyone can draw a bow enough to reach the farthest target, so find your range and practice there. As you get better, you may wish to reach a target farther out." He walked the length of the walkway, spacing the archers out evenly. "Take a close target and when you can place ten arrows in it without a miss, move out to the next target."

Both men and women practiced with the bow, and the results for most were impressive. An attacking force would need to dismount a distance away from the wall and approach with raised shield. Often times an arrow from the side may not be seen and the practice sessions led to the process of taking a target straight ahead, then take one to the right and one to the left.

"Daily practice will make us all better." said Grian, "I can now strike all three targets at twenty yards out as quickly as I can notch an arrow."

Muirin placed an arrow in a target at thirty yards, then a second arrow missed her target to the right by about ten feet and a third arrow fell short of the target. "I think I will wait until they are a little closer," she said to Grian. "If I am no threat at an angle, then they just hold up their shield and we waste arrows." She took another arrow and struck a target at twenty yards, then two more in rapid succession. She looked at Grian, twenty yards it is then."

Grian looked out over the open field, "Let's try the targets at thirty yards again."

The two women waited until others had finished their supply of arrows and everybody walked out across the bridge to collect arrows and javelins from the targets. As they were pulling arrows from the straw, Conall gathered a number of warriors and began a practice session on the open plain behind the wall. The men worked with wooden weapons and Conall and Deaglan watched. "I think we should invite Olaf to join us," said Deaglan.

"Do you mean 'Olaf the Slow' or 'Olaf the Fat' as we knew him at Ceann Coradh?" asked Maolan with a grin.

"Yes," answered Conall, "you will practice on both the brothers Olaf." He noticed several pickets cut for the wall that were not being used. "I see a post there and the hole can be dug where you stand, Maolan."

The day finished with Maolan and two others digging a pit as the people practicing on the wall gathered the final volleys of arrows, javelins, and stones. When all of the weapons collected, cleaned and checked, they were spread out along the wall on the walkway along with stones and arrows. Two guards were posted on the wall and two others were left to sleep under the walkway as the second shift in the middle of the night. The others returned to the south plain and their tents and a blast on a horn was returned with another from the wall. All was well for the night.

* * *

The days of summer passed, and the autumn breeze brought a chill to those still in tents. A small harvest was gathered from the fields and meat was cut and hung. Glaisne made regular forays into the sea catching sea bass and eels. A large gathering house had been built and meals were often a cooperative enterprise accompanied by conversation, games, and drinking. Glaisne had distinguished himself as a maker of mead and Grian could sing songs that tickled the little children with laughter.

The foundations of all twelve roundhouses were set and the main poles were in place. Weaving the wattle walls took time and the rains frequently interrupted progress. Conall and his sons went from house to house, helping with the heavier work and thatching of roofs. The daub plastering into the walls was left to others. By the time the first freezing rain fell, all twelve roofs were in place, hearths were actively supporting burning fires and most of the wall covering was in place. They were ready for winter.

Conall and Earnan organized a regular meeting of the adults to discuss the progress of building, planting, hunting and practice at the walls and with Olaf. The people were encouraged to talk, make suggestions, and offer advice. The two brothers were determined to make Draighean Cnoc a safe place to live and raise families. They encouraged input from everyone, and discussions sometimes resulted in agreements, and sometimes in argument. Conall stood more than once between disagreeing parties saying, "We will work this problem out together with talk, there will be no fights within these walls. If you cannot agree, I will decide, and that will be the end of it." Nobody was willing to argue with the giant warrior and several disagreements were mediated by Conall and settled amicably.

Grian had explored the caves with several of the older children and suggested they would make a good place to store food, valuables and hide the children if an attack were to go badly. "I know it sounds like play, but the caves could be used if we were attacked, or if there was a great storm."

"My boat," said Glaisne, "I should move my boat to the cove below us, much closer than it is now." He paused and continued, "As long as I am moving the boat, I will try to catch a fish or two to add to the food stores." He paused, then added, "I think some of you should join me and learn the ways of sailing a boat." He sat down and stood again, "I have always thought the long ships our enemies from the north use would be easy enough to sail, if I had enough men to man the sheets and take direction." He looked about, "They do make a fine boat and we may be able to get one from them, next time they come to visit." The crowd laughed at the thought of taking a boat from the Vikings.

Meallan stood and offered, "The boat, we should learn to sail, all of us should learn." He looked around at the gathering, "The more each of us can do, the stronger we will be as a group."

Deaglan leaned toward Conall, "Your son speaks with more wisdom than most. He is also a very capable warrior; I want to put him in charge of a team of warriors."

Conall responded, "He is my eldest and I want him to be tall and strong. I am not sure my judgment is best where he and my other sons are concerned. Your words give me a comfort in what I see in him."

Earnan joined the two men, and they discussed various tactics which could be employed in the event of an attack. "We can fight from the wall for just so long and sooner or later we will have to meet the enemy on the ground," said Conall. "I want to develop a strategy for just this situation."

Earnan said, "I have stood on the wall and watched the archers as they practice, they can clear an area in front of the wall allowing warriors to cross the bridge safely. It is then, the problem would arise." He paused, then continued, "Remember, these attackers will be mounted, carrying only what they need to attack a farm or a normal village. They will not be prepared to lay siege to a wall such as ours with more than grappling hooks and ropes. They may try to pull our wall to the ground and attack through a breach, but they will not have war machines to hurl stones or towers to climb above our wall. They will loose a volley of arrows, throw burning oil on the pickets, but our advantage is greater over them from high on the wall. We will keep water to douse the fires and our arrows, stones and javelins will push them back. As you say little brother, sooner or later, we must meet them on the ground outside the wall."

Conall picked up a stick, tapped it against his head and said, "Brian often talked of the Romans and their battle formations. They did not rush into battle, rather they formed lines and marched toward their enemy. If we are to meet an attacking force on the ground outside the wall, we should have a means of forcing them back toward the woods without scattering and leaving gaps in our lines."

"The wood," said Deaglan, "there we have the advantage.

"We do," said Earnan, "but as we push them back, they will soon be out of range of our arrows."

Conall smiled, "Yes, if the archers stay on the wall."

Earnan and Deaglan both knew what was coming, "The archers will come out as well," said Earnan.

"Yes," said Conall. "Mounted with a supply of arrows. As we advance, the archers will loose volley after volley, when the attackers are in range."

"If our arrows can reach them, theirs can also reach us," said Deaglan.

"True," returned Conall, "but we will loose our arrows together, then raise our shields and advance and when another volley is needed, we do the same, loose a volley then raise our shields and advance."

The three men looked at each other, thinking. Then Conall continued. He drew a series of lines in the ground. "If these are the cliffs to the east and west and this is the trench and wall. Here would be the gate, and here the north wood." The three men looked at the drawing on the ground.

Earnan began, "The archers will keep an attacking force back this far," he said, scratching another line with the stick, "allowing us to cross the bridge." He thought for a moment and continued, "Warriors with shields should move out and stand ten yards in front of the trench from east to west, evenly spaced." He drew another line, "Behind the warriors will be our kerns with javelins, slings, shields and swords ready to follow the warriors. Then, behind the kerns, archers, mounted with shields and bows." He looked at the lines in the dirt, then at Conall, "Is that what you intend?"

"Yes," said Conall, "we gauge the distance and march, until they are in range, allow the archers to do as much damage as possible, then raise their shields, everybody will have a shield, as large a shield as we can all carry and advance, slowly."

Deaglan nodded, "When we have them in the wood and we are close enough for combat with the sword, we may drop the shields and then charge." The conversation continued into the night and the next morning an assembly of warriors, archers and kerns was called at the wall.

Conall stood on the walkway facing the assembly, "We have identified a problem in dealing with attackers at this wall. We're very effective in pushing an attacking force back away from the wall, but only to a distance out of range of our archers. The movement we will try today will get us out through the gate and ready to finish the battle."

Deaglan stood next to Conall, "Archers, leave your horses below, come up on the wall and assume your positions."

Earnan walked out across the bridge and waited. He waved at Conall, "I'm ready."

Conall turned toward the assembly, "Warriors, come to the gate and wait. Kerns, assemble behind the warriors."

As soon as everybody was in position, Conall ordered the gate to open, the bridge to lower. "Now, warriors, follow me out through the gate." He walked through the gate, across the bridge and stood next to Earnan.

Earnan said to the warriors, "Every other man to the left and others to the right, spread out to cover the length of the wall. Stop when you have reached your position and wait."

The warriors in place, Conall walked back inside the wall and said to the kerns, "Now you cross the bridge and line up behind the warriors. Cover the distance from one end of the wall to the other."

They crossed and dispersed as directed. Conall now stood on the bridge and called to the archers, "Every other archer, go to your horses and come out behind the kerns. Keep your bows at the ready, and you on the wall stay where you are until these archers are in place and have notched an arrow each. Then, take to horse and join the others behind the kerns."

When the force was arranged outside the wall, Conall looked at the people still inside and said, "Raise the bridge, stand on the wall, take up a bow and stand ready." He walked out in front of the three lines and said, "Now we march across the field toward the enemy. Archers, look to the targets we have stood near the wood. When these are in range, you will loose three volleys into them. We continue to march, and the archers stay behind us. Kerns, when we are in range for your javelins, we will throw them into the same targets, slings, cast your stones when the javelins are being thrown. When you are out of javelins, and stones, draw your sword and hold your shield high. And we continue to march toward our enemy."

They ran through this scenario five times that morning, making little adjustments as the morning passed. By noon, the entire process was learned, and each man and woman could see the advantage of a coordinated attack.

"Tomorrow we will do this again," said Conall. "We will do it every day so it becomes habit, and we will be able to do it when necessary."

*　*　*

58

1027 AD Munster, Éirinn
An chéad Gheimhridh … The first Winter

The winter of 1027 was the first spent at Draighean Cnoc. Southern winds kept the air warmer than the people were accustomed to and work continued on fences, walls and removing stones from the planting fields. Glaisne ventured out to sea with two or three others as the weather permitted and they brought in fish to help feed the ever-growing village.

Grian made several torches and explored the caves below their new home, finding passages to several large caverns and a stream flowing south to the cliff face. She found the caves to be cooler than the ground level above and suggested it serve as a place to store food.

"Food and other valuables," suggested one of her friends.

"Yes," agreed Muirin, "and a place to set up a surgery, where we could keep supplies for a physician to work his magic whether it be for injuries incurred in battle or accidents working in the fields."

Everybody in the settlement was required to go to the wall several times every week and learn a task to be employed in a defense of their homes. Warriors practiced with their weapons, archers practiced hitting targets on the ground outside the wall and those capable of riding a horse and hitting targets both moving and fixed with arrows, javelins or spears rode a course of targets daily. These practices on or around the wall continued daily, through the winter and into the spring months canceled only when the weather was extremely difficult.

The approaching summer brought a new series of raids by small bands across the land. The new village was ready. Two guards mounted on horseback patrolled the northern plain, ever watchful for roving bands. They had practiced warning the people working in the fields outside the wall and helping everybody getting across the little bridge before an enemy could attack.

The practice sessions were so frequent and demanding that some of the people began to complain and some found excuses to miss a number of sessions.

Then came a cloudless day in May, when Osan, one of the outer guards sighted a band of men moving quickly across the open plain.

"They come this way," he muttered to himself as he waved to his companion and the two met near the center of the tree line. "This is no longer a practice session," he announced. "There are at least twenty, maybe more. "You take the lead and I'll follow."

Finnen turned his horse into the wood and rode as fast as he could through. He sounded the alarm as he broke through the final stand of trees, the people working in the fields stood, looked and most thought it was just another practice exercise. Finnen charged across the open area yelling that this was not a practice session and the people finally heard and understood.

Tools were tossed onto carts that stood at the ready and the fields emptied of workers, horses and implements in an almost orderly fashion. Finally, Osan came through the wood and hesitated, scanned the fields and seeing them cleared, spurred his mount toward the bridge.

A band of thirty-seven raiders had seen the village fires the previous night from the mainland coast north and east of the island. They didn't know what they would find, but many raids were like that. One didn't know until he'd battled the resistance and killed as many people as possible and began to search their homes.

Everybody safely across the bridge, the ropes pulled the bridge up and blocked the opening. The horns were blasted in warning to the south plain and with older men and women left to care for the children, every able body came to the wall. They climbed to the walkway and spread out as practiced and waited for the raiders to appear from the north wood. Then they came, all thirty-seven, mounted, hardened warriors, looking to take what they wanted and leave no living person behind. They immediately saw the wall and hesitated at the tree line. There was discussion amongst several of the visitors, then one broke from the group and slowly crossed the open fields.

Conall and ten of the men, all well trained and battle tested warriors, stood ready at the gate. Earnan was atop the tower and watched as the apparent leader of the raiders rode closer to the wall.

The rider stopped twenty yards short of the tower, looked from east to west, grinned and said in a booming voice, "Lower your bridge and we will let you live. Leave it as is and we will burn it to the ground."

Muirin looked at Earnan and said mockingly, "A fire, a warm fire may feel welcome," she turned, looked at the raider and smiled, "a fire?"

Earnan replied, "We will allow you to turn around and leave this place alive, but we will not lower the bridge."

The raider again scanned the wall, "You are old men, children and women and you seem to limp as you walk. Who do you think you are?"

Grian stood on a box so she could see over the wall, "This is Earnan, a warrior who fought with the great King Brian. And who are you?"

"I am Olaf, son of…"

A great round of laughter drowned out Olaf's continued words and Olcan, now in his ninth year called out, "Be that Olaf the Slow, or Olaf the Fat?"

Another round of laughter and Olaf furiously signaled the rest of his raiders closer, "You will all burn for this."

Muirin looked down at the ten warriors behind the gate and laughed, "I suggest you leave us, 'Old and Fat'. You are no match for what is behind this wall."

Olaf called for the grappling hooks and four men approached on foot with hooks and ropes. The hooks were thrown onto the bridge and the men ran out to a distance of thirty yards, tied the ropes to horses and started to pull.

Muirin looked at Earnan. He looked down at Olaf and said, "If it is battle you want, then it is battle you shall have." He turned to the side and shouted, "Archers, at will." He looked at Olaf, smiled and walked away from the edge and down to the ten warriors waiting for the bridge to drop. "Give the people up there a chance to thin their ranks, little brother. Then the rest are yours."

The group of warriors laughed as the people above began their work, loosing volley upon volley into the ranks of the raiders.

"Another," called Grian.

"Again," said Tuathla as the raiders fell one after another.

The archers took eight of the thirty-seven, javelins another four and the remaining twenty-five raiders fell back out of effective range. Conall signaled for the bridge to be lowered and ten warriors walked out across the bridge. They spread out across the open field and waited. Earnan then signaled to a group of kerns who ran across the bridge and took positions behind the warriors. Twelve mounted archers then rode out behind the kerns and as soon as they were in place, Conall raised his great sword and the force marched north toward the attackers. Olaf looked at the force of men and women coming at him and thought his men could defeat them and decided to meet them in battle. The archers were at the ready and reaching a reasonable distance, loosed a volley of arrows. The kerns didn't have to wait long and as the archers were on their third volley, twelve javelins flew over the warriors' heads and each man moved his shield to the front and drew his sword.

Olaf's opening threat was met with a slash of Conall's sword across his shield. Olaf staggered back and tried to regain his balance when a second slash sent him to the ground. Olaf's last vision before his head was split in two was of the twelve mounted women notching another volley of arrows.

The battle was brief and the last two raiders tried to run for their horses. They were cut down with several arrows, each from the women on horseback. The battle was over, all the raiders were dead and none of the people of Draighean Cnoc was seriously hurt. Conall looked about and four warriors replaced four of the mounted women and rode out through the north wood looking for any others of the raiding party.

Earnan crossed the bridge in a cart as the four returned from the north wood. The horses were given back to the women and the four warriors assumed a defensive position, facing the north wood. The others quickly stripped the raiders and placed bodies in the cart. It took seven trips to the west cliff where all thirty-seven raiders were thrown over into the surf a hundred feet below. Their dirty clothes were piled up and set afire, weapons and mail were collected and taken back across the bridge to the caves and the booty, leather and reusable clothing the raiders wore or had amassed in their raids was spread out south of the wall, below the walkway where it could be inspected.

Conall and Earnan inspected the weapons and supplies the raiders had with them. "There is no booty, no riches from other raids other than the purses carried by a number of them and the jewels encrusting their weapons. These men are not the whole of their group." He looked at Earnan, "We'll send out a party of four to look for the others of this band." He scanned the weapons again, "Send another rider north to Riordan's village and hope they are alright."

Earnan found Meallan, "Take three others and look for the rest of this band of raiders. If you find them, keep them in sight, send one back here with word and we will be ready with a mounted force to deal with them."

Meallan took his brothers and Ciaran, then rode east along the cliffs edge looking for signs of the extended raiding party. Laisren was sent north. "If you see anyone who has been attacked, tell them they may come here to Draighean Cnoc, to claim anything these raiders may have left behind, and if they wish, perhaps they will stay and increase our numbers," said Conall. He looked at Earnan and said, "We could add more round houses between the wall and the south wood and when that is full, more north of the wall."

Earnan looked at Conall, "Perhaps we'll need another wall, little brother, out at the beginning of this fine peninsula."

"If enough join us, we may well be building that second wall," replied Conall.

* * *

59

Tola walked the length of the wall on the walkway, looking out over the trench and back to the north wood. As he paced eastward, the sun was at his back and his view was of the open plain and the ocean beyond, both bright and clear. He watched the people working in the fields below, tending to the crops planted earlier that year. Reaching the far eastern end of the walkway, he turned his face to the sun and glare off the ocean west of the land bridge. Shading his eyes, he walked the length of the wall westward and turned again to the east. At the mid-point and the small roof over the gateway tower, he paused and scanned the edge of the north wood. A rider appeared, moving quickly and waving the several people in the fields, back behind the wall. As he crossed the bridge behind the last of the field workers, Osan appeared again, moving quickly. He reached the bridge and crossed it as Tola, standing guard on the wall saw movement near the east cliff. Horsemen, eight, ten, twelve of them, armed and moving quickly. He raised the horn at his belt and gave a blast, warning the people in the field behind him and the other warriors in the south plain. Two blasts repeated twice more brought Conall and three warriors along with twenty women ready to mount the wall in another defense.

"Conall, armed men approach," called out Tola. "They are twelve, and now coming slowly."

Conall climbed to the walkway, looked out as the horsemen neared, "Ah, it's Riordan and some of his men." He patted Tola on his shoulder, smiled, waved the group to the gate, and called out to the men standing below, "They're friends." He climbed down and met Riordan at the gateway. "Riordan, what brings you this way, old friend?"

Riordan dismounted and walked to Conall, "I've come to ask for your help. My daughter and two of her cousins have been taken by a band of raiders not two days ago. They came this way."

"Yes, we were attacked yesterday, and we defeated them here on this field. They had little with them, a cart with food and weapons, but no captives," said Conall. "How many were there?"

Riordan hung his head, "I don't know, the fighting was fierce, it went on through the morning and suddenly they turned and ran with what they had taken. There may have been sixty or more, I couldn't count them. We lost twelve of our men and took six of theirs, the rest escaped and came this way."

"How many are left in your village," asked Earnan.

Riordan shook his head, "I'm not sure, perhaps thirty-five, several men, the rest are mostly women, children and a few more wounded or dying."

Conall put his hand on Riordan's shoulder and said, "Send a rider to your home and bring the rest of your people here to this place, they will be safe until you return."

Earnan approached, "Conall, we have eight men and seven women ready to ride out now." He looked at the men with Riordan. "Your men look tired, and some are injured." He looked at Conall, "Brother, what do you think we should do?"

Conall turned to Earnan, looked at Riordan and said, "Leave your injured men here, our people will tend to them. We will send those able to travel back to your village along with some of our people. They will collect everybody and return here where they will be safe behind this wall." He looked at Riordan's men and continued. "You and your men will rest and eat. The horses will be fed and watered. We will prepare to set out upon the return of our scouts. We'll find this band of raiders—and finish them."

Riordan looked at his tired and near beaten men, then at Conall's eight men and said, "Your eight and three of my men with the two of us is only thirteen," he breathed deeply and looked at Conall. "They have many more than us."

"Thirteen men and seven women," came a voice from the mounted warriors. "We ride with you."

Riordan looked at Conall with a blank stare and Conall smiled, "My niece, Tuathla." He extended his arm toward one of the straw targets thirty yards out and said in a loud voice, "An enemy."

Before Riordan could speak, the target had seven arrows sunk deeply into it and the women had spread out in a line loosing another arrow each, striking the target seven times again from as many angles.

Conall looked at Riordan, "Tuathla and her friends."

Riordan looked at Conall, then at the women, now collecting their arrows from the target, "We are twenty then," he said with a smile.

* * *

The group rode out of Draighean Cnoc and north to the path taken by the raiders where they were met by Lonan. "We've tracked them to their camp near the coast about ten miles away. They may be waiting for the others, but some of them have loaded a boat and set sail."

Conall looked at Siollan, "Take Lonan's horse, tell Glaisne to set sail immediately, come up the coast and we will meet him where these thieves wait for their friends."

Siollan looked at Conall, "Yes, and I'll be with him." He left the group and the others followed Lonan back to the north and the rest of the raiders. When they arrived, Meallan had a report for them. "They move slowly," he said, "I count thirty-one remaining on shore. As they continue to the north, the two ships parallel them."

"I don't see their ships," said Conall, "have they left them already?"

"No," replied Meallan, "the ships have gone ahead a short distance and wait for them."

"Yes," said Conall, "these few wait for their friends, but stay on foot." He looked at Riordan, "As we did two years ago Riordan, we'll get ahead of them with seven of our number, another ten to the side and the last four will close the rear." He looked at Lonan, "Go ahead and find a place for this trap." He turned to Tuathla, "When Lonan has chosen a place, take the archers and three men with javelins. Stay in the wood with their path between you and the river, then wait hidden in the wood. When you see me raise my sword, loose your arrows."

He turned to Deaglan, "You have the rear with three men.

As the three groups were about to move in different directions, Lonan returned from his scouting mission. He went directly to Conall, "There's an opening ahead, they'll be against the water, and there's good cover to their left for Tuathla."

"How far?" Asked Deaglan.

"Less than two miles, we must move quickly," said Lonan.

Conall looked at Deaglan, "If you see the hostages, protect them."

Deaglan nodded and mounted his horse.

Conall looked at Lonan, "Lead us."

Lonan led them farther away from the river to get around the band of raiders. They reached the clearing well in advance of their enemy and all assumed positions. Deaglan moved his group of four where they could easily move in behind the raiders as they passed into the opening and Tuathla aligned her archers to allow a good line of sight for each. The all dismounted and found a place to hide and wait for the raiders to enter the clearing.

Conall and the six warriors moved to the north end of the clearing. As the raiders broke into the opening, the archers readied their bows. When the last of the raiders was in the clearing, Deaglan fell in behind them. No hostages were visible and Conall moved his horse into the clearing directly in front of them. He was seen, but not as a threat. The raiders slowed but continued and Conall raised his sword.

The raiders laughed and then as quickly as they began to laugh, four of them fell to the ground with arrows protruding from necks, chests and backs, another went down with a javelin in his chest. The second volley of arrows and javelins came before the wounded hit the ground and a third was issued as they drew their swords. Their number was reduced from thirty-one to eighteen after the third volley. The raiders turned their shields toward the woods and caught another volley of arrows when another attack came from the rear. Four more javelins flew into their midst, taking two more. The ensuing confusion caused some of the raiders to turn toward the rear attack and exposed them to a frontal surge of javelins and another volley of arrows from the side. Their number fell again to twelve.

Another volley from the archers took two more and the warriors from both front and rear slowly moved in. The raiders formed a small shield wall and waited for the onslaught. One pulled a javelin from a comrade and threw it toward Conall, striking Laisren in his leg. Just as suddenly, a flood of arrows took that raider to the ground. The remaining nine men saw no hope of winning and panicked. Two ran into the water where they sank from sight, weighted down by their mail and armor and three tried to run north. They were immediately cut down with swords by the warriors at the north end. The last four dropped their weapons and pleaded for mercy.

Conall and Riordan dismounted and approached the captive raiders. "Where are the girls taken from my village?" demanded Riordan as Conall looked at Laisren's wound.

The four men were on their knees and one spit at Riordan's feet. This was met with a fierce blow of Riordan's sword to the man's head, and he turned to a second man. The man shook but seemed unwilling to talk. As Riordan raised his sword, Conall said, "Riordan, do you remember the last time we asked questions and they chose to remain silent?"

Riordan paused, slowly lowered his sword, and looked at Conall, "Yes, I do."

Conall said to Deaglan, "Do you have a knife I can use?"

Deaglan fought back a smile and said, "'Tis a bit dull and to do a proper skinning, it should be sharpened," he pulled a knife from his belt and handed it to Conall, "but it'll still cut."

"Strip him and hold him, I don't want to be kicked by this piece of wolf bait like the last one did," said Conall.

"Yes, but it was a fine wolf we caught that day. Do you still have the hide?" asked Deaglan.

"The wolf's, yes, the man's, no. We let the other wolves finish his skin as well," said Conall as he turned to the naked man being held down. "My friend will ask you again while you can still talk."

Roirdan stepped closer, "My daughter . . .?"

"They took them to the ship and sailed last night," cried the man.

"And where did they go?" demanded Riordan.

"I don't know," replied the terrified man.

Roirdan angrily slashed the man across his chest with his sword, "Damn," he roared, "this one is dead, bring me another."

Riordan held his knife to the man's throat and demanded to know where his daughter had been taken. The man's eyes were wild with fear, and he babbled in a tongue not familiar to Riordan.

"This one does not speak our language," he roared and angrily slashed the man's throat with the knife. Riordan looked blankly at the knife and handed it to Conall, "It needs an edge."

As the next man was being stripped and Conall was sharpening the knife with a rock, the man screamed, "I'll tell you, but let me live."

"Tell me or I will ask this man to peel your skin off," said Riordan.

"They sail for Gwynedd," screamed the kneeling man.

"He may keep his skin," said Roirdan. "Tell me, how many sailed to Gwynedd?"

The man was terrified and quickly replied, "Six, yes, six and the three girls."

"Have they been harmed in any way?" asked Conall.

The man hesitated, "No, they are unharmed."

"Why does he hesitate?" asked Conall, quietly to Deaglan.

Riordan relaxed, assuming his daughter was still alive, "Conall, what do we do with these three?"

"I would ask another the same questions," said Conall.

Both remaining men told the same story and thought they might live. Conall said to Roirdan, "These things are yours to do with as you please."

Roirdan turned toward the two and said, "You killed my people, you took my daughter, you burned my village." He slashed and hacked both of them apart, leaving a bloody mess where they knelt.

Conall ordered Laisren, four of the women and two other men to load the carts with weapons and booty from the raiders and return to Draighean Cnoc. "Laisren needs to be treated for that wound and we shouldn't leave the wall undefended for this long. There could be other raiding parties roaming the country."

* * *

Glaisne sailed up the east coast and found the group near a river outlet to the sea. He came in close to shore and Conall asked him if he could see the other ships.

"No, but I can ease my way north a bit more and look," returned Glaisne. "After all, I'm just a fisherman lookin' for my evening meal," he said with a laugh. The little boat sailed out into the river and turned north. As they moved through the water, Glaisne said to Maolan, "put your sword down and look like we're fishing."

Moalan put his sword down and picked up the corner of a net, "Can you really catch fish with this net?"

"That I can, but today it's a much bigger animal we'll catch," replied Glaisne. They sailed slowly about a mile up the coast and finally saw two longships beached in a small cove and a fire on shore. He turned his boat and eased it south again.

"There are two boats in a little inlet near a mile up the coast," he told Conall. "Give me those three archers," pointing at Tuathla, "and we will block their exit from the cove, the rest is for you to handle."

Conall smiled, "Glaisne, I like the way you think." He turned to the people with him, beckoned Tuathla over, "Take two of your archers and go with Glaisne, don't come closer than needed, but keep them in that inlet."

Maolan came ashore and joined Conall as three women boarded the boat. Glaisne eased the boat out and turned north. Conall with the other nine warriors mounted their horses and moved north along the shore.

Soon, Conall had the raiders in sight and Glaisne had moved into the cove. The boat was anchored and Glaisne began to move his fishing nets about with the help of Tuathla and her friends.

The men on shore saw him and began to yell and wave at him to move away.

Glaisne returned the waves as if he were greeting old friends. The men on shore started in his direction, but he was in water over their heads. "I can't hear what you're saying to me," Glaisne hollered back, "I'll cast a net a few times and be on m'way."

Conall smiled and looked at Riordan, "Glasine is going to drown them if we don't step in and help."

Riordan laughed, "Then by all means, we should drag the man out of the deep water."

They rode into the camp and dismounted. "You people have something of ours and we want it back," said Riordan.

These six, the last of the raiders didn't know their comrades had been killed. "We have nothing of yours. Look around you, see there is nothing."

"Why are you camped here?" asked Conall.

"We wait for friends to join us," replied one of the men.

"I don't think they will be coming," said Conall.

"Yeah, they're right behind us, coming this way. Should be here any time now."

Conall smiled, "No, we met them just south of here. I know they won't be coming."

The raiders looked puzzled and Roirdan stepped forward, "They said you'd be here, and you were going to follow your friends when they arrived. Where were you going to go?"

"Nowhere you'd be welcome," said one of the raiders.

Glaisne saw the gathering on shore and moved his boat in closer, enough to wade ashore. "No fish out there, maybe there are some in here," he smiled.

Roirdan grinned, "Glaisne, are you usin' a proper bait for the fish?"

Glaisne knew where this was going, "Well, actually, fish here about like a little meat now and again. A nice tender bloody meat."

"Like from a rabbit, or a squirrel?"

"Oh no, but if I cut my finger and put it in the water, they'd came quick for a nibble and a bite."

"So, if a man were to be serious wounded, he should stay out of these waters?"

"Right you are old friend, you'd be picked apart by the little fishes, they'd clean you to the bone." He smiled, "Like those men down river we pitched into the water. They'd be all eaten by now."

Conall stepped forward, "No time for conversation now," he looked at the raiders, "Tell me where our friends are, or I'll let these two turn you into fish-bait."

The raiders looked concerned but didn't believe Conall. He repeated his question and with no answer, he said to Riordan, "Cut one of these pieces of bait and pitch him in the river."

Riordan drew his sword and slashed one of the men across his chest. The man fell and two warriors dragged his body to the boat. "Where do we drop him?" asked one of the two.

Glaisne said, "We'll take him out to the middle and drag him. The little fishes will come, they're always hungry."

Riordan grabbed another man and said, "Where did they go?"

The man answered immediately, "They've sailed for Gwynedd, near the little island, across from Dubh Linn."

"I know where that is," said Glaisne. "I've been there several times for the fish."

"The little fish that bite?" asked Maolan.

Glaisne smiled, "No m'boy, these fish don't bite."

Riordan watched the remaining two prisoners, looked at Conall and said, "These swine?"

"They are yours, perhaps they will feed Glaisne's fish," replied Conall. "Whatever you do, be done with it soon, we sail for Gwynedd."

*　*　*

60

1028 AD Gwynedd
Gwynedd

Glaisne's small boat was not big enough to carry four men with horses, and return with the addition of three girls, so he boarded the smaller of the two long ships used by the raiders and decided he could handle it with a few helping hands. "Conall, this boat is large enough to transport everything you have in mind and a little more if needed."

Conall looked at the craft then scanned the open water, looked questioningly at Glaisne, "Can you sail this pile of timber and not get us all killed?"

"The beginning may be a bit rough as I get the hang of steering this beast," said Glaisne with a laugh in his voice, "but with a proper crew, it should be no problem." He looked about and said quietly, "I've been aboard a few of these things in the past and this one will be no problem."

Conall thought for a minute and said, "What do you need to make this work?"

"I'll pick a crew of four men to work the rigging and six more to help pull on the oars," said Glaisne.

Deaglan nodded and Conall said, "Pick a crew. How quickly can you teach them what they need?"

"Not very long, we can leave while there is still light. It may take half the day tomorrow to reach Gwynedd."

"You are sure you know the way to this place," asked Deaglan.

"Yes," returned Glaisne. "I'm sure it's the same place I have been fishing many times over the last few years."

"Pick your crew," said Conall, "and let's be out of here as soon as possible."

Glaisne looked about the men present and selected ten to join him on board. They tested the rigging, raising and lowering of the sail several times. He had them all take an oar, and they eased the ship away from shore, then

Glaisne had the men row for a bit as he managed the steering board from the stern. Finally, they let the sail taste the wind and Glaisne called out to the men on the sheets to turn the sail and catch the wind moving them across the water. He steered the ship out and away from land and disappeared. They returned sometime later with the sail full of wind, moving across the water as if the crew had been sailing all their lives. The ship turned toward shore and the sail was again lowered, stowed, and secured as the men took to the oars waiting for Glaisne's orders. The ship eased up to the shore and Conall saw Glaisne at the stern with a big smile on his face. Two men jumped over with lines and waded ashore. Glaisne waited until all was secured, and he came ashore, walked up to Conall, and said, "A fine ship it is, my friend and we're ready to take you to Gwynedd, at your convenience."

The men were ready to leave as soon as the ship was seen coming back from the open water. Planks were set for the horses to board and as soon as all was secured, the men were at the oars, Glaisne took the rudder and called out, "Your oars, men touch the water and give me a long gentle pull." The men pulled on the oars and the ship eased back out into the cove then Glaisne told them to turn around and pull again as he steered the ship farther away from shore.

Glaisne waited a short while as the ship moved across the waves. He felt a slight breeze and called out, "The sail, men raise the sail." Six men stayed at their oars and four moved to pull the spar up the mast. As soon as the sail was full of wind, the oars were brought in, and the crew took turns manning the sheets.

"We sail north in sight of land until we see Dubh Linn, then east to Gwynedd," said Glaisne.

The light of day allowed the ship to see the shoreline for a while. Then as the sun left the sky, Glaisne looked to the stars and continued to sail through the night. They were offshore of Dubh Linn as the sun brightened the eastern horizon in the morning and Glaisne adjusted his course east into the rising sun. "Now we cross Muir Eireann and look for land straight ahead, it'll be the coast of Gwynedd and our destination."

Conall stood near the bow, holding onto a sheet, steadying himself as the boat pitched and rolled its way eastward. He was not a sailor; he was very much a man of the land and wanted solid ground below his feet. "How much longer, Glaisne?" he shouted back to the sailor at the steering board.

"Before the day is done, we'll be landed on Gwynedd's shore, my friend," returned the little man with a laugh.

Conall lifted his head as a splash of sea slapped his face and he again strained his eyes looking for land.

The others took seats along the sides of the ship and busied themselves in light conversation, cleaning weapons, eating from the bags of dried meat and drinking.

"Conall, you've not eaten today," said Deaglan as he held up a slice of meat, "here, put something in your belly, before you waste away."

"Not now," returned the big man. "That which I ate yesterday I left in this angry sea this morning. I'll wait 'til we're standing on dry land."

"Conall, you'll not be worrying about the rough seas," said Glaisne, "I've seen many worse and still, here I am."

Conall turned away from the wind, stepped to the deck and said, "Aye Glaisne, the sea is a little rough this day, but not a concern. The wonder in my soul is for what I will find on that shore we approach."

"I've never known you to be a man fearing the unknown ahead of himself," said the old salt.

"Fear is not what stirs me, old man. Just the wonder of the place, the people that I may meet and will I be bringing home three young girls or their corpses." Conall moved across the open deck to a fence and the horses within. He moved near a large black horse, reached through the rails with a piece of fruit in his hand and the animal approached. "There you be Horse, dry land soon enough and grass on which to graze." He turned and walked slowly back to the fore rail, wrapped his massive hand about a sheet to steady himself and put his face into the wind. He stood, nearly frozen in place until he saw land protruding through the low-level mist, "Land, Glaisne, I see land."

"I'll bring us about again and we make for that gap in the hills ahead. As I recall, there is a small pier sturdy enough for you and the horses, but I'm not sure about the two horses at once," Glaisne laughed, "or one horse and you," he chided Conall. "But take it slow and easy and all of you will be safely ashore soon enough."

"You've done us a service, Glaisne, and I am indebted to you," he replied as he went below to gather his weapons and supplies.

Glaisne turned his face to the shore then to the sky and brought the ship about to begin his run to the shore. "Ah Conall, you have done more for me than I can ever repay," muttered the old man as he smiled and breathed in the sea air, "So much more."

The others returned to the deck with their kits in hand and Conall said, "Looks a fine summer day, this. I'll hope we'll be back here in two days with or without our friends, Glaisne."

"Yes, Conall, and I'll be here also. Be careful old friend, remember, we're not as young as we were at Clauin Tarbh."

"Ah, Glaisne, it's been a few years since then and much has passed. We're older and wiser now."

"And still alive," laughed Glaisne.

"Yes, such as it is," returned Conall.

Conall opened the fence around the horses and led the largest to the gangway, down to the pier and together walked its length to solid ground. Deaglan followed, then Riordan and Meallan. Conall didn't hold a rein, the horse walked by his side until they were on solid ground. After the four men had led their horses ashore, Glaisne directed the men on board to pull on the oars to move out of reach of land to wait for Conall's return.

"We will linger offshore and catch fish," Glaisne said to Maolan. "Everyone, keep one eye on the shore and the other on the open sea as we wait. We must be ready to move away if challenged by a larger force. These men may have other friends."

* * *

Conall brushed his horse's mane with his hand and said, "Go horse, taste the grass of this land, eat your fill, we have a full day ahead of us." The large horse lazily moved out into an open meadow to graze followed by the other three, and the four warriors began an investigation of the ground, looking for tracks.

"Deaglan, what do you think now that we're here?" asked Conall.

"I didn't see another boat," he replied. "They may have come ashore somewhere else, or the boat has left them here and gone."

Conall smiled, "We should move out in four directions and meet back here as soon as we can. We'll look for signs of these people and then we can plan our next move."

Riordan was anxious, "I worry about my daughter, and I want to get started as soon as possible."

"Yes, and we know from the six men back on our soil, they are now seventeen able men with two wounded and three hostages in tow."

"And whatever booty they amassed," added Deaglan.

"We should be careful, they outnumber us and staying hidden may be our greatest ally." Conall scanned the open field and said, "I'll go that way," pointing east and north."

"And I will look east of that," said Riordan.

Meallan and Deaglan looked at each other, "I'll go to the right," said Deaglan.

"Back here before the sun is highest?" said Meallan as he marched toward the wood ahead and the only direction left.

"Yes," replied Conall.

All four started out on foot and soon were deep in the wood or around a hill, but not in view of each other. Meallan happened upon a patch of open ground that had been trampled, he saw freshly broken tree branches and grass crushed by a horse drawn cart. He advanced and as he approached a clearing ahead, he heard voices. Closer investigation proved the seventeen estimate was right and they were resting as a fire warmed food. He saw two men lying on the cart and two girls, one tied to each of the wheels. "The wounded," he muttered to himself. "But I only see two girls."

The four met back at the meadow as planned and Meallan's report had them gathering their horses and moving out immediately. They moved to a position about a half mile from the raiders camp. Conall dismounted, "We will go from here on foot and see how they are set. I prefer to take our young friends home with us, so we must be careful, no attack yet, we observe and come back here to plan our next move."

"Agreed," said Roirdan, "It will be difficult to hold back, but Conall is right, we want to take both of the girls home with us. I hope my daughter is one of them."

Deaglan said, "I'll check their camp from the far side."

Roirdan removed his small weapons from his belt and stabbed his sword in the ground, "I'll go with you and take only my bow, we should stay in the cover of the wood."

Conall and Meallan split the open ground, Meallan crawling through the open meadow, staying low in the grass, and using a series of small rolling knolls as cover. His view of the seventeen was better than he had hoped, and he noted the men were eating and drinking heavily.

Reassembled and eager to take advantage of surprise, Conall decided an immediate strike was best, "Their bellies are full, and they have drunk more than normal. They think themselves safe."

"Seventeen, Conall, more than we should try, even if they are drunk," said Deaglan.

"Ah, yes," agreed Conall, "But if we can separate them, make two or three of them come to us." He looked at the three men with him and said, "Roirdan, if you were to walk out in the open with bow in hand, as would a hunter, they may come to investigate."

Meallan said, "Yes, walk away with your back to them. When we see they are coming, turn as if you see a deer and slowly come back here, we'll be ready."

Roirdan notched an arrow and started his slow walk. He was about three hundred feet from the raiders when they spotted him. As Conall suspected, three of the men stood and slowly walked toward Roirdan. They called to him, and he ignored them, continuing to walk away, as if he heard something. He turned toward his three comrades, raised his bow, and stalked carefully out of view of the fourteen, still at their campfire. The three hurried their pace, trying to catch Roirdan before he went too far. As the three pursuers turned and rounded a thick grove of trees and brush, Roirdan turned and released an arrow into one of them. The other two immediately drew their swords and charged Roirdan. At a distance of twenty feet, Conall, Meallan and Deaglan stepped out of the brush behind them and Roirdan drew his sword. The remaining two fell immediately and Meallan crept to the edge of the wood to see if any others were coming. Five men were standing and scanning the open area where their friends had gone. They called to their comrades and with no answer, the five began to move in their direction. They called again and hurried their pace. As they rounded the end of the grove an arrow found the first of them.

Conall stepped out into the open and two men moved toward him, the other two charged Roirdan. Meallan broke cover and stopped one of the men attacking Roirdan with a hard slash across the man's mid-section. The raiders were not dressed for combat, mail and armor had been taken off before they began their eating and drinking. They were not accustomed to fighting with exposed flesh and they hesitated too often. Deaglan met the largest of the group and was slashed on his leg above the knee. He stayed on his feet and managed to find an opening to the man's throat with his sword. Roirdan dispatched another with a series of violent blows to his sword and finally to his head.

Conall walked slowly to the last of them and spoke to him in Irish. The man didn't seem to understand and as he puzzled over the words, Conall surprised him with a swing of his big sword, taking the man's head.

The raiders still at the camp were puzzled at the disappearance of their comrades and another four men began to cross the open field. Deaglan's leg was bleeding freely, and Conall threw a quick bandage around his thigh, tied a knot, and put a stick in the bandage, "As tight as you can, my friend." He helped Deaglan to his horse, "I have a few more to attend to, be ready to ride."

Riordan held the reins to his horse and Meallan's. "Another four come this way, mounted," he said. The two men looked at Conall and in silent agreement, they moved around behind the raiders camp.

Deaglan notched an arrow and moved quietly close to the woods, out of sight. The four riders rounded the end of the grove and slowed to a walk. One of the riders saw Conall and shouted, "Old man, why do you pursue us?"

Conall leaned on his big sword, "You have killed my friends and taken their daughters. I want the girls."

"Then what? Will you go away with them?" asked one of the riders.

"No, I will send them home with my comrades and then I will kill you and the rest of your filthy friends."

The raider laughed, "Great talk from one man, one old man."

"Ah, yes, old," said Conall. "Old, but very much alive and better than the lot of you." He laughed then his face grew stone cold, and he continued, "Ask your friends," he pointed at the five bodies on the ground.

The raiders started to move toward Conall. Deaglan loosed an arrow and one of the men fell dead.

Conall looked at the other three, "That would be my friend," as he raised his great sword and attacked the nearest horseman, taking him to the ground with one blow and splitting his chest open with a second slash.

Deaglan put another arrow in one of the two remaining riders, unhorsing him, and another arrow through the man's throat killed him.

The last man, obviously full of mead and not well mounted, charged Conall on horse. Conall moved quickly to his right, bringing his sword in an arc, finding a mark above the horseman's knee, and taking the lower half of his leg. The man paled as blood flowed from the stump and he dropped his sword and shield.

Conall quickly ripped a piece of cloth from the man's back and tied a tourniquet around his leg. He looked at Deaglan, "There are now ten. This one may be of use later."

Deaglan said, "I'll go to the opening and draw more this way, when they attack, I'll come back. Be sure your aim is good." He eased his horse out in the open, noted that they saw him, feigned panic, and hurried back toward Conall.

Three mounted their horses and raced after him, as he passed Conall, he turned, grabbed his bow, and notched an arrow. As the three raiders turned the corner, both Conall and Deaglan loosed their arrows, bringing down another two. Another volley of arrows wounded a horse and it stumbled. Conall dropped his bow, pulled his great sword out of the ground and he raced toward the fallen rider. Conall parried a slash from the raider and returned with a solid blow to his shield. The man stopped as if he ran into a wall and Conall again raised his great sword and began a swing. The sword struck the man's shield a second time, knocking him to the ground and breaking his arm. Conall finished the exchange with a hard blow to the man's head, splitting it open and spilling his brains onto the dirt.

The one-legged raider sat on his horse, semi-conscious and staring blankly at the ground. Conall approached him and looked back at Deaglan, "Let's ask him a question first, Deaglan, then perhaps we let him live."

"Where do you and your friends go with my three girls?"

The man continued to stare at the ground and Conall hefted his great sword, ready to slash his throat.

Deaglan smiled, "I think we should let him live; I'm enjoying his pain far too much to end it."

Conall turned toward Deaglan and said, "You're right good friend." He loosened the tourniquet around the stump of the leg and patted the horse on its rear, sending horse and rider back out into the open meadow.

"Conall, he may not survive the ride back to his friends," said Deaglan.

"Then he should ride fast, eh Deaglan," returned Conall as he again picked up his bow. "His friends should be along now to help him. We now have seven to deal with and Roirdan and Meallan should be in position behind them. He adjusted his heavy gloves and again picked up his great sword. Then in a deep and serious voice he said, "Stay out of sight until they are very close, I expect two or three will come this way leaving the others to guard the girls and their booty."

Deaglan nodded in agreement, "Those left with the girls?"

"Meallan and Riordan will kill the first two and we will take the two that come our way. Then we have to get to the others before they can hurt the girls or get away."

Deaglan nodded in agreement and notched an arrow, "Whenever you're ready."

Conall casually walked out from the cover of the grove and started slowly toward the remaining seven raiders. They saw him, stood, and began to walk in his direction. All seven men took several steps before one of them said, "No, you two stay here with the girls, we will take care of this fool."

The five continued toward Conall. He slowed, stabbed his great sword in the ground and checked his two short swords. When the five were closer to him than the girls, he raised his great sword over his head as a signal to Meallan and Roirdan.

Meallan immediately put an arrow in one as Riordan killed the other. Then Meallan looked at Roirdan, "Take the girls back to the boat, we'll finish this business here and be with you soon enough." Meallan hesitated, then added, "Tell Glaisne to move offshore until he knows it's us coming. If it's someone else, leave us here. We can find our way home."

Roirdan breathed deeply, "I'll not leave here without you," then he rushed to the girls, thanking his God that his daughter was one of them. He hurriedly cut them loose from the cartwheels and the three ran back into the woods and disappeared.

Meallan notched another arrow and started after the five men approaching his father. Conall saw the girls being taken back into the woods, smiled and slowly backed up, making the five raiders walk faster, "The farther away, the better," he mumbled to himself.

The raiders were fixed on Conall and seemingly gave little thought to the two girls and their two friends. Then, one casually turned to look back and seeing Meallan, yelled at his comrades, "A trap, it's a trap." An arrow from Meallan's bow silenced him and the four remaining spun around, not sure of what they were facing. Meallan was twenty paces behind them and Conall twenty in front of them.

Deaglan moved slowly out of the wood coming to within fifty feet of the four men. He sent three arrows into their midst in rapid succession, taking one man and wounding another.

Meallan remembered his practice sessions at Draighean Cnoc and yelled, charged and engaged two of the men. Conall immediately attacked from the front and swung his great sword wildly, crashing into a man's shield, he repeated the blow three times pushing the man into his two remaining friends, giving Meallan an opening. He slashed one of the raiders across his gut, spilling his entrails as he fell to the ground screaming. Conall finished the man who had fallen and the last man slashed Conall across his back and side. The cut was deep and brought Conall to his knees. Meallan quickly charged the man taking his arm in one slash and crushing his skull with a second. He looked at his father, ripped off his shirt and wrapped it around Conall's waist. The bleeding was severe, but it was slowed by the bandage.

Deaglan turned his horse toward the raider's campsite in time to see one of the wounded men notch an arrow, as another flew past and into the dirt. His second found Conall's back and as he notched a third, Deaglan was on him with his sword. A single blow to the man's shoulder near his neck took him to ground and Deaglan quickly dismounted. The archer was dead, the other wounded man was cringing in fear and Deaglan crushed his skull with two solid blows. He quickly grabbed the reins of the cart, climbed on and guided the horse back to Conall and Meallan.

The arrow in Conall's back had sunk in deep, but the shaft fell off easily while the iron arrowhead remained in the wound. The two men helped Conall onto the back of the cart and Conall sat down on top of the booty taken in raids. Deaglan took the reins, Meallan mounted a horse, and they left the raiders with their weapons in the open field. The extra horses were set loose, and they hurried back to the boat. They were about halfway there when Roirdan came through the woods.

"What happened?" asked Roirdan.

"The raiders are no more," said Meallan, "but Conall has been cut deeply and we have to get him back home where his wounds can be treated properly."

They hurried back to the pier, found Glaisne waiting. Conall could stand and walk, but it was very painful. He was helped off the cart and began to walk to the ship, "Bring all that is in the cart," he ordered and stepped on board.

Meallan assessed the situation, said to Deaglan, "We could cut another of the horses loose, it would lighten our load on the ship."

Deaglan replied, "Agreed, we will take only two horses, the others run free."

The horses and booty were loaded, all the men and the two girls were aboard, and the other horses were set free. The crew then pushed away from the pier and dipped their oars in the water. The wind was fair and out of the northeast, making the voyage home much quicker than the one to Gwynedd.

"We sail south and west, look for land and we'll be home in half the time it took to get here," said Glaisne as he pointed the men to setting the sail. The seas were light at first but grew angry as the day faded into night. Sailing by the stars and keeping a watch to the west, they sighted land as the sun cast first light over the eastern horizon. "We'll sail this ship straight to Draighean Cnoc," he said, "it should be faster than going by land."

Conall had been bleeding, slowly but constantly and Riordan's daughter, Sheila, washed the large wound, keeping it moist and applied pressure at two different points, slowing the bleeding. "If I had needle and thread, I could close this wound, but it may continue to bleed inside. I think we should get the arrowhead out first and close it later." She had tried to dislodge the arrowhead, but it was too deep, and the barbed edges secured it in place, "I'll need a long thin knife and a spoon to pull this one out and there's no honey to treat it with, my friend. Can you wait till we reach the other shore, and I may find help there?"

Conall looked at her and said, "You remind me of my wife, Tressa. I will trust your judgment, leave it open if that is best and I won't die before we reach Draighean Cnoc."

The sea voyage was nearly over when they cited the cliffs around their destination. Glaisne guided the ship toward the little cove below the cave entrance and told Meallan to stand on the bow and let the people see him, "Wave and call out, let them know it's us come home and not a raiding party of Norse."

Both Conall and Deaglan were below deck and Sheila tended to them with her friend's help. In a moment of calm, Conall thought about the last few days and their purpose in going to Gwynedd. "I see only two of you," he said to Sheila. "I thought there were three of you taken."

"Marga," said Sheila, "she was used by them on the boat and when they finished, she was thrown into the sea." She paused, checked their wounds and continued, "One of the wounded men at their camp, he was the one who threw her off the boat." She wiped her eyes and added, "I hope you killed them, those wounded men."

The ship neared shore and Glaisne ordered the sail be lowered. The men rowed the ship to the beach and Glaisne muttered, "We should build a pier," he paused and continued, "with a ship this large, we could really use a pier."

Conall stood and tried to take a step. The pain in his side was too much and Meallan and Maolan each took one of his arms across their shoulders and carried him ashore. Muirin came immediately and ordered someone to bring a stretcher. Conall was carried up to the caves where Muirin had set up a surgery that had been used several times after battles and accidents. Conall was made to stretch out on a table and Muirin looked at his wounds. "Who cleaned this cut?" she asked.

"T'was I," replied a young girl, "I am Sheila, Roirdan's daughter. This man's wounds are deep, and I thought the cut should heal inside himself first, then allow the healing to come outside." She stepped closer to Conall and touched the arrow wound in his back, "This one needs a good knife and a spoon to pull it out. I hope no infection has set in."

"Well then, Sheila," said Muirin, "my brother owes you his life, you did a good job of tending to him." She wet the wound again and asked another woman to bring her a sharp knife, a spoon, and the honey. "I would like you to stay here with me and help me finish treating my brother." Muirin looked at the two who carried Conall to the surgery and continued, "You two will hold his arms as I cut him, hold him very still."

Meallan looked at his brother and said, "We'll do the best we can."

Sheila beamed with pride, hearing that she had done the right thing, "I would be happy to stay and help, but my father may wish to go home."

Roirdan, hearing Sheila's words said, "Ah, girl, I think we are home. The house we lived in is burned to the ground, too many of our villagers were killed and these people have offered us a safe place to live. I think we'll stay here."

Muirin cleaned the knife blade as much as she could, looked at Maolan, Sheila and Meallan and said, "Are you ready?"

* * *

61

1029 AD Draighean Cnoc
An Mhainliacht … The Surgery

Time heals many wounds, but not all. The sword slash to Conall's back was deep and long. The arrowhead lodged in his back required cutting, digging, and pulling to remove. As Muirin made the first cut toward the arrowhead, he passed out. When they had finished removing the piece of iron, they cleaned the wounds and stitched them closed.

Conall's sons stayed close and held onto his arms as Muirin and Sheila worked on him. Finished and concerned about tearing open the wounds, Muirin had Conall strapped firmly to a pallet that could be tilted halfway from horizontal to vertical.

"He'll sleep a while now," said Muirin. "We'll keep a close watch on him, check on the bandages frequently and when he wakes, we'll have to keep him still, no movement. He'd tear those stitches and bleed to death."

Meallan and Tola took the first watch. As night fell, Grian arrived with Muirin. "Has he moved at all?" asked Grian.

"No, not a twitch. I keep looking close to be sure he's still breathing," said Meallan.

Muirin walked over to his bed, she touched his head and said, "No fever, and that's a good sign." She looked at Meallan and continued, "You two go get some food and let the people know he's still sleeping, and he has to remain quiet. Grian and I will keep watch now."

The night passed quietly, and morning came with another cloudless sky and a gentle breeze from the south and west. Muirin walked out of the cave as she addressed Grian, "I'll go get food for the two of us and be back quickly." She hurried up the walkway and toward a crowd of people at the large fire pit.

Conall woke and as he tried to move, he felt the deep cut into his body and the stitches holding it closed. Grian had been sitting nearby and saw him stir. She stood, put her hand on his shoulder and said, "You're to stay where you are, don't move and I'm going to call Muirin. Now stay still and we'll be

425

right back." She ran to the path and was about to go up to the open plain when Sheila came down the path. "He's awake," said Grian.

Sheila's eyes widened and she said, "I'll get Muirin, you stay with him."

Muirin was nearly back when Sheila reached the top of the walkway and waved frantically. They hurried down the path and back into the cave. Muirin handed the bowl of food she had acquired to Sheila and went to her brother.

"You'll not like what I say, little brother," she said, "but these are my orders." As she talked, she tilted the pallet up and stood in front of her brother, "If you stand or roll over, you may tear the stitches, so until this thing heals some, you'll be on your belly." She stood and stared at him ready for an argument. None came.

"This pallet can be tilted up a little more than it is now and made flat all while you stay where you are and don't move."

Conall opened and closed his eyes several times, cleared his throat and groggily said, "How long do you think it'll take before I can stand?"

"A few days, maybe more," she answered. "Now, we'll tilt you up to talk, eat and drink and tilted back down to sleep."

Conall forced a slight smile and said, "You remind me of Mam when she last scolded me."

* * *

Four days later, Conall was ready to stand and walk, or so he thought. "I'm as healed as I need to be," he bellowed.

"That you may be, but not without two of your sons to hold you up if you're not," retorted Muirin.

"Alright, alright, bring the children in to help the old man," he replied sarcastically.

Meallan, Lonan, Maolan, Cirian and Tola all came to the cave. The bed was tilted as upright as it would go and Conall looked angrily at the assembled group and said, "I can stand on my own." As he spoke, he tried to step away from the bed and stumbled. Meallan grabbed his left arm and Tola immediately took the other.

Muirin stood in front of him and glared, "Now do as I say and don't argue."

Conall grumbled as he attempted a second step and felt no strength in his legs, a third and a tingle in his thighs meant there was life in his limbs. Several more attempts had the aging giant walking like a drunk and within a few minutes he could negotiate himself across the room alone. He stood as straight as he could and felt the cave around him tilt and spin. Then, holding on to anything he could, he walked from the cave to the path up to the open plain. All five who came to help him, stayed with him as he made his way up the path.

"You see girl," said Deaglan, "he's too mean and hard to die from a little arrow in his back and a slash across his belly."

Muirin frowned, shook her head, and followed her little brother to the open air.

*   *   *

Standing still for a moment seemed to clear Conall's mind, he stood as straight as he could and said, "Better, I still feel the place where I was struck, but I feel better."

Deaglan slapped Conall on the back near the wound. When Conall grumbled, Deaglan said, "You cry like a woman." Conall forced a laugh as they walked across the open plain. Each step seemed to have Conall standing taller and as he breathed in the salty air, his demeanor brightened. They walked about for a few minutes and Conall looked for a place to sit down.

"I'm tired, Deaglan," said Conall, "I've rarely been wounded this badly before and it takes my strength away. The last time I was this injured, Tressa helped me. She made me eat and rest. I now feel I should rest again."

As the two old warriors were walking and talking, Sheila saw them and approached. "Conall, you should be resting, allow the wound to heal."

Conall looked at Deaglan and shook his head.

Sheila moved in front of Conall, looked up at him and said in a scolding voice, "If you do too much, you'll tear the stitches inside you and bleed to death. Now, you come with me, we will go to the meeting building, and you can rest and visit with everybody." She looked at Deaglan, "Your leg needs the rest as well, tall man. Now both of you come with me." The meeting building was less than a hundred feet away and that walk was all Conall could take. He sat on a large chair covered with hides and soon fell asleep.

Between Muirin and Sheila, Conall was watched every minute of every day through the healing process. As winter approached, he was more able to stand, walk and even try to practice with his smaller swords, but only for a few minutes at a time.

"The spring will bring new beginnings," Grian would say. "Both you and your brother have had your day of battle and now my large friend, 'tis time for the young men to do as you did and time for you to watch," she paused, smiled, and said, "watch and teach."

* * *

62

Glaisne had suggested the longships be taken back to the cove where he kept his little boat. "It's a good little boat for fishing, I can handle it myself." He continued, "Maolan knows how to sail it as well, if I had a few men with us, we could sail both of those longships back here." He scanned the room, looking for approval, then he added, "We could move so much more with those longships than we can with my little boat."

Conall thought for a moment and said, "They had two longships, I wonder if they are both still there." He looked at Glaisne, "If there are two, are you sure you could bring them both back?"

Glaisne replied, "Give me Maolan and one more for my little boat, eight more for the first longship and Tola with another eight for the second longship. As we sail north, everybody will learn as much as they can, and we'll stay close on the journey home. Perhaps we'll bring all three back here."

Conall looked at Earnan then at Deaglan, both returned his questioning look with an approving smile. He looked at Glaisne, "Pick your crews and leave when you are ready."

Six days later, Glaisne sailed into the little cove at the base of the north cliff on Draighean Cnoc. The boats were beached and tied down and a crowd gathered to see their new navy. Deaglan patted Conall on his shoulder and said, "I remember when Brian had but two or three ships."

"Ah, Deaglan, I am not a king."

"And just who's to say you're not?" returned Deaglan.

Conall frowned, staring at friend, "Deaglan!"

"Well, you are a chieftain, one step removed from a king."

"No, I am a warrior, now become a farmer. I help lead these people the best way I know, but I am not a king and I'll hear no more about it."

Deaglan knew when to stop with this aging warrior. He could push, but only so far, then stop if he says stop, and leave it there. Conall was getting older, but his mind was still sharp. His legendary strength had ebbed some and the wounds had left him with aches and pains when he moved, but he was still a formidable force in battle; not a man to be teased or pushed.

Glaisne climbed the path from the beach and approached the two men, "Well now, we have three ships, and I think a proper pier is in order," he said looking at Conall. "We've cut enough oak for the wall, so, a few more pieces, a little more work and we'll have a pier."

"Glaisne, you've done a fine thing, bringing these ships here. A pier may be just the thing they need," replied Conall.

Deaglan added, "Do you think we could get rid of those heads of beasts at either end?"

"Give me the men to help and we'll build the pier and kill the dragons," replied Glaisne.

Conall looked about himself at the people standing and watching, then with a smile, "Glaisne, make it happen."

The crowd rumbled in approval and as Glaisne began to pick out men to help him, Grian, standing close by said, "You'll need a new sail for each of your boats," she smiled, "with our colors."

Glaisne was thinking more of the condition of the wood on each of the ships. "These ships are over fifty feet long and every inch of timber must be inspected regularly and repaired immediately when a flaw is found." He looked at Grian, "Yes, sails. We will need new sails soon enough. These that brought us here from Gwynedd are in poor repair and should be retired."

Grian took on the task of making the new sails. She garnered the help of several women from the growing village and the two sails were taken down, washed, and cut into useable sections. Then Grian patched together a single white sail from the reusable pieces, and she configured them such that the center of the sail had a dark green wolf's head stitched in place. With a few remaining pieces she cut four triangular banners, each with another dark green wolf's head. Two of the banners were taken to the wall and placed atop the central tower over the bridge.

When Conall finally was able to walk to the wall again, he went with Deaglan and the main core of warriors to practice their crossing the bridge and prepare for battle. As they approached the wall, Conall saw the banners for the first time.

"Banners, we look like a castle," he looked closely and saw the wolf's head. "A wolf, why do we have a wolf?"

Grian responded, "Because your name is Conall, and it means the wolf."

As she said, "the wolf," the assembled crowd raised a cheer and shouted, "Conall, the wolf!"

*　*　*

In his fifty-second year, his aches and pains aside, Conall's strength was still greater than most men and he could still wield his great sword effectively, although not as long as years ago when he could stand with the warriors through an entire battle.

A raid on the wall in the spring by a horde of some seventy men brought him once again into a battle. As their number was reduced to thirty, following several barrages of arrows and javelins from the wall, the marauding horde retreated toward the north wood.

Once again, they employed the tactic of assembling a force outside the wall. Conall now had a contingent of fifteen warriors, including his six sons to establish the front line. The gate was lowered, and the men emerged, made their way over the bridge, and spread out before the raiders. His warriors were followed immediately by nearly thirty kerns and finally, Tuathla and a band of twenty archers, on horse. The combined force of sixty very angry men and women moved across the open field. They surrounded the horde on three sides and began their execution of the remaining force. As the raiders numbers were severely reduced, their backs were to the wood and the last twelve turned to run on foot through the trees and brush. Conall stabbed his great sword in the ground, drew his short swords and along with his contingent of warriors, pursued the raiders on foot.

When they returned to the gate, Conall was exhausted, cut in several places and bleeding. Muirin took him into the cave and began to clean the deeper cuts. "Brother, you are not the warrior you used to be, but your sons take after you. They are big strong warriors and you, Earnan and Deaglan have trained them well. It's time for the three of you to pass on the swords and stay behind the wall."

Cut, bleeding and feeling these new wounds as well as the old ones, Conall was forced to agree. Then again, not agree. "I'm a warrior, not a farmer. I tried to raise crops, tend to cattle and horses but each time we need men with swords, I'm there." He paused, thought and continued, "I know you're right, but if the day comes again where we are attacked, I know I will be in the thick of it, little sister. It is what I am, it is what I will do."

Muirin knew all too well, he was right. Battle was his calling. Fighting to protect his family was not an option to Conall, it was his responsibility, his only way to continue. "If I stay on the wall and let the others fight the battles, each one who dies will be because I was not there." He bowed his head as Muirin stitched closed a slash wound across his upper right arm. As she pulled the final stitch, he said, "Our mother died because I was not there, Tressa died because I was not there. No Muirin, I cannot put my swords down and hide behind a wall. I will fight as long as I can breathe, as long as I can stand and hold my sword."

* * *

The summer passed with no further raids on Draighean Cnoc. Reports of raids in other areas were heard in the great hall during gatherings and Conall took the opportunity to reinvigorate his warriors, to call them to more practice sessions. "We will be ready if they ever come this way again."

Each village or farm that was attacked brought more people to their gate. The population of the village grew to nearly four hundred people. The men were all required to practice with the warriors, the women all learned the bow and practiced with the sword.

Glaisne had finished supervising the construction of a pair of piers in the cove and the ships were moved to the piers and tied in place. "Now to modify the ships," said Glaisne, "we have one ready to transport livestock and we should have another to move people in bad weather." His construction force was reduced to several carpenters and the task of enclosing the middle of one of the longships began.

There were fifty roundhouses now south of the wall and discussion of a new wall, north of the north wood was no longer a thought, but rather a reality.

Every able-bodied person: men, women and children did something to help in its construction. Some used shovels, some lifted stones and others cut the timbers from the north wood and slowly, but surely, the new wall grew out of the ground across the peninsula.

Spring of the following year brought new threats by bands of outlaws roaming the countryside. Conall met with his most trusted friends and warriors, and the decision was made to patrol the land along the southern coast from ten miles inland to the north and east along the river to twenty miles west and south near the coast. Patrol units of ten men would take near two full days to complete this route and their presence was welcomed by the people they met on these treks. Often the mid-point of their two-day patrol landed them in a village or at a farm where warm food and shelter were gladly provided. The reputation of Draighean Cnoc grew. Families who lost their fathers to battle and were otherwise destitute were welcomed in this new growing village. Young fatherless families drew young warriors looking to start a family. The village grew steadily, and the new north wall eventually contained an additional thirty roundhouses.

As each group of warriors returned from their patrol, another made preparations to leave. These were warriors, keeping the peace, and as they covered the area north, east and west of Draighean Cnoc, the outlaw bands found other targets to attack. The name of mac Laoghaire was known to these attacking foreigners, and they kept their distance. As the patrols moved farther north and west, the occasional conflict did occur. Each skirmish experienced was reported back at the great hall to the council and some of these encounters resulted in injuries and even death to warriors.

"This is the price we pay to keep out village safe," said Conall. "If the patrols are meeting larger bands of raiders, we will make our patrols bigger. If the outlaws run from us, we will pursue them, but always with the memory of Sulcoit in mind. There, with Brian they trapped the Norse, there they won a great victory, but the same could happen to us. Beware as you pursue, the enemy may be drawing you into a bog, and from there you may never return."

The fall of 1041 brought a band of foreigners to the gates of Draighean Cnoc. Demands were made and the force assembled behind the wall. Conall was still leading the force and as they assembled, Earnan stood on the walkway.

"We will allow you to leave without battle," said Earnan. "We want no blood shed on this day."

The leader of the outlaws called back to Earnan, "You are an old man, you have only women on your wall, what can you do to stop us?"

"This is the village of Draighean Cnoc, home of the Clann mac Laoghaire," replied Earnan, "you will not fare well here."

"Ah," replied the foreigner, "I know of this name, and the name Conall. Is he one of you?"

Earnan looked at Conall, turned toward the attackers and responded, "Yes, he stands behind this gate, ready to come out and do battle if necessary."

"Then send him out, we will give him battle and then we will kill him," laughed the outlaw.

Earnan looked at Tuathla, then at the outlaw, "Move away if you wish to live." He nodded to Tuathla and stepped away from the wall.

The first barrage of arrows took nine of the raiders and the rest retreated to the wood. The bridge was lowered and as before the warriors walked out, taking positions along the trench. When the force was fully assembled, Conall led them across the field toward the raiders carrying his great sword and two short swords in his belt.

At a distance of fifty feet from the wood several archers stood and loosed arrows at Conall. He was not carrying a shield and was struck in the chest and left leg. He staggered, the mounted archers immediately returned with another volley of arrows and the kerns found several targets for their javelins. Conall fell to his knees and angrily pulled an arrow from his chest, then another from his leg. He stood as Deaglan stepped closer and two other warriors stepped in front of him.

"Pull that damned arrow out of my leg, Deaglan," demanded Conall.

Deaglan took the shaft in hand and pulled, removing the shaft but not the arrowhead. It was imbedded deep inside his leg.

Conall gritted his teeth, "Now the other."

Deaglan did as he was asked and said, "You're bleeding too much, let me finish this battle and these men will help you back to the wall."

Conall rolled his head, flexed his shoulders and drew his two short swords, "Not yet, old friend, there's work to do here."

Deaglan didn't argue, the battle was on and the two warriors in front of them needed help. Both Deaglan and Conall stepped into the fray and fought as if there was no wound.

As the raiders' numbers fell, the few remaining started to look for a way out. Five of them fell on Conall and with fury hacked and slashed at him. He continued to fight with two arrowheads buried in his body and now three slashes across his back and arms. Conall was tiring and his swords slowed. Two raiders managed to stab him and one paid with his life. The other stabbed again, this time a thrust toward the heart and Conall was down again. The raider turned and ran into the wood along with three others.

Deaglan was cut across his leg and Meallan had taken an arrow in his left shoulder. The battle was over, the warriors pursued the outlaws into the wood but didn't know how many there were. Darkness fell and a cart was brought out to carry the wounded back behind the wall. Conall was the second to be reached and loaded on the cart.

"I think he's dead," said one man.

"No, he can't die. This is Conall. Quick, let's get him back behind the wall." They moved as fast as they could, and the cart was met by Muirin.

"Oh God," she cried and rushed to feel for life. "He's alive, quick to the cave with him." She ran by their side as the two men pulled the cart to the path down to the caves. Inside and laying on a stone slab in the cave, Conall was losing blood and life. Muirin closed the wounds she could and as she was starting to look for a spoon, Sheila came into the cave.

"What can I do?" she asked Muirin.

Muirin was shaken and replied, "The spoon, there's an arrowhead in his chest and another in his leg."

Sheila found the spoon and stepped in front of Muirin, "Allow me Muirin," and she proceeded to dig out the arrowhead from Conall's chest. As she pulled it out, she looked at Muirin, "Should we cauterize the wound or stitch it closed?"

Muirin hesitated, then quickly turned to the fire, and picked up the hot iron. The two women tried through most of the day to close his wounds and keep him alive, but it was a losing battle. Conall was slowly slipping away.

Earnan and Deaglan were brought to the cave. "He is dying, and I can do nothing," cried Muirin. "We have tried everything we know and still he bleeds."

Deaglan said, "He took four arrows and there were slashes on his back and shoulder. Then, I saw him stabbed near his heart, two times."

Conall woke for a brief time, and looked at Deaglan, "You were right, old friend. It makes little difference if your opponent is skilled or lucky, either can kill you."

His sons and Fiona all came into the cave. Meallan looked at Muirin, "How much longer does he have?"

Muirin's eyes were wet, "Soon, before this day is done, I don't know." Fiona stepped closer to Conall and touched his shoulder where the wound bled and then his chest where the sword touched his heart, "Da, can you hear me?"

His eyes opened and he looked at Fiona, "My little girl, you have your mother's eyes." He drew a breath and obviously felt pain, "Look to your brothers, they will take care of you now."

She held his large hand in hers and cried softly, "Da." Conall did not draw another breath. Sheila touched his neck and said, "He's gone."

*　*　*

CLANN MACLOAGHAIRE

63

Conall's family was with him when he died. The entire population of Draighean Cnoc mourned his passing and there was a gathering at the first wall where people stood and remembered his life, his great victories and his leadership. Several men stepped up onto a small earthen mound near the wall so all could see and hear them. They began with shouts of praise for their leader, citing his victories in battles from Ghleann Mama and Cluain Tarbh to the rescue of the two girls in Gwynedd.

Muirin and Earnan approached the crowd, and a path was opened for them to reach the earthen mound. As they stepped up the rise, Muirin stumbled, and a large hand reached out and caught her fall. Her eyes widened, it looked as if Conall's hand had touched her arm and stopped her fall. She looked up in awe into a dark figure blocking the sun directly overhead. The massive arms, the sand-colored hair and the shoulders of a giant gave her pause.

Then a deep voice quietly said, "Careful now, Aunt," and Meallan supported her as she regained her balance.

She held onto Meallan's arm as she stood, and the light finally showed his face. The face of a young, very alive Conall. "You look so much like your father," she whispered, offering a sad smile. "Please, help me to the top of this little mountain."

As Meallan held Muirin, Lonan helped Earnan up the rise as well. Muirin looked out over the assembled crowd of several hundred people. She cleared her throat and raised her hand to speak. The crowd quieted and Muirin tried to raise her voice for all to hear. She paused and looked at Earnan, "I can't speak loud enough to be heard."

Earnan coughed, raised an eyebrow, and replied, "Nor can I, little sister."

Meallan put his hand on Muirin's shoulder, "Tell me the words, Aunt, and I'll pass them on to the people." He lifted his arm as the crowd began to mumble again. Then there was silence.

Muirin smiled and said in a voice few, if any could hear, "Thank you for honoring my brother," her eyes turned up to Meallan, "this man's father and father to seven more."

Meallan repeated her words and Muirin spoke again, "Conall was the great strength we all gathered around and found peace, safety and comfort." She listened as Meallan repeated her words and she spoke again, "Now he has passed on and we remain, but not alone. He not only stood tall but taught us all to stand tall. We built this wall years ago and learned to defend it. Then we moved out farther and built another wall and learned to defend it. There is safety behind these walls, in part because they are tall and strong, but even more so because we have stood on these walls and defended them." She paused again as Meallan relayed her words.

"My brother was a great warrior, one of the greatest. Something like these walls that are built from strong oak trees, Conall stood in battle and all respected him. These pickets stand in these walls, strong and upright. But even these sturdy oak pickets age and soon rot away, so too do warriors. They stand tall, they fight and some die, but all come to an end sooner or later." Meallan continued with Muirin's sentiments, "Like a great picket in our wall, Conall has reached his end, but his words and his teachings are still with us. We are now a force in this world. We have all learned to use our weapons and we have learned to fight as one from this wall and beyond it."

Meallan paused before speaking her final words, "The people who stand on this wall and the outer wall are his monuments. Those who learn to work together as one are his monuments. Put your time and your energy into your training and providing for your families. Make this village, this Clann, work and grow. There can be no better monument to Conall."

The gathered people raised their voices in support of Muirin's words and enthusiastic conversations broke out throughout the crowd. As the people began to disperse, a small group paused and seemed to be in serious conversation. Meallan helped Muirin down from the earthen mound and immediately was approached by three men.

"Meallan, we have concerns and wish to talk with you."

"Can this wait 'til my father has been buried?"

"No," replied one of the men. He stood tall and continued, "Conall must be buried, but where? No matter where we choose to place his grave, someone, sometime will try to dig him up. To have his sword or his bones. He must be buried in secret."

Meallan stood silent as Muirin stepped up, "I hear your concerns and it troubles me," she said. "This is something I had not considered."

Meallan put his hand on Muirin's shoulder, "Conall has often brought the elders together in council. I think we should do that again, perhaps even tonight."

"There are several points to discuss," offered another of the three men. "We should decide who will lead this village, who will be our new chieftain."

Meallan looked about as Earnan and Grian approached. Lonan was near and Meallan called him and Olcan to join them. "Brothers, friends, we will meet in council tonight. Spread the word. The elders must be there."

Earnan knew what was being planned and he nodded in approval, "The night looks to be fair, we can assemble at the large fire pit in the center of the open ground."

An informal custom of each man bringing a log or two to an open-air meeting for the fire had most bringing two or more. The attendees saw it as a long meeting, and none wanted to be left out.

The fire was started as the sun approached the western horizon over the ocean. Meallan stood and began, "Today as we met near the first wall, some expressed concerns and we meet here now to discuss them." He looked to the man who approached him at the wall, "Aonghus, stand and ask your questions."

The man stood, he was a large man, advanced in years and had fought alongside of Conall several times. He was a well-respected man, and all listened intently. "Conall was a good man, a good friend and I wish to honor him with a large monument. But I listened to Muirin's words and there is wisdom there. We should honor our chieftain by continuing to act as if he was still here. Work together as one, fight together as one and we will continue." He paused and took several steps, "Conall is to be buried, but where? No matter where we bury him, someone will try to raid his grave and steal his bones or his sword. I think we should hide him, bury him in secret where he can rest in peace."

The crowd began to talk quietly and Earnan stood, "My brother was not a man to wear gold or jewels. He was not one to paint his face before battle and he was not one to pick the wealth off the dead after battle. He would not want a great monument built for himself and he may be well served with a hidden burial. I propose his sons find a quiet place and take his body there. They can be trusted to keep his burial secret."

The crowd again began to mumble in low conversation and Grian stood. "I know a place we all know. A place where he can rest forever, and we need not worry about him being disturbed." She walked over to Muirin and whispered into her ear.

Muirin looked about and called Conall's children to her. Grian knelt in their midst and in less than a minute, all stood and Meallan extended his hand toward Grian, inviting her to continue to address the crowd.

Grian began, "The caves below us go in many different directions. Some wander below the little mountain, others out toward the sea. There are many and probably more we have not yet found. I'd pick one that ends with only one way out and place him there. Then we block the entrance and collapse the roof of the passage to him." She bowed her head, "We could never visit him, but he'd be safe from everybody and could rest in complete peace."

The crowd approved and Meallan stood, "Then it is to be done. Grian will find an appropriate cave and my brothers, and I will gather as many large stones as we can carry into the cave and he will be buried."

Earnan stood and raised an arm, "We have followed the lead of Conall for near 20 years and he has often referred to us as the Clann MacLaoghaire. That is who we are and who we shall continue to be under our new chieftain. Now is the time to select that new leader, our new chieftain."

The gathered people agreed, and one man stood, "Earnan, you have been as much a leader as Conall, I say you should be our Chieftain."

There was a rumble of approval and Earnan stood, "I thank you for the vote of confidence, but I grow older every day and I think we need a younger man to lead us." He paused and walked toward the fire, "Over the last several years, I have seen Meallan in battle and he is formidable. I have listened to him at the council meetings, and he has been wise in his words. I watched as he helped my sister this afternoon and he was kind and gentle. I have seen him about this new home of ours as he has helped other people. I think he would be a good chieftain, a good leader. I propose we elect Meallan as our chieftain."

The crowd was silent, people looking back and forth, then Torcan and Lonan both stood, "I would follow my brother wherever he leads," said Torcan. "As would I," Lonan added.

Men and women stood one at a time and said in loud, determined voices, "Meallan!"

Earnan walked over to Meallan and clapped his shoulder, "Chieftain."

As the crowd tried to approach Meallan to congratulate him, a path opened for his sisters, Neanhain and Fiona. They carried the great sword of Conall over their heads and stopped in front of him.

"Take this sword, brother, and you will be our chieftain," said Fiona.

The crowd roared in approval as Meallan took the sword and raised it over his head with one hand.

* * *

The morning came with a brisk wind off the ocean and the smell of salt air. The sun promised a warmth soon enough and Meallan and his brothers began gathering large rocks, carrying them into the cave. Grian had scouted the system of caves so many times, she knew four that would do well as tombs for Conall. She finally decided on one that had several turns and two low passageways. The cave ended in an open almost circular space about twelve feet across and near ten feet high.

Conall's body was washed and dressed in a plain tunic. His short swords were heated and bent, then placed in a crossed pattern on his chest. He was carried through the caves to this tomb on a wooden pallet and placed in the middle of the open area. The pallet was raised a few feet and rested on wooden beams. After the family had their final farewells and vacated the tomb, the rocks gathered by his sons were placed blocking the narrowest part of the passageway. Then the walls and overhead of the passage were loosened and allowed to collapse through to the next narrowing some twenty feet away.

* * *

The fall went into winter and life at Draighean Cnoc became normal again. The spring rains brought new life to the flowers and crops were planted on the open plains. People were busily going about their lives when a band of nearly one hundred approached the gate. Two blasts on the horn brought the entire village to the wall. The archers assumed their positions and the warriors theirs. Earnan went to the tower over the gate and looked down on the thirty-four warriors, led by Meallan standing at the ready. He turned, looked out over the wall at the emissary sent to negotiate terms with the village.

"What is your business here today?" asked Earnan.

"We've come to sack this village," replied the emissary with a laugh. "Lower your gate, lay down your arms and we won't kill everybody. Just a few."

"And if we don't?" asked Earnan.

"Then we'll burn down this wall, kill all your men, rape all your women and sell those we don't kill as slaves."

Earnan looked out over the north plain. Out of reach of their bows were about one hundred raiders ready to attack. "You may tell your leader that this would be a great mistake," said Earnan, "no, we will not open our gate for your people to attack us. If battle is what you want, it is battle you shall have." He looked at Tuathla and nodded.

Tuathla notched an arrow and let it loose.

"Ha," laughed the emissary, "you didn't come close to me."

Earnan said, "Look behind you, fool."

There stood a target, the size of a man with Tuathla's arrow in the center of the target's chest.

Earnan smiled and left the tower. The emissary's face drained pale, he turned his horse and returned to his leader near the woods.

"They said no," reported the emissary.

The leader signaled to one of his men, "Are you certain this giant; this Conall—is dead?"

"Yes," replied the man, "I slashed and stabbed him myself. Stabbed him in the heart."

As they spoke, the bridge came down and the leader said, "There, they surrender. Ha."

As he spoke, a tall warrior, with broad shoulders, wielding a long sword and carrying two short swords in his belt, crossed the bridge. He was taller than most men, heavily muscled and with sand-colored hair that fell to his shoulders. He stepped to the right of the bridge and five paces forward, stabbed his long sword in the ground in front of himself and folded his arms. He looked like the images the leader of the raiders had of Conall.

Slightly taken aback, the leader asked, "Who then might that be?"

As he asked, another warrior crossed the bridge. Tola walked up to Meallan touched his shoulder and moved to the other side of the bridge, stabbed his sword in the ground and folded his arms.

The raider looked puzzled, then he saw another tall warrior walk across the bridge, "Look, there's another giant." As he spoke, a fourth and then a fifth, very tall imposing man crossed the bridge and finally the sixth. The six brothers spread out in front of the wall, standing about ten feet apart. Each similarly armed with their great swords stabbed in the ground in front of them.

"Six warriors. More than I expected, but we still outnumber them," said the leader. "If that's all they have, we'll send ten or more against each. We still win."

Then Tanai walked across the bridge and stood between Meallan and Tola and immediately nearly sixty more men carrying javelins and shields with swords in their belts, crossed the bridge and spread out behind the six warriors. There was a pause, then Tuathla led forty mounted archers across the bridge and positioned themselves evenly spaced amid the kerns.

Neamhain and Fiona crossed the bridge, carrying the great sword of Conall. They handed it to Meallan. He lifted it above his head to the shouts of over one hundred people standing on the platform behind the wall. Each was armed with a long bow or held a supply of long, heavy arrows for the archers. Finally, several more young men crossed the bridge, carrying large shields and spears.

Conall's great sword was then passed to each of the six brothers, each holding it high over his head to the same approving shouts of the people on the wall. The sword then returned to Neamhain and Fiona, together they held it high and carried it back across the bridge.

Muirin stood on the wall with Earnan and said, "This family will continue. You and Conall made a place for us to be safe together and grow and that is what we will do. These raiders will soon see we are not to be played with."

Earnan looked at Muirin, "I think Conall still lives in his sons."

"Yes," she replied, "and his daughters."

* * *

GLOSSARY

Aidhne

Historical location: Territory in southern Connacht, Éirinn

Ainle

Fictional Character: Born: 958 AD Died: 1014 AD

A spy in Dubh Linn for the Dal gCais

Ainnir

Fictional Character: Born: 983 AD Died: 1032 AD

Mother of Moalan (1005) with Conall

Alba

Historical Location: Scotland

Amhra

Fictional Character: Born: 1005 AD Died: 1070 AD

Son of Earnan and Grian

Brother of Soillan

Brother of Flann

Aodhan

Fictional Character: Born: 970 AD Died: 1043 AD

Blacksmith, Armorer

Aralt mac Imair

Historical Character: Born: (Unknown) Died: (Unknown)

Son of Ivar of Limerick

Ally of Donnuban mac Cathail in the Battle of Cathair Cuan in 977 AD

Ard Ri (Ri Eireann)

High King of Éirinn

The High King of Ireland claimed lordship over the entire island

Armagh

Historical Location: Northern Éirinn

St Patrick's Cathedral

Burial place of Brian mac Cennetig

Axe

Weapon

Several Configurations, lengths …The Irish Battle Axe was made with short handles less than two feet in length to longer weapons with handles near six feet in length. The axe heads also varied from narrow heads to wide curving heads

Banshee (or banchee) (<u>ban-shee</u>) (from <u>Irish</u>: bean sí)

Mythological Character

Woman of the <u>barrows</u>; omen of death;   messenger from the underworld

In legend, a <u>fairy</u> woman who begins to wail if someone is about to die

Bardan

Fictional Character: Born: 863 AD Died: 918 AD

Farmer, warrior

Uncle to Brighid

Bealach Leachta

Historical Location: Munster, Éirinn

Battle in 978 AD between Máel Muad mac Brain from South Munster and the Dal gCais under Brian mac Cennetig. The battle resulted in a Dal gCais victory and Brian assumed the title of King of Munster.

Beallach Mugna

Historical Location: Éirinn

Battle on August 16, 913

Cormac mac Cuilennian, King of Munster is killed

Be Binn

Historical Figure: Born: c. 898 AD   Died: c. 986 AD

Wife of Cennetig mac Lorcain

Mother of Brian mac Cennetig

Blathin

Fictional Character: Born: 1009 AD   Died: 1025 AD

Mother of Neamhain (1008) with Conall

Bow and Arrow (Bogha   Saiget)

Weapon

Iron arrow heads

Brat

Clothing

Woolen cloak normally be fastened by a crios (belt) and dealg (brooch).

Men fasten the dealg on their shoulder,

Women fasten the dealg on their chest.

Breasal

Fictional Character   Born: 861 AD   Died: 914 AD
Father of Brighid
Brother of Bardan
Farmer, Warrior

Breifne

Historical Location:Northern Éirinn
Between Connacht and Northern Ui Neill

Brian mac Cennetig (Brian Boru) (Brian Boraime) (Brian Boruma)

Historical figure: Born (926) (941) AD Died 1014 AD
Date of birth is uncertain. It may have been as early as 926 AD and as late as
941 AD. Date of death April 23, 1014 after the battle of Clauin Tarbh
King of Munster: 978 AD – 1002 AD
High King of Éirinn: 1002 AD – 1014 AD
Son of Cennetig mac Lorcan and Be Binn
Father of Murchad
Father of Conchobar
Father of Flann
Father of Tadc
Father of Donnchad
Father of Sabd
Father of Slaine
Brother of Marcan
Brother of Latchna
Brother of Dub
Brother of Finn
Brother od Donnchadd
Brother of Echthighern
Brother of Mathgamain

Brighid

Fictional Character: Born: 896 AD Died: 956 AD
Daughter of Breasal
Wife of Scolai
Mother of Daigh

Brocc

Fictional Character: Born: 869 AD Died: 903 AD
Nephew of Niall

Brodir (from the Isle of Man)
Historical Character: Born: (Unknown) Died: April 23, 1014 at Battle of Clauin Tarbh
Killed Brian mac Cennetig (History / Myth)
Killed by Wolf The Quarrelsome (History / Myth)

Brogan
Fictional Character: Born: 946 AD Died: 1023 AD
Member of Brian mac Cennetig's band of warriors
A spy in Dubh Linn

Buachailli(Irish)
Translation: Boys

Cairbre
Fictional Character: Born: 867 AD Died: 922 AD
Wife of Niall
Adoptive mother of Scolai

Caman (Hurley)
Game Equipment
Stick used in the game of Hurling

Capall   (Irish)
Translation: Horse

Cairell
Fictional Character: Born: 917 AD Died: 976 AD
Son of Cassair

Cairbre
Fictional Character: Born: 867 AD Died: 922 AD
Wife of Niall
Adoptive mother of Scolai

Cashel
Historical Location: Tipperary, Munster, Éirinn
Rock of Cashel
Residence of Kings of Munster

Cassair
Fictional Character: Born: 895 AD Died: 964 AD
Dal gCais Warrior

Cathair Cuan

Historic Location: Limerick, Munster, Éirinn
Battle in 977 AD or 978 AD
Dal gCais under Brian mac Cennetig defeat Norse of Limerick under Donnuban mac Cathail

Ceann Coradh (Kincora)

Historical Location: Killaloe, Clare, Éirinn
"Head of the Weir."
Home of Lorcain, Cennetig, Brian

Ceara

Fictional Character: Born: 879 AD Died: 894 AD
Mother of Scolai

Ceithernach (Irish) (Kern)

Military
Light Infantry, Combatants, With Slings, Javelins, Bows

Cellachain mac Buadachain (Cellachan Caisil)

Historical Figure: Born: c. 900 Died: 954 AD
King of Munster
Eoganacht Chaisil
Defeats Cennetig and the Dal gCais at Gort Rotachain in 944 AD

Celts

Historic Culture
Originating in central Europe.
Migrated to Pretanic Islands, Modern day Britain and Éirinn, around 500 BC

Cennetig mac Lorcan (Cendetigh) (Ceinneidigh) (Kennedy)

Historical Figure: Born: c. 896 AD   Died 951 AD
King of Tuadmumu
Father of Orlaith, Dub, Finn, Donncuan, Echthighern, Latchna, Mathgamain, Brian

Ciaran

Fictional Character: Born: 996 AD   Died:1058 AD
Son of Deaglan and Muirin

Cillian

Fictional Character: Born: 996 AD   Died: 1048AD
Spy

Claideb (Irish) (claideamh)
Weapon
Long sword designed for slashing or cutting.

Claíomh gear (Irish)
Weapon
Translation: Short Sword

Clann(Clan)
Descendants
Clauin Tarbh (Chluain Tarbh) (Clontarf) (The Meadow of The Bull)
Historical Location: Near Dubh Linn, Leinster, Éirinn
Cath Corad Cluana Tarb, Battle in 1014 between Irish under Brian mac
Cennetig and Rebel alliance between Norse and Irish

Clondalkin
See Cluain Dolcáin

Clonmacnoise
Historic Location: Offaly, Connacht, Éirinn
Monastery

Clontarf
See Clauin Tarbh

Cluain Dolcáin (Clondalkin)
Historical Location: Near Dubh Linn, Leinster, Éirinn
Tower over 80 feet in height built c. 790 AD

Cnoc Gorm (Blue Hill)
Fictional Location: Munster, Éirinn
Home of Laoghaire and Deidre

Cnoc Toirneach (Thunder Hill)
Fictional Location: Munster, Éirinn
Home of Tressa and Conall

Conall mac Laohgaire
Fictional Character: Born: 978 AD   Died: 1042 AD
Son of Laoghaire and Deidre
Brother of Muirin and Earnan
Father of Meallan (998) with Liamhain
Father of Lonan (1002) with Eithne
Father of Moalan (1005) with Ainnir
Father of Neanhain (1008) with Blathin
Husband of Tressa

Father of Olcan (1018) with Tressa
Father of Torcan (1020) with Tressa
Father of Seanan (1021) with Tressa
Father of Fiona (1022) with Tressa

Conghalach Cnogba (Congalach mac Máel Mithig)
Historical Figure: Born: (unknown) AD Died: 956 AD
High King of Éirinn (Ard Ri): 943 AD – 956 AD

Connacht (Connaught) (Cuige Chonnacht)
Historical Location: Province of western Éirinn

Corcaigh: (Cork) (marsh)
Historical Location: Corcaigh, Munster, Éirinn
Founded in 6th century as a monastic settlement
Became a trading port under Norse settlers in early 10th century

Cork
See Corcaigh

Cormac mac Cuilennian
Historical Figure: Born: (Unknown) Died: 908 AD
King of Munster: 902 – 908 AD
Killed at Battle of Ballaghmoon (Belach Mugna) Sept 13, 908

Crios
Clothing
Belt

Cu Chulainn, (Setanta)
Mythological Character:8th Century Irish Hero
Trained by Scathach

Curnan
Fictional Character: Born: 947 AD Died: 1024 AD
One of Brian's Commanders
Battle of Cathair Cuan
Da
Irish
Father; familiar form

Dagger (scian)
Weapon
A knife with a sharp point

Daigh mac Scolai
Fictional Character Born: 917 AD Died: 969 AD

Husband of Saraid
Father of Garbhan
Father of Laoghaire
Father of Tanai

Dalcassian
See Dal gCais

Dal gCais (Dalcassian)
Tribe
Branch of the Desi Muman
Descended from Cormac Cas

Darts
Weapon
Thrown, shorter than an arrow

Deaglan mac Aodh
Fictional Character: Born: 967 AD Died: 1042
Husband of Muirin
Father of Tuathla
Father of Ciaran
Father of Tola

Dealg
Clothing
Brooch

Deirbhile
Fictional Character: Born: 1011 AD, Died: 1068 AD
Daughter of Laisren and Tuathla

Deirdre
Fictional Character: Born: 948 AD, Died: 991 AD
Daughter of Fearghal
Wife of Laoghaire (967)
Mother of Muirin (969)
Mother of Earnan (974)
Mother of Conall (978)

Diarmait mac Máel na mBo
Historical Figure: Born: c.990 AD, Died: 1072 AD
King of Leinster
High King of Éirinn

Domnall ua Neill

Historical Figure: Born: c. XXX AD Died: XXX AD
High King of Éirinn (Ard Ri): 955 AD – 978 AD

Donncuar mac Cennetig

Born: 921 (?) AD Died: 949 AD
Killed during the invasion of Munster by Congalach Cnogba

Donnchadh Donn

Historical Figure Born: c. 880 AD Died: 944 AD
High King of Éirinn (Ard Ri): 918 AD – 942 AD

Donnchad mac Briain

Historical Figure   Born: c. 980 AD   Died: 1064 AD
High King of Éirinn (Ard Ri):   c. 1022 AD – 1064 AD
Son of Brian mac Cennetig and Gormflaith ingen Murchada
King of Munster
Half Brother of Tadc
Lost his right hand in 1019
May have ordered the assassination of Tadc in 1023

Donnuban mac Cathail (Dondubain) (Donovan)

Historical Figure Born: (Unknown) Died (Unknown)
Led the men of Munster and foreign allies against Brian mac Cennetig in
the Battle of Cathair Cuan

Dub mac Cennetig

Historical Figure Born: c.919 AD Died:944 AD
Killed at Battle of Gort Rotachain

Dubh Linn (Dublin)

Historical Location   Leinster, Éirinn
Modern Day Dublin

Dublin

See Dubh Linn

Dubliners

The people of Dublin,
In the late ninth and tenth centuries, predominantly Norse

Eadan

Fictional Character Born: 986 AD Died: 1047 AD
Tanai's Wife

Earnan

Fictional Character Born: 974 AD Died: 1044 AD

Son of Laoghaire and Deidre
Brother of Muirin and Conall
Husband of Grian
Father of Amhra (1005), Soilan (1007), Flann (1008)

Echthighern mac Cennetig

Historic Figure Born: c. 922 AD Died:950 AD
Killed during the invasion of Munster by Congalach Cnogba

Éirinn (Ireland)

Island nation in the North Atlantic Ocean
West of England and Scotland

Eithne

Fictional Character: Born: 981 AD Died: 1048
Mother of Lonan with Conall

Faolin

Fictional Character Born: 975AD Died: 1016 AD
Father of Tressa

Fearghal

Fictional Character Born: 930 AD Died: 994 AD
Father of Deidre

Fergal

Fictional Character: Born: (???) AD Died: (???) AD
Dal gCais Warrior

Finguine Cenn nGecan Mac Loegairi

Historical Figure: Born: (unknown) AD Died: 902 AD
King of Munster

Finn mac Cennetig

Historical Figure: Born: c. 920 AD Died: 944 AD
Killed at Battle of Gort Rotachain

Fiona

Fictional Character: Born: 1022 AD Died: 1078 AD
Daughter of Conall and Tressa

Flann Sinna

Historical Figure: Born: 847 AD Died: May 25, 916
High King of Éirinn (Ard Ri): 879 AD – 916 AD

Flann

Fictional Character Born: 1008 AD Died: 1063

Daughter of Earnan and Grian, Sister of Amhra and Siollan

Four Masters
Historic Figures
17th Century Compilers of The Annals of The Masters

Gambeson
Clothing
A padded jacket

Garbhan mac Daigh
Fictional Character Born: 937 AD Died: 950 AD
Laoghaire's brother
Killed in the invasion of Munster

Glaisne
Fictional Character Born: 962 AD Died: 1047 AD
Warrior at Clauin Tarbh
Two sons killed at Clauin Tarbh

Glen Mama
See Ghleann Mama

Ghleann Máma (Glen Mama) (The Glen Of The Gap)
Historic Location: County Kildare, Ardclough near Lyons Hill
Site of Battle (Cath Ghleann Máma) 999AD
Battle between Brian mac Cennetig of Munster with Máel Sechnaill II of
Meath against Máel Morda of Leinster, Cuilen son of Eitigen, Sigtrygg of
Dubh Linn and Harold Olafson

Gilleagan
Fictional Character:Born: 943 AD   Died: 1014 AD
One of Brian's Commander
Battle of Cathair Cuan

Goban
Fictional Character: Born: 857 AD Died: 945 AD
Slaver, Instructor at warrior school

Gormflaith ingen Murchada
Historical Figure: Born: c. 960 AD Died: c. 1030 AD
Daughter of Murchad mac Finn, Sister of Máel Morda mac Murchada,
Wife of Olaf Cuaran, Mother of Sigtryyg Silkbeard Olafson, Former wife of
Máel Sechnaill (Malachi II)
Third wife of Brian mac Cennetig
Mother of Donnchad mac Briain

Gort Rotachain

Historical Location:Éirinn
Battle of Gort Rotachain: 944 AD
Dal gCais under Cennetig mac Lorcain defeated by Cellachain mac
Buadachain , King of Munster

Greaves

Early Irish armor for the arms and legs
The use of hard-boiled cow hide, used to make chest armor

Grian

Fictional Character: Born: 979 AD Died: 1051 AD
Wife of Earnan
Mother of Amhra (1005), Soillan (1007), Flann (1008),

Gudrik

Fictional Character: Born: 866 AD Died: 894 AD
Viking Raider
Father of Scolai

Gwynedd

Historical Location: Modern day Wales

Herlu

Fictional Character:Born: 868 AD   Died: 918 AD
Viking Raider

Hurley

Sport Equipment
Stick used in Hurling

Hurling

Sport
Hurley or Hurley and Sliotar

Iberian Peninsula

Historical Location: Modern day Spain and Portugal

Inimar

Fictional Character:Born: 958 AD   Died: 991 AD
Norse raider, pirate

Ireland

Mogern Day Éirinn

Irish

The people of Ireland, Éirinn

The language of the Irish

Ivar of Limerick
Historical Figure: Born: (Unknown) Died: (Uncertain)
Norse King of the city state Limerick, (King of the Foreigners),
(King of Hlymrek)

Javelin
Weapon
A light throwing spear

Karl, Son of Halldor
Fictional Character: Born: 881 AD Died: 912 AD

Kerns
See Ceithernach

Killaloe
Historical Location:County Clare, Éirinn
On the River Shannon

Kincora
See Ceann Coradh

Knarr (Knorr) (Knerrir plural)
Ship
Norse cargo ship, Clinker built
Up to 60 feet long and beam of 15 feet
Three decks, Single square sail
Ocean capable

Laisren
Fictional Character:Born: 987 AD   Died: 1037 AD
Husband of Tuathla
Father of Deirbhile

Land of The Shadows
Mythical location
Home of Scathach

Laoghaire mac Daigh
Fictional Character:Born: 940 AD   Died: 978 AD
Killed in the Battle of Belach Lechta
Husband of Deidre,
Father of Muirin

> Father of Earnan
> Father of Conall

Latchna
> Historical Figure: Born: c. 930 AD Died: 953 AD
> King of Tuadmumu 951 AD to 953 AD

Leif son of Rodmar
> Fictional Character: Born: 981 AD Died: 1014 AD
> Norse Warrior

Leine
> Clothing
> A loose fitting long-sleeved tunic made from wool or linen
> The common garment of the time for both men and women.
> The men wore the léine down to the thigh or knee region,
> The women wore theirs much longer.

Leinster
> Historical Location:Province of Eastern Éirinn

Liam
> Fictional Character: Born: 1018 AD Died: 1081 AD

Liamhain
> Fictional Character: Born: 980 AD Died: 1012 AD
> Mother of Meallan with Conall

Limerick (Luimneach) (Hlymrekr)
> Historical Location: Located on the River Shannon Estuary

Linen
> Common material used in making clothing

Lonan
> Fictional Character: Born: 1002 AD Died: 1059 AD
> Son of Conall with Eithne

Longship, Dragon-ship
> Long wooden ship, low draft, capable of ocean and shallow water travel.
> Dragon ships have heads of dragons, fore and/or aft.

Lorcain mac Lachtnai (Lorean mac Lachtnai)
> Historical Figure:Born: c. 856 AD Died: 942 AD
> King of Munster, (King of the Dal gCais) (King of Mumhan)

Lough Derg
> Historic Location: Lake in Munster on the River Shannon

Máel Morda mac Murchada

Historical Figure: Born: (Unknown) Died: 1014 AD
King of Leinster

Máel Muad mac Brain

Historical Figure: Born: (Unknown) Died: 978 AD
King of Munster
Killed in the Battle of Bealach Lechta

Máel Sechnaill mac Domnaill (Malachy II)

Historical Figure: Born: 949 AD Died: 1022 AD
High King of Éirinn (Ard Ri): 979 AD – 1002 AD
High King of Éirinn (Ard Ri): 1014AD – 1022 AD
King of Mide
Defeated Olaf Cuaran at the Battle of Tara in 980. Succeeded by Brian
Boru. Allied with Brian Boru at the Battle of Clauin Tarbh, but withdrew
before the battle began
Ard Ri restored following Brian Boru's death at Clauin Tarbh.

Mahon

See Mathgamain mac Cennetig

Malachi II

See Máel Sechnaill mac Domnaill

Mam

Irish
Mother, Familiar form

Maolan

Fictional Character: Born: 1005 AD Died: 1051 AD
Son of Conall and Ainnir
Half brother of Meallan, Lonan, Neanhain, Olcan, Torcan, Seanan and
Fiona

Marcan

Historical Figure: Born: c. 920 Died: c. 1000
Son of Cennetig

Mathgamain mac Cennetig (Mahon)

Historical Figure: Born: c. 930 AD Died: 976 AD
King of Cashel
Son of Cennetig mac Lorcain
Brother of Orlaith, Marcan, Latchna, Dub, Finn, Donncuan, Echthighern,
Brian

Meallan
Fictional Character: Born: 998 AD Died: 1063 AD

Meath
Historical Location:County in Éirinn north of Dubh Linn

Mor
Historical Figure: Born: c. 945 Died: c. 970 AD
First wife of Briar Boru
Mother of Murchad, Conchobbar, Flann, Sadhbh and Blainaid

Morann
Fictional Character: Born: 915 AD Died: 967 AD
Brother of Saraid

Muirin
Fictional Character: Born: 969 AD Died: 1047 AD
Daughter of Laoghaire and Deirdre,
Sister of Earnan and Conall
Wife of Deaglan
Mother of Tuathla, Ciaran and Tola

Munster
Historical Location: Province of South West Éirinn

Murchad mac Brian (Murrough)
Historical Figure: Born: 966 AD Died: 1014 AD
First son of Brian Boru. Killed at the Battle of Clauin Tarbh

Neamhain
Fictional Character: Born: 1008 AD Died: 1063 AD
Daughter of Conall and Blathin

Neasan
Fictional Character: Born: 893 AD Died: 912 AD
Warrior in training

Naill Glundibh mac Aodha
Historical Figure: Born: 830 AD Died: 919 AD
High King of Éirinn (Ard Ri):915 AD – 917 AD

Niall mac Morann
Fictional Character: Born: 860 AD Died: 921 AD
Foster father of Scolai, husband of Cairbre

Norse
Ethnic Group

People from Scandinavia: Norway, Sweden, Denmark
Northmen

Northman

See Norse

Nuala

Fictional Character: Born: 898 AD Died: 962 AD
Wife of Cassair, Mother of Cairell

Ogan

Fictional Character: Born: 953 AD Died: 1014 AD
Father of Ruarc

Olaf

Fictional Character: Born: 985 AD Died: 1024 AD
Viking raider, pirate

Olaf the Fat and Olaf the Slow

Training Equipment
Names given to the training posts

Olcan

Fictional Character: Born: 1017 AD Died: 1074 AD
Son of Conall and Tressa

Olgar

Fictional Character: Born: 854AD Died: 894 AD
Viking Raider

Orkney

Historical Location: Archipelago along the north east coast of Scotland

Orlaith

Historical Figure: Born c. 917 AD Died: 940 AD
Daughter of Cennetig mac Lorcain

Osan

Fictional Character: Born: 890 AD Died: 912 AD
Warrior in training

Osgar

Fictional Character: Born: 987 AD Died: 1043 AD
Dal gCais scout

Pitch

Sport
Playing field in the game of hurling

Ragnar Son of Meldun
Fictional Character: Born: 983 AD Died: 1014 AD
Challenged Conall to single combat at the Battle of Cluain Tarbh

Ri Eireann
Irish
English Translation: King of Éirinn

Ringard, Son of Olaf
Fictional Character:Born: 983 AD Died: 1014 AD

Rioghan
Fictional Character: Born: 893 AD Died: 947 AD

Riordan
Fictional Character: Born: 983 AD Died: 1047 AD

River Shannon
Historic Location: River flowing through central Éirinn
Passes through Lough Derg,
Passes Ceann Coradh
Passes Limerick
Empties into the Atlantic Ocean on Éirinn's western coast

Roghanna (Irish)
Choices

Ronan
Fictional Character: Born: 939 AD Died: 1003 AD

Ruarc
Fictional Character: Born: 975 AD Died: 1038 AD
Hurling, Broken Ribs

Saraid
Fictional Character: Born: 920 AD Died: 969 AD
Sister of Morann
Wife of Daigh mac Scolai, Mother of Garbhan, Laoghaire and Tanai

Scannal
Fictional Character: Born: 991 AD Died: 1057 AD

Scathach
Mythical Character
The Shadowy One
Teacher of Warriors

Scéalta (Irish)

Stories

Scian

Weapon
Long dagger

Sciath

Weapon
A shield, a must for any warrior of the time;
Used to protect the body from incoming blows,
Also used as a weapon,

Scolai

Fictional Character: Born: 894 AD Died: 944 AD
Fighter, brawler, Warrior
Son of Gudrik and Ceara (Foster parents Niall and Cairbre)
Father of Daigh mac Scolai
Husband of Brighid

Seanathair (Irish)

Grandfather

Seanmháthair (Irish)

Grandmother

Seanan

Fictional Character: Born: 1021 AD Died: 1082 AD
Son of Conall and Tressa

Setanta

See Cu Chulainn

Shannon

See River Shannon

Sheila

Fictional Character: Born: 1009 AD Died: 1062 AD

Shield

Weapon / Armor

Shield wall

Military practice
Cooperative placing of Shields to form a wall

Sigtrygg Silkbeard Olafsson (Sitric)(Sihtric)(Sitrick)(Sigtryg)

Historical Character: Born: 9xx AD Died: 1042 AD

> King of Dubh Linn
> Son of Olaf Curaran and Gormflaith

Siollan
Fictional Character: Born: 1007 AD Died: 1054 AD
Son of Earnan and Grian
Brother of Amhra and Flann

Slings
Weapon

Sliocht (Irish)
Sept, a division of a family

Sliotar
Sport equipment
Ball in the game of Hurling

Soarla
Fictional Character: Born: 874 AD Died: 907 AD
Connaught woman, Ceara's Friend

Southern Ui Neill,
Historical Location

Sparth
A large axe Spear
Weapon

Starkad
Fictional CharacterBorn: 943 AD Died: 991 AD
Norse, Raider, Pirate

Sulcoit Hill
Historical Location:Éirinn
Battle in 968 Between The Dal gCais under Mathgamain mac Cennetig
and The Norse of Limerick under Ivar of Limerick
Victory to Mathgamain mac Cennetig
Norse numbered about 1,000
Dal gCais numbered less than 1,000
Cavalry was used by both sides
Casualties are noted as high for the Norse and light for the Irish
After the battle, the city of Limerick was undefended
Irish attacked, sacked and burned Limerick the following day

Sword
Weapon

Short sword, Irish short sword
Long Sword

Tadc

Historical Figure: Born: c. 970 AD Died: 1023 AD
Son of Brian mac Cennetig
Assassinated at the direction of Donnchad, his half brother

Tadhg

Fictional Character: Born: 857 AD Died: 932 AD
Warrior / teacher of warriors

Tanai mac Daigh

Fictional Character: Born: 943 AD Died: 1036 AD
Son of Daigh and Saraid, Brother of Garbhan and Laoghaire

Thomond

See Tuadmumuh

Thorkel

Fictional Character: Born: 861 AD Died: 922 AD
Viking Raider, Helmsman

Tipperary

Historical Location: Éirinn
Modern day county east of the Shannon in central southern Éirinn

Tola

Fictional Character: Born: 1001 AD Died: 1056 AD
Son of Deaglan and Muirin

Torcan

Fictional Character: Born: 1020 AD Died: 1091 AD
Son of Conall and Tressa
Brother of Olcan, Seanan and Fiona
Half brother of Meallan, Lonan, Moalan and Neanhain

Tordhelbach

Historical Figure: Born: 999 AD Died: 1014 AD
Son of Murchad, grandson of Brian mac Cennetig

Torna

Fictional Character: Born: 894 AD Died: 944 AD
Warrior in training

Tressa
>Fictional Character: Born: 997 AD Died: 1024 AD
>Daughter of Faolin
>Wife of Conall
>Mother of Olcan (1017) Torcan (1020) Seanan (1021) Fiona (1022)

Trodai
>Irish
>Translation: Fighter, warrior

Truis (Irish)
>Clothing
>A type of tight fitting trousers, but otherwise were bare legged.

Tuadmumuh (Thomond) (Tuadhmhumhain)(Tuamhain)
>Historical location: Éirinn
>Northern Munster surrounding the Shannon, Limerick and Ceann Coradh
>Home of the Dal gCais

Tuagh (Irish)
>Weapon, Battle axe

Tuathla
>Fictional Character: Born: 992 AD Died: 1064 AD
>Daughter of Muirin and Deaglan
>Sister of Ciaran and Tola
>Wife of Laisren
>Mother of Deirbhile

Ulidia
>Historical Location: Kingdom in north east Ireland

Viking
>Ethnic Group
>Seafaring Scandinavian warriors and traders

Waterford
>Historical Location

Westmeath
>Historical Location

Wexford
>Historical Location

Wolf The Quarrelsome
>Historical / Mythical Character

John B. Wren

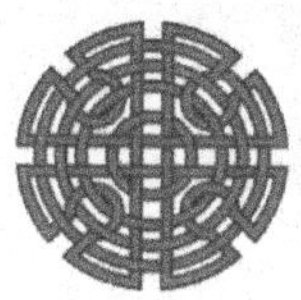